THE GHOST THAT GOT AWAY: COFFEE AND GHOSTS 2

THE COMPLETE SECOND SEASON

CHARITY TAHMASEB

COLLINS MARK BOOKS

COPYRIGHT

CONTENTS

COFFEE AND GHOSTS 2

AUTHOR'S NOTE

COFFEE & GHOSTS is a cozy paranormal mystery/romance serial told in episodes and seasons, much like a television series. Think *Doctor Who* or *Sherlock*.

I've recently consolidated the episodes into three season bundles. This makes the episodes easier to find and—I hope—more enjoyable to read.

~

If coffee hasn't yet topped your list as the most versatile substance on Earth,
consider
"The Ghost in the Coffee Machine" by Charity Tahmaseb.
~ **Lori Parker, Word of the Nerd**

COFFEE AND GHOSTS, THE SEASON LISTS

Season 1:
Episode 1: *Ghost in the Coffee Machine*
Episode 2: *Giving Up the Ghosts*
Episode 3: *The Ghost Whisperer*
Episode 4: *Gone Ghost*
Episode 5: *Must Love Ghosts*

Season 2:
Episode 1: *Ghosts of Christmas Past*
Episode 2: *The Ghost That Got Away*
Episode 3: *The Wedding Ghost*

Season 3:
Episode 1: *Ghosts and Consequences*
Episode 2: *A Few Good Ghosts*
Episode 3: *Nothing but the Ghosts*

COFFEE AND GHOSTS 2

THE COMPLETE SECOND SEASON

PART I
GHOSTS OF CHRISTMAS PAST

COFFEE AND GHOSTS SEASON TWO,
EPISODE 1

CHAPTER 1

I T'S TWO WEEKS before Christmas, and I'm crouched in our storefront display. Morning sunlight shines through the gold lettering on the glass and casts the words *K&M Ghost Eradication Specialists* along my arms. The velvet beneath my shoes makes it tough to gain purchase. My thighs ache. My palms sweat. The scalding cup of coffee I'm holding threatens to spill.

Passersby stop and stare, mouths open. I catch sight of Police Chief Ramsey, but all he gives me is a smirk. He doesn't believe in ghosts, not even when they're right in front of him. If I had any sort of presence of mind, I would've thought to print out a sign, something along the lines of: *Demonstration in progress.*

But that would be a lie. This is no demonstration. The sprite careening around the display window really is agitated. I really need to catch it. I'm really not certain this single cup of coffee will do it. Not this time of year.

There's something about December that brings out the worst in ghosts.

I'm about to admit defeat. The coffee's cooling too rapidly to tempt this one much longer. The sprite shoots back and forth, whipping around the samovar and percolator we keep on display, nestled in the velvet. It slips inside the samovar. The whole thing shakes, then teeters off its perch.

I pitch forward to catch it. My fingertips skim the metal. The coffee in my other hand sloshes, soaks my sleeve, and splatters the window. I'm flat on my stomach in the middle of the display. The sprite does a victory lap around my head and I glance up into the perplexed gaze of my business partner.

He's standing on the other side of the glass. His lips twitch. Malcolm Armand (the M in *K&M Ghost Eradication Specialists*) was once my rival and is now my partner—and sometimes there are benefits with that arrangement. He doesn't move from his spot outside our window. In fact, he looks like he's about to settle in for a show.

"Help?" I mouth.

I can't hear his laugh, but I can see it, head thrown back, the way it lights his eyes. He vanishes from sight and a moment later, the chime over our door rings out.

"Katy, what on earth?"

"We have a sprite," I say.

He sticks his head into the display area. "We have a sprite?" He glances about like he's tasting the air. "Oh … we have a sprite. Any idea how that happened?"

"None."

The sprite shoots past Malcolm and heads for the conference room.

"Damn," he says. "Is Nigel in yet?"

"Not unless he came in the back way."

Without another word, Malcolm sprints toward the conference room. I crawl from the display as quickly as soggy velvet will allow. Nigel, Malcolm's brother, was once addicted to swallowing ghosts. Granted, there isn't much to a sprite, but it's better if he isn't tempted.

I'm at the threshold to the conference room when Malcolm emerges.

"All clear." He holds up a sealed Tupperware container. "Look what I got you for Christmas."

"Seriously? You caught it that fast?"

He shrugs. "I'm just that good."

He is, actually, but I'm in no mood to admit it. I cross my arms over my chest and stare hard, waiting for the rest of the explanation.

"And I think you wore it out," he adds.

I study the sprite trapped inside the Tupperware. It floats lazily about, giving me a single thump against the side in agreement.

The chime above our door rings for a second time that morning. Nigel strolls in. His shock of white hair always takes me by surprise. Although he's only a few years older than Malcolm, he wears the legacy of his addiction in his hair and in the lines around his eyes and mouth.

Today a grin brightens his face. He looks almost boyish. His steps are quick and light. I think he might break into a song or possibly execute some sort of dance step. Instead, he merely nods at the sprite as he passes by.

"Good work," he says, and heads into the conference room where we keep the computer.

Malcolm and I stare after him. A tune reaches my ears, the melody off key but buoyant.

"Is he whistling?" I ask Malcolm.

"I think so."

"Does he do that often?"

I've only known Nigel for about four months, Malcolm a touch longer. Both brothers still hold a great deal of mystery for me. I couldn't tell you if Malcolm whistles.

"I don't think I've ever heard him whistle before," he says.

Malcolm creeps toward the conference room door and peers inside. Then he whirls, eyes wide, lips pursed as if he's trying to hold in laughter. He crosses to the far side of the reception area, gesturing for me to follow. We bend our heads close together.

"Nigel went over to Sadie's for dinner last night."

I nod. This, I know. Sadie Lancaster is my neighbor. I swept her house for sprites about fifteen minutes before Nigel was due to arrive. It's become an evening ritual.

"Well," Malcolm says now. "He never made it back to the apartment."

"Never made it ..." I trail off, the obvious hitting me with enough force I almost gasp. "You mean they ... that he ... he stayed the night?"

"That's exactly what I mean." Malcolm grins and leans in even closer. "I think it explains his mood, don't you?"

I clamp a hand over my mouth so I won't giggle or do anything else juvenile. Sadie deserves some happiness. So does Nigel, for that matter. Still, Malcolm and I are responding with all the maturity of a couple of twelve-year-olds.

Maybe that's because we haven't taken that step. We're not even close to that step. We are, by my calculation, at least five miles from that step. My gaze drifts from the conference room door to the display window. From here, I can make out the sodden velvet and the way the gold lettering makes it glow.

K&M Ghost Eradication Specialists

My eyes lock with Malcolm's. His are a deep brown, close to black, like an excellent dark roast. We both know why we haven't taken too many steps. What happens to *K&M Ghost Eradication Specialists* if K&M the couple doesn't work out?

"Katy," he begins. His voice is soft, devoid of that earlier glee. He sounds like he might say something quite serious.

Before he can, my phone buzzes in my back pocket. I tug it out, and Malcolm sighs. I can't tell if I hear regret or relief in it, so I focus on the text instead.

Sadie: Katy, can you come over

I hold the phone so Malcolm can read the message. "I just cleared them last night."

"Maybe it's time we took them farther out."

"Maybe."

Sadie's two sprites adore her. They are, I think, like the children she never had. But they're not children; they're sprites. Like the one thumping the Tupperware container Malcolm is holding, they cause trouble. Sprites love to play pranks, get a reaction, soak in attention.

"If Nigel …" He nods toward the conference room. "I mean, if this is getting … permanent, they can't hang around."

No, they can't. Nigel's addiction makes that impossible. But something about losing them for good makes my chest ache, just a little.

My phone buzzes again.

Sadie: Katy please

I tuck my phone back into my pocket and hold out my hands for the Tupperware.

"I might as well go. I have coffee at home, and I can lose this one and the other two while I'm at it." I give my soggy sleeve a shake. "And change. I should probably change."

My hands are on the container, so when he pulls it toward him, I come with it. We're close now, with just a sprite and some plastic between us.

"I probably smell like the Coffee Depot," I say, and my voice has gone all breathy.

"I'm not complaining."

Between us, the sprite thumps the sides of the Tupperware, and my heart picks up its beat. If I smell like the brew of the day, then Malcolm spices the air with a strange mix of Ivory Soap and nutmeg—it's warm and exotic all at once. Malcolm's gaze is locked on my face. I couldn't look away even if I wanted to.

And I don't want to.

My phone buzzes a third time.

Malcolm sighs again and then gives me a grin of resignation. We are *K&M Ghost Eradication Specialists* and this is how we pay the bills.

"I'd better." I wave a hand toward the door.

"Yeah. You'd better."

When I'm outside, with my truck rumbling to life beneath me, I can't tell if it's regret or relief that will follow me on this call.

SOMETHING GREEN IS HANGING from my door. The wreath looks festive, like Christmas, but it wasn't there this morning. The front walk bears the slightest imprint of someone's boots, a pair much larger than I wear. Instead of heading around back to the kitchen like I normally would, I follow those snowy footsteps up my walk.

A mistletoe wreath is hanging from a hook on my door. It's an old-fashioned arrangement, the perfect complement for the old Victorian house, and the sprig of holly berries glow blood red against the white of the door. In the center, stuck beneath a plaid bow, is a card.

I strip off my mittens and tug at the card. The entire wreath wobbles, then plunges to the ground. I balance it against one boot while I read the note.

For one speaker to the dead from another:
Did you know that the French once referred to a bough of mistletoe as a
specter's wand? They believed that not only could the holder see ghosts, but
could induce them to speak as well.

Of course, we don't need those sorts of tricks, do we? Still, what would the holiday be without such ornaments as this?

The card is unsigned. I turn it over, check the envelope, but there's no clue to who might have sent the wreath. Malcolm, possibly? Was that why he was a few minutes late this morning? I frown at the card. It doesn't really sound like him.

"It's bad luck, you know, to let mistletoe touch the ground."

A voice echoes around me, low and masculine. I shove the card into my coat pocket and whirl to face it.

No one is there. Not on the sidewalk or the street. No one has crept up behind me on the walkway, although my heart is thudding like someone has. I scan the area, my back to the door. Without taking my gaze from the street, I bend down and pick up the wreath. It takes three clumsy tries before it lands on its hook once again. Then I decide the best place to be is inside the house.

Without shrugging off my coat, I brew a quick pot of Kona blend. If Sadie's sprites are back so soon, I'll need extra enticement to get them to leave. They've been stubborn lately. Maybe it's the holiday. Maybe it's because they're lonely.

Maybe I don't blame them. I haven't climbed the stairs to the attic yet to bring down the decorations. I haven't bought a tree. Whenever my mind drifts to this first Christmas without my grandmother, I force myself to think of something else.

Like now. I'll go catch some sprites and breathe in all that is Sadie's house at Christmastime—sugar cookies and gingerbread houses, strings of popcorn and cranberries, spiced apple cider.

Although first I take a quick look around outside, but the street is late-morning quiet with children at school and people at work.

The door to Sadie's house is ajar. Warm, scented air greets me when I push it open all the way.

"Sadie?" I call out.

I stop at the threshold, pulling in a few deep breaths, tasting the air. Sprites have such a slight presence that sometimes it's hard to tell if they're in residence at all.

Something otherworldly is here. That much I can tell. Normally, when the sprites act up, Sadie will be somewhere they are not. I call out again.

Nothing.

I pull out my phone. On the screen is one final message.

Sadie: he

He? Is there someone—or *something*—else in the house? Or is it the start of a word—a word like *help*? I don't think, don't question what I should do next. I dash up the stairs to the second floor, taking the steps two at a time. I call out again, my voice ragged.

"Sadie, are you okay?"

I don't want to barge into her bedroom, but that's the most logical place to search. I push open the door, the sight that greets me freezing me in place.

Sadie, on the floor, clad in a silk robe of deep gold. Her face is far too pale. She is far too still. My thumb is on the phone, ready to dial 911. I step into the room, but before I can cross to Sadie, a force surges into me.

The cold envelops me first. This is no sprite. Its presence fills the bedroom with resentment and dread, the air so stale and sharp it pricks the inside of my nose. A hot trickle of blood runs down my lip and the quicksilver taste fills my mouth.

The thing shoves me against the shuttered doors of the closet. The flimsy wood buckles under my weight. I grip the frame and try to regain my balance, my breath, cursing myself for walking into an ambush.

This ghost is fierce and angry. It moans, the sound like an accusation. Then the room is silent.

In the quiet, I glance around. The thing is still here; that much I know. With my coat sleeve, I wipe away blood. My phone is where?

I can't fight this ghost on my own. In fact, I haven't encountered one this aggressive for a while. I need Malcolm. Sadie needs an ambulance. But first, I need to cross the room to where my phone has landed, next to the vanity.

I'm halfway there when the air shifts behind me. It feels like a gathering storm. I launch myself those last few steps. All I need to do is send a text. The ghost slams into me, the force propelling me against the vanity and its mirror, with all its glass.

The room explodes in shards. My head slams against something hard. I crumple to the floor, lungs searching for air, fingers groping for the cell phone. The moment I reach it, an icy blast sends it skittering away.

My vision blurs both with tears and an approaching darkness. I need my phone. I need to tell Malcolm about this ghost.

But it's too dark and too cold and my phone is too far away. I close my eyes. I tell myself it's only for a second so I can catch my breath. But my eyelids are heavy, and the dark washes over me. I taste regret along with the blood in my mouth. What I want is to hear Malcolm's voice. That feels like the most important thing of all.

THE INSISTENT SOUND of the ringtone penetrates my skull. This is the fifth time someone has called my phone. However, it's only the first that I'm coherent enough to do anything about it.

My world is still very much a black tunnel. I crack open my eyes, wincing against the sun streaming through lace curtains. I don't dare move too much or too quickly. If this ghost is still here —and I suspect it is—I don't want to alert it that I'm now awake— or mostly so. Not that my head, in its current state, will let me move too much or too quickly.

I crawl, a slow, agonizing trek across the hardwood. Beneath me, I leave a trail, a smear of blood, I think.

My phone stops ringing.

I sag against the floorboards in defeat. But with my ear pressed against the floor, I hear the rumblings in the house. A scraping, a crash, a shattering of glass. It's the sound of a Christmas tree toppling over.

If the ghost is downstairs, then he can't keep tabs on me, not if I'm quiet about it. I renew my journey across the floor and toward my phone. When my fingers graze its edge, it rings.

My first impulse is to answer the call, cry out, but I still my hand. This ghost is too aware, too calculating. I feign unconsciousness, enduring each ring and praying that the caller has patience.

On the seventh ring, I answer.

"Katy? Where on earth are you?" Malcolm's voice fills the room and my head. My heart beats hard with hope and reassurance even as a spike of pain travels my skull. "Did you drive out of cell phone range? It's been hours."

Hours. I crane my neck but can only glimpse Sadie's feet. Malcolm's voice is so strong and sure—and loud. I feel the buzzing, that otherworldly static, fill the air before the ghost flows into the room.

"Sadie's," I cry out, but my voice is rough, the word slurred. The ghost plummets and sends the phone careening against the wooden footboard.

This time I know it won't ring again.

CHAPTER 2

SINCE MALCOLM'S CALL, I've drifted in and out of consciousness. I know I must move, crawl if I can't walk, stay awake if I can't do either.

But my eyelids are so heavy. The icy dread that fills the room makes it difficult to breathe. The ghost isn't letting down its guard this time around. Forming complete thoughts is a challenge, never mind forming a plan to escape this thing. My head aches every time I try.

I know my grandmother faced such ghosts during her life. I remember a showdown in an old barn on the outskirts of Springside when I was barely eight. I remember that particular ghost lifting my grandmother as if her bones were hollow and tossing her into an empty stall.

We hadn't even used coffee to defeat it, although we'd started there. We always started there. All ghosts want something. Sometimes that something is to simply feel human once again, which is why coffee works so well to catch them. The steam. The aroma. Maybe it's simply nostalgia. I never questioned my grandmother on why it works.

But sometimes ghosts want more.

That particular ghost wanted forgiveness, something my grandmother figured out by lighting a bit of hay on fire and shutting the barn doors. The ghost whirled and swooped, pushing open the doors and urging nonexistent horses to escape. Then it charged my grandmother as if it could smother the flame with its ethereal form. I caught it with one of our extra-large Tupperware containers.

But what this ghost wants? I can't begin to say.

Panicked voices fill my head long before I can make sense of any words. Footsteps pound, the vibration traveling through the floor, along my jaw, around my skull.

"Sadie!"

I squint. Behind me, Nigel crouches, touches Sadie's forehead and brings his cheek to hers while his fingers travel her neck in search of a pulse.

"Thank God." He scoops her up into his arms and stands. "I'm going to take her next door to Katy's."

"I've called 911," someone else says, the voice familiar, but I'm certain it isn't Malcolm.

I push against the floor. I should help. I should at least walk out of here under my own power. My arms tremble and I collapse against the hardwood. Then a hand is on my shoulder and that voice is in my ear, a tenor with just a hint of a southern drawl.

"Katy? Katy Lindstrom?"

I push against the floor again. This time, two strong hands hold me steady. Slowly, I inch upward until I sit. I blink and the man who's holding me comes into view.

"You're not Malcolm." It's the only thing I can think to say.

The man gives a soft laugh and shakes his head. "No, I'm not. Sorry to disappoint. I'm a friend of his, though. Carter Dupree."

"Do I know you?" My head swims and Carter's face distorts. He has four blue eyes, then two. He is so very blond and bright it makes me wince.

"I'd remember meeting you." He grins at me, and even his teeth are bright, so much so that I want to shield myself from the glare. "Here. Can you stand?"

He offers his hand and I take it, my knees wobbly. For a moment, I sag against him, then stand on my own.

"Where's Malcolm?" I ask, my words mostly air.

"Downstairs, holding off the ghost until we get out of here."

"Is he okay? It's …" I touch my head. My fingertips come away stained with red. "It's bad."

"I can see that. Let's get you out of here and to the hospital."

We pass Malcolm on the way out. On the threshold of the living room, a samovar sits, the aromatic steam filling the air, the scent exotic and distracting. The ghost rattles about, still angry, but the aroma diverts its attention.

Malcolm throws a worried glance over his shoulder. His gaze lands on me, his gaze stricken.

"Christ, Katy—"

"I've got her," Carter says. "Follow as fast as you can."

Behind us, something shatters. Carter urges me toward the entrance.

We step outside and into the crisp air of December. The midday sun makes me duck my head and hide my eyes. The wail of a siren grows closer. By the time I can crack my eyes open again, an ambulance has pulled to the curb in front of my house.

Carter holds me steady until the EMTs can load the stretcher with Sadie into the back of the ambulance. Then, they come for me.

"I—" My mind is too foggy to calculate the cost of an ambulance ride or remember if we even opted for this under our small business insurance.

"You need to go with them," Nigel says. He eases me from Carter's grip and toward the nearest EMT. "If not for yourself, then for Sadie. They won't let me ride with her because we're not related."

I let the EMTs lead me to the ambulance. Carter peers in after me.

"I hope the next time we meet it's under better circumstances, Katy Lindstrom." He touches his brow as if tipping a hat.

The doors shut. The ambulance pulls forward, rocking me back and forth. I reach for Sadie's hand and squeeze her fingers.

She doesn't squeeze back.

DESPITE MY PROTESTS, I'm admitted to Springside Hospital for an overnight stay.

"Observation," the doctor intones, looking very serious right before she winks. I've known her all my life, and this isn't my first trip to the emergency room. When she adds, "Your grandmother would never forgive me if something happened to you," I know she's sincere.

But I'm alone in my own room. No one will tell me how Sadie is. The room phone is out of my reach. I don't have my cell—and even if I did, it's probably broken—so I can't call Malcolm. The television makes my head ache even worse. Someone with a sense of humor selected my hospital gown. I stare down at the print.

Dozens of little ghosts and jack-o'-lanterns stare back.

I wait, worry eating away at my insides. My head is throbbing, so I shut my eyes and concentrate on the footfalls that echo outside in the corridor. Some whisper. Some clomp. Then I hear steps that have a familiar cadence, footsteps that have shadowed mine.

I open my eyes in time to see Malcolm enter the room. Part of his forehead is covered with a bandage. I open my mouth, but before I can say anything, he waves away my words.

"Just a graze," he says. "Damn thing threw a vase at me."

"And?" I'm certain this is not a full report.

"And maybe a few bruises." He pulls up a chair and sits at my bedside. He reaches toward me as if to brush hair from my face but pulls his hand back. "I'm fine. It's you I'm worried about."

"And Sadie? How is she?"

He sighs. "She's fine, physically, according to the doctors. But she's still unconscious. They'll run more tests in the morning, but she's not injured—well, not like you are. They're letting Nigel stay with her."

I start to nod, then my head decides that's a bad idea. I swallow back the pain. I want to talk, not be coddled, so I school my face.

"What do you think it is?" I ask. "I mean, is it more than a ghost?"

It wasn't so long ago that I freed Malcolm—and myself—from an entity. This ghost in Sadie's house doesn't feel as calculating or intelligent as that other being was. True, Sadie's new ghost flavored the air, but it didn't change it, didn't manipulate, didn't suck the life from everything. I remind myself that not only did I banish the entity, I'm the only one who knows how to invoke it. Even so, I feel as if I should glance over my shoulder once in a while, just to make sure it's truly gone.

"It feels like a ghost to me," Malcolm says. "Completely nasty, but just a ghost. We used to get the really horrible kinds once in a while when I was living in the frat house. I used to catch them—" He breaks off, eyes widening, a look of chagrin painting his features.

"In my samovar," he finishes. "I had all those ghosts in there when it exploded at Sadie's," he says. "What if this is my fault? Nigel will never forgive me."

"But that was months ago. Why now?"

"It hates Christmas? It's holiday central at Sadie's. Or at least, it was. The place is a mess."

"I don't think that's it, and I don't think it's your fault either."

His jaw tenses, his lips a thin line. No matter what I say, he'll blame himself. With my eyes closed, I cast my mind back to Sadie's bedroom. The ghost attacked so fast and so hard, I barely had time to get a read on it. But I spent plenty of time on the floor before help arrived.

"Suffocating," I say, testing the word for how it feels.

"Is that what it wants?" Malcolm asks.

"How it feels, what's left of its personality. Suffocating." I want to elaborate, but my thoughts are too fuzzy, my mind too dull to grasp the right words for it.

He nods as if I've made perfect sense. It's one of the things I love about working with him. He connects the dots between my random thoughts.

"And it's not leaving," he adds. "We'll have to eradicate."

"And clean up the mess." Not just the one it made, but the coffee-soaked one we're bound to create getting rid of the thing.

Malcolm manages a short laugh. "Yes, and clean. When you're up to it."

"Thank you," I say, something else occurring to me.

"What are partners for?"

"Well, that, but I meant the other, for the wreath. I just saw it this morning."

His brow crinkles. "What wreath?"

"The one on my door. You sent it, right?"

He gives his head a slow shake. "No, I didn't, but I'm thinking maybe I should have sent something."

"If you didn't send it …" My mind gropes for an answer or at least a clue. Then I remember. "My coat. I shoved the card into my pocket before I went to Sadie's."

Malcolm rummages in the built-in closet and pulls out an envelope.

"For one speaker to the dead from another," he reads before skewering me with a look. "Really, Katy? You thought I wrote that?"

"Who else would?"

"It's terrible." He makes a face. "Plus, it isn't signed. Trust me, when I send you something, you'll know it's from me. This?" He waves the card in the air. "This is just creepy."

I let out a breath, all relief and no regret. I knew it didn't sound a thing like Malcolm.

"But if you didn't send it, who did?"

Malcolm turns the card in his hands, studying it, holding it up to the light. His features shift from grim to amused. He throws his head back, but his laugh lacks its usual warmth.

"It seems they're courting you already," he says.

"Who's courting me … and why?"

"You met him today. So that's why he's in town." Malcolm shakes his head, self-recrimination painting his features. "I should've known."

"Who?"

"Carter Dupree."

"So he's a friend of yours?"

Malcolm snorts. "That might be pushing it."

"He said he was."

"Yeah, well, Carter says lots of things he shouldn't and not enough things that he should."

"Even without the head injury I'm not sure I'd know what that means."

He doesn't laugh, but the smile he gives me is indulgent and dazzling. After a quick glance at the door, he scoots his chair closer to the bedside.

"He's like us," Malcolm says. "A necromancer."

"I'm not a necromancer." We've had this conversation. Right now I'm in no shape to have it again.

"Whatever. Only with Carter it's different. He's part of a necromancer … guild, I guess you could call it."

"Such a thing exists? What do they do? Go through training?"

"Yes, but it's more like a consortium, or maybe a cabal, a syndicate."

"That sounds shady," I say.

He raises his hands, palms skyward. "It does, doesn't it?"

What is he saying, exactly, and why won't he spell it out? An awful thought strikes me, sends a second spike of pain through my head.

"Are *you* part of this thing? Is Nigel?"

He leans forward, so close I can smell the Ivory Soap laced with his sweat from this afternoon's battle. He is both warm and safe. I'm praying he won't say something to change that.

"Honestly? I don't think I ever made it onto their radar. That's maybe just as well." He pauses as if considering his next words. "Besides, the Armands have always been ... free agents. We'll consult with each other occasionally, but this is the longest Nigel and I have ever worked together." This time when he reaches out, his hand does travel my forehead and sweeps strands of hair from my face.

Shady cabals and families filled with lone wolves. Both options strike me as unbearably sad. There are many reasons I refuse the label of necromancer. I've now added two more to the list.

"Why is he here?" I ask.

"Ghost gossip."

"Ghost gossip?"

"You can't banish an evil entity without that fact getting around. One sprite told another, that one told a ghost who told another who has a ... pact with a necromancer."

"And then that necromancer tells all the others."

"Well, in this case, yes. I'm surprised it took them this long, now that I think of it."

"What do they want?"

"You."

"Me? What on earth for?"

"Less earth, more otherworldly. You called forth that entity once, right?"

Despite the ache in my head, I manage a small nod. Yes, I did, and we both wear the scars from that. There's still a faint blue cast to my left cheek from where the entity marked me. Malcolm's ebony hair has a touch of gray, especially around the temples.

"That means you can do it again," he says now.

"I don't want to do it again. That would be stupid."

"They don't think so. In fact, that's how they ... work things. They find the most powerful ghosts they can and then use their membership to leverage them."

"That sounds awful. It sounds ... cruel."

Again, Malcolm raises his hands. "I'm not disagreeing, just telling you how it is."

Dinner arrives then, in a clattering of the cart across the linoleum floor (*loud ... so loud*) and the scent of turkey with gravy. The meal includes pumpkin pie with a dollop of whipped cream on top. I plan to skip straight to dessert.

"That looks almost edible," Malcolm says.

The remark earns him a glare from the nurse entering the room.

"I think, young man, it's time to end your visit."

He turns one of his dazzling smiles on her and melts some of her ice. Her own smile in return is indulgent.

Oh so predictable.

"I just wanted to make sure Katy's okay for the night," he says.

"We'll be watching her." The nurse holds up her hand, five fingers extended. "Five minutes and no more."

Malcolm leans close as if to give me a goodbye kiss. Instead, he says, "We'll sort through this tomorrow."

I start to agree, then a panicked thought strikes me. "I left a sprite on the counter in my kitchen, and Belinda can't stay the night with that ghost next door."

Belinda Barnes is my roommate. She's also a magnet for the nastier ghosts that haunt this world. The one next door fits the profile perfectly.

"I called the Pancake House to warn her. She says she has a

place to stay and will grab something to eat before she goes off shift."

She does? Before she moved in with me, that place was more often than not some back alley.

"Really?" I say, because Belinda having somewhere new to stay is a curious development.

He shrugs. "Don't think too hard on it."

With that, Malcolm leans even closer and places a gentle kiss on my forehead. I want to tell him he can do more than that—my lips are in perfect working order. But there's so much tenderness and concern in that one simple gesture that I decide to simply savor it instead.

"I'll be here in the morning to pick you up."

And then he's gone, out the door in five minutes as promised.

A HOSPITAL IS an eerie place in the middle of the night. I sample the air, but nothing supernatural flavors it. All that lingers on my tongue tastes antiseptic and medicinal. I want to ask for another piece of pumpkin pie, but except for the occasional shuffle of soft-soled shoes, the hallway is silent. I suspect the cafeteria is closed for the night.

I stare up at the ceiling, my eyes wide open, growing unease gripping my stomach. My limbs ache; I'm starting to feel the after-effects of the attack. I reach for the call button, but I don't know what the night-shift nurse could do except hand me some Tylenol. Still, I clutch the cord. When a voice sounds near the end of my bed, I yank it closer.

"Good evening, Katy."

My heart pounds, feels as though it might shoot out of my chest. It's a good thing I'm not hooked up to any monitors—I would've sent the readings off the chart. I bolt upright. My entire skull protests the sudden movement. I sink back down against my pillow, fingers searching for the call button.

It's nowhere to be found. Or rather, the shadowed form at the end of my bed is holding the cord.

"I didn't mean to startle you," he says.

"Yes, you did." The accusation bursts from my mouth as my mind scrambles to assemble the pieces of the puzzle. I've met that slight southern drawl, recognize his voice. The light in my room is too dim for me to fully discern his features. Considering how bright Carter Dupree is, that's just as well.

"You're right," he says, his voice both quiet and filled with humor. "I did. And I apologize, but think of it as a demonstration."

"Of what? How to creep someone out?"

"No." This time, there's a slight edge to his voice. "The power of necromancy."

"I'm not a necromancer."

"That's not what we've been hearing."

"And you've heard what, exactly?"

I'm not up to this. After that jolt of adrenaline, my muscles are sluggish, and my head throbs. Despite being wide awake moments before, I feel waves of sleep crash over me.

"Ghosts talk. I'm sure you know that. We have a pretty good idea what happened."

"Great. Then you can let me sleep."

"Are you tired?"

"Very. Please leave."

"All right, Delilah," Carter says to the air. "That's enough."

All at once, a fog lifts. My eyes flutter open. My heartbeat climbs again, and I'm certain if I lunge, I can grab the call button from Carter. I also feel another presence in the room, unfamiliar, but definitely otherworldly.

"Delilah," I say. "I don't think we've met."

"She's not much for small towns. This may be her first trip down here," Carter says. "She's rather sophisticated."

"She's your ghost?"

"Not exclusively, but we work well together, so for all intents and purposes, yes."

Once upon a time, Malcolm had a ghost. Selena. She helped him play the stock market, propelled him into being named Broker of the Year. But that was before he came to Springside, before … everything.

"Don't you see, Katy?" Carter says.

"You've lost me. I have no idea why you're here, in the middle of the night, and if I could call the nurse, I would."

"I'm here, in the middle of the night, without any detection or consequences—"

"None yet."

"Because of Delilah and the power of necromancy."

I glance toward the nightstand. It's still more than an arm's length away. I could try diving for it, but I'd only catch air. Next to the phone, something glimmers, but with Carter in my room, there's no time to investigate.

"Okay, great," I say. "You can sneak around."

"And throw my voice."

"Mistletoe and bad luck? That was you?"

"It was, and I can get you out of the way of a very angry ghost."

Delilah's presence is a tangible thing. She flits around the room. Strong—oh, she is very strong, and yet, at the same time, tethered, like she's on a leash.

"Thank you, Delilah," I say. "That was quite a shield you created."

"Hm." Carter folds his arms over his chest, the cord for the call button dangling from his grip. Any moment, he'll start tapping his foot with impatience.

"What?" I say. I'm in no mood to be grateful. "If you'd been there alone, that ghost would've thrown a vase at you, too."

The air vibrates, the feel of it like delight, like laughter building in the back of your throat. I think Delilah *is* laughing. I tilt my head because I'm not sure I've heard a ghost this strong laugh before. Sprites don't count. Their default setting is laughter.

All at once, the sparkle of the otherworldly drains from the room, as if it's being sucked up by some supernatural vacuum. Delilah's presence slips away, and the stale ordinary returns, the air filled with that medicinal, antiseptic odor.

Then I know. Carter has pulled her back inside himself, and the room is lonelier for it.

"There you go, Katy. The power of necromancy. Aren't you intrigued?"

"Not really."

"Don't you see what this means? What you can do?"

"I'm a ghost hunter. I separate people from ghosts." I pause, then add, "When they want to be separated." Lately, I've also brought people and ghosts together.

"So none of this tempts you?"

"Should it?"

"Oh, it should, and greatly. Perhaps I've done a poor job in showing you just how amazing necromancy is."

"No, I don't think it's you. It's me." I nod toward the call button. "You can give that back to me or I can start screaming. Either way, you're out of here."

Carter drops the call button on the end of my bed, then raises his hands in a gesture of surrender.

"You win, Katy, this round. But I came to Springside to convince you, and I'm not leaving until I do."

I pull the cord to me and hover my thumb over the button. "Three ... two ..."

Carter backs out the door. His footfalls are nearly nonexistent as he makes his way down the hall, but I catch a telltale hint of them. Delilah's doing, perhaps? It almost has the feeling of a gift. I wrap the cord around my wrist and sink back against the pillow.

Before I can close my eyes, that glimmer on my nightstand

teases my peripheral vision. I sit up, lean across the bedrail, and inch the nightstand closer.

A single rose in a vase is sitting next to the phone. I pluck the card free with two fingers. There is just enough light that I can make out the scrawled message.

Katy,

Sleep well tonight. I'll see you in the morning.

Malcolm

I hold the card in my hand and do what he says. Despite my still-pounding heart and late-night visitors, I sleep amazingly well.

CHAPTER 3

I N THE MORNING, before leaving the hospital, I visit Sadie. Someone has dragged an actual armchair into her room. It's there that Nigel is curled, a thin hospital blanket tossed over him.

Sadie appears serene, or nearly so. Her mouth isn't slack, as it would be in sleep, but tight, like she's worried about something. My gaze drifts to Nigel. I wonder if that something is him.

I ease the bag I'm carrying onto the floor. During my short stay, I have collected an astonishing number of things: tiny lotions, fuzzy socks with sticky tread on the soles, discharge papers, and information on head injuries. In my other hand, I hold the vase and its rose. This I clutch close.

With my free hand, I touch the back of Sadie's. Her skin is smooth, not too cold, not too warm. Any other time, I'd agree with the doctors. There's nothing wrong with her.

Except for one extremely nasty ghost.

I step back and jostle the IV stand. I steady it, but it jangles, the noise loud enough that Nigel stirs. The blanket slips from his shoulders, and he sits up. He stares at me, bleary-eyed.

"Katy?"

"Sorry. I didn't want to wake you."

"No ... no. It's fine. I want to be awake." He nods toward Sadie. "I don't want to miss anything. I really don't want to miss it if she comes to."

"I don't think she has." I want to explain why, but before I can, his gaze moves from Sadie to my hand—or more precisely, the rose in my hand.

A smile lights Nigel's weary face. "I'm guessing that one is yours." He nods at the vase. "Not Sadie's."

Her room blooms with plants and flowers. I suspect the lovely fern is from Nigel himself, a replacement for the one her sprites constantly uproot. I glance at my rose. Heat washes across my cheeks, and I nod.

"From your brother," I say.

"Ah, I see he decided to go with 'low key and elegant'."

"There were other options?"

Nigel gives a soft laugh. "Lots of them. We grabbed some coffee in the cafeteria before they closed last night." He shudders. "Speaking of which, if you get a chance, will you bring me a thermos of yours?"

"Of course," I say, my mind half on coffee and half on Nigel and Malcolm discussing flowers.

A rap on the door has me turning. There Malcolm stands, pressed and presentable, as always. For a moment he grips the doorframe, not moving, a smile tugging the corners of his mouth.

"How are you this morning?" he asks, voice quiet.

"Better." I touch my head. "Still hurts. The doctor said that's normal." I hold up the vase, the rose swirling in the glass. "Thank you. It's beautiful."

I should say more. I should tell him about Carter Dupree's strange late-night visit, and get Malcolm to poke holes in my theory about Sadie's state of unconsciousness. But at the moment all I can do is gaze at him, and he seems content to do the same.

"I'm fine, too," Nigel calls out. "So thanks for asking and all."

Malcolm peers around me and skewers his brother with a look. But when he enters the room, his expression is nothing but concerned.

"Sadie?" Malcolm asks.

Nigel shakes his head. "The same. The doctors have no idea why she won't wake up."

"I do," I say.

I know I shouldn't blurt it like that. And as expected, my declaration gets attention. Nigel shifts in the chair. Malcolm frowns, touches my elbow.

"Katy, I don't think—"

"Hear me out," I say. "Please?"

I focus on Nigel and he gives me a tentative nod.

"I think it's the ghost in her house. She was unconscious when I found her, but she wasn't injured, right?" I glance toward Nigel. "The doctor said so."

He nods.

"But I was. I don't think the ghost wanted to hurt Sadie so much as to ... have her?" I'm not sure of this last, but it's odd that I was hurt and Sadie not at all. "I think if we can drain some of its power or even capture the thing, she'll regain consciousness."

Nigel's gaze goes from me to Malcolm and back again.

"It's a really strong ghost," Malcolm says at last. "It's possible that it has some sort of agenda and it's causing this." He gestures toward Sadie. "There are cases that back this up."

"Do you think you can capture it?" Nigel asks. "I was there yesterday. It's not going to be easy."

Now Malcolm turns toward me. "I don't even need to ask, do I?"

"We can try," I say. "Of course we're going to try."

～

WE'LL TRY, but not right away. This is Malcolm's only stipulation.

"I can't go in without you," he says, "and you can't go in until you're better."

This gives us time to plan a massive eradication. I order special beans from the Coffee Depot—the usual Kona blend and their new fair trade holiday blend. Malcolm makes a quick trip to Minneapolis to buy spices from A Taste of Persia, the restaurant and market where he gets all his supplies for tea. For this ghost, we'll need every trick in our arsenal.

He even sketches a floor plan of Sadie's house. We pore over it, looking for places a ghost might use to ambush us—and vice versa. We set a date for the Saturday before Christmas. With luck, we'll eradicate the ghost and be able to clean Sadie's house all before Christmas Eve.

And maybe she'll get to come home.

IT'S the eve before our planned eradication, and I've gone over our notes so many times, I can't stand the sight of them. I'm sitting on the sofa in the living room, playing with my new cell phone and listening for the scrape of a key in the kitchen door lock.

I gave Malcolm one a week ago, and now he enters, bringing a blast of icy air with him. He smells like snow and cold and outdoors. There's a sprinkle of snowflakes clinging to his dark hair.

He shrugs off his coat, revealing a button-down shirt newly decorated with splotches of coffee and tea.

"A rough go today?" I ask. He's been taking all our routine calls, insisting that I must rest. Now I wonder if that was wise. He's the one who looks like he needs a rest.

"There's an overabundance of ghosts at Springside Long-term Care," he says.

"Happens every year, especially after they show *It's a Wonderful Life* or *A Christmas Carol.*"

"So, the ghosts think it's funny?"

"They do, and the residents are highly suggestive as well. It doesn't take much activity to get everyone in a frenzy. Plus, I sometimes think the residents are in cahoots with the ghosts." I've liberated my share of ghosts of Christmases past over the years, and I've chalked it up to holiday tradition. "And for some of the residents, ours is the only visit they get over the holidays. I mean, not counting the ghosts."

Malcolm's jaw tenses, and he gives me a terse nod. "Yeah, I guessed as much. Maybe we could go back the day after Christmas and—"

"Bring them some sprites?"

"Yes." He grins now. "We'll bring them some sprites." He taps the papers on the coffee table and takes a seat next to them. "What about you? Any new thoughts?"

"I just ..." I shake my head, wishing that would shake in the answers that elude me. "Why Sadie? I know she has her two sprites, so yes, there's that connection. But they adore her. If they weren't such pests, I could leave them be."

"I sent this thing's profile around to a few necromancer buddies to see if they recognized it, but came up empty." He takes up a perch on the coffee table. "It's not local because then you'd recognize it."

I would, or at least should. "I feel like I'm missing something." I consider Malcolm's statement, then ask, "When you say 'necromancer buddies,' you don't mean Carter, do you?"

He snorts. "No. I simply contacted a few other ... free agents. It's a courtesy as well. When we catch this thing, we'll have to set it free somewhere. A heads-up is always appreciated."

There is so much I don't know—and I'm not sure I want to know—about necromancy.

"Malcolm, can I ask you something?"

Maybe it's the tone of my voice, or that I'm leaning forward, nearly off the sofa and onto the coffee table, but his eyes brighten. He gives me that smile, the one that can make you forget the next words you planned to say.

"You can ask me anything."

He may regret saying that when he hears my question.

"When you were with Selena, was she free to come and go?"

A shadow crosses his face, douses that grin. I don't know what it's like to have a long-term partnership with a ghost, only that it's an intimate thing, and this feels weird and awkward, like I'm asking about an old girlfriend.

"Part of our ... arrangement was that she'd be around during work hours. And of course, I held up my end by doing those things she wanted." He gives a little shrug. "I think I told you art museums were her favorite. We went to a lot of gallery openings, too."

"But you didn't control her."

A frown crinkles his brow. He gives his head a quick shake.

"She wasn't a pet," I say to elaborate. "You didn't have her on some kind of leash."

"It's a mutually beneficial agreement. It's always been that way between ghosts and necromancers."

"Always? With all necromancers? Even that guild thing you told me about?"

He blows out a breath. "Katy, what are you getting at?"

"When I was in the hospital, Carter Dupree came to visit me and—"

"Wait!" Malcolm shoots up. "You're telling me this now?"

He paces the living room. His strides are long and each step holds frustration. "You're telling me this now," he mutters. "Seriously? Now?"

He continues the litany, although it's really more *about* me than *to* me.

"I forgot," I say when his steps and words slow. I tap my forehead. "Head injury, remember?"

Malcolm halts, hands on hips, eyes narrowed in my direction. I take that as my cue to tell him about Carter's visit, the parlor tricks, and the odd obedience of Delilah the ghost.

"It was horrid," I tell him. "Like she was a dog that he could tug along on a leash, or a servant ... or worse. I felt so sorry for her, and I liked her. She was strong, but she wasn't that sort of ghost." I gesture in the direction of Sadie's house. "And she did shield me from that thing over there."

Malcolm returns to the coffee table. He sits so close, our knees brush. He takes my hands in his, and his skin is so warm. He rubs my fingers, and the resulting heat threatens to obliterate all my coherent thoughts.

"It wasn't like that with me and Selena," he says. "It's never supposed to be like that. I don't know what, exactly, Carter and the rest of his bunch do, but it's a power I've never learned, or at least, it's not one my grandfather taught me."

"Do you miss her?"

He hesitates, his gaze drawn to the ceiling, before he speaks again. "I did, especially when I first came to Springside and didn't know anyone here."

"You came to Springside and ended up the most popular guy in town."

"That doesn't mean I had any friends."

How lonely was he during those first weeks in town? All I could focus on was how he was stealing my clients. I never considered that someone new in town, someone so good with people *and* ghosts, might lack friends.

"You do now," I say.

He eases one hand from mine and uses his fingers to tuck a strand of hair behind my ear. And even though we have things to do, things to discuss, for a moment, the two of us together, like this, is enough.

"So, tomorrow," he says at last, his voice quiet. "Do we risk brewing on the premises?"

"I think we'll have to." I cast a glance toward the kitchen. "Even with the thermoses and the short walk, the coffee will cool too much by the time we get it over to Sadie's. We'll need it fresh-from-the-percolator hot."

"As much as I hate the risk, I agree."

"I'm going to use the Kona blend," I add. "I don't want to tackle this thing with an untested coffee."

He nods. "Agreed."

"What about your samovar? That seemed to distract it."

"Let's hope I can replicate the recipe."

Malcolm stands, the movement so sudden, the coffee table scoots backward in his wake. "I should let you rest, and I promised Nigel I'd stop by the hospital for a bit."

"There's a thermos of coffee if he wants it," I say.

"I'm sure he does."

I walk Malcolm to the kitchen and then to its door. We stand there with it wide open, snow swirling. I wonder if he might kiss me. I even rise on my toes as if my feet have anticipated such a thing. But after a moment, I wonder why he won't.

"I have no plans to become a necromancer," I say to break the silence. "Especially that kind."

Why he might doubt this, I don't know. But it's like he wants something from me. My only guess is he wants to hear this. He tilts his head, but the smile on his face tells me that the message has been received.

"I know." He leans in and plants a gentle kiss on my forehead. "I've always known that." With that reassurance—and no other kiss—he leaves.

I hold in my sigh until the door has closed behind me.

Really, my lips are in perfect working order.

～

BETWEEN US, we maneuver a crate with all our supplies from my backyard to Sadie's. We have a key from Nigel, and Malcolm unlocks the kitchen door and opens it in increments.

"At least it's not keeping us out," he whispers.

There's that. Battling this thing and a full-on ghost infestation might be more than the two of us can handle.

Slowly and with as much stealth as possible, we lug all the items we'll need into Sadie's kitchen. Percolators and the samovar. Freshly ground coffee. Sugar and half and half. I've added in a set of twelve china cups I picked up at Goodwill. I don't want this ghost destroying any more of Sadie's things.

And, of course, the Tupperware container with an extra tight lid.

I'm standing in the middle of the kitchen when the feeling of the place washes over me. The walls have absorbed the ghost's malevolence, the atmosphere like that of an abandoned building, of some place that is truly haunted.

"I don't like this," Malcolm says, his words barely audible.

I don't either. "Start the samovar. That will help."

Once upon a time, I would've sworn you couldn't catch a ghost with tea—I mean, who ever heard of such a thing? But Malcolm can and does, and some ghosts (the odd ones, admittedly) prefer his concoctions of tea leaves and exotic spices. In any case, the aromatic steam will do this place—and us—some good.

"It's a Christmas blend," he says.

"Sadie would like that."

Without another word, we get to work. Malcolm starts the samovar going near the kitchen entrance. If the ghost interrupts our preparations, it will need to breach the steam. That will slow it down and give us time to react.

Or so we hope.

I brew the coffee; we'll need lots, so I set three percolators going at once. Between the scent of freshly brewing coffee—the

Coffee Depot's very best blend, their Kona blend—and Malcolm's tea, the kitchen glows with steam and warmth. It feels like Sadie's kitchen again.

"Better?" he says, scooting past me, a hand on my waist.

"Better."

"Where do you want to start?"

While we've talked through the options, you really need to breathe in a place this haunted before making a final decision. I do that now, shutting my eyes and inhaling.

"The dining room. There seems to be an abundance of ..." I trail off, the word elusive.

"Resentment," Malcolm finishes.

"Yes. That. That's it, exactly." I turn to him, and I'm certain I look as curious as he does. "I can't imagine Sadie making anyone or anything feel resentful." I inhale again and consider our other options. "Living room, and master bedroom. Those are the three main spots."

Coffee brewed, we set to work. Always twelve cups, always the same combinations: three black, three with sugar, three with half and half, and three extra sweet and extra light.

I pour while Malcolm follows, adding and stirring. His touch is deft. I don't think the man has sloshed coffee into a saucer even once. My grandmother would've been impressed.

He insists on the master bedroom, leaving me with the task of placing cups in the dining and living rooms. The air grows tense, as if it would love to absorb this warmth we're offering but something is holding it back.

"Do you feel that?" Malcolm calls from the bedroom.

"I do. Be care—"

A crash cuts off my warning. A howl shakes the house. Picture frames rattle against the walls. China in its cabinet clatters. Above my head, the chandelier sways and jangles, the trajectory threatening. Any moment, the thing will come crashing down on the table —and me.

Malcolm pounds down the stairs. The apparition looming behind him is so strong, so angry, it appears nearly solid. Except for the entity of a few months back, I've never encountered anything with so much substance.

Just a ghost. Just a ghost. I chant it silently, over and over. Just a ghost. Out loud, I say, "Living room."

I've already deployed the four cups of coffee in there. There's a couch to hide behind and several other pieces of furniture to use as shields.

Malcolm dashes past me. Before I can follow, the ghost diverts its course and flows into the dining room. It swirls around the chandelier. The crystals cry out almost like they're in pain. Why this thing hates the dining room so much, I can't say.

But it does. I glance around, trying to discern why. What is so offensive about this space? Sadie had—and has—an open invitation. After a long day of ghost hunting, my grandmother and I ended up here more often than not. And more often than not, it was the three of us, since Sadie's philandering husband was usually out ... philandering.

Malcolm's footsteps sound in the hallway. A moment later, he bursts into the room. He glances upward, eyes wide.

"Damn."

That one word sums up both our feelings. The ghost covers the entire ceiling, its form churning as if it's being boiled. The chandelier makes a pathetic sort of jingle.

"It doesn't seem to be going for the coffee," he says.

No, the coffee hasn't helped at all. If anything, it's as if we've fed its anger and resentment. Steam is still rising from the cups, but if the ghost isn't tempted, won't dip down for a taste, then we can't capture it. I'm about to suggest the samovar and tea when Malcolm's cell phone buzzes.

"What the—" He pulls out the phone, brow furrowed. "I don't get it ... I don't know what ... It's Nigel, but I don't understand what he's saying."

"What does he say? Is it Sadie?"

At my words, the ceiling quakes. Plaster rains down and coats my arms and the table, and covers the coffee in a light dusting.

"It's just one thing, over and over again." He looks up at me. "He says: It's Harold, it's Harold, it's Harold."

Harold? My gaze is drawn upward. Nothing in the whirling form looks familiar or even remotely human. But I sense it the moment the name pops into my head.

Harold Lancaster. Sadie's husband. The man who died in another woman's bed. The anger, the resentment—they simply don't add up. Sadie was the wronged party. Even Harold would've admitted as much. But this thing festering inside the house? Where does its resentment and anger come from?

"It's Harold Lancaster," I say, "but I can't figure out—"

"I can." Malcolm tucks the phone back into his pocket. "I recognize the feeling now. It's not resentment. It's jealousy."

"Jealousy?"

"Because Nigel slept with Sadie."

And Harold slept with half the town. "That's a bit hypocritical."

"Some people ... ghosts ... are like that."

Something pings in the back of my mind. I've forgotten something, I'm certain, something important. On the table, the dusty coffee is cooling. What's there now wouldn't tempt the most desperate sprite, never mind a ghost of this caliber.

"I haven't tapped into the third percolator yet," I say.

"I'll get it. I'm closer."

When he leaves, the room seems to contract as if I'm not enough to fight this thing on my own. I widen my stance, plant my hands on my hips, and stare upward. The ghost is everywhere, easy to see, and yet I feel as if I can't keep track of it.

I hear the clank of a percolator. Cups and spoons rattle. It's then that I remember. It's then that I know this is absolutely the wrong move. Malcolm enters the dining room and I meet him, hands outstretched to take the percolator from him. I will grab it and run. Before I can, it slips through my grasp and shoots toward the ceiling.

One moment, I'm staring, open-mouthed, as the percolator zooms on a collision course with the decorative plaster. The next, I'm on the floor, Malcolm sheltering me from the coffee that's raining down.

Scalding coffee.

He swallows back a cry, but I hear the pain in his voice. He sits up, his fingers fumbling with the buttons on his shirt. I have no time for such niceties. I grip the sides of his shirt and yank. Buttons scatter across the floor. He shrugs off the sleeves, grips his t-shirt, and pulls it up and over his head.

"Let me look." I don't dare touch him for fear of causing more pain.

His back is bright pink, all of it. Scalding is an occupational hazard, but a burn this large means a trip to urgent care.

"We've got to," I begin, but a rumbling from the ceiling drowns out my words.

I glance upward. This is bad. This is very bad. Of its own volition, my hand finds Malcolm's. More plaster falls. With his back both bare and damp, the dust sticks. No doubt it stings. The lines around his eyes and mouth are carved with pain, but he doesn't utter a word or a cry or even a protest. All he does is give my hand one quick squeeze.

"I'm sorry," I say.

"It's not your fault." His breath is ragged, but the words come out strong.

"Actually, it is. I forgot."

"Forgot what?"

"Harold Lancaster hated coffee."

His gaze meets mine. We don't discuss. We don't even need to confirm. We leap to our feet at the same moment and run.

Harold's ghost follows us as far as the front door. With a burst of supernatural wind, we're shoved from the house, down the porch steps, and into the snow-covered yard. Malcolm flops onto his back and releases a sigh.

He knows as well as I do the best method for treating scalds; rolling around in the snow isn't one of them. But I let him. We've been through too much in too short a time. And if I'd been thinking, this wouldn't have happened at all.

I gaze up at Sadie's house, then turn to track the flashy yellow van rumbling up the street. On its side the words *Ghost B. Gone, Gregory B. Gone, Proprietor* remain, although Gregory has traded his so-called ghost evictions for substitute teaching at Springside High School.

The van jerks to a halt and both Gregory and my roommate Belinda hop out.

"Katy?" Belinda rushes over, her boots stabbing the snow, her hair a blonde explosion between two neon green earmuffs. Her gaze falls on Malcolm. "What happened?"

"Scalding," I say. "I'm fine, but I need to get Malcolm to urgent care."

"Or just leave me here," Malcolm says. "Here is good."

"Frostbite isn't going to help." I reach down, offer him my hand, but he waves it away.

"One more minute." He shuts his eyes. "That's all I ask."

"I take it the eradication was a no-go," Belinda says.

"You'll need to stay ... somewhere else. I may need to stay somewhere else. That." I point at Sadie's house. "Is the ghost of Harold Lancaster."

"Seriously?

"Malcolm thinks it's because Nigel slept with Sadie."

Belinda's eyes go wide, her mouth an o. I consider that maybe I shouldn't have blurted that, but it's too late now.

Her expression shifts, a knowing smile lighting her face. She nods. "Yeah, he's right. Some guys are like that. I can totally see Harold Lancaster being one of those guys."

Gregory kneels next to Malcolm. He urges him to sit up and he gives Malcolm's back a quick inspection. His eyes narrow, and I have to fight my own urge to tramp across the lawn and check on him myself.

I'm about to ask Belinda where it is she's been staying when rotating lights and a single whoop of a police siren catch all our attention. A patrol car pulls up and out steps Police Chief Ramsey.

He doesn't so much look at us as judge us, and that judgment passes from Gregory to Malcolm to Belinda. At last, it lands on me. Of all of us, I suspect I'm the biggest disappointment.

"Call came in about some vandalism and a possible home invasion," Chief says.

Yes, because tiny Springside Township gets so many of those.

"Thought I'd check it out myself, seeing Sadie is in the hospital and all."

He strides past us, up the porch stairs, and rattles the handle to the front door. Nothing. It's locked. Or rather, my guess is it's supernaturally frozen. The brass glimmers, and I suspect a full-on ghost infestation. Usually you need a bevy of ghosts for that. But this thing? This particular ghost is strong enough to pull one off all on its own.

Chief Ramsey walks around to the back door, presumably to repeat the same exercise with the same results. Handcuffs jangle at his side. A frown creases his brow. He takes in the four of us again, and I think he regrets not being able to use them.

"And what are you doing in Mrs. Lancaster's yard?" He directs this at Malcolm, who is still shirtless and sitting in the snow.

"We're making snow angels," Belinda says, her voice light and sweet. "For Sadie, as a way to welcome her home. You know how she loves Christmas."

Chief exhales, shakes his head, then points a finger at each of us in turn. "You four are more trouble than the kids from the high school. And you." He points again at Gregory. "Are double-parked."

No one says a word as Chief Ramsey lumbers down the sidewalk and into the cruiser. In another burst of lights and siren, he leaves. The quiet in his wake feels ominous. Sadie's house appears benign, and it's just as well that Chief Ramsey couldn't peek inside. It's a coffee-soaked, plaster-covered mess.

Of course, that means we're not getting back inside either, at least not anytime soon. My normal procedure of warming up a ghost infestation? Plenty of Kona blend. I have no idea how we'll rid Sadie's house of Harold's ghost. But first ...

"Urgent care?" I direct this at Malcolm. He's shut his eyes again.

"I'm ... fine."

"No, you're not," Gregory says and turns to me. "I can drive him over, or we could call 911..."

Malcolm opens his eyes and we exchange a glance. No, we can't afford another ambulance ride, not so soon after the last one. He pushes to his feet.

"No ambulance," he says.

"Why don't you ride with Gregory," I say. "Belinda and I will follow in my truck."

It's only after they've left that I turn to Belinda, and it's only now that I notice the bag slung over her shoulder.

"So ... you've been staying where?" I ask, but I have a fairly good idea.

She holds up a hand. "Don't even start with me."

"I thought you said he was obnoxious."

"I did."

"But?"

"But he's the least mystical person I've ever met. It's like he repels ghosts. Sprites can't even stand him. You should probably send him in there." She points to Sadie's house and then shrugs.

"It's a relief, really, not to have to worry about waking up to Casper the less-than-friendly ghost."

"And?" This can't be the whole story.

"And I figured it was just a rebound thing. He and Terese were together for a long time. I'm not looking for anything serious. So ... it works." She adjusts the bag's shoulder strap. "I was actually just going to switch out some clothes and stay over for another night—or two."

"You *should* stay somewhere other than here tonight." Here is bad for Belinda, especially with Harold's ghost so recently agitated, especially since I'm the one who caused all that agitation. Revenge isn't out of the question.

"What are you going to do?" she asks.

I study Sadie's house and shake my head. "I don't know."

"Know what I'd do?"

"What?"

"Get out of here for a night and offer to play nursemaid to Malcolm. He's going to need someone to wrap his back in gauze and check for blistering, right? That might as well be you."

Despite the cold and the light breeze, my cheeks burn.

"Tell me you didn't notice him in all his shirtless glory," she adds.

"I take it you did."

She raises her hands as if this goes without saying.

"We're business partners," I say. Now is not the time to think of Malcolm's naked back. It only makes my cheeks burn harder, and Belinda smirks.

"*Just* business partners?"

I don't answer. I'm not sure I know the answer. Instead, I head for my house. I can't imagine Malcolm wants any coffee, but Nigel might. I need to check on both of them, and Sadie too.

Belinda falls into step next to me. "Five minutes and I'll be ready."

"Take your time," I say. "I need to brew some coffee for Nigel."

I also need to think, and consider, and grope for answers. The kitchen is a good place for that. But as I stand in its center, listening to the percolator work its magic, I can't conjure up anything that might resemble a solution to all this. Even if I had an idea of our next steps, I doubt it would work.

There's something about December that brings out the worst in ghosts.

CHAPTER 4

"SHE WOKE FOR A BIT."

Nigel hasn't even poured the first cup of coffee when he tells me this.

"When?"

"About one thirty, I think."

"We were at Sadie's then," I say. "Just our presence must have drained some of its power, at least at first."

"She called out his name." He stares down at the thermos as if he doesn't want me to see his face. "I thought at first she was calling *for* him."

Oh, poor Nigel. I hadn't thought of that. "But it wasn't that," I say. "Right? It was a warning."

Nigel pours and considers the coffee in his cup. I think he won't meet my eyes, but a moment later, he glances up, gives me a wan smile, and offers the thermos to me. I shake my head. I've had enough of coffee for one day.

"Didn't think so," he says. "I'm guessing Malcolm won't want any either."

"You're right."

A voice comes from the doorway. There Malcolm stands, hand braced against the frame, his grip tight as if he's holding himself up.

"How are you?" I ask.

"Not in the mood for coffee."

"But how are you?"

"Lucky." Now he grins, and if it isn't as bright as it normally is, it's still just as warm. "Only two small blisters, and the rest like a bad sunburn. You ripped my shirt off me in time."

"You know," Nigel says, and he takes a long draw of his coffee. "Under different circumstances, I might want to know more about that."

For the second time that day, I feel the rush of blood to my cheeks, like tiny pinpricks. I eye Nigel, who only laughs, and then work up the nerve to look at Malcolm.

His smile hasn't faded and he holds out a hand. "I feel like I'm about seventy, though."

I grab his hand and help him to a chair.

"Sadie woke for a bit," I tell him. "She tried to warn us about Harold."

He nods. "So that confirms the connection."

"I'm thinking that if we can drain its power, capture it, and take this thing far, far away, that will do it." My gaze drifts to Sadie's form, so still in the bed. "He'll let her go—or be forced to. Whatever this connection is, it won't hold."

We fall silent. I'm hounded by the notion that all ghosts want something, but I can't figure out what it is Harold wants. Is it this? Sadie in a forever sleep, like some fairy tale queen? Or is it something else, something I'm missing?

I was so young when Harold and Sadie moved in next door. She seemed old to me. She was, in a way—a married grownup, after all. Harold was even older. It's only recently that I've begun to think of Sadie as my friend rather than my grandmother's. It's only recently that I've seen how young she still is. The man keeping vigil at her bedside has a lot to do with that.

We sit. After a while, Malcolm's hand finds mine. I find Nigel's. The vigil doesn't help Sadie, but we're not doing it for her. I think we're doing it for us.

IT'S NEARLY ten at night when I return home. I'm clutching the takeout containers left over from dinner at Sadie's bedside. The spicy scent of Szechuan chicken warms the air and stings my nose.

I stand on the sidewalk outside Sadie's house. The windows are black. The place looks curled in on itself, as if it might crumble into dust. I remain there for so long, cold sneaks through the soles of my boots until my toes ache.

"He's gone, you know."

The voice makes me jump. My heart thuds, the beat of it quick and annoyed. This is a voice I recognize, and this is the third time it has startled me. I swallow my first question, which is: *He is?* I go with the one that I think will irritate Carter Dupree as much as he irritates me.

"Who's gone?" I ask.

"The ghost." And there he is, Carter Dupree, sliding soundlessly to stand at my side.

"What ghost?"

"Don't play dumb with me, Katy. We both know what's been going on." Although it's dark, I think I detect an eye roll. "Please. I carried you out of there."

He points to Sadie's house. Then, as if to prove a point, he strides up the walk. He halts on the porch, strips off his gloves, and touches the doorknob with bare fingers. He doesn't bend over in pain. His hand doesn't suffer from frostbite.

The door swings open. With the house so dark, I can barely see the decorative wreath Sadie keeps just inside the entryway. The infestation truly is gone. Now that I can taste the air from inside, I realize that so is Harold's ghost.

"See?" he says, and closes the door. "No ghost."

My fingertips itch. I want to pull out my phone. I want to text Malcolm or call him so he can eavesdrop. Instead, I tilt my head and keep my expression as bland as possible.

"Oh." It's all the reaction I plan to give him.

"You wouldn't know what happened to him, would you?" he says.

"Are you asking me or baiting me?"

"What do you think?"

"I think I'd rather talk to Delilah. Is she here?"

If she is, I can't sense her. The air is so devoid of anything supernatural, I'd almost welcome the appearance of Sadie's mischievous sprites.

"Delilah is always with me."

"Even when you sleep?"

The streetlamp casts a yellow glow. There is just enough light that I can see his left eye twitch. It isn't much of a tell, but it's enough to go on.

"Even then," he says at last, the words clipped.

"How can you be sure? I mean, you're asleep, right?"

A touch of the otherworldly invades the space between us. It doesn't warm the air, of course, but it gives the cold some extra bite.

"Delilah," I say, letting my voice ring loud. "Next time you want to hang out, just wait until Carter goes to sleep and come on over. We don't have much nightlife in Springside, but I can brew you some Kona blend."

The air around us shimmers, the feel of it light and joyful. I think it must be Delilah. Even with the lockdown Carter has on her, he can't suppress every last reaction. My guess? She's laughing.

"Hm." His voice is terse. "You may regret that invitation."

"I doubt it."

"Then I'll leave before you do."

Without another word—and with that strange threat in the air —he turns from me. I'm determined to track his progress up the street. I see no car. All the houses are dark, front porch lamps extinguished for the evening except for my own. I hold Carter Dupree in my sights for as long as I can, eyes wide open.

The air is so cold, his walk so long that tears brim in my eyes and travel down my cheeks, hot trails against chilled skin.

Then he vanishes. He isn't so far away that I merely lose sight of him. One moment he's beneath a streetlight, the next nothing is. I stare at the empty space until my gaze is drawn, once again, to Sadie's house.

My feet start moving before I've really decided. I walk to her porch, touch the knob for myself, and then step inside.

THE FIRST THING I do is lock the door behind me. The second? Pull out my brand-new cell phone and speed-dial Malcolm. I'm halfway to the kitchen door when he answers.

"Jesus, Katy, are you okay?"

"Relax. I'm fine." I lock the kitchen door as well and flip on the lights.

Coffee stains the countertops. On the floor, near the refrigerator, a pool of half and half has congealed. I tuck the takeout containers inside and continue my inspection. My boots crunch spilled sugar and shards of broken china. One Goodwill cup remains, the lone survivor of the mêlée.

"It's a mess in here," I say, more to myself than Malcolm.

"What's a mess? Where are you? Don't do this to me."

"Sorry, sorry. I'm at Sadie's. Harold's ghost is gone."

"How do you even—?"

"I ran into Carter Dupree. He told me." I crunch my way from the kitchen, intent on inspecting the rest of the house.

Malcolm swears, colorfully and for several seconds. "Funny how he shows up when I'm not around."

"Yeah, it feels less like courting and more like stalking."

The line goes silent. This worries me, as does the coffee stain on the living room's cream-colored rug. The spot is the size and shape of a Great Dane. It's going to take more than a can of carpet cleaner to get rid of that.

"Malcolm?"

"Still here. I'm just … worried. Are you sure you should be at Sadie's?"

"The ghost isn't here. Carter isn't here. Besides, I locked the doors."

"And he has a powerful ghost at his disposal."

"Delilah? I like her."

"Well, don't get too attached. One, she's under his control. Two? The powerful ghosts are the most capricious."

"Was Selena?"

He falls silent again. I don't think he expected that question. Maybe it was unfair of me to ask it.

"She was," he says at last. "A little high maintenance too, as far as ghosts go."

"I think Harold's ghost has her beat."

To my relief, he laughs, the sound of it warm and sweet, a dark roast on a cold day sort of a laugh.

"Speaking of Harold," I say, although I hate to hear the humor drain from Malcolm's voice. "Carter was asking whether I knew where he … it … the ghost went. Why is he so interested?"

Malcolm swears again.

"What?" I prompt when he doesn't elaborate.

"I'm starting to think that this has been a setup."

"You mean Harold's ghost."

"That's exactly what I mean."

I move on to the master bedroom. Compared to the rest of the house, the damage is minimal in here, the most significant being my blood on the corner of the vanity and the floor. Jars and bottles are scattered everywhere, but everything is made of plastic or thick glass. Nothing is broken.

Except the mirror. I did that. Or rather, Harold did that, using me. Who gets that piece of bad luck?

"So, are you saying that someone like this necromancer cabal or whatever it is, tracked down Harold's ghost, captured it, and then set it free at the moment it would do the most damage?"

"That's exactly what I'm saying."

I step over shards of shattered mirror. "Do you know how paranoid that sounds?"

"Do you have a better theory?"

I don't, except that Sadie falling in love might have triggered something like this. Even in death, Harold has managed to control major pieces of her life. He owned the house she lives in, the car she drives. What happens when the grieving widow no longer grieves? What happens when her attention turns to someone else? Someone alive and worthy and oh so perfect for her?

"Is this something this guild thing is capable of?" I ask Malcolm.

"Possibly. Probably. Okay, yes. They've been in existence for a hundred years. They have ... accumulated wealth. But it's not like they advertise their abilities, not like we do. They don't want people knowing what it is they do or can do."

"Then why?" I ask. "Why do this to Sadie?"

Silence on the line greets my question.

"Malcolm?"

"It's not so much Sadie as it is you," he says, and reluctance is thick in his voice. I wonder if there are things he's not telling me. "It all comes back to you."

"I'm nothing."

"Don't say that. You're not only powerful, but ghosts like you."

"Not all ghosts."

"Forget Harold's ghost. Those kinds of ghosts don't like anyone. You know that. You have a sense for ghosts. You draw them out. Seriously, you keep us in business."

"You're good with ghosts. I couldn't do this without you."

"Thanks. My ego needed that. But how many times do sprites hit me on the head during any given week?"

Okay, the answer to that is: more than I can count. I see the gesture as a ghostly buddy-shove, but maybe Malcolm has a point.

"I can catch ghosts," he says. "I was a pretty good necromancer. Not so good that the cabal started courting me, but I held my own. They want you, Katy, because you have an innate affinity I don't think any of their number has. It's a whole lot easier when the ghosts come to you."

I'm in the dining room now. I've saved this space for last. The chandelier is hanging by wires. I don't dare turn on the lights, but the ones in the hallway shed enough light that I can see. Coffee has dried all over the dining table, ruining its finish. My silver percolator is resting on the floor near the sideboard, dented and concave. I will have to retire this one from service.

"Okay," I say to Malcolm. "Let's say this is a setup, and Carter brought Harold here. Where is Harold now? Not under his control, that's for sure."

"I don't know." Doubt echoes in his voice.

"Sadie," I begin. I'm about to dash from the house and rush over to the hospital.

"I'm with her, and Nigel will be back soon. He needed a shower and a change of clothes. I said I'd sit with Sadie until he got back. But I'll stay the night. I can't sleep on my stomach, so there's not much sense in going home."

"I feel like I'm missing something." I scan the dining room as if that something is here, spelled out in the coffee stains on the walls and across the floor. There's more to this than Malcolm's crazy conspiracy theory. I'm certain of it.

"Why don't you go home?" he says. "Get some sleep. There's not much you can do at eleven at night."

He's right, of course. But after we've hung up, I can't force myself to leave Sadie's house. If Malcolm can't sleep because of his injured back, then I can't sleep, period.

I spend the night cleaning what I can. The big chores—like the Great Dane on the carpet—will have to wait until the stores open in the morning. But at sunrise, when I leave, at least the place no longer reeks of stale coffee.

CHAPTER 5

B ELINDA BRINGS THE steam cleaner. She and Gregory
carry it up the front porch steps and into Sadie's house. They
head straight for the living room.

All this in response to a single text I sent her an hour ago:

Ghost gone. You can come home.

"How did you know?" I ask, raising my voice to be heard over
the rumble of the machine.

The thing throws steam into the air. Too bad Sadie's sprites
aren't here. They'd love to dance in that.

"Did you look in the mirror anytime yesterday?" Belinda says.

Okay. She has a point. I may not be able to wear those jeans
again—except on another eradication. My hair held so much
plaster it needed three washings.

"I figured the house had to be worse," she adds.

With patience and undeniable practice, Gregory sets to work on
the Great Dane. Already the stain has shrunk to standard poodle
size. Chihuahua can't be far off.

I nudge her. "Man knows how to use a vacuum."

"Shut up."

I laugh, but I do shut up because she bites her lower lip and the start of an honest blush creeps up her cheekbones. I won't tease her about this, not too much. Still, he's only been in town for a few months. He can't be too obnoxious if he's willing to pitch in and clean a near stranger's home.

We're in the kitchen, scrubbing coffee stains from the floor tile's grout, when Malcolm stumbles in.

And he does stumble. Gregory holds out a hand to steady him, but Malcolm waves away the offer. He blinks against the scent of the cleanser as if it stings his raw and weary eyes. His normally smooth hair is rumpled; so is his normally pressed shirt.

I open my mouth. I'm about to ask. I'm sure the question is there on my face.

"Been driving around all night," he says before I can utter a word. "Went out to the old barn, even drove all the way over to the mausoleum." He shakes his head. "Nothing. I didn't see any signs of a ghost that powerful. I didn't even run into any sprites."

And we haven't received any calls, either. Some people ignore the sprites, chalk up their mischief to bad luck or Mercury in retrograde, but most can't ignore a ghost so powerful it can toss people against walls and mirrors.

"Well, if he showed up here and then left," Belinda muses, "maybe he went back to his old job?" She looks to me, both eyebrows raised. "Do ghosts do that?"

"Sometimes, but usually only one thing drives them, one passion from their old life."

"Have you tried the bars?" Gregory offers.

"The bars?" I say, skeptical. I'm pretty sure my grandmother never eradicated a ghost from a bar, and I certainly haven't.

"So, passion, right? He comes here." Gregory waves a hand, indicating Sadie's house. "Then Sadie leaves."

"Actually, the ambulance came to get her," I say.

"Narrow the lens." He brings his hands together. "The ghost doesn't know that. All he can see is betrayal and abandonment. It doesn't matter if he caused all the problems; he's still going to throw himself a pity party, and he's going to do that with alcohol."

The room falls silent. Belinda's expression shifts to something both thoughtful and tender.

Gregory strokes his beard, his own expression contemplative. "Trust me, I know a little something about that."

Malcolm clears his throat. "What do you say, partner? Want to hit the bars later tonight?"

I feel as if I'm missing something crucial in all of this. We all are. But I nod.

"Sure," I say. "Let's go out drinking."

MY TRUCK IS IDLING in front of the Last Ditch Bar and Grill. The neon illuminating the D barely flickers, so Malcolm and I peer up at the Last Itch Bar and Grill. My hands are on the steering wheel, his on the dash. So far, Finnegan's Pub, the American Legion, and the bowling alley have yielded zero ghosts but plenty of questioning looks.

I'm stiff from the cold and too little sleep. Malcolm's head bobs. I suspect the dash appears as tempting as a pillow at this point. But he heaves a sigh and pushes himself upright.

"Maybe I should go in alone," he says.

"Why?"

"This place looks a little ... rough."

The bar is technically outside of Springside Township, but there's a Dairy Queen a quarter mile down the road, so I'm fairly certain the clientele can't be too questionable.

He doesn't move. Neither do I.

"What do you know about Harold?" he says instead.

"I told you most of it. I remember his lawn. He was forever

doing something to the lawn, and when he ran out of his own, he moved on to ours. And I remember Sadie coming over for coffee. I remember the tears." As I speak, my voice lowers, and I catch the echo of the confused child I used to be. "I wasn't supposed to be eavesdropping, and there was so much I didn't understand."

I do now, of course.

"Sadie didn't grow up here, didn't have many friends," I add. "That can be hard."

"Yeah. Tell me about it."

Again, I swallow back a dose of guilt.

"She has a sister in Illinois," Malcolm says. "Nigel's been talking to her, keeping her up to date on Sadie's condition."

"This just seems so unfair, for both of them."

"You know," he says, his voice lower, filled with what sounds like admiration, "the nurses on the floor call him Sir Nigel since he's hardly left her side and he's so gallant."

Now it's my turn to heave a sigh. "We've got to fix this." I undo my seatbelt.

"You—"

"I'm coming with you." Before he can launch a protest, I switch off the ignition and hop from the truck.

The wind batters us. My jacket with its down filling feels thin and flimsy. The neon from Last Itch drowns out even the chance of stars, and I squint in its glare. It's late; we're both exhausted. And this feels like a fruitless effort.

"We really should be home in bed," I say.

My words hang in the air for so long that I think they might freeze and shatter on the ground. Then it hits me: what I've just said, what it sounds like.

"I—" My cheeks blaze, and even with the wind and the icy air I'm not sure they'll cool any time soon.

Malcolm laughs, grabs my mittened hand, and gives it a squeeze. "Come on. It's cold out here."

A haze of beer and hard liquor flavors the air. But the brass along the bar gleams, and the mirror reflects an array of colorful bottles. The few patrons look depressed rather than dangerous.

"Sense anything?" he asks.

I shake my head.

Malcolm nods toward the bartender. "Let's see what he has to say."

We navigate the maze of chairs and tables. At the bar, a large man is sitting, head down. He wobbles his beer bottle back and forth as if this is his sole entertainment for the evening.

The moment we reach the polished wood, the large man glances up, his gaze meeting mine in the mirror's reflection.

Police Chief Ramsey.

My grip on Malcolm's hand tightens until I'm certain I'm cutting off his circulation.

"Katy, what the ... *oh.*"

Chief Ramsey spins around, wobbles, then rights himself. Although his gaze is a little bleary, it's just as relentless and judgmental as ever.

Malcolm tugs me closer. "Well, this is different."

Chief Ramsey points his beer bottle at me. "What are you doing in here? You're underage."

"No, I'm not."

"Well, you should be," he says. "And you." The beer bottle shifts and accuses Malcolm. "This is no place to bring a girl."

"Actually, we drove here in my truck," I tell him, "so technically, I brought Malcolm."

Malcolm snorts and gives my hand a quick squeeze.

Chief harrumphs, swivels in his seat to face the bar, and continues the back and forth dance with his beer bottle.

"Pity, party of one?" Malcolm whispers, but his tone is compassionate rather than cruel. "Chief's married, right?"

"As far as I know."

"*Still* married?"

The wedding band on his left ring finger would indicate yes, but people—and ghosts—have a hard time letting go.

"I don't know."

I wonder if I should start paying more attention to relationships in the here and now. I have no ambition to become the town gossip, but if the ghosts insist on making it personal, maybe I need to as well. It might make our job easier.

Malcolm tugs me closer still, his gaze scanning the booths, the pool table in the back, the ancient jukebox in one corner that has an *Out of Order* sign duct-taped to its front.

"Why don't you pretend to head for the restroom and do a quick circuit?" He nods toward the bar. "I'll talk to the bartender."

He lets me go and I do just that, my path through the place haphazard, as if I haven't noticed the sign for the restroom. Since it's an index finger with the words *Little Ladies This Way* painted on it, I'd have to be fairly dim not to.

No one here cares. Even the guys playing pool don't seem all that invested in their game, despite the bills stacked to one side. Near the back, I catch the sensation of the otherworldly, the presence slight and light.

I whirl, searching for the source. Nothing stands out. I take a few steps, and a pitcher of beer catches my eye. Normally, they don't wobble of their own volition, but this one does. I inch closer to confirm my suspicions, but don't get too close. I know what comes next.

The pitcher upends, coating the tabletop, the floor, and the two guys sitting in the booth.

One of them shouts. The other swears. At the front of the room, the bartender slaps the counter with his rag in frustration.

"Really, guys? Really? That's the third time tonight."

The sprites careen toward me, pleased and drunk and seeking attention.

"Not funny," I tell them.

They ruffle my hair and stream off, unconcerned. I don't have coffee. My Tupperware containers are in the truck. They know I'm not here for them. And I know, thanks to them, that Harold's ghost can't be here. Sadie's two sprites still haven't returned to her house. Sprites will not be where that particular ghost is.

I thread my way back to Malcolm, who's standing at the bar, head bent in conversation with the bartender and Chief Ramsey. Malcolm takes an occasional sip from a Heineken. I suspect he paid with a twenty and let the bartender keep the change.

Chief has moved on to something amber in a tumbler. The bartender is drinking Perrier. And as odd as this threesome is, the second I'm in earshot, their chatter dies. All three turn to gaze at me. I feel as if I've forgotten to pull on pants, or possibly zip them, but resist the urge to check.

The bartender smiles, then Chief does, and the whole thing goes from odd to creepy.

Malcolm raises an eyebrow. It's a small, almost-not-there sort of gesture, but it floods me with reassurance. He bids the men goodnight and heads for the door, catching me on the way with a hand at the small of my back.

"Outside," he says before I can ask.

The cold clears my head and my lungs. After the dank and murky bar, the air feels crisp and I think I could spend a good ten minutes in deep breathing exercises.

"That was interesting," Malcolm says.

"You had a nice chat, then?"

"No ghost, at least not the one we're looking for," he says. "I managed to find that out before Chief Ramsey butted in."

"Two sprites," I say. "You probably saw them."

"I offered our services, but Jeff—the bartender and owner— wasn't interested. They actually make him money. People keep buying new pitchers to replace the spilt ones. He promised to call if something other than that starts happening."

Sprites are one thing, but I think Harold's ghost might be bad for business.

"So ... what did you three guys talk about?"

He nods toward the truck. "I'm freezing. Get in and I'll tell you."

He's dragging this out, but I comply. Malcolm's expression is both mirthful and a bit mystified, and he knows how to leave me in suspense. He doesn't start speaking until I put the truck in gear and pull onto the highway that leads back to Springside.

"I was getting a little fatherly advice," he says at last.

"About?"

"You."

"Me. For real?"

"Apparently," he says. "According to them, I'm going about it all wrong."

"Going about what?"

"Everything, if you believe them."

The tires hum against the road. Wind carries snow across the double lane. The flakes swirl in the headlights. The effect is hypnotizing. I need to keep the conversation going, if only to stay awake.

"So, are you going to take their advice?" I ask.

Malcolm coughs out a laugh. "Not at all. One." He holds up a finger. "I want you to keep speaking to me."

"Do I even want to know?"

"Trust me, you don't. And two." He adds a second finger. "Chief is sleeping at the station tonight. You don't want to know about that, either. As for Jeff, he's on..." He trails off, touching his thumb to each finger, first on one hand, then the other.

When he reaches double digits, I ask, "Wives? Girlfriends?"

"Yes."

"Wives or girlfriends?"

"Wives *and* girlfriends."

"At the same time?"

"Often."

I can't help it. I laugh.

"When I take advice," Malcolm says, "I like to consider the

source. And in this case—" He casts me a sidelong glance. "I'll wing it."

The heat returns to my cheeks with a vengeance, and it doesn't fade until I pull up in front of Malcolm's apartment complex.

"It looks like we've hit a dead end." He shields his eyes against the glare of the streetlamp and gazes through the windshield. "Can you think of any place we haven't tried?"

I can't.

"Maybe Belinda was right about his work," Malcolm says. "He was in sales, right?"

"I think so. He made a lot of money. That's all I really know."

"I'll call around in the morning to some of our business contacts, see if they're having any issues."

Our contacts? More like *his*. He's the one with the gift for networking and talking and generating leads. I shift in my seat so I can look at him full-on. We're in the black this month, even with my hospital stay. Some of that is the holiday bringing out the ghosts.

A lot of that is Malcolm.

"Thank you." I mean to say it forcefully, like a business partner. It comes out soft, more like a friend.

"Hey, it's what we do, right?" His grin starts off businesslike but transforms into something far sweeter.

That sweetness invades the cab of the truck. I feel as if I should hold my breath or make a wish or something. Every part of me insists I should lean closer to him. He seems caught by something and reaches out a hand to brush a strand of hair from my cheek.

I remain absolutely still. It's so quiet I'm certain I can hear my heartbeat. I think I might hear his.

"It's late," he says, breaking that stillness. "Even ghost hunters need sleep."

He unhooks his seatbelt and opens the passenger side door. "See you in the morning ... well, later this morning."

I swallow hard and nod.

He jumps down from the truck. I wait until he's inside the building and the light flickers on in his apartment's living area.

"It's what we do," I echo, putting the truck in gear.

I drive home, certain that when it comes to both this particular ghost and Malcolm, I'm missing something crucial.

THE CALL COMES at three in the morning. No name, just a local number that blurs before my eyes. I don't think I can handle a ghost eradication on only two hours of sleep. But it's December, and that brings out the worst in ghosts. I answer because—to quote Malcolm—it's what we do.

"Is this Katy Lindstrom?" a voice asks, husky and feminine and completely unfamiliar.

"Yes." I'm oddly reluctant to respond. Maybe it's the hour or the woman's tone. I blink and taste the air. I almost never end up with even a playful sprite, but something feels off kilter to me.

"And you're the ghost catcher, right?" the woman says.

"I am, along with my partner, Malcolm Armand."

"Oh, he's the cute one."

I haven't conducted an actual survey of how many cute guys live in Springside, but I'm pretty certain Malcolm isn't the only one. Besides, he's more … suave than cute.

"Yes," I say, because the woman has fallen silent. "Can we help you? Do you have a ghost?"

"I think so … I mean, I've never had one before, but I'm pretty sure this is one. I'm Misty Sandborne, by the way."

Something about her name pings in the back of my mind. I don't know her; she's obviously not a repeat customer. Yet, as the silence extends, it's clear she's expecting me to respond.

When I don't, she adds, "I … knew Harold Lancaster."

Oh? *Oh.*

"Yeah, I know," she continues, although I haven't said a word. "It doesn't make me the most popular girl in town. I could tell you stories, though, about some of these so-called upstanding citizens—"

"The ghost?" I prompt.

"Right. Of course. Well, this guy said he could handle it."

"Guy?" I ask.

"A real cutie—not your cutie, but a different one."

See? Springside does have more than one cute guy.

"I don't have a cutie," I feel compelled to add, but I'm not certain Misty hears me.

"Anyway," she continues, "he said he could handle it and now he's out cold on my living room floor, and this ghost thing is ... pouting."

"Pouting?"

"Just hanging in the air. You can see its outline and everything and it's just ... sulking. *Gawd*, it reminds me of the way Harold used to get."

I bolt upright, then freeze. For a moment everything seizes: my muscles, my thoughts, any words I might say.

"You still there?" Misty asks.

"Yeah ... I am, and my partner and I will be right over."

"Oh! You're bringing the cute one?"

Yes. Yes, I am.

I TEXT Malcolm Misty's address and add:

It's Harold's ghost. Bring extra Tupperware. And anything else you can think of.

In the kitchen, I consider the percolator, the Kona blend, our field kit for toting coffee when we don't brew on the premises. But

Harold Lancaster hated coffee, and his ghost has shown us—in no uncertain terms—how it feels about the stuff.

Coffee won't work. Maybe nothing will.

Misty lives in a duplex a few blocks from Malcolm's apartment. He's on the porch, stamping his feet against the cold and blowing air against his hands when I pull up in my truck. He has a bag slung over one shoulder filled with Tupperware and a small electric samovar.

I've arrived empty-handed.

"She's not answering?" I ask when I reach the porch.

"Decided to wait for you. What's up?"

"I'm pretty sure it's Harold's ghost," I say.

"And he's here ... why?"

"Misty Sandborne was one of the women Harold had an affair with."

So, yes, Malcolm is suave, the sort of guy who's hard to ruffle. But in this instance, I manage to do so. His mouth hangs open, and he blinks a few times before an incredulous look spreads across his face.

He recovers, because Malcolm always recovers, and says, "We're missing something, aren't we? Something obvious."

"There's ... yes, something. A connection? A pattern?" I shake my head. "But what it is, I don't even have a clue."

Malcolm rings the bell and we wait. A shuffle sounds behind the closed door, then it opens as far as the security chain will let it. I peer inside but can't see a thing.

"Hi, I'm Katy Lindstrom, and this is my partner, Malcolm Armand. We spoke on the phone? You have a ghost?"

"Oh, thank goodness!" the husky voice from the phone greets us.

The door shuts, the chain rattles, and then the way is clear.

"Watch out for the body," Misty says as we make our way down the hall.

Three feet inside, where the entryway meets the living room, a body is sprawled face down on the carpet. Malcolm steps over it first and then offers me his hand.

"Oh, a real gentleman," Misty coos.

We ignore her. We're too riveted by the sight of the inert form just lying there as if it's part of the decor. The question in Malcolm's eyes mirrors my own.

What the hell is Carter Dupree doing here?

I crane my neck to get a better look. With slightly more presence of mind, Malcolm takes a knee and checks for breathing and a pulse.

"Oh, he's fine," Misty assures us. "Just out cold."

I decide not to ask why or how. In that moment, the real reason we're here oozes its way into my consciousness. I recognize Harold's ghost. From the way it surges forward, I suspect it recognizes me as well. I brace, waiting for the inevitable—a vase careening toward my head, another encounter with sharp-edged furniture.

Instead, the thing simply hunkers down, morose and melancholy, filling the room with undeniable gloom.

"See?" Misty says. "I'm supposed to live with that? I was going to call you from the start, honest." She adjusts her emerald silk robe and gives Malcolm a little finger wave. "But he"—she points at Carter—"said he could fix everything."

"What happened?" Malcolm asks.

Misty shrugs. "He was muttering some things, crazy words—I'd never heard them before—then he opens his mouth real wide, like he was trying to swallow the thing whole. Then, boom!"

"Boom?" I say.

She extends a hand toward the body on the floor. I notice then that her long, lacquered fingernails match her robe exactly. "Out cold."

A knowing look crosses Malcolm's face. He gives his head a shake, like he can't believe the thought that's just crossed his mind. His sardonic smile tells me he does.

"Remember my theory, Katy, about why Carter's appearance coincided with Harold's ghost?"

I consider the events of the past few weeks, from the wreath on my door to Carter Dupree unconscious on Misty Sandborne's floor. My gaze travels from him to the dour mass that is Harold's ghost. I'm not entirely certain I believe Malcolm's conspiracy theory, but the proof of it is right there on the floor.

"But why? Why would he do that?"

Malcolm stands and nudges Carter's side with the toe of his boot. "You'll have to ask him that."

"Then what happened here?" I point at Carter and then to the ghost. This, I suspect, is a necromancer thing.

With movements practiced and cautious, Malcolm eases toward the ghostly shape. Its form covers the sofa and it seems to have settled there, its focus on the flat screen television rather than us. I have a strange urge to hand it the remote control.

"I think," he says, reaching a hand out, gauging the ghost's strength, "that it overpowered him. It's grown stronger in the past few days." He turns to me. "Do you feel it?"

I do, and the idea fills me with dismay. We've been doing all the wrong things with this eradication.

"Carter can't hold it and his other ghost at the same time, not anymore." Malcolm gestures toward the floor. "That's the end result. Only a really strong necromancer could do that. Nigel could, before the addiction took its toll."

At these last words, Misty places a hand on Malcolm's arm, her green nails shining like Christmas ornaments against his white shirt. "Oh, sweetie, that must have been so hard. Your brother, is it?"

Malcolm gives an awkward sort of nod, pats Misty's hand, and backs away with all the grace of Frankenstein's monster. I realize then what he probably has from the start.

Misty is wearing absolutely nothing beneath that emerald silk.

The ethereal form on the couch roils at this interaction. Misty whirls, silk swirling, hands on hips.

"Now, Harold Lancaster, you behave yourself. Yes, I know who you are and I'm not impressed."

The ghost shimmers, the result throwing a glow over the three of us. We stare, caught up in this spectral lightshow. It has our attention, and that's what most ghosts want, one way or another.

I cast my mind back to when I was younger. I didn't understand Harold's philandering back then. Even when I did understand the concept, it was only much later that I truly understood—the pain, the sorrow, Sadie's tears, my grandmother's troubled looks.

But I also remember Harold Lancaster, the man who always ran his snow blower along our sidewalk and driveway every winter. He would—assuming he was home—come over to take something down from a high shelf, or lug the Christmas decorations from the attic. He'd oil the hinges on the garden gate without anyone asking him to.

"Malcolm," I say, working to keep my voice even. "Can you go grab some Tupperware?"

He backs toward his bag, more stuttering monster steps. "What do you have in mind?"

"If I can drain its power, do you think you can catch it?"

"Depends on how much you drain it, but yes, you do that, and I'll do the rest."

I turn to Misty. "Do you have an apron?"

"I have one left over from a French maid's costume I wore at Halloween."

Of course she does. "Can I borrow it?"

She heads toward the bedroom and I call after her.

"And a hair binder or two?"

When she returns, I knot the apron around my waist and use the rubber bands Misty hands me to secure my hair into a bun at the nape of my neck.

Malcolm raises an eyebrow at my impromptu costume. "I'm afraid to ask what it is you think this ghost wants."

"Trust me?"

He gives me one of those sweet, dark-roast grins. "Always."

I bustle into the kitchen area of Misty's apartment. The only thing dividing it from the living room is a long breakfast bar. I'm in full view of everyone. I turn, stand on tiptoes, and strain toward the top shelf above the sink.

"Oh, if only there was someone around who was tall enough," I say, making my voice quake the way my grandmother's used to, all low tones and a certain amount of bite.

"I'm sure he's tall enough." Misty jabs a finger toward Malcolm.

I shush her. "Now, Katy-Girl, don't you go crawling on the counters. That's dangerous. You might fall and hurt yourself."

A choking sound comes from Malcolm, like he's trying very hard not to laugh. Misty stares, wide-eyed. She throws Malcolm a questioning look, and her hand twitches, like she's *this close* to calling 911.

"I would love it if someone would help me." I punctuate this with little jumps toward the shelf.

Behind me, a groan sounds, eerie and possibly irritated. There's a rumble. A moment later, a soft exhale escapes Malcolm.

"Whoa," he says.

I peer over my shoulder to see the ghost slide from the couch, its form spreading out over the floor, like a bank of fog rolling in from the ocean. It flows from the living area to the kitchen until the mist is swirling around my feet.

Then the ghost pulls itself together into an almost humanlike mass.

"Oh, Harold! It's you!" I clap my hands together. "You're here to help!"

Harold's ghost rattles the dishes on the top shelf. One teeters and plunges to the floor, missing me by mere centimeters. It splinters into pieces.

"Hey!" Misty cries out. "That's my Martha Stewart collection!"

Another choking sound comes from Malcolm. I turn in time to see him jam the Tupperware under one arm and pull out his wallet. He hands Misty twenty dollars. She takes the bill and tucks it inside her cleavage.

How it remains there is a physics problem I don't care to contemplate. Besides, I have an entire kitchen yet to ruin.

One hand on my hip, I use the other to point, direct, cajole, and praise. Harold's ghost pushes the broom across the floor before shattering three glasses within the confines of the sink. The refrigerator door flies open. Cartons inch forward and then fall over the edge. Yogurt splatters across the tile.

With each effort, I praise. With each effort, Harold's ghost shrinks until at last it's opaque and puny. It still wants to help, circles me as if begging for another chore. This might be the saddest thing of all. It would do anything if only I praised it one more time.

My gaze meets Malcolm's, and I give the barest of nods.

He launches himself across the room, Tupperware clutched in both hands. His aim is perfect. He catches Harold's ghost in the exact center of the container and crashes to the floor.

With the ghost trapped, the otherworldly presence in the apartment dissipates. I draw a full breath. So does Misty.

"It's like smoke clearing." She fans herself, those long green nails blurring with the effort.

I glance down at Malcolm, still on the floor, still gripping the Tupperware for all he's worth.

"How'd you know?" he asks.

I shrug. "I didn't, not really. It was a guess, something I remembered from when I was little."

I think it was one of the reasons my grandmother always looked both sad and troubled around Harold. Yes, he hurt Sadie—and badly, too. But how awful is it to go through life craving constant praise and attention?

I kneel next to Malcolm to help him secure the container's lid. The Tupperware rocks, but the fight has mostly drained from this ghost. The only thing left to do is drive it somewhere far away. I unknot the apron and pull the rubber bands from my hair. Malcolm double-checks the container's lid. We're both eyeing the door.

"And I suppose you expect me to clean up this mess?" Misty is standing in front of us, hands on hips, emerald silk robe dangerously close to not being there at all.

Malcolm reaches for his wallet again, but she laughs.

"Oh, honey, I was kidding. I'll clean up. I'm just so glad to get that thing"—she flings a hand toward the container—"out of here."

"What about him?" I nudge Carter's foot with my own.

Misty cocks her head. "Naw, you can leave him. He's a cutie."

"He's kind of a jerk," I say.

"So was Harold."

Malcolm clears his throat. "It was nice to meet you, Misty." He extends a hand, the one not clutching the Tupperware.

"Oh, a real gentleman," she coos in a reprise from earlier.

I want nothing more than to leave, drive Harold's ghost far, far, far away, and then sleep for eighteen hours. But I turn to Misty and say brightly, "Call if you get anymore ghosts!"

Malcolm shrugs on his coat and steps over Carter Dupree. I do the same, a mere three feet behind him. The door opens, blasting us with icy, predawn air. He steps outside. I'm about to do the same when the door slams shut.

CHAPTER 6

THE DOOR'S OAK paneling frosts over immediately. I know a ghost infestation when I see one. Even so, I touch the doorknob. I yank my hand back, fingers stinging with freezer burn.

I'm about to pound with my bare hand, but think better of it. I pull on a mitten and start hammering on the door.

"Malcolm! Are you okay? Did the ghost escape?"

"Did it ... what?" The door—and whatever else is between us—muffles his voice. "I have it right here."

"Then what is this?"

The door is now hoary with frost, and crystalline patterns spread across the doorknob. Even through the mitten, the cold brass bites my skin. I try the knob several times, because none of this makes sense and I'm feeling more stubborn than smart.

"Katy, Katy, stop it. You're not helping."

He's right. I give the knob one last rattle for good measure before giving up.

"Do you sense anything?" I ask through the door.

"Not a thing. Look, I'll do a circuit around back. You look inside."

I turn to face Misty. Her face is nearly as pale as her frosted door. Her hands clutch her arms, the nails fading into the green of the robe. I find myself contemplating that rather than my current predicament. I don't know where to look or what I'm looking for, and my mind is so clouded from lack of sleep, I'm not sure what I'd do if I found something.

"I could use a cup of coffee," I say.

That's when an icy glimmer chases across my neck.

"Maybe I'm not the only one?" I ask the air.

"Who ... who are you talking to?" Misty demands.

"I'm sorry," I say—to her this time. "But I think you have another ghost."

I hover impatiently by the door until Malcolm completes his circuit. His thump against the wood makes me jump, heart thudding.

"Nothing," he calls out. "We could maybe try the neighbors—"

"I think it's a ghost."

"But—"

"What happened to Carter's ghost when he passed out?" I ask before he can say more.

Silence greets this question. After a moment, I hear some stomping and throat clearing.

"Are you telling me that it was there in the apartment the whole time and we didn't sense it?"

"*She* was there the whole time, and no, we didn't, because I think that's her specialty."

I turn in a slow circle, my gaze scanning Misty's apartment. Other than that glimmer across my neck—and the frozen door, of course—I have nothing else to go on. But I doubt it's Carter Dupree who has been the master of stealth all this time.

"Delilah? Is that you?"

The air shimmers and sparkles, Delilah's presence filling the small space. She's strong, and lovely, and awe-inspiring. Misty gazes at her, slack-jawed, and I feel very much the same.

"I hope I'm that hot when I'm dead," she murmurs.

I ignore this and call through the door to Malcolm. "It's her. It's Delilah."

"Well, get her to let you out," he says.

"How am I supposed to do that?"

"Oh, come on, Katy. What do most ghosts want? What do most ghosts want from *you*?"

Is he crazy? Can't he feel how strong she is? Why would a ghost with so much power want a measly cup of coffee? Then I cast my thoughts back to that night when I invited Delilah to my house and the air shimmered with her ghostly laughter.

"Delilah?" I say. "Would you like some Kona blend?"

The door springs open. Malcolm reaches for me. Before he can grab my wrist, I'm yanked backward, a set of deadly green nails puncturing my down jacket.

"That one, honey?" Misty whispers in my ear, voice urgent and fierce. "He's a keeper. Grab him while the grabbing's good. You'll regret it if you don't."

With the force of the supernatural at my back, I'm ripped from Misty's grip, propelled down the steps, and dumped into the snowbank at the edge of the walkway.

I emerge from the snow, eyelashes fringed with flakes, cold rivers running down my spine. Malcolm stares, his gaze filled with concern. But really? Beneath that concern, I think he's trying very hard not to laugh.

"Here," he says, a hand extended. He pulls me from the snow and I topple forward into his arms.

I peer up at him, still snow-covered. Now he does laugh, but it's soft and sweet. With the gloved fingers of his free hand, he brushes the melting snow from my face.

"You okay?" he asks, and there's something more in his question, something I'm missing.

I nod. Cold sneaks through my jacket. The back of my shirt is soaked. I probably look like I tumbled from bed and into that snowbank. Malcolm doesn't seem to mind.

"Katy, I—"

Before he can say more, that supernatural force batters us both, urging us toward my truck.

"I think someone wants her coffee." He adjusts his grip on the container and takes my hand.

When we reach my truck, the entire thing is frosted over. He grabs my wrist before my fingers graze the door handle. I turn to him.

"If she wants coffee, why is she freezing my truck?"

He gives his head a slow shake and searches the air. The space around my truck shimmers and sparkles. The truck itself glows like it's been doused in glitter.

"I don't understand," I say. "I thought she wanted coffee."

"You could ask her."

"Ask ... her." I take a step away from him and fold my arms over my chest. "You mean necromancer style?"

"That's exactly what I mean," he says.

"I'm not a necromancer."

"Come on, Katy. You've done it before."

"I was trying to save your life. There are exceptions to rules."

"Why is it a rule in the first place?"

"It's not what I do. It's not who I am."

"It truly won't hurt you," he says.

"Addiction?"

Doubt clouds his eyes. It was, perhaps, a low blow to remind him of Nigel like that.

"You're stronger than that," he says.

"You don't know that." I believe there's a reason my grandmother never told me about necromancy, that she did it to keep me safe. Until I understand why, I'm not about to dabble in it.

My jeans are stiff with cold. Malcolm winces against the light breeze that chases a few flakes into his hair. And my truck shines like the star on top of a Christmas tree.

Then he holds up a hand as if conceding—for now. "All right. Maybe she'll talk to me." He turns in a circle, projecting his voice. "Delilah, would you agree to a simple exchange of information?"

The air vibrates; Malcolm smiles and hands me the Tupperware. He stands straight, eyes closed, head tipped back slightly, arms at his sides, the palms turned skyward. The glimmer descends on him. He stiffens before relaxing again. Then he laughs, low and rich, his coffee laugh.

"Yes," he says. "She's very stubborn ... We manage, despite that."

What? Are they ... talking about me? I want to interrupt. I want to defend myself, but I don't know what I could say.

"Oh, of course," Malcolm continues. "I should've thought of that. I think Katy will be more than amenable once she understands."

Understand what? This is driving me crazy. Part of me regrets not speaking to Delilah myself.

The glow fades from Malcolm. He doubles over, releasing one giant cough. Then he stumbles backward, against my truck. He braces a hand on its side and then sinks to the ground.

"It's been a while since I've done that." His breath is ragged, cheeks flushed. His eyes hold a glazed look. He blinks as if he can't quite focus. "Wow. She's strong."

"Um, maybe you two would like to be alone?"

Malcolm coughs out a chuckle. Around us, the air shimmers with glee.

"A little help?" He holds out a hand.

I tug him to his feet. At the last second, I decide not to pull him in to me. It's tempting, but I'm too curious about what Delilah said. He's still too shaky. Besides, I doubt I can compete with something that sparkles the way she does.

He brushes off his trousers. "Here's the thing. She's only ever dealt with necromancers. Since she's accepted your offer of coffee, she needs to provide you something in return."

"Really? Like what? How does that work?"

"Usually it's something comparable."

I shake my head. "I don't need anything." I turn, addressing the air around me. "I'm sorry, but I can't think of anything."

"Here's the other piece of it. She's still tethered to Carter, but if you complete the pact, accept something from her in return, she'll be free to go."

"Free and not have to go back to him?"

"Exactly."

"Oh, Delilah. Okay, hang on, let me think." I squeeze my eyes shut. I take several deep breaths, the scent of wet wool and stale ice surrounding me. What I need is that cup of coffee waiting for us at home. I'm pretty sure I haven't had a coherent thought since before Misty's phone call of hours before.

I open my eyes and find Malcolm's. "Comparable, right?"

"Yes."

"So it doesn't have to be a huge thing."

"Not at all. Just a fair trade."

"Like the coffee."

"Sure." He gives me a wary look. I must sound punch-drunk to him. "Like the coffee."

Oh. *Coffee*. Of course.

"Delilah, I know I promised you Kona blend, and you can still have some, but I bought a new holiday blend from the Coffee Depot the other day. I have no idea if ghosts will like it. Will you give it a taste test for me?"

The air around us sparkles with renewed vigor. A moment later, all the ice on my truck evaporates.

~

TWO THERMOSES of the Coffee Depot's holiday blend rest between Malcolm and me on the truck's front seat. It's his turn to drive, so I clutch the Tupperware container that holds Harold's ghost. It swirls inside, still fairly weak. I thought about offering it a hot chocolate, but I don't dare crack the lid.

After much debate among the three of us—me, Malcolm, Delilah—we decide to head east into Wisconsin. The highways are clear in that direction. North is out of the question. It makes no sense to head toward the Twin Cities and the necromancers who would no doubt like to capture both Delilah and Harold's ghost.

East also isn't quite as desolate—or dangerous—as the Dakotas. Snow, wind, a sudden storm, and we could end up trapped for days.

When we cross the Mississippi, Delilah ricochets around the cab of the truck. She gives us each a ghostly kiss on the cheek before streaming through the crack at the top of the window.

"Goodbye!" I call after her. "It was nice to meet you."

Malcolm laughs.

"What?" I say, rolling up the window. "It's true."

"She ... you ... you've made a powerful ally."

"I don't want an ally."

"I'm afraid you have one."

"I just wanted her to be free," I say.

"Which is why you have an ally."

"My grandmother always said that we're doing everyone a favor by separating people and ghosts. I always took that to mean the people benefited." I stare out the window, twisting in my seat to see the Mississippi wandering south. "I wonder if she meant the ghosts as well."

"Well, there's a lot of good haunting between here and New Orleans. Delilah should have a grand time."

"It wasn't that hard to free her," I venture. Really, a taste test?

"Well, Carter was unconscious, so his additional hold on her—

whatever that was—had weakened. Also, he might be more skilled, but I think you have more innate ability."

"So, what you're saying is that it wasn't a fair fight this time around."

"Maybe not, but, Katy, don't doubt your ability as a necromancer."

"I'm not a necromancer." I sigh. How many times must I say this?

"You don't have to act on it." He casts me a sidelong glance. "But you should probably acknowledge it, for your own ... safety."

"My safety? Am I in danger?"

This time, Malcolm doesn't glance my way. His hands grip the wheel in the classic ten and two position, his knuckles tightening beneath the leather gloves, his gaze straight ahead.

"I don't know," is all he says.

WE DRIVE WITHOUT DESTINATION, leaving behind the towns close to the river and heading into the prairie. At last I spot a sign for a nature preserve. I point.

"Romance Prairie State Nature Area," Malcolm says. "Are we allowed to drive in?"

"Will it matter?"

His sigh sounds as weary as I feel.

"I have cross-country skis," I say. "I can ski to a secluded release point."

"You're not going alone. You have rules about necromancy? Well, I have rules, too, and one of them involves not wandering into a deserted nature preserve alone."

He's right, of course. It's a foolish thing to do, especially in the winter with a dangerous ghost along for the ride.

"You're not dressed for this." I'm wearing boots, at least, and I have the ski gear in the back of my truck.

"Doesn't matter. I don't think we'll have to go far."

Malcolm has an unerring sense for these things. The truck jostles over snow-packed ruts and careens onto something I'm not certain is an actual road, but after a quarter of a mile it lands us in a parking area.

The space is forlorn, abandoned. Wind whips my hair, nearly steals the Tupperware from my grip. No one is coming out here until spring. I glance at Malcolm.

He nods, once. Yes. This is the place.

I wade into the snow-covered prairie, pushing through matted grass and drifts that reach my knees. I walk far enough that sweat blooms along my spine and the cold air makes my lungs ache. I find a dip in the terrain, a shielded area, and turn around. I hold up the container.

"Do we uncover it?" My voice rings hollow in the empty air.

That's always been our policy. Catch and release. But this isn't a normal ghost eradication. This is personal. Back in Springside, Sadie is still in a coma. I don't know which is the worse fate for a ghost—released into the wilds or trapped inside a plastic prison. I suspect the latter but really have no proof.

Sadie's my friend, but Nigel is Malcolm's brother. I'll give his wishes more weight.

If he'll tell me, that is.

He stands there contemplating the surroundings. I shiver, the wind biting into my skin through my jeans. My arms tremble slightly, although the container isn't heavy. His gaze scans the horizon to the east, passes over me, and surveys the west. Then his eyes lock with mine. He's far enough away that I can't read their expression.

"Crack the lid," he says.

"Are you sure?"

"No. Not in the least. But to do it any other way would be ... violating something."

So I do. I ease back one corner enough that—if the ghost wants

—it can stream through to freedom. Instead, Harold's ghost churns, slow and sad. Waves of dejection roll off of it. A surge of pity hits me.

"There are other ways to get attention." I place the container in the snow, digging it in so the wind won't catch it and tumble it across the prairie. "You know that, right? You don't have to hurt anyone."

I clomp from the field, collecting weeds and clumps of snow along the way. When I reach the edge of the parking lot, Malcolm pulls me up and out of the snowbank. He holds me close against his chest. I nestle there, arms around his waist.

"Thank you," he says, his breath warm against my scalp.

I'm not sure what I've done, but I nod anyway.

IT'S hours later when I wake in the crook of Malcolm's arm. The remains of our breakfast litter the table in front of us. The half booth we're snuggled in shields us from most of the diner's other patrons, but the clatter of dishes reaches my ears. The pancakes I ate are heavy and warm inside me. My lips taste like maple syrup. I feel grubby, un-showered, and I'm not exactly sure what my hair is doing, but I'm certain it's frightening.

All I want to do is close my eyes again, because in this moment, I'm content.

"You awake?" Malcolm says, his voice low. From its tone I know that he'd let me sleep for as long as I like.

"Just woke up. How long have we been here? Are they going to kick us out?"

"Only an hour and a half." His fingers play with the sleeve of my shirt. It's a slow, comfortable caress and might be the reason I fell asleep to begin with.

"The rush is over, so they don't really care," he adds. "Besides, I sweet-talked our waitress."

Of course he did. Sweet-talking waitresses is one of Malcolm's many skills.

"She keeps trying to serve me coffee." He shudders. "It smells like someone dipped a brown crayon into hot water. You've ruined me, Katy. I will never drink restaurant coffee again."

I can't help but laugh, and he tugs me closer. A slight buzzing comes from the pocket of Malcolm's jacket. He shifts without letting me go.

"Hang on, let me get this."

He pulls out his phone. Because I'm resting against his chest, I feel his quick intake of breath. It's an excited, happy thing. Before I can ask, before I can crane my neck to peer at his phone, he turns the screen toward me.

Nigel: She's awake. Whatever you did, it worked. Thank you.

Malcolm pulls me closer still, folding me into his arms. He squeezes, just once. "Looks like it's going to be a Merry Christmas."

THE TWO SPRITES float lazily in the Coffee Depot's holiday blend. They've had their fill, and I will need to scoop them back into their container soon. For now, I let them bask in the steam and Sadie's attention.

"They missed you." I realize now that the sprite bent on destroying the K&M storefront display was one of Sadie's. "This one—or maybe this one." I point. "Tried to warn me."

"They tried to warn me, too," she says.

Sadie is sitting at the kitchen table, her chin in her hand. Her salt and pepper curls are tipped in red and green. Tiny replicas of Christmas ornaments dangle from her ears. She's been baking all day long and her entire house smells warm and alive again. Rich chocolate, something savory with sage and onion, and something else that's gingery with a lot of bite. No wonder the sprites love it here. I'm not certain the coffee is enough to tempt them away.

Her gaze is tender as she watches them dip and dive in the steam. "When Nigel left that morning—" Here, a blush colors her cheeks. "They burst in and tore around the place. I couldn't get them to stop. I'm afraid I scolded them."

"Sprites are immune to scolding."

"I'm just glad..." She trails off and sighs. "And sorry. I'm so sorry Harold hurt you and Malcolm."

"It wasn't really Harold," I say, "but his ghost. There's a difference."

I've tried to explain this to her already. Harold's ghost was alone and confused—and possibly under Carter's influence. With time, he might make a fine ghost. But now that doesn't matter. What matters is Sadie's quiet Christmas with Nigel, so I scoop up my charges and pull on my coat.

"It's so cold out," Sadie says. "I hate the idea of the nature preserve."

I hold the Tupperware at eye level and frown at the two sprites. "I do have another idea, but they'll have to behave themselves."

It's sunset on Christmas Eve. My truck meets hardly any traffic as I drive to the Springside Long-term Care facility. There, it's quiet too. Many residents visit family over the holidays. I wave at the night manager on my way in.

"I don't think you've ever brought us any ghosts before," he says to me.

"These two could use a little mothering. If they get out of hand, I'll come back. I'm on call over the holiday if you need me."

Mrs. Greeley's room is dark, but I doubt she's asleep. She's blind, and my guess is that she's heard my clomping boots from the moment I entered the facility.

"Katy, dear? Is that you?"

"It is," I say. "And I've brought you something." I've barely eased back the lid before the two sprites spring out, darting about like puppies or five-year-olds.

"Oh, my. They *are* active."

"They could use—"

"A visit with a grandmother?" Humor fills her voice.

"Exactly!" I pull up a chair. "I've already told them that they need to behave."

"It will be like having my own here, although at least I don't need to worry about finding them snacks."

"I'll stop by with some coffee." I eye the glimmer near the television set. "Do you two hear that? Behave and you get the Kona blend."

Mrs. Greeley's own grandchildren are away this holiday, at Disney World. I decide that when I come back tomorrow I'll spend the day with everyone. Belinda is up north with her mother at some fancy lodge. Malcolm has gone to visit a fraternity brother. Sadie and Nigel are spending the first of what I hope are many Christmases together.

"How about you, my dear?" Mrs. Greeley asks.

"I'm okay."

"That doesn't sound like an honest answer."

It isn't.

"I miss her," I say.

I want to add a litany of things to this list beyond how I miss my grandmother. How I haven't decorated the house, or put up a tree, or even have a single sugar cookie to eat. How none of that matters since my grandmother isn't here to celebrate. I don't want decorations or a tree or any cookies, not without her.

I hoped her ghost might return for Christmas, but I know that was wishful thinking.

Mrs. Greeley doesn't tell me everything will be okay. Instead, she takes my hand, the way my grandmother used to, and gently strokes my fingers.

I stay until the last of my tears have dried against my cheeks, leaving the skin scratchy and raw and my heart empty.

CHAPTER 7

I SEE THE FIGURE on my porch when I'm half a block from my house. For a second, my heart leaps. Tall, broad-shouldered. I'm certain it's Malcolm. But when he glances around—in a way that looks more than a little guilty—I know it can't be.

Besides, Malcolm has a key.

I park the truck three houses from mine, slip out, and ease the door closed. The temperature has dropped, so I tug my hood up and over my head. My boots squeak against the snow. In the quiet, the sound is loud, but whoever is on my porch doesn't seem to notice.

By the time I reach the end of my walkway, he's doing something with the mistletoe wreath, the one that I haven't bothered to take down and toss on the compost heap. Beneath the glow of the porch lamp, his hair gleams. I take a deep breath. Then I yell out.

"Boo!"

Yes, it's childish. But when Carter Dupree jumps about three feet into the air, it's worth it. He recovers, bracing a hand on the stair rail, then pulls it back because his fingers are bare and the metal handrail is like ice.

He's still blowing on his fingers when I land on the porch.

"Nice trick," he says.

"There's no trick."

"Really?"

"Yes, really. I'm not a necromancer."

"That's where you're wrong."

"Why did you bring Harold here?" I ask, deciding to skip over the small talk. "Why would you even do anything like that?"

"To show you your potential, to show you how you're *wasting* your potential." He shakes his head as if he can't believe my naïveté. "Besides, don't you have a powerful friend to call upon?"

I don't know what he means, but I also don't want to admit that—not to Carter Dupree. "So the part with the hospital means what? Nothing?"

"And everyone's okay, right?"

"Coma, concussion? Sure, we're great," I say.

He stands there, arms crossed over his chest, one eyebrow cocked in a look that's both smug and condescending. "And, speaking of necromancy—"

From the mistletoe wreath he pulls an envelope, different from the first one I found there a few weeks ago. He hands it to me. The edges are embossed in gold. The paper feels heavy in my hands. The whole thing has the elegance of a wedding invitation and the gravitas of a summons.

"Go on." He nods toward the envelope. "Open it."

I do, enough to read the gold lettering on the top of the card inside.

The Midwest Necromancer Association

Really? The shady cabal exists? And they have such a ... boring name?

You are cordially invited to a gathering of prospective members...

I read no further. Instead, I shoot Carter a glare.

"You're a shoo-in, you know," he says, "being legacy and all."

"Legacy? How can I be legacy? My grandmother wasn't a necromancer."

"No, she wasn't."

"Then?" I point to the invitation.

"Think about it, Katy. Think about what 'legacy' means and how that can apply to you."

I nod, but I have no plans to think about any of that.

We stand there in the cold, the night so still around us I can hear the faint crack of an icicle as it falls from the eaves. I suspect he wants me to invite him inside—yes, after everything. So I stand there, chin tilted in a gesture that means he should start walking down my porch steps.

"I'll be seeing you around, Katy." He brings two fingers to his brow in a salute. "You can count on that."

I remain on my porch until he's ducked inside a black sedan and driven away. Only then do I pull out the card.

You are cordially invited to a gathering of prospective members. Come meet your fellow necromancers for an evening of networking and socializing. Learn what the Midwest Necromancer Association can offer you—and what you can offer us.
Black tie recommended.

Oh. Well. I guess I'm not wearing the skater skirt, then. I roll my eyes, not that there's anyone around to see.

Below the embossed lettering is a handwritten scrawl:

You have something of mine. I'd like it back.

My gaze is drawn to where Carter's car was sitting moments before. Doesn't he know I set Delilah free? I think about what he said, something about a trick and a powerful friend, and realize that no, he thinks I'm using Delilah.

Because that's exactly the sort of thing he'd do.

I'm about to trek back down the sidewalk to my truck when my phone buzzes.

The text is from Sadie. The moment I see it, my heart seizes.

Sadie: Katy, can you come over? We need your help.

Oh, no. *No.* I told them to behave. I divert my path, heading for Sadie's instead of my truck. When I pass the recycling bin, I drop the invitation and its matching envelope inside.

It's not Sadie who greets me at the door. It's not Nigel. No, it's Malcolm. Malcolm, who's supposed to be in the Twin Cities. Malcolm, who's standing there in a pressed shirt and trousers, not a hair out of place and a shave so fresh, the lingering scent of shaving cream fills the air between us.

Humor lights his eyes. This is most likely because I'm standing there speechless. The cold against my teeth and tongue tells me my mouth is hanging open.

He grabs my hands and pulls me inside. With gentle fingers, he eases the hood from my head. I manage to unzip the thing on my own and hang it on the coat rack.

"What are you doing here?" I ask. "I thought—"

"Seriously, Katy? Did you think we'd leave you alone on Christmas? *This* Christmas?"

From the living room comes a laugh, full and throaty.

"Is that—?"

"Belinda," Malcolm confirms. "Gregory's here too. And of course Nigel. We even invited Chief Ramsey."

"No. You're kidding."

"He was alone in the station when I was locking up the other day. I felt kind of sorry for him." Malcolm shrugs. "He brought a Yule log and some rum for the eggnog."

I laugh and start for the living room, but he slips his hand in mine and tugs me back.

"Katy," he says, and now his eyes are darker than I've ever seen them.

We're in the shadows of the entryway, the space filled with the aroma of pine. I stare up at him, trying to fathom the expression that crosses his face. He looks like a man teetering at the edge of a cliff.

"What I'm trying to say—" he begins. "What I've been trying to say for a while now is—"

"You don't know what comes next?"

"That's just it. I do. This comes next. You, and me, and ghost hunting. People search a lifetime trying to find something meaningful to do, a calling. I used to think that was necromancy. I used to think that the next big market win would make me happy. But it never did, not like this."

"So ghost eradication is better than being Broker of the Year?"

He laughs, head thrown back, that rich, dark roast of a laugh. I want to drink in the sound of it, memorize it, remember it forever.

"Much better," he says, "believe it or not."

I do. That's why the rest of it—the part where it's Malcolm and me without the ghosts—is so hard.

"But then there's us," I say. "You and me. No ghosts."

His forehead rests against mine. "And then there's us."

"Do you want there to be an us?" I don't like how small my voice sounds, but there's no helping it. My question comes out small because part of me hopes he won't hear it.

He does, of course. "That's the question, isn't it?" When I don't respond, he adds, "What do *you* want, Katy?"

Is this what he's been waiting to hear all this time? I've been answering one question, but he's been asking another. My throat tightens. I'm not certain I can push words through it. My heart pounds in my chest so hard, I'm afraid it might bruise my ribs.

"I want there to be an us."

Can you feel someone smile? Does it change how they stand,

how they breathe? In that moment, Malcolm shifts. He inches me closer. His hands thread through my hair.

"Look up," he whispers, his breath soft against my cheek.

I do. Above our heads, a tiny, perfect bough of mistletoe is hanging from a velvet ribbon, a silent witness to our entryway confessions.

He kisses me then, a kiss full of nutmeg and spice, his warm Ivory soap scent mixing with the pine. This is what Christmas smells like and feels like, and I'm relieved to discover that yes, my lips *are* in perfect working order.

For the record?

So are Malcolm's.

PART II
THE GHOST THAT GOT AWAY

COFFEE AND GHOSTS SEASON TWO,
EPISODE 2

CHAPTER 1

T HE DISPLAY WINDOW of *K&M Ghost Eradication Specialists* is littered with hearts. Pink hearts. Glittery hearts. Blood-red hearts. The sign suspended above the Valentine's Day explosion reads:

Don't let the ghosts of past loves haunt you.
Two-for-one eradication special.
Now through the end of the month.

I doubt Springside Township is teeming with the ghosts of past loves, but my business partner, Malcolm Armand, assures me seasonal advertising is the way to go.

Inside our office, things are quiet, if no less glittery. A trail of the stuff runs from the display window back to our conference room and work area. We still can't afford a receptionist, so the front desk sits empty. The clatter of the keyboard tells me Nigel, Malcolm's brother and our tech support, is already hard at work.

"Katy?" he calls from the conference room. "Is that you?"

"It is."

"Malcolm with you?"

I hesitate a fraction of a second before responding. "No."

Nigel appears in the doorway and crooks a finger at me. "I want to show you something."

I shrug off my coat and follow him into the conference room. I'm guessing he's found an interesting ghost sighting online or has updated our website. But he doesn't head for the computer. He simply stands there, gaze landing everywhere but on me, fingers tapping against his thigh.

"Nigel?

"What?" His eyes are a little wide, as if he's startled or wary. The shock of pure white hair only makes him look that much more anxious.

"You wanted to show me something?" I prompt.

"Yeah ... yeah. I do." Those nervous fingers reach into his jeans pocket. "This. I want to get your opinion on this."

From the depths of his pocket he pulls out a velvet-covered box, one small enough to rest in the palm of his hand. With a deep breath, he eases open the lid.

"What do you think?" he says, his words rushed. "Is it good enough? Big enough? What do you think of the design?"

Inside the box, nestled in midnight-blue velvet, sits a diamond engagement ring. Marquee cut, I think, although I hardly ever wear jewelry and I barely know anything about gemstones. Despite this, something tells me the ring is perfect for its intended recipient.

For a second, I can't actually respond. My mouth is an o. Then I exhale, words and breath coming at once. "It's gorgeous. When are you going to ask her?"

He shrugs. "Maybe Valentine's Day, but then I thought that's too cliché."

I give my head a quick shake. "Sadie loves the holidays. Valentine's would be perfect."

"You think?"

Now I nod, just as vigorously, and run the risk of injuring my neck. "Of course."

"And you really think I should propose?" The doubt in his voice chills me more than the negative ten degrees outside did.

"Why wouldn't you?"

For a long moment, Nigel studies the ring and then snaps the lid shut. He tucks the box into his jeans pocket and leans against the conference room table.

"Honestly?" he says. "I'm not sure I'm good enough for her."

I can't imagine why he thinks this. He is kind, gentle, attentive. When Sadie was in the hospital, he only left her side to eat and take the occasional shower. He was so devoted that the nurses dubbed him Sir Nigel. He's the opposite of Sadie's first husband, Harold Lancaster, who wasn't the best human being and made an even worse ghost.

The expression on Nigel's face, the worry in his eyes, tells me this is more than cold feet. This doubt runs deep.

"Look at me, Katy." He holds out his hands. "What can I offer her? I'm a recovering addict and I work for my little brother."

I cringe, inwardly, because technically, yes, that's true. He wears his former addiction—to swallowing ghosts—in the white of his hair, the deep grooves around his mouth and eyes. These facts don't do justice to who Nigel Armand really is, on the inside.

"Sadie sees all of you, not just those things. Those things don't matter."

"They do matter. A lot." His fingers start their tapping against his thigh again. "I can't give her what she deserves."

"You know what? She was married to someone who could give her everything." Only now that I'm older do I realize just how rich Harold must have been. "We both know how that turned out. She needs you. I've never seen her this happy."

He purses his lips, mouth tight with disbelief. Before I can launch another round—for Sadie's sake if not his—the bell above the front door chimes.

Nigel's eyes take on a renewed panic. "Promise me that you won't tell Malcolm anything."

"But—"

"Promise me."

"Don't you want him to know?"

"Eventually, yes. If things ... work out, I want him to be my best man."

"Then—"

"It's a brother thing. Trust me?"

I nod. I'm an only child, raised by my grandmother. Siblings are a mystery to me. The Armand brothers in particular? Even more so.

"And promise?" he adds.

I nod again. "I'll even run interference."

I dash out of the conference room and run smack into Malcolm. The cold clings to his wool overcoat. When he grips my arms, the icy leather of his gloves penetrates the sleeves of my shirt. My skin erupts in goose bumps, but that isn't entirely from the cold.

"Whoa," he says. "Hang on." He adjusts his grip so I'm embraced in a proper hug. "Morning kiss."

Then my business partner kisses me full on the mouth. This routine, this morning kiss, is one of the ways we manage the transition from couple into business partners.

"How are you this morning?" he asks, his lips at the corner of my mouth.

"Good."

"You were that last night, too."

I laugh because in truth, we merely indulged in an evening kiss. Granted, those last longer than the morning ones. Still, we're navigating our dual roles with caution. As K&M ghost eradication specialists, we work so well together.

We don't want K&M the couple screwing that up.

But I'd be lying if I said morning and evening weren't my favorite times of day.

Malcolm pulls back and smiles at me. It's that warm smile, the one that reminds me of a sweet, dark roast. If you could pour it into a cup and drink it down, it would sustain you for days. The crinkles around his eyes deepen and his gaze scans my face.

"You look like you have a secret," he says.

Oh, I'm so transparent. I consider how to respond and decide on the truth.

"I do, but it isn't mine to tell."

He opens his mouth, prepared to cajole, I'm certain. Malcolm is a world-class cajoler. The bell above our door chimes once again. Instead of breaking our embrace, he grips me tighter. We don't often get walk-ins. When the silhouette of two men in dark over-coats comes into view, I'm certain my expression is as confused as his.

"Oh, excuse me." The voice has a certain lilt, one that's out of place in Springside. "Are we interrupting something?"

My insides go as frigid as the air now swirling around our reception desk. I know that southern drawl. As the man steps closer, I recognize the glossy hair and overly white teeth. Carter Dupree gleams; he shines.

Right now, I wish he'd do it somewhere else.

Malcolm eases away from me, but the move is protective, not guilty. He stands, his body half-blocking mine. It's kind of endearing. It's also unnecessary.

"They don't have any ghosts with them," I say, my words low, only meant for Malcolm.

"Are you certain of that, Ms. Lindstrom?"

Carter's companion steps forward. He's an older, smoother version of Carter. He doesn't gleam quite as much, his hair gray rather than blond. His words, his steps—both carry weight. Despite myself, I want to stand up straighter, smooth out the wrinkles in my jeans.

"I'm certain," I say. Or as certain as I can be, under the circumstances.

"In this instance, you're correct. And I've been remiss. Allow me to introduce myself. I'm Orson Yates."

Malcolm sucks in a breath and chokes on it, his cough muted but clear.

"What a place you have here." Orson Yates surveys the front area, his gaze moving from the empty reception desk to the threadbare couch to the glitter on the floor. "It's ... quaint."

"Can I help you with something?" I tilt my head in mock concern. "Are you having problems with a ghost?"

I collect the stares of all three men. Yes, I'm pretending I don't know who this guy is, that I haven't spent the last two months deleting his emails—or rather, the ones I'm sure some assistant sends for him. I'm pretending I don't know that Orson Yates is the chairman of the Midwest Necromancer Association.

Orson himself breaks the silence with a laugh that sounds as brittle as ice.

"Oh, she's funny. Really, Carter, why didn't you tell me she was funny?"

Probably because Carter Dupree hates me.

"But I'm distressed that you didn't attend our gathering in January. You didn't even RSVP." Orson's tone implies I have all the manners of a five-year-old. I'm bracing for the *kids these days* speech, but decide to take the offensive.

"It was black tie. I didn't have anything appropriate to wear," I say. That, and I tossed the invitation into the recycling. "I only own a skater skirt."

"You gentlemen missed out," Malcolm mutters, low and under his breath.

I shoot him a look, but his entire focus—his whole being—is on the two men. He won't let down his guard, not even to receive a glare from me.

"I see," Orson says. "Perhaps the fault is ours. It's been a while since we've had a woman in our ranks. Then again, we don't have that many men, either. We're exclusive that way." He pauses, his gaze darting to Malcolm before landing on me. "Still, I can't remember our last female necromancer. I would, however, like to rectify that now by possibly adding you to our list."

"I'm not a necromancer." Really, I've said this so many times and to so many people. Why no one listens, I can't say.

Catching ghosts is my business, one my grandmother taught me. Using ghosts? To play the market, intimidate people, and who knows what else? That's necromancy, and I'm not interested.

But I'm at the point where I might invest in a nametag, one that reads:

Hello, my name is Katy.
I am not a necromancer.

And I would wear it every day.

When no one responds, I add, "I told Carter that, too. More than once."

Orson chuckles, a patronizing sort of laugh. "My child, you have no idea what you're capable of. Why restrict yourself?"

"Why would I want to be a necromancer?"

Orson spreads his hands wide. "Security. Wealth. A way to make your mark on the world."

"Why do I need your little club to do that?"

A spasm hits Orson's left eye—a tic that distorts his features for a moment. Then he's smooth again, but the façade looks more brittle than before. Malcolm steps closer and takes my hand.

"Easy," he whispers in my ear. "He's a powerful necromancer, and they're here for a reason."

I have a horrible feeling that reason is me, and they won't go until I say yes to whatever it is they want.

Before I can utter another word, or think of a way to get them out the door, Nigel emerges from the conference room. His gait is steady and strong, hands tucked casually in his jeans pockets. His shoulders are square, his mouth grim. His stride never falters as he passes us and halts before the two necromancers, effectively cutting them off from me.

"Ah, Nigel," Orson says. "Carter mentioned you were slumming it these days. Addiction, was it?"

I cast a glance at Malcolm, but his gaze is on Nigel, eyes wide with shock.

"You're not wanted here," Nigel says, tone bland as if he's merely discussing the weather. "You know that. You've known that from the moment you walked through the door."

"Your ward. Yes, I felt it. Did you think it would keep us out? This is a place of business, after all."

"It's not meant to keep you out, it's meant to encourage you to leave. You have no true business here. You can catch your own ghosts." Nigel casts me a glance. "Although these days, Katy is probably better at it than you are."

Nigel is so calm, hands still tucked in his pockets, but his words hold an authority I've never heard before—his last volley provoking a second eye twitch from Orson. I've only ever known the recovering addict, the sweet man who is quietly courting my neighbor.

I don't know this Nigel Armand at all.

Orson snorts. "What happens if I refuse?"

"You can't," Nigel says simply. "You know you can't."

Orson holds up his hands in apparent surrender. "All right, you win. For now." He clears his throat. "I'm afraid, Ms. Lindstrom, that you've aligned yourself with the wrong sort of necromancer. Pity, that. You have such potential."

He turns to leave, Carter Dupree shooting me a nasty look before he heads for the door as well. The bell chimes, and I swear I've never heard anything so wonderful as that sound. I'm about to sigh with relief when the door rings yet again.

"Now I remember!" Orson Yates declares, features bright, cheeks flushed. "Our last female member was your mother, and quite the necromancer she was, too."

The door whooshes closed as all the breath leaves my lungs.

~

WE STAND THERE, the three of us staring at each other, all of us searching for words. I don't know where to start. Nigel as some sort of badass necromancer? My own mother?

All of it is too much. I turn to Malcolm, who is still clutching my hand.

"Do you have any tea?" I ask, and it's a plaintive sort of question.

He gives my fingers a quick squeeze. "Let me brew some. Then maybe we can figure out what's going on."

This last is directed more at Nigel, who raises his eyebrows as if he's nothing but innocent.

Within minutes, aromatic steam fills the conference room. Malcolm does the honors, from brewing to pouring to pressing a glass into my hands. Warmth sinks into my fingers, which feel cold and stiff. For a moment I simply hold the tea, inhale, and let the steam fill me.

"This is different." I sniff, trying to work out what spices he's added this time around.

"It's my comfort tea," he says. "Secret recipe, emergency use only."

I manage a laugh. Malcolm pours two more glasses. Before Nigel can grasp the drink, Malcolm pulls it back, just out of his brother's reach.

"Ward?" he says. "I've never felt it."

"That's because you're not trespassing. I have one on the apartment and Sadie's house as well." Nigel's tone is still bland, but there's an undercurrent of resolve I've never noticed before. "After Carter came to town, I figured I should establish my territory."

"The apartment, too?" Malcolm shakes his head. "I should've thought of that."

Nigel rolls his eyes. "You've never been very good at them."

Malcolm scowls at this, but it's mostly in jest because a moment later he nods and relinquishes the tea. "True."

"Territory?" I ask Nigel. "Does it keep people ... necromancers out?"

"No, it establishes your right to certain spaces. Another necromancer is free to violate that, but if he or she does, there are consequences. It's like a No Trespassing sign. It's all good until Chief Ramsey catches you."

"Could you put one on my house?" I ask, leaning forward in my chair.

This, I think, would be good. This might keep Carter Dupree from leaving creepy offerings on my doorstep.

"No, I can't," Nigel says.

I deflate and he laughs.

"I can't because it's your territory as a—"

I raise a hand. "Don't even say it."

"It doesn't make it any less true. But I could teach you how, if you like. Don't ask Malcolm. He's lousy at it."

I glance toward Malcolm and he gives me a rueful smile.

"I kind of am," he admits.

I swallow down some tea, the liquid nearly scalding the back of my throat. "Why are they here?"

I have my suspicions, but all of this is still so new to me. Necromancy, an association, wards. My thoughts linger on my grandmother and why she never told me about any of this.

A look passes between Malcolm and Nigel. Some sort of silent brother debate is waged. There's a tightening of lips, a barely visible nod, then Nigel takes a deep breath.

"You, Katy," he says. "They're here for you."

"But I told them 'no' already. I don't want to be in their club."

"Keep calling it that and you'll give Orson Yates a nervous breakdown. He takes the association very seriously," Nigel says.

"Then again, a hundred years and a billion dollars is a serious thing."

"A billion *what?*" I try to wrap my mind around that. I remember what Malcolm once told me: many successful stockbrokers are necromancers. In fact, before he came to Springside, he was a broker as well. Judging by the clothes he wears and the fancy red convertible he drives, he was good at it, too.

But that was before he lost Selena to Nigel's addiction.

"Maybe they haven't noticed," I say, "but we don't make a whole lot of money eradicating ghosts."

"That's not why they want you," Nigel says. "It's your ability with ghosts. It's the fact that you invoked an ancient and powerful entity—and could do so again. Do you know what sort of power that would give them? We're talking power on a global scale."

I shake my head. "That thing's name dies with me. I will never say it again."

Even thinking about the entity makes me nervous. I know I shouldn't, but sometimes the harder I try, the more I actually *do* think of it, like when someone tells you not to think about elephants—that's all you can do.

"We should've anticipated this," Nigel says, his voice quiet, the words meant for Malcolm. "Springside is just so..."

"Nice," Malcolm finishes.

"Exactly. I was hoping they'd chalk it up to nonsensical sprite gossip, even after Carter came to town." Nigel shakes his head. "I've been stupid."

"I thought they'd give up after Katy sent him packing," Malcolm adds.

"Why would I even want to align"—I draw quotes in the air —"with someone who would hurt one of my friends? They must think I'm insane, or unfeeling, or something."

The ghost Carter unleashed—that of Sadie's dead husband— was about as strong a ghost as I've ever confronted. That it was immune to coffee made it all the more difficult to catch.

The furrows around Nigel's mouth grow deeper. "I should've been there."

"Too soon." This comes from Malcolm, the words quiet, apologetic.

I suspect for Nigel it might always be too soon before he can confront another ghost. He acknowledges this with a nod, then rubs his hands across his face.

"Do you think they've brought other ghosts to town? Could they hurt someone like Belinda?" My roommate attracts the nastiest of ghosts. If something like this is in their plans, I'm not sure how we'll cope.

Both Nigel and Malcolm swear, same word, same time, and they're so like brothers in that moment, I can't help but laugh, just a little. Their eyes meet and they both give a grudging smile.

"They're here under the guise of courting you," Nigel says. "I don't think they'll try the ghost trick again."

"If by courting you mean creepy and vaguely threatening, then yes, that's what they're doing."

"It's a show of power," Malcolm says. "Like with Harold's ghost. That was meant to impress you."

All it did was piss me off.

"They have a narrow view of what motivates people," Nigel adds, speaking like someone who knows a great deal about them. "Wealth, power, sex. For someone with a different temperament, and probably gender, the whole Harold thing might have worked. They show you their power. You prove your worthiness."

"Sounds like hazing," I say.

"Yeah." Nigel nods as if the word fits what he's been thinking all along. "It kind of does."

"What did they use on you?" I ask.

Nigel starts. Next to me, Malcolm leans forward. It was no more than a guess, but wariness crosses Nigel's face, followed by a half-smile of acknowledgement.

"They did court you, didn't they," Malcolm says, admiration

and envy warring across his features. "Why didn't you ever tell me?"

"Because it was a non-starter. It never went much past the New Year's gathering." Nigel shrugs. "What can I say? The Armands are free agents. These guys have rules and practices I don't agree with. Since then, I've had a few run-ins with Orson or one of his flunkies —hell, you know Carter."

"Yeah, well, Carter gets around. Before today, I'd only ever heard of Orson Yates. I'd never actually met him."

"There's a reason for that."

Malcolm is sitting so close that I can feel his posture stiffen. "You ... is that why I never got an invitation? Because of you?"

Nigel drains his tea glass, stands, and crosses to Malcolm.

"There's a lot you don't know about necromancy, baby brother." He pats Malcolm on the cheek and leaves the room.

CHAPTER 2

I TRY TO BROKER a peace between the brothers with sandwiches from the deli next door. Nigel eats his lunch, nose inches from the computer screen—not that I've given him anything to do.

Malcolm sits in the outer room, inspecting each layer of his sandwich and putting it back together before bringing it to his mouth. Then, without taking a bite, he sets the sandwich down and begins the routine all over again.

Despite our haunted love advertising, we have no calls to distract us. It's so cold out, I'm certain the ghosts must be behaving themselves rather than risk a trip out to the nature preserve where we do our usual release.

I wait until Malcolm stops playing with his food to say quietly:

"Would you really want to align yourself with that sort of necromancer?"

His lips twist, his expression contrite. "No. I wouldn't."

"But it would've been nice to have the acknowledgement?" I venture. "For them to come courting?"

"I knew Carter at the U of M. We were both in the business

program, both in a frat—different ones." He studies the sandwich and takes a bite before continuing. "You could say there was some friendly competition."

Or not so friendly. "And he got an invitation and you didn't."

This isn't a question. The whole scenario plays out in Malcolm's expression, the tensing of his jaw, the shadows in his eyes.

"I always thought I was the better necromancer." He gives me a wan smile. "And you've met Carter. As you can imagine, he rubbed it in."

"So, it's sort of like being asked to prom even if you don't want to go. It would've been nice, right?"

"Sort of." A bit of humor lights his eyes. "Speaking of which, you've never told me why you turned down Jack Carlotta."

Oh, there were so many reasons for that, the main one being I knew he'd end up at prom with Belinda—no matter who his actual date was. No one wants to be second place, second choice, a second thought. But I don't want to explain all this now, so I go with the answer I hope will make him laugh.

"Oh, you know, the only thing I had to wear was a skater skirt."

Malcolm laughs, head thrown back, and I know I've hit the mark. A moment later, when Nigel joins in, I think I may have brokered a peace. I bite my lip and try not to move, try not to jinx it.

"I was feeling protective," Nigel says. "I'd just come off a nasty encounter with Orson. I didn't want you near him and vice versa."

Malcolm nods, gaze locked on his lunch.

"They would've tapped you, if it's any consolation."

Now Malcolm shrugs.

"Oh, come on," I say. "Would you really want to be like Carter Dupree?" I wave my hands in the air. "All shiny and fake?"

"You don't think he's handsome?" And the way Malcolm says this has me tilting my head and leaning forward to catch the meaning in his words.

I wrinkle my nose. "He's *handsome*, I guess."

Malcolm's face goes blank. Really, I don't think I've ever seen him without some sort of expression.

"But you're the truly handsome one." He is. Women go nuts for him. The female residents and staff at Springside Long-term Care practically have their own fan club for him. "And you're interesting. You can brew tea and do magic tricks and make people laugh."

I lean closer to touch the gray at his temples. It's so recent and premature; I think maybe he's self-conscious about it.

"Listen to Katy if you're not going to listen to me," Nigel adds.

Malcolm laces his fingers through mine. He kisses them quickly, a there-and-gone brush of the lips. Then he lets go as if K&M the couple never made an appearance.

"I've been thinking," Nigel continues, "and doing a little searching over lunch. We haven't talked about the bait they're using on Katy." He looks at me now, his expression tender, brotherly. "Do you have any evidence to support their claim?"

I know so little about my parents. Pestering my grandmother with questions only deepened the frown she so often wore. I hated to do that to her.

"They died soon after I was born, in a car accident."

Again, they do that brother thing, eyes meeting, Nigel mouthing a silent question, Malcolm nodding his answer.

"Malcolm told me about necromancers dying in car accidents," I say.

"Leading cause of death. Never get into a car with an angry, uncontained ghost."

This, I know. This is why we trap ghosts in Tupperware to begin with and they ride in the back of my truck when we head out to release them. There are rare exceptions—like when we caught Harold's ghost. In those cases, they need to be contained and always in sight. You don't want ghosts of that caliber bouncing from the flatbed and vanishing into some cornfield.

"Do you have things like birth certificates, and—" Nigel hesitates.

"Death certificates?" I finish for him.

He winces, then nods.

"I can get all that for you. Social Security numbers, that sort of thing?"

"Yes, I'll use all that when I search. Are they buried here in Springside?"

"Next to my grandmother," I say. "There's..."

The words, *there's an extra plot*, freeze on my lips. It was the one meant for my grandfather. A chill runs through me. I try to shake it off and shake off the notion that the person who ends up in that extra plot will be me.

At last I do chase away the chill and gaze up at the two men. I have their full attention, their full concern.

"You know what I think?" I say. "I think I've aligned myself with the right sort of necromancer."

THAT NIGHT'S evening kiss tastes sweeter and lasts a whole lot longer than any before it. We're in my truck outside Malcolm's apartment building, engine rumbling against the cold. We've done a good job of fogging up most of the windows.

He cups my cheek, fingers threading into my hair. "You okay?"

"Why wouldn't I be?"

"After today? Your parents? I thought you might be feeling ... sad."

"I never really knew them. My grandmother raised me, and I miss her. I'm curious, and skeptical, but really, if it means banishing Orson and Carter from Springside, I'd be fine with never knowing."

He pulls me close for another kiss. "You're something else, you know that?"

I smile against his lips, my entire face on fire with a blush I suspect not even the dark can hide.

"Hey," he adds, voice low. "I just thought of something. Let's go somewhere for Valentine's Day."

"Uh, where?"

Springside is a wonderful small town with much to offer. Romantic restaurants don't make the list.

"We could drive up to the Cities, maybe eat at A Taste of Persia. I need supplies for tea, and I want to pick up some basmati rice."

"You know," I say, not entirely certain how to broach the subject. "Last time we went to the Twin Cities, there was that necromancer surprise."

His laugh is soft and maybe a little apologetic. "What if I promise, no necromancer surprise? Will you go?"

Considering what we've been through since then, and the fact I don't think there are many surprises left—at least not necromancer ones—I can't think of a reason not to go.

"Yes," I say at last. "I will."

"We'll go early, right after my appointment at Springside Long-term Care. Drive up, have dinner, walk around, and drive back?"

"I'll wear the skater skirt."

"I was hoping you'd say that."

He leans in for another kiss. The moment our lips meet, the cab of my truck fills with flashing red lights. The rearview mirror reflects the image of a patrol car. Between the dark and rotating lights, I can barely discern the bulky form of Police Chief Ramsey.

"That's my cue." Malcolm steals a quick kiss. "Text me when you get home."

He hops from the truck and strolls over to the patrol car. The lights cut off. Malcolm crouches to speak to Chief. I take that as my opening, put the truck in gear, and drive home.

I STAND on the sidewalk in front of my house, an old Victorian that belonged to my grandmother. Icicles hang from its eaves. Snow shrouds the lilac bushes. The windows are dark.

And once again, Carter Dupree is standing on my porch.

"Good evening, Katy." He's as cool as an ice statue, gleaming in the light of my front porch lamp.

I feign disinterest by pulling out my phone as if someone far more interesting than Carter Dupree has sent me a text message. Instead, I start one to Malcolm. I get as far as *Carte* when he speaks again.

"You have something of mine."

His words make my fingers jerk. I press send by accident but don't have time to follow up with an explanation. Beneath the calm tone lies a threat. Without looking away from him, I tuck my phone back into my pocket.

"I don't have anything of yours," I say, and my reply sounds lonely in the night air.

I'm cursing myself for not asking Nigel to show me how to create a ward. Not that it would do me any good now. Carter is already inside my territory and blocking my way.

"Delilah," he says. "What have you done with her?"

"I haven't done anything with her. She's a ghost, not your property."

"Where is she?" He takes the stairs with deliberation, each step making my heart spike. His hands are tucked in the pockets of his overcoat. Somehow, this makes him all the more threatening.

"She isn't here," I say. "I don't have her. I let her go."

At my words, he halts. Three feet of icy air separates us, but the way Carter glares at me lowers the temperature by ten degrees.

"You let her go?" His voice is so brittle that it cracks.

"Why wouldn't I?"

"Do you understand how powerful she is, how valuable?" He tips his head back and sends his disbelief skyward, as if I'm the stupidest person he's ever met. "I can't believe you did that."

His Adam's apple bobs. I think he might be crying; I think he might be experiencing actual remorse, but when he looks at me again, the smile on his face is like nothing I've ever seen. It goes beyond icy.

He takes a step forward. I take one back. I dart a glance toward Sadie's house. The windows are glowing with warmth. She's home. I suspect Nigel's there, too. I'm in boots; Carter is wearing loafers. I can run across the ice and grit of the sidewalk much better than he can.

Before I do, headlights flood the street. A red convertible careens to a stop, one wheel bumping up and over the curb. Malcolm bursts from the car and races across the yard.

He slams into Carter, the force of it sending them both into a snow bank. A shower of ice fills the air. And then it's arms and legs and fists. I inch forward, but when they roll in my direction, I jump back. Someone's foot connects with my shin.

I stumble toward the sidewalk. When my boots find purchase, I run. I'm out of breath when I reach Sadie's. I pound on the door, but my mitten absorbs all the sound. I yank it off with my teeth, try again, and I still have a mouthful of wool when Nigel opens the door.

"Katy, what the—"

I point to the battle currently being waged in my yard. Nigel grabs his coat and follows me. But when we reach my sidewalk, he simply stops, sticks his hands into his pockets, and watches, an amused smile on his face.

"Aren't you going to...?" I gesture toward the fight. "Help?"

Carter lands a punch that makes me wince, but Malcolm rallies with a knee to Carter's stomach. They roll again, snow spreading across the shoveled walk, flakes dancing in the air.

Nigel tilts his head as if considering. "No, I don't think so. He seems to be holding his own."

I release a disgusted sigh. "Really?"

He shrugs.

Before I can cajole or break up the fight myself, Sadie tears from her house, a huge pot clutched in her hands. She marches down the sidewalk, her destination clear. She takes a wide stance before Malcolm and Carter and heaves.

Water splashes. Steam rises. Shouts and curses echo in the night.

Carter staggers to his feet first, whirling on Sadie. "Holy hell, woman! It's below freezing out."

Now Nigel moves, inserting himself between Carter and Sadie. He shoots an arm out, connecting a palm with Carter's shoulder.

"Leave." Nigel's command is sharp, cold, and nonnegotiable.

Carter is drenched. He steps back, wiping a hand across his brow. Malcolm surges forward, but Nigel catches him around the waist.

"You, too, baby brother. Get out of here before someone calls Chief Ramsey at home."

"But Katy—"

"Is a grown woman and can take care of herself," he finishes. "Besides, Sadie's right next door, and so am I."

Carter remains immobile, an ice statue once again. Malcolm pants, breath ragged, a bruise forming beneath one eye. The sound of a car engine fills the night, and momentary panic grips me. I'm convinced someone has already made that call. This is Chief Ramsey, and Malcolm is headed for a night in jail.

Instead, a yellow van with black lettering pulls up. My roommate Belinda jumps from the Ghost B Gone vehicle. Gregory rounds the front, his form cutting through the van's headlights. They cast each other a look as if retreating back into the van is the better option.

I don't blame them. It probably is.

Nigel turns to Carter. "Where are you staying?"

Carter simply scowls.

"You can answer that," Nigel says, "or we can wait for Chief Ramsey to show up."

Carter wipes his mouth with the back of his hand and leaves a smear of pink across his cheek. "Springside B&B."

Gregory surveys the scene, his gaze going from me to Carter and then to Malcolm with his budding black eye. A crooked grin spreads across Gregory's face as if everything he needs to know is here in its aftermath.

"Need an escort service?" Gregory asks Nigel, with a nod toward Carter.

"Would you?"

"Leaving now." He pecks Belinda on the cheek and then takes Carter by the elbow. "That your fancy car down the block?"

Carter gives a single, terse nod.

"Then let's go."

At the wheel of the Ghost B Gone van, Gregory tracks Carter's progress down the sidewalk and into the sleek black sedan. The wheels squeak against the packed snow, and in the quiet that follows, I can hear Malcolm's still-ragged breathing and the soft rumble of his convertible.

"Now it's your turn," Nigel says to him.

"But—"

"Go. You'll see Katy tomorrow."

"Don't worry," Belinda chimes in. She drapes an arm around my shoulder. "I've got her."

Malcolm shoots me a look, one filled with doubt.

"Text me?" he mouths.

I nod.

We wait until Malcolm drives off. Only now do I feel the cold. I shiver against it, the chill penetrating through my coat and all the way down to the bone. Nigel picks up the pot and takes Sadie's hand. He nods at us, and together they retreat back up the walk and vanish inside Sadie's house.

Then Belinda and I are alone in the night.

"What was that?" she asks me.

I shake my head. "I don't know."

"Don't you?" she says, and her voice turns sly. "Didn't you once say you weren't the sort of girl guys fight over?"

"I'm not."

"Doesn't look that way to me."

I sigh, but it comes out more like a growl.

Belinda laughs. "Come on." She tugs me toward the door. "Let's go inside."

Before I shut the door, I scan my yard and the legacy of the fight. I wonder if I should dash over to Sadie's and ask Nigel to teach me how to create a ward. But I don't think I could make one big enough to hold the entire town of Springside.

CHAPTER 3

T HE NEXT MORNING I'm the first one through the door of
K&M Ghost Eradication Specialists. I pace between the front
window display and the conference room, tracking glitter in my
wake.

I peer out at the street, searching for that head of ebony hair.
Even in the winter, Malcolm walks to work in the morning. When
he doesn't appear, I pull out my phone and reread his final text
from last night.

> **Malcolm:** I'll apologize again in person in the morning. Meet
> me early?

Meeting early promises an extra-long morning kiss. So I wait. I
pace. My heart jumps at the sound of footfalls on the sidewalk
outside. At last, the bell above the door chimes. I whirl around.

And find Nigel shaking off the cold.

"Eventful night last night," he says.

I roll my eyes.

"He means well," Nigel adds. "Malcolm, that is. I don't know what the hell Carter wants."

Oh, but I do. I swallow back the dread. I haven't seen the last of Carter Dupree.

"Malcolm already apologized for going crazy," I say. "And it's not that..."

Although I worry that Carter might press charges. I worry he's done so already and that's why Malcolm hasn't walked through the door.

"This is new for him, Katy." Nigel hangs his coat on the rack.

"It's new for me, too," I say.

"Thing is, he knows how to get a girl's attention, but he hasn't had much practice in keeping it." He drapes his scarf over the coat. "Partnering with Selena ... well, it kind of kept him from figuring out the whole relationship thing. A ghost girlfriend is a whole lot easier than a real one. And as far as Carter goes, it's only natural that Malcolm would see another necromancer as a threat."

"Can he really be jealous of Carter?" I ask. "I don't even like Carter as a human being, and he really doesn't like me."

"Doesn't matter." He crosses to me and cups my shoulders. "Give Malcolm some time. He'll come to realize that he doesn't need to surround you with a ward or beat his chest or any of that."

I nod. I'm not as upset about last night as maybe I should be. I don't know what Carter planned to do, or what would've happened if Malcolm hadn't shown up. I glance toward the door. We are officially open for the day and the prospect of an extra-long morning kiss is diminishing by the second.

I reach for the canvas bag I use for porting thermoses of coffee. Today I've included a folder of information that Nigel asked for.

"It's all I could find." I hand him the folder and he pages through the contents.

"Have you thought of asking around?" he says, peering over the top at me.

"Asking ... around?"

"Springside. The people who knew your grandmother. The older residents." He slaps the folder against his leg. "What about the long-term care facility? Mr. Carlotta or Mrs. Greeley? They might know."

Of course they might, but I wouldn't know how to even start asking. I nod and tell Nigel thanks. I'm still leaning against the reception desk, my thoughts far away, when Malcolm flings open the door and brings in a flood of cold and energy. He shrugs off his coat, tosses it onto the rack, and then crosses the room to grab my hands.

Then he's swinging me around, his expression joyful. A deep purple bruise lines one eye, but that can't hide the delight in them. He's saying something, but his words are so rushed, so frantic, I can't make them out.

At last our whirling slows, as do his words.

"She's back! She's back. She's back, Katy. We were up all night."

I shake my head. I don't know who he's talking about or why he's so excited.

"She's here right now. Don't you feel her?"

I pull my hands back, tilt my chin up, and sample the air. With the cold and Malcolm's excitement, I missed the otherworldly presence that fills the space. Although how I could have is hard to say. It's so strong I suspect that if I reached out, my fingers would meet resistance.

"Selena's back," Malcolm says. "She found me."

"Selena," I echo, and my voice is thin.

"I couldn't wait for the two of you to meet."

Oh, I could've waited. Judging by the way Selena flows and buzzes around me, my guess is she could have as well. Her form shoves me, a cold caress that radiates up my spine. This Selena is territorial. If she could, I suspect she'd create a ward around Malcolm.

"Nigel's here," I say. "I don't think a ghost should be, especially this one."

While neither brother has admitted it, I believe that when Nigel —in the throes of his addiction—swallowed Selena, it caused a falling out between them. It wasn't long after that that Malcolm left Minneapolis and came to Springside.

He cringes. "You're right. I wasn't thinking. I'm just too ... I mean, I'll"—he points to the doorway—"just take her ... somewhere."

"Why don't you take the day off?" I suggest. "You were up all night, right?"

"Yeah, but I'm not even tired."

Maybe, but his eyes gleam with a frantic look, like someone who has taken a hit of a mind-altering drug. A crash is inevitable.

"Go on. Take the day." I nod toward the door. "Get reacquainted."

Part of me insists this is the wrong thing to say. That part insists I bring out my thermos of Kona blend, find some Tupperware, and catch this Selena. Then I'd go somewhere—preferably somewhere far, far away—and drop her off. And if she's lucky, I might crack the lid.

"Are you sure?" he asks, and his eyes appear preternaturally bright.

A drug, I think, and a powerful one. "Of course."

"You're the best."

He kisses me, a quick peck on the cheek, and dashes out the door, one arm flailing to find the sleeve of his coat.

I sink against the reception desk because suddenly my legs won't hold me. I stare at the closed door, the hint of cold—and supernatural—hanging in the air. I'm still there when Nigel ventures from the conference room.

"Katy? Was that Malcolm?"

"It was."

"And he left?"

"He did."

He takes a few cautious steps forward. "Is everything okay?"

"Selena's back."

Nigel exhales and swears under his breath. "This won't change anything. It really won't."

But he doesn't meet my gaze, and I know:

It already has.

THE VERY BEST place to drown your sorrows is the Springside Pancake House. I get a booth to myself, in Belinda's section, and she doesn't even bother to take my order. She knows.

All-you-can-eat dollar-sized pancakes and a large orange juice.

She eases the plate in front of me, her smile fading. "You okay?"

I manage a nod.

"I'd say you look like you've seen a ghost, but that's kind of every day for you."

Now I manage a laugh.

Her gaze flits toward the entrance. "Malcolm?"

I shake my head.

"Last night? I mean, did you guys fight or something?"

"No, it's ... complicated."

Really, how do I explain? That I'm jealous of Selena? That I'm afraid she'll ruin everything? That I risk losing my business partner and a friend and ... something more than that, something I haven't really given a name to. I didn't want to jinx it.

I suspect this is the reason why.

"Tonight, we can talk if you want," Belinda offers. "You know me. When it comes to guys, I never run out of advice."

And when it comes to guys, Belinda never needs it.

I'm almost done with my first plate when a well-tailored figure slides into the seat across from mine. In the late morning sunshine that streams through the windows, Carter Dupree gleams fiercely.

He grins, teeth so white that I hold up a hand to ward off the glare.

"Could you turn that off?" I say.

"Rough night last night?"

"I could ask you the same."

"Rough morning?" His voice is sly and smooth.

I peer at him, searching for signs of last night's scuffle. Malcolm got in several good punches, but not a single scratch mars Carter's face. His knuckles are free from bruises, his nails short but perfectly manicured.

"So," he says, inspecting the cuticle of one of those manicured nails. "Did Malcolm like my present?"

Once, not too long ago, a ghost—an entity, really—choked me, cut off all my breath, made it impossible to breathe. Like then, I can't pull any air into my lungs. I want to claw at my throat, but I know that won't do any good. That I can't actually speak is a blessing. Any words I might say would come out garbled and pathetic.

"You met her, of course," Carter says. "I mean, he can't help himself." He taps his head. "He's not very bright that way. He thinks you'd want to meet her, and vice versa." Carter rolls his eyes.

"I don't know what you're talking about."

I'm proud of these words, but they wash right over him and leave me hollow.

"Not that I blame him," Carter continues. "Selena is one strong, sexy ghost. She's literally the one who got away. There's a special bond between a necromancer and the right ghost." He props his chin on a fist and contemplates the air somewhere above my shoulder. "Having the perfect woman inside your head, one who understands all your thoughts, your feelings? Indescribable, really. Delilah and I had that."

"Of course." I manage an eye roll of my own. "That's why she couldn't wait to leave."

Nothing. Not a twist of the lips or an eye twitch. He's nearly as icy as he was last night.

"It seems like we've both lost something, then." He leans forward, hands clasped now. "I'd call that even."

Belinda comes bustling by, her gaze flitting over Carter. The only evidence that she's seen him is the slight crease in her brow. She whirls, and the pitcher she's carrying tips precariously.

Orange juice splashes from the rim and drenches Carter's white dress shirt. He bolts upright, rocking the table between us. My plate and glass skitter and slide, but I catch them, one in each hand.

"Oh, I'm so sorry, sir." Belinda pulls a rag from her apron. "Here, let me help—"

He holds up both hands. "That won't be necessary. I was just leaving."

She beams at him, gives him the dazzling Belinda smile, and his scowl softens. He almost looks human like this, a little rumpled, not so shiny and pulled together. He eases from the booth and studies her nametag.

"Belinda, is it?"

She tilts her head, her explosion of blonde hair bouncing in its ponytail, customer-service smile still in place.

"I'll be sure to remember that," he adds.

And I don't like the way he says it at all.

We're silent as he leaves the restaurant. And there it is: a telltale limp in his gait. Only when the door has closed behind him do I let myself lean back against the booth. I wish she hadn't done that, but I can't find the words to tell her so.

Belinda, on the other hand, whistles while she wipes down the table. She gathers up my plate and glass and returns moments later with a fresh version of each.

I cut my pancakes into tiny pieces. I dip each bite in maple syrup and contemplate how vindictive Carter Dupree actually is.

My guess is *very*.

CHAPTER 4

Don't let the ghosts of past loves haunt you.
Two-for-one eradication special.
Now through the end of the month.

I STUDY THE VALENTINES scattered in our display window and wonder if I can hire myself to eradicate a ghost. Although, really, if I could, would I? As if in answer, my reflection shakes its head.

No, I don't want to be someone's second choice, a second thought, a better-than-nothing. I also can't face Nigel's pity, and that's what it will be, no matter how hard he tries to hide it. Down the street, I catch sight of Chief Ramsey pushing through the doors of the Springside Police Department.

If I can't face Nigel's pity, then the least I can do is take his advice.

Inside the police station, Penny Wilson darts about as if Chief has given her twenty different tasks and she's uncertain which one to complete first. I stand at the front desk, head tilted, and taste the air. The space is close and dank, filled with the scent of stale snow mixed with sand. The aroma of charred coffee comes from the sideboard.

The two spites that normally haunt here? Hunkered down and miserable. I don't blame them. Penny has such a high tolerance for the otherworldly that she doesn't notice their existence. Chief doesn't believe in the supernatural. As a result, I'm never around, offering up the Kona blend.

Something feels off, so I taste the air again. Scared? Yes, they both are. I glance around, searching for a reason, but before I can uncover anything, Penny halts in front of me.

"Oh, Katy!" Penny juggles today's newspaper, which I gather is for Chief Ramsey, two coffee cups, and a container of non-dairy creamer.

I should come back with some real coffee and half and half. It would be a public service.

"Can I help you with something?" she asks.

"Is Chief in? I mean, is he busy? If not, I'd like to talk to him."

"I ... I can check." Doubt flavors her words, her expression. She gives me a once-over, perhaps checking for trauma.

Chief and I have often had words, and in that, I'm merely following in my grandmother's footsteps. She never stopped by for a chat. To needle him? Maybe. But not like this, and not like what I have in mind.

Penny vanishes inside Chief Ramsey's office. She's gone for so long, I suspect the answer will be no. She's gone for so long, I consider investigating what has these two sprites on edge. Not even my full attention is enough to draw them from their hiding spot.

Penny emerges from his office minus one coffee cup and the newspaper. She nods. "You can go on back. He doesn't have anything scheduled until noon."

Chief is bulky, his office tiny. He's sitting behind his desk, gaze on his coffee cup, his expression dour.

I don't blame him; it smells terrible. I'm afraid the aroma might damage the inside of my nose.

He shakes his head and sets the cup down. "She means well, but..."

"The Coffee Depot delivers," I say.

"It would break her heart."

"I could teach her?" I venture. Maybe. I've tried to teach Malcolm, but when it comes to coffee, I'm either the world's worst instructor or he's an unusually slow learner. Why he can concoct amazing tea but his coffee tastes like a vending-machine special, I'll never know.

"You didn't come here about the lousy coffee," Chief says.

"No." I'm grateful for the excuse to shove Malcolm from my thoughts.

"So maybe it's about the disturbance in your yard last night?"

Of course some tattletale called Chief Ramsey. "Disturbance?" I go for all innocence, making my eyes wide and voice light.

He grumbles a sigh, rubbing his temples with his left hand. The wedding band is there, where it should be. But whether this means he's still married or is simply bad at letting go, I can't say.

"I have a personal question. If you don't mind, that is." I don't wait to see if he does. "You knew my mom, didn't you?"

Something changes in that moment. Chief drops his hand. His spine straightens. He leans toward me, as much as his bulk and the desk will allow.

"Yes, I did. We went to high school together."

"Same class?"

He nods. "She was the first person who ever spoke to me at school, maybe in all of Springside." Chief pauses as if he's considering what to reveal, or perhaps how much. "It wasn't the easiest thing, moving from Minneapolis to Springside. At least, not for me."

"So, what did she say?"

"That they gave me the haunted locker and to let her know if I wanted her to take care of that."

"Oh, yes. Locker 35. It's always been haunted."

The spirit that occupies the space is so benign, most people can't feel its presence. Except on pep rally days. Then it expels the contents of the locker as if it can't contain its excitement.

Chief eyes me, but continues. "She waved me over to her table at lunch that first day." His lips compress into a grim line. "I'm embarrassed to admit I thought the school administration put her up to it, so I just ... walked on past. But that wasn't your mother. I figured that out later."

This woman I never knew is starting to captivate me. We walked the same halls, the same streets, eradicated ghosts from the same school lockers.

"And when she came back to Springside after college, already engaged, she broke a lot of hearts, too."

Chief's included? His eyes hold a tenderness I've never seen before.

"Did you know my dad?"

"I did. He was a fine man. Trust me, I would've had something to say about it if he hadn't been."

Oh, yes, I think. Chief included.

He smiles at me now, the look indulgent and fatherly. "Why all the questions, Katy? Surely your grandmother—"

I give my head a vigorous shake. "She couldn't talk about it. It ... hurt her, so I stopped asking. But recently, I've been curious about my mom, my dad, and what they were like."

"I understand, perhaps more than you realize." He stares out the small window as if the icy patterns on the glass enthrall him. He keeps his eyes there when he speaks again. "Their car accident. I was the first officer on the scene. I was still green, too. So green, this was the first time I'd ever..."

Something clicks in my mind. I wonder if my grandmother

blamed Chief for not being able to save my mom. I don't know. I doubt I'll ever know. But all their years of animosity take on a fresh meaning.

We're both silent. I nod so Chief knows he doesn't need to continue the story. I've heard enough, and I can see this is a wound that has never fully healed.

After a moment, he coughs, clears his throat. Then he straightens again. He is less fatherly and more Police Chief Ramsey.

"It's interesting that you're asking me this now," he says, and his tone is far more no-nonsense than a moment before.

"Is it?"

"Because yesterday, I see this fancy Mercedes roll down Main Street. I get curious when a stranger comes to town driving a car that costs more than most of the houses around here. So, I ran the plates."

My heart is thumping so hard it makes my ribs ache. My throat is tight, and I have that feeling where I can't breathe again.

"Orson Yates," Chief says. "Thought the name sounded familiar, so I had Penny do a search on our old case files. Know the last time he was in town?"

Something tells me I do know, but would rather not acknowledge it. I shake my head.

"The week of your parents' accident. I interviewed him as a witness. He saw the car plunge into the ravine. You know the one, outside of town on the way to the nature preserve."

I know that ravine. I drive past it every time we do a catch and release. I wonder how my grandmother drove by it for all those years—there's no other route to the nature preserve, no other close-by place to release ghosts.

I wonder at her strength.

"What caused the accident?" I ask. "Can you tell me?"

"Faulty brakes. Your grandmother ... pushed for a more thorough investigation, but there was no denying bad brakes on an old car."

Could a ghost do that? Could a powerful one lie dormant until the perfect moment? Could you unleash something like that, the way Carter unleashed Harold's ghost on Sadie?

Not to mention unleashing Selena on Malcolm. I bite my thumbnail in thought. This is information I never expected. It's information I can't use. It simply is; a past I can't change.

"Katy, what's going on?" Chief is frowning now, his expression both fatherly and official.

"I really don't know."

"Give the word and I'll start the paperwork for a restraining order."

And how would that work against ghosts?

"I don't have..." What? I'm not sure of the word I'm looking for, but at last I go with, "I don't really have any evidence. Orson Yates hasn't done anything except stop by K&M Ghost Eradication Specialists. His ... friend, Carter Dupree, is creepy, but it was Malcolm who started the fight last night."

At this, Chief actually chuckles. "I know. Carter Dupree was in earlier, asking for one against Malcolm."

Of course he was. I lean forward, wondering if this is yet another problem. "And?"

"I told him if he didn't like the residents, he could leave town." He jabs a finger at me. "But you tell that young hothead of yours to watch it."

"He's not mine," I say.

"Sure he isn't." Chief settles back in his chair, far too smug. "Tell him anyway. And you tell me if something else happens. Anything, even if you think it's no big deal. Call the dispatcher and they'll call me at home."

I nod. "Thank you. I ... hope I won't need to."

I'm at the door, ready to leave, when Chief calls out one last time.

"Katy? Know what I think?"

I shake my head.

"Your mother would be proud of you."

I leave the police station with my eyes damp and my heart beating a strange, erratic rhythm in my chest.

THE SETTING SUN is painting the snow pink by the time I reach home this evening. The windows of Sadie's house are glowing brightly, the light warm and inviting. Two shadows move from one room to another. When they meet, they pause for what I guess must be a kiss.

I hate to interrupt that.

I trudge up her steps anyway. A moment after Sadie flings open the door, she pulls me inside and into a hug.

"Oh, my dear. Nigel said you had a rough day."

Over Sadie's shoulder, I spear Nigel with a glare. He shrugs and mouths an apology while she rocks me. At last, I push away with gentle hands on her shoulders.

"I'm fine," I say. "Really."

"Still, you shouldn't worry," she says, patting my arm in a consoling manner. "A ghost can't replace a human being."

This I'm not so sure about, but I nod.

"And stay for dinner. I baked pecan pie for dessert."

Because I haven't drowned my sorrows in enough carbs and sugar yet today. This might push me over the edge.

"Actually," I say, "I was hoping Nigel would show me how to do something. A necromancer thing."

He raises his eyebrows. "A ward, perhaps?"

"Yes, a ward. Would you?"

"You don't have to ask twice." Already he's reaching for his coat and within a minute, we're outside, trudging through snow in the winter dusk.

We walk the perimeter of my property, along the picket fence between my yard and Sadie's and the taller, cedar fence of the neighbor to the rear. Occasionally Nigel stops, crouches, touches something—the base of a pine tree, the lilac bushes, the garden shed I never use because I never garden.

"Interesting," he says at last. "Your grandmother must have been extremely powerful. I'm picking up remnants of a ward she put in place years ago."

"But she wasn't—"

"A necromancer?" He gives me a sly look. "Are you one?"

I concede his point, although I don't consider this true necromancy. This has nothing to do with ghosts and everything to do with other human beings.

"So, she had a ward in place?" I ask.

"Several, I think, over the years. The vibe I'm getting is 'back off, big city necromancers'."

Despite myself, I laugh. That sounds like my grandmother. "I don't sense anything."

"Well, you wouldn't. This has always been your home. I'm only sensing it now because I'm searching for signs of a ward. It's not intact and its hold has depleted, which is why I haven't noticed it before."

"And Malcolm, too, right? He would've noticed it if it was intact."

"And my stupid brother, yes."

"He's not stupid," I say, although why I'm defending Malcolm is beyond me.

"All right, he's acting stupid and if he doesn't stop, he'll regret it."

"So how does a ward really work if a necromancer can walk right through it?" I want to change the subject. I want to know how this is going to help if someone like Orson Yates can breeze into K&M Ghost Eradication Specialists without recourse.

"This is important," I add. "Belinda spilled orange juice on Carter Dupree this morning."

Nigel snorts. "On purpose?"

"Yes. That's why it's a problem. I don't know if he recognized her from last night, but he made note of her name."

He swears, and his breath chases snowflakes from the slender branch of a sapling. "And that will lead him back here."

"Exactly. She's been ghost-free and alcohol-free for months now, but it wouldn't take much. One nasty ghost and she'll lose everything all over again."

"I know how that goes," he says.

"So, how does it work? Is it like insurance?"

"Sort of. The reason most necromancers won't violate a ward is the threat of retribution. Other necromancers will band together and deliver ... justice. Even if we can't stand each other, we'll work together to set things right or make sure it doesn't happen again. It's the principle of the thing."

"Retribution," I echo. "That sounds unpleasant."

"Trust me, it can be."

"This retribution wouldn't be one of your run-ins with Orson Yates, would it?"

Nigel laughs. "Very astute. Even he thinks twice before violating a ward, but he's one of the worst offenders."

"Speaking of Orson," I say, "I don't think he's bluffing about my mom."

The story comes tumbling out, everything Chief Ramsey told me about my parents and Orson Yates. We stand in the cold, the sun fully set, the yellow glow of the back porch light from Sadie's house illuminating us.

Nigel grips my arms as if he needs me to hold him up as much as I need someone to steady me.

"Katy, I'm sorry. I spent the day searching, but I haven't come up with much. I also reached out to some of the older necromancers I know, but I haven't heard back yet. Some of them don't even use email or the internet."

"But how do they—"

"Sprites, ghosts, telephone." He shrugs and gives me a crooked grin. "This time around, I used the telephone. I left lots of voice messages."

I want to laugh at this but only manage a sigh. "I suppose in the days before telephones and telegraphs, that could make a necromancer pretty powerful."

"You suppose right."

"And today, too," I add, thinking of Malcolm again and his time as a stockbroker with Selena retrieving information for him.

Will he go back to that? Part of me insists he won't; he loves what we do, even if he doesn't ... I can't finish the rest of that thought. Part of me wonders how anyone could resist the temptation. He could work for another brokerage firm or even start his own business. Scratching out a living as a ghost catcher can't compare.

"Hey." Nigel's voice is as soft as the snow. "Let's get your ward in place."

I shake off my thoughts and the cold eating at me. "What do I need to do?"

"A couple of things. A ward is deceptively simple. You pick a few anchor items, place the ward on them, and call it done. But it's all in the choosing of the right items, truly identifying what belongs to you, and not picking something that will up and leave— or get uprooted—any time soon."

I scan my property. "So, everything inside the anchor points is under protection?"

"Yes. This is where Malcolm always messes up. He'll pick things in a hurry and not truly consider how permanent something is, or whether it's his to begin with. For instance, the picket fence. That belongs to Sadie, which makes it a poor choice for you."

I walk toward the fence, place my hand on it. I turn and glance over my shoulder at Nigel. "But a good choice for you?"

"Try it without the mitten."

I pull off my mittens and shove them into my coat pocket. With bare fingertips, I touch the fence. The paint feels brittle, and my skin aches with the cold. Beneath all that comes a sensation. Words and images fill my head. I laugh.

"What do you sense?" he asks.

"Something along the lines of: *Go away! She's my girl.*" I spear him with another look. "That's very ... middle school."

He shrugs, hands in pockets, expression mild.

"And kind of chauvinistic. Sadie can take care of herself."

"I know. Still." He tilts his head toward the fence. "Message received, right? Short, no room for questions. Complicated wards disintegrate too quickly and are too easily circumvented."

"I'm guessing the one on K&M Ghost Eradication Specialists isn't so ... strident."

"No, because you might want to collaborate with necromancers and ... others. But you're right. It's more complicated and will wear off more quickly. Together we should be able to keep a solid one in place. So?" He raises his eyebrows at me. "Ready to try?"

I point to the items I've identified as anchors. "Willow tree."

"Good," Nigel says.

"Lilac bushes."

"Another good choice."

"The handrails out front, by the sidewalk?" This one I'm not so sure of, but I would love nothing more than to never see Carter Dupree on my porch again.

"You'll need to reinforce it with a few more anchors," he says. "Let me show you how to place a ward, and then we'll move to the front."

We start with the willow tree. Nigel kneels at its base and digs through the snow until he exposes the trunk near the frozen earth.

"Most necromancers will respect a ward placed anywhere on an anchor, but others will simply duck under one placed up high and then claim they never felt it."

"That sounds like a technicality."

"It is."

"It sounds like something Orson Yates or Carter Dupree might do."

This time, Nigel grins. "Absolutely."

He takes my hand and places it against the cold bark. "Now concentrate. Pick a few words or a phrase that encompasses your message."

"Does it matter what it is?"

"Not as long as it's clear."

I close my eyes, letting thoughts and images fill my head: Belinda, Sadie, Nigel, Malcolm. Friends. Safety. Protection.

"Whoa," Nigel breathes. "Glad I'm your friend."

"You're getting the message?"

"Loud and clear. Let's connect the dots so everyone else will too."

We trudge through the snow. By the time we're done, I've placed six anchor points around my property. We stand on the sidewalk staring up at my home as if we can admire my handiwork.

"You can come over for dinner," he says. "I owe you that. You know how it is. Sadie asks about my day, and things just come out."

"You're like an old married couple already." I cast him a look from the corner of my eye. "I'm guessing you haven't—"

He sighs. "Not yet. Valentine's, for sure."

"Or tonight," I say. "You could always ask her tonight."

He laughs, a self-effacing sound. "Not tonight, but dinner still stands."

"I'll order some pizza when Belinda gets home."

"All right. Goodnight, Katy."

"Goodnight," I echo. "And thank you."

He raises a hand as if to wave away my gratitude. I watch as he enters Sadie's kitchen and she envelops him in a hug. I remain on my front walk, gaze touching each anchor point. It's a start, but a shield isn't enough, not one as insubstantial as this.

I want Orson Yates out of Springside, and that's going to take something more than a flimsy ward. I know of only one thing powerful enough. My fingertips come to rest on my left cheek, on the faded blue mark the entity left.

I refuse to let my thoughts drift any further.

CHAPTER 5

THE MORNING AIR is bitter, the sun brilliant. My face aches from the short jaunt from my truck to inside the office. I'm pressing my fingertips against my cheeks in an effort to warm them when Malcolm bursts through the front door.

The bell chimes; his face is glowing from excitement and the cold. He scoops me into a hug, tucking me inside his overcoat.

"You owe me a morning kiss and an evening kiss," he says.

Inside the wool, the world is warm and safe. It smells of nutmeg and Ivory Soap frosted in winter. I nuzzle closer, intent on remembering how this feels, his arms around me, the thrum of his heartbeat. I hold still, hold on to the moment—this exact moment, the one before everything changes.

"Hey." He clutches my chin and raises my face to his. "What's wrong?"

"Carter Dupree brought Selena to Springside," I say, because delaying will only make it worse. "On purpose. To..." I trail off. To what? Hurt me? Obviously. To distract Malcolm? Maybe. But what else? Is there something I'm missing?

I brace for denial, for an outburst—for Malcolm to call me a liar. Instead, he tips his head back and laughs.

"Is that all? I already know that. Besides, Carter only thinks he's done that. Selena used him to find me. She told me all about it. He thinks he's this slick necromancer." Malcolm laughs again and gives his head a shake. "Trust me, he's not half as good as he thinks he is. Remember how easy it was to free Delilah?"

I nod slowly. This, I'm not so sure about. But Malcolm is as bright and brilliant as the day. He positively glows. That's when it hits me.

I've never seen him look so happy.

"Is that what's bothering you?" he asks.

"I'm worried," I say. "I'm worried that they came to town and haven't left and I don't know how to make them leave. I'm afraid they'll hurt even more people."

He cups my face. "We won't let them. Me, you, Nigel. We won't. I promise you that."

He kisses me then. I don't know if I believe the promises in either his words or his kiss. But I do know this:

There is nothing in the world I want to believe more.

IT'S TOO cold out for over-the-knee stockings. I grew up in Minnesota, and any sensible Minnesotan knows that winter weather and bare skin don't mix. Still, part of me is tempted to show some of that skin, opt for the stockings rather than the far more practical—and thicker—tights.

Part of me knows it's too late for that. It's the same part of me that has Carter Dupree's voice on a constant loop in the back of my mind:

Selena is one strong, sexy ghost ... there's a special bond between a necromancer and the right ghost.

Not that Malcolm has canceled the date. But the only time he's mentioned it all week was to insist that, weather permitting, we would drive up in his car, not my truck.

"My pickup is better in the snow," I said.

"My convertible is better for everything else," he countered. "It's Valentine's Day. I want to zip you up to the Cities in style, not in your grandmother's old truck."

Even I had to admit that my grandmother's old truck isn't all that romantic.

Now I stand in the living room, shutters partly open so I can see the street. I won't miss the flash of red. Malcolm's convertible is very hard to miss. Even so, I pace, gaze darting to the curb outside my house, dread building in my stomach. Every so often, I glance down, inspect a leg, and reconsider whether the black tights with pink hearts are cute enough.

He's fifteen minutes late.

I force my mind to turn to other things, like the lack of customers this month. Perhaps on Valentine's Day, everyone wants to cling to past loves. Our two-for-one eradication special hasn't brought in any business. Even the sprites are behaving themselves. I haven't gone out on a single annoyance call all week.

Worse, a fancy Mercedes is still sitting outside Springside B&B, although Carter Dupree has not darkened my doorstep since I put the ward in place.

Nigel has still not asked Sadie to marry him. He has nine hours left in the holiday to do so.

Malcolm is twenty-five minutes late.

At the forty-five minute mark, my cell phone rings. My heart leaps, my fingers fumbling with the phone. I answer so fast, all I catch of the caller is one small fact:

Not Malcolm.

"Katy, I'm sorry to bother you at home." It's Vanessa, the manager of Springside Long-term Care. "And really, I hate to bother you at all. I know you don't charge for your visits."

Springside Long-term Care has always been a gratis account; my grandmother insisted.

"What's wrong?" I ask. Perhaps this is where all the past loves have taken their haunting. That makes a certain amount of sense.

"Malcolm was scheduled to visit this afternoon. We were going to have a little party. Many of the residents wanted to give him valentines."

By *residents*, I'm sure she means the female residents and members of his fan club.

"Oh, and you have a valentine, too, Katy. From Mr. Carlotta."

Yes. I have a fan club of one.

"They were so disappointed, but I'm certain something came up. I told them that the two of you must have gone out on an emergency eradication, but they insisted I call and—"

"Vanessa, hang on. Are you saying Malcolm didn't show up today?"

"He was scheduled for one o'clock, like always."

Malcolm never misses his weekly visit, although truthfully, he does so little eradication while he's there you could hardly call it part of our business. It's all coffee and tea taste tests, magic tricks, and of course, a massive amount of flirting.

"Katy?"

That earlier dread—born of jealousy—shifts, turns cold. I close my eyes and see that black Mercedes in front of Springside B&B.

"Is everything okay?" Vanessa prompts.

"I don't know," I tell her. "But can you let everyone know that he didn't forget? It wasn't on purpose?"

"Of course."

I hang up and immediately send Malcolm a text:

Are you okay?

I wait a whole thirty seconds before calling him. His phone rolls straight to voice mail. For a moment, my mind blanks. I don't know what to do next. I peer out the window, like an idiot, as if Malcolm will suddenly pull up in the convertible, like the last hour hasn't happened.

Then my limbs spring to life. I pull on my coat, pull the keys for my truck from the hook by the kitchen door. I throw the deadbolt and push the door open ... and a force sends me backward, into the kitchen table and onto the tile floor.

The otherworldly presence that has invaded my space is so strong that it looks like a layer of fog is covering the ceiling. I stand and flick on the light, but the glow is anemic, at best.

The ghost whirls; the walls shake. Waves of frustration roll off the thing. I don't know what it wants. I reach upward in hopes of gauging its intentions. My fingertips meet icy resistance, and I jerk my hand back.

This ghost?

Does not like me.

Then a shiver crawls down my spine, the sensation familiar. Now I know why this ghost doesn't like me.

This ghost is Selena.

But if she's here...

"Selena? Is that you?"

The walls rumble again, and I take that as a yes.

"Where's Malcolm?"

The shaking moves into the foundation. I'm fairly certain she'll shake my house to pieces at this rate.

"Stop, stop. I don't understand you. Where's Malcolm?"

As if in answer, the fog on my ceiling descends. It forms a shape that's vaguely humanlike, or more accurately, womanlike. Curves. This ghost has curves, and she's stalking me in what looks like an otherworldly pair of high heels.

She surges against me, shoving me back toward the living room. She pushes, and I stumble, until at last I land on the couch.

I try again. "Where is he?"

She whirls around while flyers, junk mail, and napkins from the takeout pizza place swirl into a small cyclone. The temperature in my house has dropped at least ten degrees. We're about to go into a full-on ghost infestation at this point.

I don't think even my best Kona blend will stop her.

I hold up my hands in surrender. "Selena, listen. I get it. Something's wrong, but I can't understand you the way Malcolm does. Spell it out. Assume I'm stupid."

At this last, the air shakes with what feels like laughter. Oh, she already thinks I'm stupid.

Her presence contracts until she's a nearly solid form across from me, perched on my coffee table, one ghostly leg elegantly crossed over the other. Tendrils that look very much like fingers extend from her, their trajectory on a collision course with my face.

This could be a bad idea. Even so, I hold still. She reaches me, wisps of her flowing around my head, invading my ears, my nose, my mouth.

That's when the images flash, one after the other. The road to the nature preserve. A red convertible in the parking lot. A dark-haired body slumped over the wheel.

I spring up. For a moment, the two of us occupy the same spot. More images, a jumble of them. I get a flash of other places, other people. The Minneapolis skyline. Carter Dupree. An old warehouse on some lonely road. The Springside Cemetery.

Selena shoots toward the ceiling and takes the images with her. I gasp for breath, winded, although I've done nothing more than view these things. But I'm still in my winter coat. I still clutch the keys to my truck. I study the shoes on my feet. Mary Janes.

That won't do. I kick them off, shove my feet into boots, and race out the door.

AT THE TURNOFF for the nature preserve, the steering wheel

freezes. I yank on it, feel the ache in my shoulders from the effort before noticing the cloud around my legs.

"I can't go that way!" I kick with my left foot, for all the good it will do me. "I'm not a ghost. I have to drive the long way around."

The cab shakes with Selena's frustration.

"Go on ahead," I tell her. "Check on him. I'm right behind you."

She sticks with me as if she doesn't quite trust that I'll follow through. The truck rocks down the road. I'm grateful for the light traffic—and the fact that I've made it this far without encountering a patrol car.

It's only when I tap the brakes for a yield sign and meet no resistance that another notion creeps into my mind. Instead of Carter Dupree haunting my thoughts, I hear the echo of Nigel's warning:

Never get into a car with an angry, uncontained ghost.

And I've done just that.

I swallow back my panic and try for nonchalance, although certainly Selena can tell this is an act. I grip the wheel and sense its range tightening. Soon I won't be able to turn it at all. My brakes are all but useless. I pump them to no avail. All I can do is ease off the accelerator. Even that becomes a chore. My foot feels like it weighs fifty pounds.

Thoughts batter me from all sides. Can ghosts lie? Sprites play pranks, but can ghosts fabricate the way Selena has, showing me images of things that don't exist? Is Malcolm actually hurt? Is he even at the nature preserve?

Or is this an elaborate trap that I've walked right into? One orchestrated by Orson Yates and Carter Dupree?

The ravine is coming up on my right, that same ravine where my parents died. Like this? I wonder. An old car, an angry ghost, and no hope. Except I do have hope. I have Malcolm.

"Let me steer," I say to Selena, my voice as stern as I can make it. "If you don't let me steer, I can't save Malcolm."

She buzzes about the cab, agitated, her worry a tangible thing. Yes, Malcolm is hurt.

"You can't save him," I add, "but you know I can. That's why you found me, right? But if you don't let me drive, I can't do that."

Up ahead a sign looms, the one alerting me to take the turn at twenty-five miles per hour.

I'm going fifty.

"Selena, let go of the steering wheel. If I drive into the ravine, you might get rid of me, but there won't be anyone around to save Malcolm. Carter Dupree won't. Orson Yates won't."

The tires inch from the asphalt and onto the gravel of the shoulder. The silver guardrail flashes into view. I'm wrenching the wheel so hard, I'm nearly flat against the driver's side door with the effort.

All four tires are rolling across gravel now. The front grill of the truck will meet the guardrail first. At this speed, I'll plow right on through. My seatbelt is buckled, but I doubt that will matter.

I'm gripping the wheel with all my strength. When it turns freely in my hands, I'm thrown sideways against the window. The wheel slips through my fingers. The truck's grill scrapes the guardrail. I jerk the wheel farther, and then I'm jostling back onto the asphalt. The truck crosses both lanes and bumps against the row of pines that line the opposite side of the road.

I pull into my lane, heart pounding, hands shaking. Either my windshield or my vision is fogged. I swipe a hand across the glass and consider that maybe it's both. Cold sweat blooms across my skin. The sharp taste of copper fills my mouth. I wipe at it with the back of my hand and leave a smear of red across my skin. I'm bleeding, but don't have time to figure out from where or how much.

The fogged windshield clears and Malcolm's red convertible comes into view. The truck jumps forward, although I can't tell if it's Selena or me doing the driving. We skid into the parking lot, fishtailing to a stop.

I leap out and circle Malcolm's car. I try each door. I pound on the driver's side window. He's slumped over the steering wheel, absolutely still, his bulky winter coat blocking my view of possible injuries.

Except for the blood. I assume it's blood. A dark stain is spreading across one leg of his trousers. I pound some more, but he doesn't stir. With the coat in the way, I can't tell if he's breathing.

I pull out my phone and call 911. I don't stay on the line after I give the dispatcher the basics. I go back to circling Malcolm's car, trying the door handles again, tugging on the trunk's latch.

Selena is a blur above us.

"He's bleeding," I say to her, although I'm certain she knows this. "Can you get in? Unlock the door? Something?"

Certainly she's strong enough, but she flutters around as if there's a barrier keeping her away from the vehicle. I pull off a mitten and press my hand against the icy glass of one window. A cold ache invades my fingers, and I detect something else, something that feels supernatural.

What it is, I can't say. But if Selena can't get in, that leaves me. I race back to my truck and scramble into the back. Could I smash a window? Slice through the convertible's top? I find the flat tire kit first. The tire iron is heavy and cold in my hands.

It's perfect.

On the passenger side, I take up a wide stance and swing at the window. The blow bounces off the glass and the force sends me backward. All I manage is a tiny crack. I don't see the sense in trying again, but Selena is pushing at my hands, forcing my arms upward. Although I can't truly hear her, the air vibrates with the message.

Try again.

I do.

Another blow, another crack. The chip in the glass is deeper, a spider web of fissures branching across the window.

Again Selena urges me, so I swing a third time. If the crack is any deeper, I can't tell. I'm no closer to breaking the window than I was before I started. My arms ache, the tire iron weighing them down. I strain my ears in hopes of a siren, but hear only wind chasing ice crystals across the snow and the sound of my own ragged breathing.

"I can't break it," I say into the air.

Instead of urging me on, Selena spirals into tighter and tighter circles until at last she appears as thin as a wire. I'm certain if I touched her, she'd have actual substance.

I see then what her target is. Perhaps I've broken more than I thought. Or maybe it's just enough. She burrows into that small crack; it's a hole, not only in the glass, but also in the supernatural field that surrounds the car. Her form spreads through the fractures.

Then, with the force she demonstrated in my car and my kitchen, Selena vibrates. I don't think to turn away or step back. When the glass shatters, I'm standing right there. Shards rain down on me. I duck behind my hands, but glass tangles in my hair, cuts my skin, sticks to my tights.

I ignore it all in my lunge for the door. I yank it open from the inside and crawl across more glass to reach Malcolm.

I ease him back from the steering column. He is so heavy in my hands. My fingertips snake along his collar and dip beneath it. I hold my breath while searching out a pulse. It's there, strong beneath my fingers. With my cheek next to his, I feel his warm exhale against my skin.

Flashing lights fill the car. A siren I can only now hear wails. I manage to unlock the driver's side door before someone tugs me from the car. Two EMTs take over, leaving me in the cold and underneath the glare of Police Chief Ramsey.

CHIEF RAMSEY TOWERS OVER ME, unsmiling, arms folded across his chest. This is not the man who laughed at ghost stories on Christmas Eve. Neither is he the man who shared his memories of my mother mere days ago.

This is a man who may pull out his handcuffs and slap them on my wrists. He has a fierce look about him, a mix of disappointment and something I can't name. He takes deliberate steps and stops when the toe of his boot bumps against my phone. He leans down and picks it up.

"I thought I told you to call me."

He hands the phone to me and I tuck it into my pocket. Beneath his glower, I can do little more than swallow hard and nod. The urge to turn from him nearly overwhelms me. I want to track the EMTs' progress with Malcolm, make sure he's okay. I don't dare, not even when something clanks and rattles. A stretcher, I think.

"What the hell happened here?" Chief is still glowering at me, still fierce and unrelenting.

"I ... we..." I glance around.

Selena's presence no longer fills the air. She is either gone or has made herself so slight, I can't detect her. A wave of sudden exhaustion fogs my mind. I'm not sure I can make up a story, not one that will satisfy Chief.

But I try. "Vanessa from Springside Long-term Care called me because Malcolm missed his weekly appointment. I got worried when he didn't answer his phone, so I went looking for him."

There's nothing in my statement that isn't true. I take a breath, relieved I've made it this far with Chief.

"What about this." With a foot, he taps the shattered glass that litters the parking area. In the sunlight, the shards sparkle, and the light crunch of stretcher wheels running over the debris reaches my ears.

"This is safety glass," he continues. "Do you know what that means?"

I shake my head.

"It means that there's no way you used that"—he points to the tire iron—"to shatter the window so ... completely. Mind telling me what really happened here?"

I can only stare back at him, mute. No, I can't tell him what really happened; he'd never believe me. My legs shake as if the adrenaline is already seeping from my feet and into the ground. I may follow, curl up into a Katy-puddle among all the shards of glass.

"Hey, Chief," one of the EMTs calls out. "We're about ready here, and I'd like to check Katy, make sure she isn't injured."

Chief Ramsey blinks, gives one terse nod, and turns his back on me. The EMT leads me to the ambulance with a gentle hand on my arm.

"Are you okay?" she asks.

"I think so. I'm covered with glass." I wave a hand up and down. As if on cue, a few splinters from the window fall to the ground.

"You should probably come in to the ER. The glass might have scratched your eyes."

"Is Malcolm—?"

She nods. It's a noncommittal sort of gesture and I take it that way. Malcolm still is. For now that's enough.

"Why don't you ride in the back with him?" she says.

"But my truck—"

"I'll take care of your truck," Chief says.

How he went from convertible to ambulance without my seeing him, I don't know. But I think it means that, yes, I *should* ride in back. I should go to the ER. Even so, I turn and call out a second protest.

"And Nigel—"

"I'll call Nigel," Chief replies. "He'll probably beat us to the hospital."

Feeling chastised and childish, I let the EMT direct me into a seat next to Malcolm's stretcher. I can reach his hand, and for this I'm grateful. His skin is warm against mine.

I hold his hand for the entire ride to Springside Hospital. Every few blocks I give his fingers a gentle squeeze.

He doesn't squeeze back.

CHAPTER 6

A NICE NURSE PRACTITIONER helps me pick the glass from my hair and clothes. She cleans all the cuts and scrapes. A doctor is confirming that my eyes are scratch-free as Sadie arrives with a change of clothes and an extra-large hot chocolate.

"Oh, Katy, dear." Her hug is a cautious, gentle thing but so warm and safe that for a moment, tears fill my eyes.

"Malcolm?" My voice rings plaintive and scared around us. I haven't sounded this way since my grandmother died.

"In a room, recovering. He has some broken ribs and a concussion. They want to keep him for a few days to make sure there isn't any internal bleeding. Nigel's up there now."

"Can I ... I mean, will they let me see him?"

Sadie smiles at me and cups one side of my face with her hand. "They'd better. He's been asking for you. He's more concerned about you than his own injuries."

I clasp Sadie's hand—the left, I realize. It is smooth and unadorned. There will be no proposal tonight, I'm certain. The thought adds a layer of sadness to the entire day.

Nigel meets us outside the door to Malcolm's room. He pulls me into a hug, one with far more intensity than Sadie's.

"Thank you," he whispers. "Thank you. We have our differences, but he's—"

"Your baby brother," I finish.

He grips my shoulders. "Yes. That. And you." His fingers hover over the scrapes on my face. "Are you okay?"

"Mostly."

"Would seeing Malcolm get you all the way there?"

"I think it would."

"They've got him doped up on painkillers. If he falls asleep, don't take it personally."

"I won't," I promise.

Nigel releases me and I slip through the small opening in the door to Malcolm's room. The lights are dim. Beneath the antiseptic hospital odors, I catch a hint of something, something that smells like nutmeg and Ivory Soap.

Dark lashes grace his cheekbones. Both eyes are bruised now. A bandage is wrapped around part of his skull, and I wonder if that was the source of the blood. But his mouth looks soft, relaxed.

This might be the result of the painkillers.

His eyes flutter open, and he gives me a smile just this side of goofy.

It's most definitely the painkillers.

"Hey," I say, keeping my voice low and quiet.

He twitches his fingers, a *come here* sort of gesture, and I inch forward.

"There you are." His voice sounds rough. "Lifesaver."

I shake my head. "It wasn't just me. Vanessa called, and Selena—"

He grips my fingers and gives them the squeeze I so longed for in the ambulance.

"You," he says, a simple statement to end my protests.

I pull up a chair as close to the edge of the bed as I can. Malcolm takes my hand again, laces our fingers.

"What happened?" I ask. "Do you remember?"

"I was ... showing Selena what we do, my new life here. How we catch and release, although I couldn't even find a sprite to demonstrate. Our next stop was the party at Springside Long-term Care. Something attacked us, or really, me. It had no interest in Selena."

"A ghost? Something else?"

"A ghost, I think. A really nasty one."

"So, not like that entity?"

Malcolm shuts his eyes. "I don't think so. I think if it were something that strong, I'd be dead right now. It probably had a little direction and a boost from a necromancer, though." He sighs. "How did you get me out?"

I cringe to even say it. "A tire iron."

His eyes fly open. "You what? Smashed a window? Have you been working out in secret?"

I shake my head. "I could only make a tiny crack, but it was enough for Selena to sneak in and do the rest."

"Necromancy," Malcolm says. "A containment field. It can be used to keep ghosts out—or in. I used one on my samovar. It's how I stored so many inside there."

"A samovar is pretty small," I point out, "compared to a car."

"An easy trick for a powerful necromancer."

Our gazes lock, although we both remain silent. We don't need to confirm out loud what we're both thinking, how we happen to have two too many necromancers in town.

"I remember promising you no one else would get hurt," he says.

I think I might cry. Tears from earlier—from this entire week, really—blur my vision. I sniff, once.

"Hey, don't. Don't do that." He touches my cheek and catches a teardrop. "It's okay. I'm okay."

Except it's not okay, and he's clearly not okay.

A soft knock on the door has me sitting up a bit straighter, although Malcolm clutches my hand, keeps me from going too far.

"You need your rest," a nurse says to him, her admonishment gentle but firm.

This is my cue to leave. I don't want to. The hardest thing I've ever done is let my fingers slip from his. I'm at the door when he calls out, voice scratchy but filled with humor.

"Can I get a rain check on that date?"

I nod, push tears from my cheeks with my palms, and then I'm alone in the hallway. I stand there, outside Malcolm's room. I don't know what to do next. I don't know where to turn.

I don't see Nigel and Sadie on my way out. In truth, I don't search for them. I'm halfway down the sidewalk in front of the hospital when I spot my truck in the visitors' parking lot.

The keys are on the front seat, weighing down Chief Ramsey's business card.

I SIT cross-legged on the reception desk of K&M Ghost Eradication Specialists. It's far too early to be open for the day, but it's also far too early to visit Malcolm, which is the only item on my agenda. The only other business open at this hour is the Springside Pancake House. I have a takeout container of pancakes and a large orange juice, courtesy of Belinda.

And I have coffee, courtesy of my own kitchen. I will use the time to think, to plan, to strategize. That black Mercedes is still sitting outside the bed and breakfast. I'm starting to loathe the sight of it, its presence a dark, malevolent thing.

I'm five minutes into strategizing—with not much to show for it—when the bell over the door chimes.

Orson Yates walks in, black wool overcoat dusted with a few

snowflakes, a fedora giving him a polished air. He pauses at the threshold, removes the hat, and then tilts his head.

"Oh, my. That's an impressive little ward you've got going there."

"Then you know you're not wanted here."

He's quite possibly the last person I want to see—well, second to last. I dislike Carter even more.

"Ah, but the rules differ for a place of business." He drops his hat onto a coat rack hook as if he plans to stay a while. "Trust me. We have business."

"Did you lose a ghost or just your shadow?"

Orson purses his lips as if he's trying to swallow a smile. "Yes, Carter. I left him behind this time. I believe he has a tiny crush on you." Orson pinches his index finger and thumb together. "His judgment is off."

My appetite is off. My stomach rolls over on itself, and I'm afraid I'll lose all of my breakfast pancakes. I shut the lid on the remaining two and push the container to the far side of the desk. The thought to call Chief flashes across my mind, but Orson hasn't broken any laws—that I know of. He hasn't threatened me.

And informing Chief that Orson Yates is the most powerful necromancer in town, and therefore the most likely suspect in the ghost attack on Malcolm, simply won't work.

I have no choice. I must listen to what he has to say. I lean back and pull a paper cup from the desk drawer. When the top of the thermos opens, the rich aroma of Kona blend fills the space. The moment the scent reaches Orson, his features soften; an eyebrow arches. Oh, he's interested.

It might not be alcohol, but sometimes coffee works just as well.

"Would you like some?" I ask, going for professional. Or as professional as someone can be while wearing jeans and sitting on her own reception desk.

"I would. Believe it or not, the coffee-making ability of the

161

Lindstroms is legendary. Your grandmother had quite a reputation for excellent brew, and there was more than one man who would've married your mother for her coffee alone."

I don't like that this man knew my mother. I don't like that he knows things about her that I may never know. I really don't like that he's old enough to be my father.

I offer him a cup anyway. "How do you take it?"

"Black."

Lucky for him. I'm not about to hop off the desk and fetch sugar and half and half. I pour a cupful for him and top off my own before closing the cap of the thermos.

Orson takes the coffee, inhales, and his expression is so rapturous it's nearly obscene.

"Your grandmother taught you well." He raises the cup. "In this, at least. Why she neglected a large part of your education, I can't honestly say. It baffles me."

"I don't know what you're talking about."

"I think you do. I think you've been wondering the same thing yourself. Have you ever asked yourself, why coffee?"

"Because it works."

"If that were the case, why not use instant or those new K-cups?"

I make a face. "You'd just end up with a mess and a pissed-off ghost."

"But ask yourself: is it the coffee, or is it the container?"

Orson points to the storefront display where, along with the hearts and glitter, an old percolator of my grandmother's rests next to Malcolm's samovar with the blown-out back.

"And why Tupperware?" he continues. "There's nothing special about it."

"It contains the ghosts until we can release them." Really, this is ghost-catching 101.

"Yes, but why, Katy? Not everyone can scoop up a ghost and seal it away for transport or ... whatever."

I shrug. "Does it matter?"

"It might, considering you claim not to be a necromancer. What if I told you that every time you catch a ghost, you commit an act of necromancy?"

"But I'm not—"

"So you say. But what keeps the ghosts in check once you catch them? Why doesn't it work for most others? It's you. Call it your touch, your innate ability. If you trap a ghost in something, it will stay there until you release it."

"Are you saying I'm magical?"

"Not exactly. What I'd like you to consider is this. Your friend Belinda Barnes can sense ghosts just as well as you can. Why can't she catch them? It would make her life so much easier."

The pit of my stomach ices over. I clutch my cup and sip, desperate for something warm inside me. I don't like that he knows about Belinda. And while his words are perfectly reasonable, his tone holds something else, something that sounds like a threat.

"You, my child, are a necromancer. Why your grandmother didn't inform you of this, I don't know." He gestures toward the display window. "That's how we stored ghosts, originally. The coffee or tea kept them from grumbling too much until the time came to pull one out and put it to use."

"I don't use ghosts. I set them free. Catch and release."

"Really? Springside has an unusual number of ghosts. Oh, and don't they adore you. I've never seen a necromancer who inspired so much affection and loyalty. If I didn't know better, if I didn't know of your aversion to necromancy, I'd say you were amassing an army."

"A ghost army?" The idea is ludicrous. "What on earth would I do with a ghost army?"

"On earth? A great many things, actually. But the fact you're amassing an army on the border of my territory ... concerns me."

"It shouldn't, and it isn't an army."

"But they've come to your aid before, have they not?"

This is something else Orson shouldn't know. Only a few people know how the ghosts of Springside helped me free Malcolm from the entity.

"They may be loyal," he adds, "but ghosts aren't very discrete."

Tattletales.

"What do you want, Orson? You said we had business. I've already told you I don't want to be a part of your club."

With this last, I set off the twitch again. He uses his ring finger to smooth his left eyebrow. He casts me a look, his expression that of someone much older and much wiser dealing with a rebellious child.

"So, what do you want?" I ask when he doesn't respond.

"It's quite simple, my dear. I can't allow you to collect so many ghosts so close to my own area of operations, so I will simply appropriate them from you. It's not like this"—he waves a hand, indicating K&M Ghost Eradication Specialists—"was going to pay the bills for long, or at all."

Will appropriate ... or already has? My mind goes to how few customers we've had this month, especially since Orson and Carter rolled into town. I think of the cowering sprites in the Springside Police Department reception area. I think how I haven't chased Sadie's two from her house in a week.

"You can't take my ghosts," I say.

"*Your* ghosts?" He raises an eyebrow. "So, you *are* amassing an army. In that case, I'm afraid I can and I will. Do you know what happens to a loyal, affectionate ghost after a few months—or years —in isolation? Oh, they become nasty, indeed. I believe you may have met a few."

My mind goes to Harold Lancaster's ghost. Then an image flashes in my mind, one Selena shared with me of a warehouse, gray and dingy. How many ghosts could you store there? I feel as though I've walked right into this—whatever this is—and don't know the way back out.

Orson Yates drains his coffee and crushes the cup in his hand. He lets the crumpled paper drop to the floor and returns his hat to his head.

"Good day, Ms. Lindstrom." He nods once. "It was a pleasure doing business with you."

I'M CROUCHED in a far corner of the Springside Police Department reception area. Penny Wilson's chair sits empty—for now—and the scent of yesterday's charred coffee is a lingering memory in the air.

I pop open the thermos and the rich smell of Kona blend banishes it completely.

"Come on, guys," I say. "I'm not going to catch you. I just want to talk."

Sprites have such a slight presence, they're often difficult to detect. But these two are still here, cowering behind a file cabinet. I doubt they've played a prank all week.

"No one's here," I add. "At least not Carter Dupree."

I suspect Chief is in his office, although the door is shut tight. I keep my voice low and encouraging.

"He's not coming back. Chief Ramsey doesn't like him. As long as you stay put, they can't take you."

I hope what I've said is true. Carter must know two sprites haunt here. He no doubt sensed them when he stopped in for the attempted restraining order against Malcolm. I wonder at that, wonder if that was simply a way to barge into one more place and take an inventory of ghosts.

After a moment, a ghostly shimmer appears in the crack between the metal cabinet and the wall. The sprites ease out, skittish, their forms barely visible. Oh, they are so puny and scared. This is nearly the same as isolation.

"Here." I place the thermos next to them.

In the rising steam, they gain substance. One whirls. The other starts a dance. I let them soak in their fill.

"Can you tell me if Carter Dupree came here more than once?" I ask them after they start floating, full and sated.

The question prompts another flurry. They twirl about, crashing into each other, rising with the steam and then sinking back down. As answers go, this is one I can't decipher.

"Bob up and down for yes," I say. "Let's try this again. Did Carter Dupree come back here?"

The bobbing is unending.

"More than once?"

Even more bobbing.

"Yesterday?"

The bobbing slows. That might be too precise a question, especially for a sprite. I've always suspected ghosts lose track of time, one day flowing into another for them.

"If he comes back, don't go near him. Same goes for Orson Yates." I doubt Orson is running around collecting sprites—that sounds like a job you'd give to a minion. "Hide back here, or in Chief's office, or even in the holding cell."

"Oh, my word! Katy! What on earth are you doing?"

I jerk up, my head connecting with the edge of a desk. Stars flash before my eyes, and I blink until my vision clears. I peer up at Penny Wilson, my fingers investigating the sore spot on my scalp.

"I..." I glance behind me. The sprites bob encouragingly. "I thought I spotted a mouse."

Penny clutches her hands together and backs up several steps. "A mouse! I'll go get Chief."

"No!" That's the last thing I need. "I think it's gone now."

But Penny is knocking on his door.

"I have to go," I tell the sprites.

This time when they bob, I swear they're laughing at me. I grab a Styrofoam cup from the sideboard and pour them some more coffee anyway. I wedge it into the crevice as best I can so it won't spill.

"Hide," I say, "and be good."

"What's this about a mouse?" Chief's booming voice fills the room. He folds his arms over his chest and locks a glare onto me. "Expanding your eradication services?"

I hop up. "No, I'm good. Thanks, Penny, for all your help."

I tread my way to the front door, hoping Penny won't ask how she helped, praying Chief won't demand an explanation. If he does, it comes after I'm out the door and on the sidewalk. The bump on my head throbs, but the cold clears my jumbled thoughts.

I don't have a plan, but at least I know what I'm going to do next.

AFTERNOON SUNLIGHT FILTERS through the window blinds, most of it spilling onto the floor. Even in the shrouded room, Malcolm winces, raising a hand now and then to shield his eyes.

"Bad?" I ask. "Can I get you something?"

"No. I just feel useless, and I hate feeling useless."

"Don't baby him," Nigel says. "He'll start to expect it."

Malcolm narrows his eyes at his brother. "Shut up."

Nigel merely laughs.

We've gone over everything we can, established that other than the sprites in the police station and Mr. Carlotta's ghost in the long-term care facility, all the ghosts of Springside are gone. I even snuck into Chief Ramsey's garden shed to confirm that the ghost who haunts the watering can was missing. The wild ghosts on the outskirts of town, in the old barn, are also absent. Perhaps they were the first to go.

Something about that makes this all unbearably sad.

"He's overstepped his bounds," Malcolm says. "Certainly we can call on someone."

Nigel shakes his head. "I tried, believe me. No one wants to go up against Orson."

Malcolm scowls and then rubs his temples as if the expression made his head hurt. "Cowards."

"Not entirely," Nigel says. "Part of it is Katy."

"Me?" My gaze darts to Malcolm, but he glances away. "What have I done?"

"They see Orson's point," Nigel continues. "You've amassed an army of ghosts here in Springside."

"But I haven't—"

"Technically, you have." Nigel holds up his hands, halting my protest. "The others in the necromancer community don't understand how you keep so many ghosts in one place and how they can be so loyal."

"Maybe because I don't actually keep any of them."

"You're an unknown quantity," he continues as if I haven't spoken. "Your grandmother was powerful, with a reputation to match, even if she didn't practice necromancy. Add in your parents' mysterious death, and they'll believe Orson before they believe you."

I turn toward Malcolm, hoping he'll see the pleading in my eyes.

He shrugs as much as the broken ribs allow. "I hate to say it, but Nigel's right—sort of. When I first came to Springside, I thought you were crazy for releasing all those ghosts. You had so many, and I couldn't believe that you'd let them slip through your fingers like that."

"My grandmother always said everyone was better off that way, ghost and human." I study my hands for a moment, noting that the most recent scald on the back of the right one is fading. Then I confront both brothers. "Do you suppose she never told me about necromancy because she wanted to change the way things were done?"

"If so, it backfired," Nigel says. "Everyone I talked to is quite baffled by you. They think you've developed some new technique and will hoard both that knowledge and all the ghosts."

"Necromancers are a suspicious lot," Malcolm adds.

Nigel nods. "One of the many reasons the Armands have always been free agents."

"But you." I point at Nigel. "And you." I target Malcolm. "They know you. Can't you tell them?"

Nigel casts his gaze downward. Malcolm's expression twists. He plucks at the bandage around his head, his hand blocking his eyes.

Then it occurs to me. Malcolm came to Springside out of desperation. Until recently, Nigel was in the throes of his addiction. Neither man was at the top of his game. And now, they catch ghosts rather than use them. I don't know much about the world of necromancy, but from what I've seen, status, power, money—it's all very important.

And it looks like we're on our own.

"I'm sorry," I say, voice contrite and soft. "If it's any consolation, I still believe I've aligned myself with the right sort of necromancer."

Nigel glances up and gives me a half grin. Malcolm's dark eyes are unreadable, the expression in them like nothing I've seen before. I can't tell if they hold regret or self-recrimination, or even disgust. Whatever it means, it's steely and unrelenting.

"Nightstand drawer," he says.

I open it and pull out a box, one that contains a Bluetooth earpiece. I don't ask how he ended up with it. No doubt a nurse or a volunteer or someone was more than happy to do him this favor. I hold it up in question.

"For your phone," he elaborates. "So you can take me with you, hands-free."

"Take you with me where?"

"When you go find our ghosts."

CHAPTER 7

MALCOLM HAS BEEN in my head all morning. He whispers in my ear, tells me jokes. I try not to laugh so passersby can see. I keep my responses muted as much as possible. But the whipping wind and the traffic on Main Street make that difficult.

Still, I try. I'm already *the girl who catches ghosts*. I don't want to add *the girl who talks to herself* to the list.

We've traveled through and around town at least three times. Or rather, I have. Malcolm's taken a virtual ride thanks to my new Bluetooth earpiece.

We haven't found a single thing.

On this circuit, something's different. The black Mercedes is missing from in front of the Springside B&B.

"It's gone," I say to Malcolm.

"What is?"

I keep forgetting he can't see what I'm doing. "Orson's car. It's not parked at the bed and breakfast."

"Did they go for pancakes?"

I make an illegal U-turn and rumbled down the opposite side of

Main Street. All the spots in front of the Pancake House are filled, but none by a black and menacing Mercedes.

"I want to go to Springside Long-term Care," I say. "I'm worried about Mr. Carlotta's ghost."

I've warned Mr. Carlotta, of course, along with both the day and night managers. It's not like they're in the habit of letting creepy visitors inside, no matter how well-dressed they are.

Still. Of all the ghosts Orson Yates could catch in town, the one that haunts Mr. Carlotta's Purple Heart is the most valuable. I make another U-turn and head away from Main Street.

The parking lot of Springside Long-term Care is also free of that black Mercedes. I hop from my truck, thermoses of coffee jostling in the canvas bag I use as a field kit. The wind whips my hair around my face, batters strands against my cheeks. With a finger, I make sure the earpiece is in place.

Inside, I'm assaulted. I'm barely past the double entry doors when residents begin to push envelopes into my hands, the paper a bright array of reds and pinks and others a more somber blue. These last, I suspect, are get-well-soon cards.

"Katy, dear, how is Malcolm?" one of the residents asks. Actually, they all ask this, in their expressions at least, each one waiting for my answer.

"Much better," I say. "The doctors say he's healing quickly, and he's sorry he missed the party."

This inspires a round of tut-tutting with suggestions for an even bigger party once Malcolm is out of the hospital. I can't possibly answer all the questions or respond to every last one of the well-wishes. They echo around me, fill the space with warmth.

"Are you getting all this?" I whisper, hoping only Malcolm will hear me.

"I am." His voice is filled with mirth. "Are you able to get to the resident rooms, or are they going have to call out the National Guard?"

I laugh and earn a frown or two. A few of the residents are

proprietary when it comes to Malcolm. In their eyes, I'm an inter-loper, at best, and I certainly shouldn't be laughing. I push on through, collecting the belated valentines and get-well cards as I go, stashing them in the field kit.

At last I reach the hallway to Mr. Carlotta's room. The corridor is serene compared to the front lobby. I can hear myself think, hear myself talk, not to mention hear Malcolm.

"They love you," I say to him. "You know that, right? I've added five pounds to my bag with all these cards."

My boots scuff the carpet as I walk. The rattle of a wheelchair and the drone of a television fill my ears. What I don't hear is Malcolm. I touch the earpiece again.

"You still there? Did we get cut off?"

He clears his throat. "No ... no, I'm a little overwhelmed, is all. I didn't realize—" He breaks off and coughs.

"That they'd end up meaning so much to you?"

"Yeah. That. You always know what I'm thinking."

Not always. I hold in a sigh.

"Katy-Girl!" Mr. Carlotta greets me, as always, with the nick-name my grandmother used. He's in his wheelchair by the window. I suspect he's tracked my progress all the way from the parking lot.

I bend so he can kiss my cheek. This also gives me a chance to take in the room, gauge it for an otherworldly presence. Ah, yes. Mr. Carlotta's ghost is still here. As soon as I sense her, something inside me unclenches.

Mr. Carlotta pulls two envelopes from the nightstand. He hands them both to me.

"One for you," he says. "And a get-well card for"—he coughs —"that young man of yours. I hope he's recovering."

"Are you kidding me?" Malcolm says in my ear. "I got a card from Mr. Carlotta? And he didn't call me a name?"

"He probably wrote something rude on the inside," I whisper.

Mr. Carlotta doesn't entirely approve of my relationship with

Malcolm. Much of that, I suspect, is because he'd prefer I be in a relationship with his favorite grandson, Jack.

"What, dear?" Mr. Carlotta says.

"Nothing, nothing," I say, feigning innocence.

Then I hold a finger to my lips. I have Mr. Carlotta's full attention. We're being sneaky, which is one of his favorite things. From my pocket, I pull my cell phone and put it on mute. I remove the Bluetooth earpiece. I give both to Mr. Carlotta.

"I need to talk to your ghost," I tell him. "No one else can hear."

He eyes the phone cradled in his hands.

"Not even Malcolm. It's for his safety, everyone's safety."

He gives me a solemn nod and wheels himself from the room. I shut the door gently behind him. A bit of guilt tugs at me. I've debated this question before: to tell Malcolm or not to tell him.

No one knows how I learned the entity's name. Malcolm has never asked, although certainly he knows I did something to find it. I tell myself that he believes as I do: the fewer people who know that being's name, the better.

That goes for ghosts, too.

I pour a cup of coffee for Mr. Carlotta's ghost. She's an old thing, ancient, possibly. He calls her Queenie, after Queen Boudicca. Although this ghost was a warrior, I have no idea if she really was a warrior queen.

She is, however, particular and morose, her presence weighing the air. As of late, she is, if not happy, lighter. The air is easier to breathe in Mr. Carlotta's room. I no longer catch and release her to give him some space. They've found a certain companionship with each other, these two old soldiers.

She oozes from her hiding spot. Most days, she's content to stay put in the nightstand drawer, attached to Mr. Carlotta's Purple Heart.

"You know what's going on," I say to her.

She continues to ease forward. I take that as a yes.

"You can't let them catch you. I know you're strong, but they're willing to wait for years, decades, even."

Queenie reaches the coffee and begins to smother it. Kona blend is her favorite, and I've splurged with fresh-roasted beans straight from the Coffee Depot. The steam glimmers, her form lumpy.

"You wouldn't want to leave him all alone, would you?" I nod toward the door.

Her form expands. She is either enjoying the coffee or I've angered her—or both. With this ghost, both is always a possibility. I know the moment she's drunk her fill. With a ghostly finger, she knocks the cup over so coffee splatters on the side table, the floor, my jeans.

"I'm telling you something you already know, right?"

I get a bounce in response, one that's almost worthy of a sprite.

"I'm just worried," I tell her. "No one knows what we know, and I'd like to keep it that way." I'm about to stand when another question occurs to me. "You wouldn't know where they're keeping the other ghosts, would you?"

Queenie's form contracts. She looks smaller, if not diminished. She retreats away from me and back into the nightstand drawer, to the Purple Heart. If this is an answer, I don't know what it means.

I pick up the cup, open the door, and then go in search of paper towels. By the time I return, Mr. Carlotta has Malcolm on speaker and is cross-examining him.

"So, she takes you around with this thing in her ear? It looks like something from *Star Trek*."

"Yes, she takes me around with that thing in her ear." Malcolm's patience is starting to crack. "That way, I can talk to her."

"What you need to do is get out of the hospital so she isn't out here on her own." While Mr. Carlotta doesn't call him anything rude, it's all there in his tone. Despite two cracked ribs and a concussion, Malcolm is slacking.

"I can take care of myself," I interject. "Besides, this way, Malcolm can look things up on the internet."

"Or even dial 911," he adds.

"See?" I say. "It's kind of handy."

Mr. Carlotta harrumphs at us. I hold out my hand. With some reluctance, he returns my phone and the earpiece. Before I can leave, he grips my wrist.

"Be careful, Katy-Girl."

"I will. I always am."

"I don't like these characters.," Mr. Carlotta continues. "They came to town before, you know. Well, not that young one, obviously. But the other one. He's all sleek and self-satisfied, was like that back then too. I remember—" He glances away.

"What do you remember?" I ask, not certain I want the answer.

"I remember how losing your mother and her husband nearly killed your grandmother. If not for you, Katy-Girl..." He trails off.

I don't ask him to elaborate.

"This isn't a coincidence, is it?" he asks.

"No." I see no reason to lie. "It's not."

"Be careful," Mr. Carlotta demands again. "And, young man? You keep your ears open."

"I will," Malcolm says before I take him off speaker and secure the earpiece once again.

Outside, I sit in my truck, letting it warm up. Or at least, that's my excuse.

"Katy." Malcolm's voice is soft in my ear. "Are you okay?"

"Thinking, or trying to."

"Your chat with Mr. Carlotta's ghost go as planned?"

"I ... sort of. I did ask her where they were keeping the other ghosts, and she drew in on herself, went back to hiding."

My first idea was to search out that warehouse from the images Selena shared with me, but there's nothing like it in Springside. After I described it to Malcolm, his guess was somewhere outside the Twin Cities. It had the look of an abandoned industrial park. If the building is close by, it's nothing I've ever seen.

"Let's assume they haven't moved the ghosts from here," I say. "You're the necromancer. Where would you store a bunch of ghosts before you could take them somewhere?"

"I used to store them in the samovar."

"And we both know what happened when it got too full."

His laugh warms my ear. "So we're looking for something bigger than a samovar."

"The high school?" I suggest.

"Too busy."

"What about the Ghost B Gone house? It still hasn't sold."

"It would work, but it's also on Chief Ramsey's radar. I'm sure they're trying to stay out of his way, not call attention to themselves. It's going to be somewhere we wouldn't think to look."

None of this inspires confidence. "Where wouldn't we look for ghosts?"

"Oh, Katy ... you're brilliant."

If I am, this is news to me.

"Where wouldn't we look for ghosts," Malcolm says, his voice taking on a new energy. "Almost never, but the one place everyone else thinks is haunted?"

It hits me then. Yes, hide the ghosts in plain sight. "The Springside Cemetery?"

"Exactly."

"Wait!" I shut my eyes, try not to see what I want to see. But no, I remember. I'm certain of it. "Selena showed me that, along with the other images. I'm almost one hundred percent sure."

I put the truck in gear and back from the parking space. I make one final illegal U-turn and rumble down the road toward the Springside Cemetery.

~

"YOU'RE RIGHT," I say to Malcolm.

Actually, I whisper it, which is silly since I'm still in the truck, still several yards away from the cemetery parking lot, but close enough to spy the Mercedes. It's like a sleek black beetle, the paint gleaming in the late afternoon sun.

I stop the truck and put it in reverse. I inch backward and park on a lightly traveled side street.

I take my field kit even though I'm not certain what good coffee will do. The thermoses rattle. I unwind the scarf I'm wearing and weave it between the metal containers.

"I'm going to hop the fence so they don't see me coming," I tell Malcolm.

"You might as well," he says. "According to the web page, the cemetery locks the gates at four."

"Really?" I ask. "They have a web page?"

"Why not? We do."

I walk the perimeter until I find a section of the rock wall that isn't much taller than I am. I unsling the field kit and ease it up and over before attempting the climb myself. In boots and mittens it's a precarious thing. My feet skid against the icy rocks. I have zero purchase with my mittens. I tug them off, and with a mouthful of damp wool, I scale the wall and tumble to the other side.

A snow bank swallows me. I am breathless and cold. For a moment, I stare up at the sky. I almost feel like a child, ready to make a snow angel.

"Katy? You've gone silent on me. Say something."

"I landed in a snow bank, but I'm okay."

I dig my way out and find the field kit, all to the sound of Malcolm's chuckle. But then he grows silent himself.

"Malcolm?" I touch the earpiece again. I'm about to pull out my phone and check it when he finally speaks.

"Maybe you shouldn't do this."

"We need to find the ghosts."

"But you don't need to have another run-in with Orson and Carter," he says. "I don't like that you're there alone. You're outnumbered."

"What are they going to do to me?"

"That's just it, Katy. I don't know."

A bit of trapped snow slithers down my neck. A shiver follows.

"I can't ... we can't just let them do this." I take a few steps forward, brushing snow from my coat and kicking it from my boots. "What if I'm sneaky?"

"You'll have to be very sneaky. They'll probably have a spy or two out."

"You mean a ghost?"

"That's exactly what I mean, so stay on high alert for all things supernatural."

Ghosts as spies. This is new. "What other necromancer tricks haven't you told me about?"

His sigh fills my ear. "Several, I'm sure. I grew up with necromancy, the same way you did with catch and release. It's not that I'm hiding anything. It simply doesn't occur to me to tell you."

He has a point—and he still can't do a release without some ghost cuffing him on the back of the head.

I shuffle forward in the snow. The gravestones around me are worn and weathered, their inscriptions barely legible, each wearing a cap of snow. Except for some crisscrossed tracks of squirrels and birds—and my footsteps—the blanket of snow is pristine. This is the old part of the cemetery, and it doesn't see much traffic.

This might be why I sense the presence immediately. It might be why I know who this ghost is. I halt. Really, I have no choice in the matter. It's like an otherworldly wall has been built in front of me. I'm not moving forward; I'm not going around, either. We regard each other, human to ghost. Then I speak very softly, just loud enough for Malcolm to hear.

"It's Selena," I say. "She's here."

"Put me on speaker," he says. "Can you? Turn down the volume if you have to, but this will go better if she can hear my voice."

I scan the cemetery. No matter how low I turn down the volume, the sound of voices will carry. But I'm not moving forward without Malcolm's help.

"Okay." I pull out my phone and tap the speaker. "It's on."

"Selena, sweetheart, is that you?"

His voice kicks up a frenzy, a mini blizzard of snow. Ice crystals strike my cheeks and his words strike a dull ache in my chest.

"I think the answer is yes," I manage to choke out. "She's causing a snowstorm."

"I'm alive and in the hospital. Thanks to you and Katy. Everything's going to be okay." His voice is patient and calming. Even though he's not speaking the words to me, I relax, if only a little. "Can you help Katy? Tell her what's going on?"

The whirling subsides. Selena's form shimmers in the light slanting through the trees. If anyone else spotted her, they might believe she's an angel.

"She's ... hovering," I say.

"Did Orson or Carter send you out as a spy?" Malcolm asks.

This is clearly the wrong thing to ask. The blizzard starts up again, this time with such force, I'm afraid she'll knock over a headstone. Instead several branches drop from the tree above my head.

"I have no idea what that means," I tell her.

Selena vanishes into the snow. A moment later, something tunnels through the smooth canvas in front of my feet. First one letter, than another.

NO

"She says no," I say to Malcolm. "Also, she thinks I'm stupid."

"I'm sure she doesn't," he insists.

The glimmering, gleeful presence says otherwise.

"Do they know you're here?" he asks.

She swirls around the letters.

"No, they don't," I say.

"Have they trapped the ghosts?"

With a single whoosh, she creates a line across her letters.

"I'm guessing that they have." I consider Selena—and consider whether she's lying. If she isn't trapped or a spy, why is she here in the cemetery?

"Do you know where Malcolm is?" I ask.

The storm she kicks up is the worst yet. I duck, clutch my hands over my head, and wait it out. Snow invades my mouth, creeps down the back of my shirt. I'm cold and achy and the wind chill in this section of the cemetery must be well below zero.

"Can ghosts navigate?" I'm still crouched, but the battering of snow diminishes.

"There's a reason we drive the truly nasty ones into the middle of nowhere, right?" Malcolm says. "We're hoping they won't find their way back."

Sometimes they do. Sometimes they seem to know where they're going, like with Delilah and the Mississippi River. But sometimes...?

"She can't find you," I say. Maybe she never could, from the first time they were separated. Carter must have enticed her with that when he caught her. I think back to when Nigel finally gave up all the ghosts and they went streaming into the air. We were nowhere near Springside. Besides, Selena didn't know Malcolm had moved away from the Twin Cities.

How long has she been searching for him? Months, certainly.

The snowstorm dies, and the cemetery is quiet again, Selena a shimmering form in front of me. From the moment Malcolm burst into K&M Ghost Eradication Specialists with her, I knew I was going to lose him. But I never imagined I'd lose him like this, here in the cemetery.

I stand, put the phone on mute, and then bring up the map. I switch to satellite view and zero in on downtown Springside.

"Here's what you do." I trace the route with a finger. "From Malcolm's apartment, go to the police station and then to our business." I glance up at her, uncertain ghosts can read maps. "See?"

Selena bobs, her excitement sparking. In this moment, she does look nearly divine, the spot we're standing in bathed in a golden glow.

"Keep to this road," I say. "You'll pass a park with a playground, and then at the end of the street, you'll see the hospital. Malcolm's on the fourth floor, room four forty."

She swirls, another frenzy that sprays snow in an arc. She follows its path. It glimmers in a rainbow of color before the whole thing collapses to the ground in an explosion of ice crystals.

"You're welcome," I say. "And kiss him for me?"

I'm pretty sure I've had my last.

Selena buzzes around the treetops as if comparing that view to my map. She swoops down one last time and swipes at my cheek. Something fizzles against my skin.

I realize she's caught a tear. If I don't get a grip, there will be several more. I press a hand against my eyes and wait for the cemetery to fall silent. When I'm alone, I push forward through the snow once again.

It takes another five minutes before I can switch the phone off mute.

YOU HAVE NO BUSINESS HERE. *Turn back.*

The thoughts pop into my head unbidden. I can't account for them. They're strange, authoritative declarations. I glance around, although I'm positive no one has spoken. Slowly, I move forward.

You have been warned. Turn back. Mind your own business.

I freeze again. I peer over my shoulder. A sensation of being watched crawls across my skin. I feel like a naughty child breaking any number of rules.

"Someone's telling me to stop," I whisper to Malcolm.

"A ghost?"

I raise my chin and sample the air. "No. Nothing like that. It's a voice, only not."

"Oh," he says, and he sounds almost amused. "Remember when Nigel taught you how to create a ward?"

"Yes."

"Well, you've just walked into one."

"Whose? Orson's?"

"What does it sound like?" Malcolm asks.

"Authoritative, yet vague. It's a *go away and ask no questions* sort of vibe."

"Yeah, that's Orson."

"But how can he create one in the cemetery? No one owns the cemetery. It's not keeping me out, right?"

"What did it make you do?"

Slow down. Stop. Talk to Malcolm. "It's a distraction."

For a moment, I consider what to do next. Do I sprint forward, or is that, too, part of the plan? Will that lead straight into a trap? The other danger is moving too slow, arriving too late to save the ghosts.

I run.

The snow hampers my steps, clings to my boots. My lungs ache with the cold. I sense something otherworldly. It's not a spy, not a single ghost, but something much more than that.

I burst through a row of pines. The toe of my boot catches on what feels like a tree root. I pitch forward and let out a yelp. Snow crashes down on me, followed by the muffled sound of Carter Dupree's laughter. Malcolm's voice is frantic in my ear.

"Katy? Katy? Who is that? What's going on?"

My face stings. My jeans are soaked. I yank at my leg to free it and dislodge another cascade of snow. I crawl forward, try to shake off the excess and blink the fringe of flakes from my eyes. I only stop when I reach a pair of legs and an extended hand in a leather glove.

Carter Dupree is as bright and smooth as ever. I refuse the offer of help, partly out of pride, partly because my attention has been caught by what's behind him.

In the center of the clearing, where some of the larger tombs form a semi-circle, there's a wall of glimmering white. I squint, picking out forms—tiny sprites, larger ghosts. Near the top, I recognize the wild spirits from the old barn. They strike what looks like air without breaking through.

They are confined, all of them, in a ghostly sort of prison.

"What have you done?" I push to my knees, my gaze never leaving that solid mass of ghosts.

They swoop and swarm as best they can in the confined space. Some, I'm certain, are calling for help. The air holds a plaintive echo, sad and heart-rending.

"What have you done?" I ask again.

"Katy, what is it? What's going on?" Malcolm's voice is low in my ear. I shake my head in answer, which is stupid because he can't see me.

"Ah, Ms. Lindstrom. I see you have no regard for wards yourself. We have that in common, then."

Orson Yates steps forward.

"Oh," Malcolm says. "That's what's going on. Be careful."

I nod, which makes me look like I'm agreeing with Orson. But I don't care. All I want is to figure out what they've done to my ghosts. I struggle to stand, again ignoring Carter's proffered hand. I take a step and then another until I'm close enough to reach out and touch the ghosts.

Except I can't. My mittened fingers meet resistance. I can't push through, and although several of them try, the ghosts can't push out. I place my hands against the invisible barrier and gaze at all the ghosts and sprites and spirits inside. How many are in there? All the ghosts of Springside minus three?

Orson moves to my side. I don't bother to glance in his direction.

"I simply can't fathom it." He waves a hand toward the ghosts. "Such loyalty, such affection. You know, of course, that all ghosts want something."

Now I do look at Orson, just barely, from the corner of my eye.

"What these ghosts want is for you to capture them, over and over again. I suppose that's a viable business model, as long as the good citizens of Springside don't catch on."

A few of the fiercer ghosts ram the barrier opposite where Orson is standing. He merely chuckles.

"You know, my dear, the offer still stands, despite everything. Your powers, while undisciplined, are impressive. Most necromancers must work for years to establish the sort of rapport with ghosts that comes naturally to you."

"Have you considered that it comes naturally because I don't want to use them, not like you do?" I turn to Orson and stare at him straight on. "I don't want money or fame or whatever it is you're offering."

"Not even the affections of a certain disgraced necromancer?"

My throat tightens. I suppose my feelings for Malcolm are hardly a secret, not with the way ghosts gossip. What about his for Selena? How much have the ghosts already gossiped about that? How much does Orson know?

"You can't buy someone's affection," I say.

"Oh, that's where you're wrong. You most certainly can, after a fashion."

"I don't want to buy anyone's affection."

"I wonder," he says, as if my declaration holds all the weight of a child's.

It's then that I notice the voice in my ear has gone silent. Has Malcolm heard everything from the past few minutes? Are we still connected? A flush invades my cheeks, a fierce one that I hope looks like the result of the cold.

I'm pretty sure it doesn't.

I don't dare speak Malcolm's name, not with Orson a few feet away and Carter within earshot. I'm afraid of what I might betray if I do say his name. Instead, I turn to Orson, arms folded across my chest.

"I've said this before, and I'll say it one last time. I don't want to join your club."

There's no eye twitch this time. The look he gives me is colder than the air. The ghosts at my side whip themselves into a fruitless frenzy. They crash against the barrier, not that they can reach me— or Orson.

He gestures with a hand. "Carter, if you will."

Carter clenches his fist. His fingers glow. I'm not sure what comes next, but I feel the hum of the otherworldly, and a fierce, angry sensation sweeps across the snow

Before Carter can take a step toward me, flashing lights paint the snow pink. A siren fills the air for a second before cutting off, and the bulky form of Chief Ramsey emerges from a patrol car.

Another patrol car pulls up, this one with Officer Deborah Millard. Orson's eyes narrow. Carter drops his hand, the glow subsiding along with that unearthly threat. I feel the cold against my tongue and teeth, and I know my mouth must be hanging open.

"Evening, gentlemen," Chief says, unlocking the cemetery gates. "I hate to inform you, but the cemetery is closed for the day and you both are trespassing. I'm going to have to ask you to leave."

I can't imagine Orson Yates hopping the cemetery fence. I study the perimeter and consider that they've been waiting for me to spring this trap, possibly for most of the day.

"And Ms. Lindstrom as well?" Orson sweeps a hand toward me. "She is also here after hours."

"Katy is a resident of Springside, and her parents and grand-mother are buried here. She has permission to visit at all hours." He nods to me before turning back to Orson. "You, on the other hand, do not. In fact, trespassing is a serious offense in Springside, but I can offer you one of two options." Chief ticks them off on his fingers. "One, leave now, and by leave, I mean Springside; or two, spend the night in jail."

"You can't do this," Orson says. "It's ridiculous."

"I *can* do this, and I will." Chief pulls out his phone and taps the screen. "Hello, Daisy? This is Chief Ramsey. You have two guests, Orson Yates and Carter Dupree. They need to leave unexpectedly. Could you have someone pack their things? They'll be by in about ten minutes to pick them up on the way out of town."

Chief hangs up and tucks the phone away. He regards Orson. Something passes between the two men, although both remain immobile. The cemetery grows colder, the sun slipping lower in the sky.

"Ah, small-town, petty tyranny," Orson says. He brushes nonexistent snow from the sleeves of his overcoat. "When it works, it works. Come along, Carter."

Carter hesitates, and he shoots me a glance. I can't read his expression. In this instant, I have no idea how he feels or what he's thinking. The moment before he turns from me, Carter Dupree rolls his eyes.

Orson pauses in front of Chief. "Ramsey, is it?"

"It is."

"Good to know."

"Officer Millard will escort you to the bed and breakfast and then to the edge of town." Chief touches the brim of his hat. "If I were you, I'd remain gone."

We wait in silence while they leave. The rotating lights on top of Officer Millard's patrol car promise it won't be an inconspicuous exit. When at last the lights have faded and quiet has returned to the cemetery, Chief speaks.

"You okay, Katy?"

"I am."

"Did they threaten you?"

"I ... I don't know. You arrived before anything could happen. And how—"

"That young partner of yours. Something about a Bluetooth earpiece and I don't know what, but he made it sound convincing enough for the dispatcher to call me."

Malcolm. Of course. I touch the earpiece, but the line is still oddly silent.

Chief stares into the center of the cemetery. I'd say he's studying the ghosts, except he doesn't believe in them. Then he speaks again.

"Can you handle that?" He nods toward the site where all the ghosts are corralled.

"You can see them?" I shout the words, my voice echoing in the cold air. This is a breakthrough.

He clamps his mouth shut, his lips a hard, straight line.

"What do you see?" I ask, making my voice as gentle as possible. This can't be easy for Chief, admitting he's been wrong about something.

He shakes his head. "I'm not sure. It looks like fog, or snow, and if things weren't always so ... strange around you, I might believe it's nothing more than that. It's odd. I went to the shed yesterday to pull out an extra shovel, and the space felt so empty, like I was missing something."

"You have a ghost that likes your watering can," I say.

He grimaces at this.

"It's not a bad ghost," I add. "It just likes your shed. I think it feels comfortable there. Some ghosts are funny that way."

"Is it in there?" He points. The ghosts swirl in response.

"I don't know. Probably."

Chief nods. "I'll leave you to it. You'll be okay?"

"Yes." I touch the earpiece again, although it remains stubbornly silent. "I have my backup."

I wait until Chief has left before placing my hands against the barrier. Ghosts swarm around my palms, but I can't break in and they can't get out. The last of the sun sinks below the horizon. I'm alone in a cemetery, in the dark, with nearly every ghost in Springside.

And I have no idea what to do.

THE SOUND of Malcolm's voice in my ear sends my heart pounding.

"Katy! Are you there? Is everything okay?"

"I'm here."

"Did Chief—"

"Ride in like the cavalry? Yeah, he did."

I tell him about the trespassing and the two patrol cars and even how, after everything, Orson still wanted me to join his club.

"You know," Malcolm says, his voice warm with relief and humor, "it's not really a club."

"Yeah, I know, and I also know it bothers Orson when I call it that."

Steam from one of the thermoses rises in the air. The scent of Kona blend is intoxicating in the cold, and it's all I can do not to drink down the entire thing. Instead, I hold it next to the barrier. With a hand, I push the steam toward the ghosts only to watch it dissipate against the invisible wall between us. They wail in frustration.

"Where'd you go?" I ask. I try to blow the steam toward them, but that doesn't work either.

"They make me get up and walk around. I put the phone on mute and stuck it in my pocket."

"Your hospital gown has a pocket?"

"I talked them into letting me wear some scrubs."

Of course he did, especially if "they" happened to be female. I roll my eyes at the ghosts across from me and shake my head.

"Have you made it home yet?" he asks.

"I'm still at the cemetery."

"But—"

"The ghosts are all here."

I place a hand on that invisible barrier, and despite this problem, something inside me relaxes. Malcolm didn't hear everything about the ghosts, which means he missed Orson's taunts as well. Relieved as I am, part of me is ... disappointed. In myself? Maybe it's better to be honest, tell him how I feel. Or maybe it's simply better to go on as K&M Ghost Eradication Specialists.

And right now, they have a huge job.

"They are?" he asks. "What are they doing?"

"They can't leave," I say. "They're ... trapped. It's like an invisible container or a barrier or—"

"Like the containment field that kept Selena out of my car?"

"Only in reverse, and much, much bigger. They're all trapped inside it."

"And they're going to stay that way. That's a necromancer trick I never mastered beyond the samovar. It must be Orson's doing. Carter isn't that good."

"But ... we can't leave them like this. I can't even get through to them."

"And I can't leave the hospital. That trek down the hall winded me. Even if I could, I'm in no shape to attempt something..." He trails off and the line goes silent again. Then he exhales and swears.

"What?" I prompt.

"I'm not strong enough for something like this, but I know someone who is."

I don't need to ask, but I do anyway. "Nigel?"

"Exactly."

"But." I point, which is utterly ridiculous. "Nearly every single ghost in Springside is in there. He can't possibly—"

"Too late. I'm calling him on the hospital line."

The second he switches to mute is obvious this time. I hear nothing. I'm destined never to know what passes between them, these two brothers. I stomp my feet and pace. I blow more coffee steam toward the ghosts, although it's cooling too fast to tempt them for much longer.

So I drink it down. I need its heat, its caffeine, its smooth warmth against my cold lips. I need to be ready. If Nigel can free the ghosts, I'll need to protect him from them.

And I'll need to protect the ghosts from him.

CHAPTER 8

"YOU KNOW THAT'S not going to work."

Nigel's voice, as always, is measured. I cap the thermos and turn to him.

"I know, but they seem to like it anyway."

Several ghosts bob and dance opposite me. I don't know if they can smell the coffee or if it's simply the idea of it that sets them off. Nigel's gaze locks on the swirling mass before his eyes clear.

He takes a few steps closer, his boots dragging in the snow. When he's at my side, he removes his gloves before reaching out and touching the barrier.

"Yes, this is Orson's work. I recognize it."

"He planted a ward, too, but I think it was more of a practical joke. I fell for it."

Literally.

"For all his pretenses, he's really nothing more than a school-yard bully on most days."

"Chief was going to toss him in jail for trespassing," I add.

Nigel snorts, but his attention soon turns to the ghosts. He exhales, his breath fogging the air, and for a moment, it looks like the barrier has been breached.

"I can't do this, Katy."

"But—"

"I can't do it, but *you* can."

I shake my head. "I can't. I have no idea what to do. I wouldn't know where to start." I hold up the thermos as proof. "See? I think coffee will work."

His laugh is warm and indulgent. "You can do it. You just don't know how. Those are two different things. Malcolm said that Orson still tried to court you, after everything. If you'd agreed, this"—he waves a hand at the barrier—"would've been your first lesson."

I look at the ghosts; I can't leave them here like this. I glance at Nigel. I can't endanger him, either.

"I'll talk you through it," he says. "Think back to when you found Malcolm in his car. What did you do?"

"I beat on the window until there was a crack. Selena did the rest."

"See that?" He gestures toward the barrier.

"No, that's the point. I can't."

"Try again."

So I do. I squint, tip my head one way and then the other. I'm about to admit defeat when the slightest outline appears.

"Oh." The word comes out with a sigh. "I never saw it around Malcolm's car."

"You didn't know what to look for. With Malcolm's car, you forced a crack in the barrier, which is pretty impressive."

"I had a tire iron," I say. "But it's in the back of the truck."

"You don't need a tire iron. Sure, you cracked the window with it, but it was your will to break through the containment field that did everything else. In some ways this"—he gestures toward the barrier again—"is easier."

"Because it's bigger?" Doubt fills my voice. I cannot imagine breaking something so big.

"Actually, yes. Something this large is hard to keep intact. Fissures, hairline fractures, cracks. It needs constant tending by the necromancer who created it. With enough time, the ghosts themselves would find holes and slip out. All we need to do is find a vulnerable point."

We trudge along the perimeter, stopping every few feet to inspect its surface. Now that I'm aware of it, the containment field seems painfully obvious. Nigel is right. It's not a perfectly round and smooth globe that traps these ghosts, but a flawed and ragged construction, hastily built.

He kneels and pushes snow away from the ground, clearing a path from our feet to the barrier.

"Do you see that?" He runs his fingers down the side, and I swear, the surface sparkles in their wake.

I nod.

"You try," he says.

I kneel next to him, pull off my mitten, and let my fingertips travel the same path. A spark kindles beneath my skin, that same glimmering light defining the crack in the barrier.

"That's your target."

We retreat a few feet back. Nigel eases behind me, positioning me by the shoulders so I face the flaw in the barrier straight on. He leaves one hand on my shoulder, the grip firm.

"I'm right here. I'll talk you through it. But if I let go of your shoulder, I want you to promise me that you'll run—"

"I won't."

"Katy, please, you don't understand—"

"Your addiction? I was there, remember? You won't let go of my shoulder. I won't let you." I lock my hand on his.

"Malcolm's right," he murmurs. "You're really stubborn."

I don't deny it. My grandmother was stubborn. I figure it's a family trait. "Now what?"

"Concentrate on the crack. Don't close your eyes, but visualize it getting larger. Think about where it's weakest, how you can chip away at it."

"Can I imagine a tire iron?"

"By all means, go right ahead."

I think about that, about breaking through that small fissure in the barrier. I remember how I created that spider web of cracks to free Malcolm. I think about how much I would like to break this thing, this prison, because I don't want anything of Orson Yates in Springside.

Nigel's grip tightens on my shoulder. "Keep going," he whispers. "You're doing it."

The outline of the barrier vibrates. I force my concentration on that weak spot, willing it to grow larger. I think of all the ghosts inside. I think about coffee, about how the steam from Kona blend might slip through and entice the ghosts out.

There's a rush for that space, the ghosts crowding so close they look like a solid bank of snow. I think maybe I've started a ghostly riot. Then that fissure expands and sends out tendrils through the barrier, one after another, until the surface resembles glass on the brink of shattering.

And then, all at once, it does.

Instinct has me ducking. I clamp down harder on Nigel's hand. I won't let him run toward the ghosts, but there's not much I can do when they come flowing out and head straight for us.

Or rather, for me. Some I recognize; their personalities are that strong. Others whip by so fast I can't get a read on them. But it's all the same, all ruffled hair and otherworldly kisses against my cheeks. A few rattle around in the field kit, searching out Kona blend.

"Go," I tell them. "Get out of here before someone else catches you." I promise them coffee—and lots of it—if only they leave now. They do, in groups and alone, until at last, all that's left are two little sprites.

These two are more than familiar.

"Go on. That includes you. I'll bring you some coffee tomorrow."

With that, the last two ghosts—Sadie's sprites—leave the cemetery.

I'm still clutching Nigel's hand. His fingers curl around my shoulder, the grip tight. His breath is ragged.

"You did it," I say.

At least, I think he has. I don't think a ghost slipped past me and into him. He turns me slowly, hand never leaving my shoulder. It's as if he still needs that last bit of reassurance. Lamplight from the street filters into the cemetery. Despite the dark, I can see the gravestones, the path we made around the now-broken barrier, and Nigel's expression.

His smile steals my breath.

"I did it," he says, his voice almost hesitant.

"You did it," I echo.

"You know why?" He releases me and digs in his pocket. "It was thanks to you, and this." In his hand, he holds the box with the diamond engagement ring. "Don't you see? Now I know. For certain. I can ask Sadie to marry me and I'll never worry that something might happen, that I'll relapse and abandon her."

I throw my arms around him. "Do it now. Ask her tonight."

Nigel nods. "Yes, tonight. I need to go find her."

A soft hum fills my ear, followed by a voice.

"She's here, at the hospital."

Even though I know it's Malcolm, I let out a yelp.

"What?" Nigel asks. "Is everything okay?"

I touch the earpiece and listen. Nigel leans closer, as if he can hear Malcolm as well.

"Sadie's visiting," Malcolm says. "She brought me something to eat. Come now. I'll make up an excuse to keep her here."

"The hospital," I say to Nigel. "She's visiting Malcolm. I'll meet you there."

He pockets the ring and races through the snow. I start the trek back to my truck.

"You okay?" Malcolm asks.

The cemetery is empty and dark. I follow the path I made through the snow on my way in. For a moment, the thought crosses my mind to visit the graves of my parents, of my grandmother, but I've had enough of ghosts for one night.

"Yeah, thanks to Nigel. And who knows, maybe business will pick up now."

He laughs.

"Orson said something," I begin, my voice thin in the cold air, "about the ghosts here in Springside wanting to be caught, that they want to be caught by me." I pause, my discomfort with the idea growing. "Are we cheating people?"

"I think the ghosts like your coffee, which is why they're willing to be caught. If you were using them in some way, they'd make it that much harder. Besides, we get our share of the mean ones."

I nod even though Malcolm can't see me.

"Unless a necromancer can find a compatible ghost," he continues, "catching them isn't all that easy. Even corralling them like Orson did wasn't simple. Why do you think he recruits necromancers in the first place? The more he has, the easier it is."

I'm not entirely convinced. And yet, I'm not unconvinced either. I want to ask how he found Selena, but I suspect she was the one to find him.

"See you soon?" he says after I've fallen quiet.

"I need to say thank you to someone first."

"Well, hurry. You don't want to miss anything."

No, I certainly don't.

THE SPRINGSIDE POLICE DEPARTMENT feels as empty as the

cemetery did, although all the lights are blazing. Penny's workstation is tidy, her computer screen dark. I swipe a Styrofoam cup from the sideboard and pour some Kona blend into it. The coffee is still hot and the steam warms my cheeks.

I know the sprites are still here. Their presence flavors the air. I breathe in their relief. True, they're still hiding behind the file cabinet, but I think that's so they can watch me crawl on my hands and knees to bring them another cup of coffee.

Sprites aren't above such things.

But I don't mind, not today. When I swap out the cold cup for the new one, their joy makes the air glimmer. Tomorrow they'll go back to playing pranks and tormenting Penny. But tonight, they're grateful.

And so am I.

On my way to Chief's office, I pull out my last thermos. His door is shut, but light sneaks through the space beneath it. I hear a squeak and the rustle of papers.

He answers my knock with a gruff, "Come in."

When he sees me, I get an almost-smile. "I hope this means you took care of the ... problem at the cemetery."

"I did."

He nods, once. "Good."

"I wanted to say thank you, for today."

He waves away my gratitude. "Just doing my job. I was looking for a legitimate way to escort them from Springside. This was as good an excuse as any."

"Even so, I want to say thanks." I uncap the thermos and pour him a cup. "This is still hot. It still tastes the way it should because it hasn't been cooking all day long." I point toward the outer office and the coffeemaker that Penny tends and then set the thermos on Chief's desk. "And it's all yours."

I'm at the threshold when Chief calls after me. He's followed me from his office and he now shadows the doorway.

"Katy, you tell me if Orson Yates turns up again, or if they contact you. I don't care what it is. Okay?"

"I will," I promise.

CHAPTER 9

SOMEHOW, I BEAT NIGEL TO the hospital. Sadie is fussing over Malcolm. His bed has precise hospital corners. She's arranged all the items on his tray table. His nightstand is spotless, and in its drawer a dozen snacks are hiding for later. She is now rearranging all the flowers everyone has sent.

When she sees me, her eyes widen. "Oh, Katy! You're soaked through. Here, let's get you dry."

She takes me by the shoulders and directs me toward the room's radiator. I cast a glance back at Malcolm.

"Oh, thank God," he murmurs. "She has another patient."

I can't help but laugh.

Sadie forces me out of my boots and socks and into a pair of fuzzy hospital ones with treads on the soles. She hangs my coat, my mittens, and my socks over the heater to dry. During all this, I send a questioning look toward Malcolm.

"Nigel?" I mouth.

He shakes his head.

"Cold feet?" Again, I mouth the words.

Malcolm shrugs.

The tiniest bit of worry worms its way through me. What if nearly every ghost in Springside was too much of a temptation for Nigel? And if so, what can I do about that?

I cast another look at Malcolm. He knows his brother better than I do, and even if he wants to, he's not going anywhere. Neither am I at the moment. All we can do is wait.

"Don't worry," he says, low enough that only I can hear.

But I do worry. For Nigel to relapse—after everything—feels like failure. It isn't fair, not for him, or Sadie, or Malcolm, for that matter.

I'm contemplating this and possible next steps when a wolf whistle sounds in the corridor.

"Looking good, Nigel," one of the nurses calls. "Or should I say *Mr.* Armand?"

Nigel's laugh echoes in return. My heart rate picks up. A curious smile tugs the corner of Malcolm's mouth. Sadie, on the other hand, is busy adjusting my damp clothes and finding me a blanket.

When Nigel enters the room it's perfectly clear why I beat him here. He's resplendent in a three-piece gray suit, a red tie knotted at his neck. His shoes gleam. His hair—as brilliant white as his pressed shirt—is smooth, not a strand out of place.

I don't think I've ever seen him in anything but jeans and sweatshirts, and maybe a button-down at Christmas. This? This is impressive. This is Nigel Armand, world-class necromancer.

This is a man on a mission.

Sadie turns, and the blanket slips through her fingers and pools on the floor.

"Nigel?" she says, uncertainty lacing her voice.

He hushes her. "Let me say this?"

She nods.

Nigel drops to one knee, that velvet-covered box open in his palm. I inch closer to Malcolm. I reach out and my hand meets his.

"Sadie Lancaster," Nigel says, "would you do me the honor of becoming my wife?"

Sadie blinks, once, twice. Her face goes pale before a blush blazes up her cheeks. "What?" she says, although it sounds more like a cry for help.

"Will you marry me?"

Malcolm squeezes my fingers, and I clutch back. I'm not sure how this will end. Even the hallway has gone quiet. We're all waiting for Sadie's reply.

"You want to marry me?" she says.

"More than anything."

When he says those words, I know they're true. He wants this more than anything, more than all the ghosts in Springside.

Sadie falls to her knees and cups Nigel's face. "Oh, my beautiful boy, you can't mean that."

"I do. I'm asking you to wear my ring, put up with all my faults, and spend the rest of your life with me."

Something cracks in Sadie's resolve. Her gaze darts downward, lands on the ring. Gently, she plucks it from the velvet and holds it up to the light.

"It's beautiful."

"Not as much as you are."

Her gaze moves to Nigel, her eyes filled with doubt. His fingers join hers, so they both hold the ring.

"Wear my ring, Sadie?"

She gives a shaky nod and together they ease the diamond onto her finger.

"Marry me?" Nigel places a kiss on her hand. "Please?" He places another kiss there before lifting his face so it's even with hers. "Spend your life with me?"

His hands thread through her curls, frame her face. He kisses her, and it's so tender, I have to look away. A moment later, Sadie's whisper fills the room.

"Yes, I'll marry you."

It's as if the entire hospital staff has been waiting for these words. Nurses pour into the room, along with orderlies, volunteers, and even a few doctors. All the nurses who tended to Sadie while she was in her coma are here. Someone breaks out an industrial-sized jug of cranberry juice and we toast the couple with plastic cups.

Tears stream down Sadie's face. Nigel holds her close, tucked in his arms. There are so many people in the room that I start to wonder if anyone is taking care of the other patients.

Malcolm tugs my hand. "How long have you known?"

"A few weeks. He wanted my opinion on the ring, like I know anything about rings."

"How does it feel to you?" He nods toward Nigel and Sadie.

I consider the question, although I already know the answer. "It feels right, has from the start."

"I think so too."

At last the nurse for Malcolm's floor clears everyone out, her voice stern.

"This young man needs his rest." She eyes him. "He's been doing far too much today."

The hospital staff vanishes nearly as quickly as they appeared. Nigel helps Sadie into her coat and they leave together, hand in hand. I'm turning toward the radiator, intent on my still-damp things, when Malcolm's fingers catch mine.

"Doesn't apply to you," he says.

"What?"

"Stay." He tugs me closer.

"I thought that maybe you'd want ... I mean, you and Selena—"

"Selena's gone."

"She's gone?" True, I haven't felt her presence, but I guessed she was hanging back, waiting for everyone to leave. "But ... where did she go?"

"Somewhere safe, where Orson or Carter won't be able to capture her. She told me about the map, how you showed her how to find me." His laugh is soft, a bit rueful. "She didn't understand why you did that."

"I wanted you to be happy."

He releases my hand and inches himself to the far side of his bed. He winces with the effort. I want to tell him to stop, but I know he won't.

"Right here." He pats the space left empty.

"But—"

"It'll be therapeutic, really. Good for me and all that. Besides, we need to talk."

I take up a perch on the edge of the bed. This, however, isn't sufficient.

"All of you," Malcolm says, "feet included."

I scoot all the way onto the bed until at last I'm flush with Malcolm, feet tucked by his ankles, my right hand coming to rest gingerly against his chest, fingertips lighting on the spot above his heart.

His sigh rumbles beneath my fingers. "Much better."

He is, as always, so warm, and still smells of nutmeg. My heart pounds because I'm not sure what comes next. I'm not sure what he'll say, only that he thinks we need to talk.

"Do you know what I was doing that day when you found me at the nature preserve?"

I give my head a slight shake.

"I was showing Selena my new life here, what it means to me, trying to explain why I wasn't moving back to the Twin Cities. I wanted her to see what I did at Springside Long-term Care, and how we catch and release."

"I thought that when she came back, you'd want to ... I don't know, go back to investing."

"I still invest. I'm not killing it, but don't you have a pretty decent start on a retirement account now?"

It's true. I do, thanks to Malcolm.

"You looked so happy when she came back," I say. "I thought you'd—"

"You thought what? That I'd want to be with her?"

I nod.

Something rumbles in his chest, another sigh perhaps. "Maybe at one time, before I moved to Springside, I would have. And I admit it, when I was living in Minneapolis, I thought having a relationship with a ghost was the answer to everything. When someone is literally in your head half the time, you never have to explain yourself. But you know what it isn't?"

I shake my head.

"Real. I was relieved when Selena came back. I spent a lot of time worrying someone like Carter or Orson might exploit her. But seeing her again made me realize what truly makes me happy."

I wait to hear what that is, my heart still thrumming, fingertips against his chest. Part of me almost wishes he won't speak. I would freeze this moment so I can stay nestled here forever in the crook of his shoulder.

"You don't know what I'm talking about, do you?" he says.

I give my head another shake.

"It's you."

"Me?"

"Of course you. I know I'm not very good at this relationship thing, but I'm willing to try if you're willing to put up with me."

"Put up with you?"

"It's a lot to ask, I know."

"You don't have to ask."

My heart pounds so hard, I'm afraid it might burst from my chest. I'm afraid Malcolm must be able to feel it. But then again, his heart is thumping beneath my fingers, its rhythm matching mine.

The lights are turned down low. Visiting hours must be over. But when a nurse bustles in on her rounds and checks Malcolm's blood pressure and pulse, it's as if I'm not even there.

"As long as you're quiet," is all she says on her way out.

"Stay the night?" Malcolm asks when the room is ours again.

"I don't think that's allowed."

"It is tonight, at least for me."

"You get away with so much."

"Well, I did bribe them, and you're going to have to bring in some Kona blend tomorrow."

I laugh, the worry, fear, and dread I've been storing inside me loosening their grip. I'm warm, all the way through, from my toes to my heart. I don't need to freeze this moment in order to savor it; I get to live it for the next eight hours.

"Stay with me, Katy?"

"Yes," I say. "I'll stay. I'll stay for as long as you want."

Malcolm closes his eyes, dark lashes gracing his cheekbones. His mouth is soft and curved with the slightest hint of a smile.

"In that case," he says, "it looks like you're stuck with me for a very long time."

PART III
THE WEDDING GHOST

COFFEE AND GHOSTS SEASON TWO,
EPISODE 3

CHAPTER 1

THERE'S A STRANGER standing on the sidewalk, staring up at my neighbor's house. In a town as small as Springside, any stranger is greeted with wariness. Ones who stare up at houses? Even more so.

Which is why I'm tracking this particular stranger from behind my screen door. I'm cradling a cup of coffee in my hands, but my phone is in my back pocket, the police chief's personal number on speed dial. Lately, whenever a stranger wanders into town, something bad always follows them. I want to make sure nothing has followed this one, because in less than a week, my neighbor, Sadie Lancaster, is getting married.

No one, not even this well-dressed stranger, will stop that. Not if I can help it.

With a shoulder, I push open the screen door and step onto my porch. The man is still planted on the sidewalk. He hasn't strayed onto the walkway itself. It's like there's an invisible barrier, one he doesn't plan on crossing. A tweed blazer is draped over one arm. His hair is dark, and smooth, and styled. All in all, he's so pulled together that I suspect I know *what* he is, even if I don't know his name.

"Can I help you?" I call out. Because, well-dressed or not, a stranger is a stranger.

His dark eyes light onto me. He smiles and then treads the distance between Sadie's house and mine, never straying from the sidewalk. He halts, turns, and clicks his heels together.

It's meant to make me laugh; I can tell. I purse my lips together in order not to. I'm still in stranger = creepy mode.

"You must be Katy Lindstrom," he says.

I swallow the urge to nod.

"I'm a friend of Nigel's," he adds, his voice low and melodious. He sounds as if he finds everything—me, Springside, this spring morning—slightly amusing. He nods toward the ground. "That's an impressive ward you've got going there. It rivals Nigel's." He waves a hand toward Sadie's house.

"And you are?" I ask.

"A necromancer who respects wards."

Well, I guessed the necromancer part. I still don't know his name or if he's truly a friend. Necromancers seem to collect a great many friends who turn out not to be all that friendly. I try again.

"And you are?"

He laughs. "Oh, of course. Forgive me. I'm Prescott Jones, and I do know Nigel. Honest." He digs around in the blazer's pocket and pulls out a wedding invitation. The gold embossed lettering glints in the morning sunshine.

My fingers unclench, slightly, from around the coffee cup. I take a sip and let the caffeine clear the last of the sleep from my head. I'm in pajama bottoms and a cami. I'm completely sloppy compared to this Prescott Jones, and I really should be getting ready for work. Instead, I remain on the porch.

"Is that the famous Lindstrom brew?"

He raises an eyebrow, a request if there ever was one. I tilt my chin in answer—a solid *no*. It's bad enough he's on my sidewalk. I will not invite a strange necromancer inside my house.

"We've met, you know," he says as if in response to my thoughts. "I was about ten years old and you were maybe ... ten months? Our parents were friends. Did you know that?"

I give my head a slow shake. "You knew my parents?"

"Not very well." He shrugs. "I was ten. I wasn't interested in what the grownups were doing, but I remember them." He pauses and looks not at me, but somewhere past me. "I remember when they died. We went to the funeral." Now he looks around as if he's just discovered where he is. "It was here, in Springside."

I'm not sure what to believe of this tale, if anything. But my heart thuds like it knows the truth of it. I grip the cup harder. My fingers feel cold and I try to catch the last of the coffee's warmth.

"And I remember." His voice has grown quiet. He speaks so softly that I can barely hear him. I want to rush down the porch steps and stand right across from him so I don't miss a word.

I stay put.

"I remember," he says again. "They—the grownups—had me play with you. We were in some side room or something, a nursery, maybe, during the actual service." He tilts his head as if seeing me for the first time. "I don't suppose that's something you'd remember."

I don't suppose it would be. My throat is tight. My heart is still thudding. And the soft words from this stranger have me transfixed.

Then something glimmers by his head. A smile replaces the pensive look, and he holds out a hand as if to catch an invisible bird.

"We also have a mutual friend. Go on, Frederick. Go say hi."

That glimmer fills the space between us, stretching thin, until it reaches me. Then I know for certain. A sprite—one with an amazing amount of strength. It—or rather, he—whizzes around my head in greeting before settling on my shoulder.

"Oh, I've caught you before," I say to him.

Frederick whirls around, the force picking up a few blades of grass and lilac blossoms. The tiny cyclone fills the air with the scent of spring—fresh-mown lawn, the light perfume of early blooms, and something that reminds me of hope.

He lands on my shoulder again and then swan dives into my cup of coffee. It's barely warm enough to tempt a sprite, never mind an actual ghost. But steam is rising in the air, and I'm drinking Kona blend, which is a ghostly favorite.

"You're quite rude, too," I say to Frederick as he floats on the coffee's steam.

Oh, this one is. This is the sort of sprite that has us using the Tupperware with the opaque sides when we go out on a call. Some sprites won't stop playing pranks—even after they've been caught —and will manifest obscene images. Some things are better left unseen.

Prescott Jones chuckles. "He is, isn't he? But he makes me laugh, so I let him tag along."

He snaps his fingers. Frederick rockets from the steam, whirls around my head once more, and then gives me a ghostly kiss on the cheek.

"I won't detain you any longer." Prescott nods. "I hope to see you before the wedding, but if not, perhaps we can speak more then."

With that, he retreats down the sidewalk until he reaches a flashy yellow car. I watch until the car and its driver are well out of sight. Even then, I remain on the porch, ears strained for any stray sound, my gaze taking in my yard and then Sadie's.

Once I've stepped inside, I bolt the door. I should shower, head in to work, ask Nigel about all of this. But Prescott's appearance has knocked me off-kilter. For the longest time all I can do is peer through the curtains at the quiet street.

~

No one hears me come in. I'm certain of this. I barely hear myself walk through the door, or the chime that rings above my head. Shouts echo from the conference room. The voices blend together, but I do know this. One belongs to Malcolm, my business partner, and the other to his brother, Nigel, our tech support.

"I can't believe you've been doing this. It's unconscionable. Really, I don't have words for it."

Since Nigel keeps on shouting, it appears that he does have more words. But they're no match for Malcolm's.

"Would you just listen? It's a simple investment. It's like getting venture capital without jumping through all the hoops of getting venture capital. In a couple of months, it will all even out and everything will be fine."

"Oh, really. And have you told Katy this? Because if you haven't told her any of this, then it isn't simple and it certainly isn't fine."

An icy silence fills the conference room. That same ice invades my veins. My fingers turn cold again. I don't know what the fight's about, but I do know this:

Malcolm hasn't told me anything.

I sigh and sag against the reception desk, the thermoses in the canvas field kit jangling. We're still not making enough money each month to hire an actual receptionist, not that we have anything for him or her to do. After all, I'm the one who makes the coffee around here. As a precaution, I've filled several thermoses this morning. Unexpected necromancers make me nervous.

To be honest, I've been dreading something like this. Malcolm is more than my business partner, and has been for a couple of months. It's been gnawing at the pit of my stomach. Needless worry, I've told myself, about mixing business and ... well, pleasure.

Maybe not so needless after all.

I almost turn around. I almost sneak out the door. For several seconds, I consider leaving and heading over to the Pancake House, because even if all-you-can-eat dollar-size pancakes don't solve anything, they certainly can't hurt.

But I want to make sure Nigel truly does know someone named Prescott Jones. I want to ask about my parents, and what Nigel thinks of this new connection, one we haven't managed to uncover on our own. I really want to talk about the wedding, complain about the final dress fitting, and all the rest.

I don't want to talk about this thing—whatever it is—that Malcolm has done. But I have no choice. I push off the reception desk and head into the conference room.

I find both brothers glaring at each other. Nigel has his hands planted on the conference table (really, it's someone's old dining room table). Malcolm is on the opposite side of the room, leaning against the wall, arms crossed over his chest.

"Oh, look," Nigel says. "Here's Katy now. Would you like to tell her, or should I?"

No one speaks.

"Tell me what?" I ask.

I can't imagine what could be so bad that they won't talk to each other. Malcolm is Nigel's best man. If they don't start speaking, it will make for an awkward wedding ceremony.

"My brother thinks he's clever," Nigel begins. "He thought we wouldn't notice, that I wouldn't notice, that *you* wouldn't." He turns to me. "Who owns this business?"

"We both do. Malcolm and I. It's a limited liability company. Malcolm filed the paperwork and everything." I cast him a hopeful glance, but the smile I receive in return is full of guilt.

"Then do you know that he's been floating the business for the past several months?"

Floating ... the business? I'm not certain what that means, but it doesn't sound good. To be honest, I've let Malcolm manage the money aspect. He has a business degree. He understands profit and loss and knows when to file the taxes.

I know how to brew a damn fine cup of coffee. I'm not sure our contributions are equal.

"What does that mean?" I say at last.

"It means we're not making any money. Malcolm has been keeping the business afloat with his own money—"

"Like an investment," Malcolm says. "If you would just—"

"What?" Nigel slaps the table. "Pretend it isn't happening? Pretend you haven't been lying?"

"Have I lied?" Malcolm turns, first toward me, and then back to Nigel. "Have I? I'm the business manager. I'm managing the business."

"We're not making money?" I say, and my voice is incredibly small compared to theirs. "But I thought ... didn't you say ... I mean..."

I'm not sure what I mean, since I can't remember—exactly—what Malcolm has told me about the business. But business was good in December; he said so. I do remember that.

"All small businesses struggle at first," Malcolm says. "Ours is no different. I'm simply providing the capital to get us going. Once we have a steady income, the business can pay me back."

"That's fine for you," Nigel says. "But you know what? It doesn't work for me. It means my baby brother is essentially giving me a handout. I'm getting married in less than a week." He pauses, scrubs his face with his hands. "I've come to terms with the fact that I'll be living in the house that Harold Lancaster bought, but I'll be damned if I'm not earning an actual salary."

Oh. *Of course.* It's not about Malcolm at all. Well, it is. Malcolm excels at lies of omission, but I've known that for a while. But this?

This is all about Nigel and Sadie, the wedding, and the specter of Harold Lancaster—who was rich, and as it turns out, an actual specter as well. We've dealt with the latter problem, at least for now.

I'm not sure how to deal with this one. This isn't the sort of ghost you can catch with some excellent Kona blend and a Tupperware container. This is the sort of haunting that can ruin a marriage.

I glance back and forth between them. I need to fix this. I give Malcolm a half-smile, just to let him know I'm working on a solution, but he won't meet my eyes. Before I can say anything—and really, I'm not sure what I plan to say—the chime over the door rings. A booming voice follows.

"Katrina Lindstrom! I respect your ward. I ask for your permission to enter your place of business."

The anger drains from Nigel's face. The smile that replaces it makes him look like he should: a man who's about to marry the love of his life. He rounds the table and grabs my hand on the way to the front entrance.

"Katy, come on. There's someone I want you to meet."

On the threshold stands the largest man I have ever seen. He must be six-foot-five, at least. In both height and girth, he's even larger than Police Chief Ramsey. This man is big and burly, with graying hair and skin a lovely shade of brown. His shirt is pressed, as are his trousers. The polish on his shoes reflects the light.

He's pulled together, the way I've come to expect from a necromancer, except everything is at least twenty years out of date.

"Katy Lindstrom," Nigel says, gesturing toward the man. "This is my good friend and mentor Reginald Weaver. As you might have guessed, he's a necromancer."

Reginald studies me, eyes narrowed and filled with discernment. "Oh, so this is the little lady causing all the trouble."

I really should take offense at that, except I don't think he means to be offensive. His tone is measured, without a trace of sarcasm. Although I would argue that I'm not the one causing trouble—that's squarely on the necromancers who keep showing up in town.

"It's nice to meet you?" I ask, and I do say it like that, as a question. Honestly, I'm not sure it's going to be nice at all.

"You have to invite him in." Nigel nudges me. "He's old school. He won't cross a ward unless invited."

"What?" I glance around as if I can see the ward I've placed on our storefront. I can't, of course. "Come in," I say, and then gesture toward my field kit. "Would you like some coffee?"

Reginald takes a giant step across the threshold. "I would, almost as much as I want to see my good friend married." He hugs Nigel then and despite Nigel's height, he's swallowed by Reginald's embrace.

Aromatic steam fills the air as I uncap the thermoses. I let everyone pour their own cup, noting that Reginald likes his coffee extra sweet.

"I didn't think you'd get word in time," Nigel says to Reginald. "We have more than our fair share of sprites in Springside, but a reliable ghost?" He shrugs. "It was secondhand, too, since I still can't—"

Reginald cuts off Nigel's words with a strong hand to his shoulder. "You don't need to explain. Malcolm's ghost came through, although apparently there was a promise of some Kona blend?"

"Did I promise a ghost some coffee?" Again, I glance around. I don't detect a presence, but I've recently learned that some necromancers can hide their ghosts.

"I'm sure Malcolm did it for you and then 'forgot' to tell you about it." Nigel draws little air quotes around *forgot*, and the anger from earlier invades his voice.

Reginald's chest heaves with a sigh. "Nothing really changes. After the ceremony I will retreat to the woods once again. In five years' time, I will emerge, perhaps to attend your wedding, Katrina Lindstrom, and these two"—he points at Nigel and then Malcolm, who is shadowing the conference room door—"will still be fighting. I miss nothing."

"Are you the one who only communicates by ghost?" I've been fascinated by that ever since Nigel told me about the necromancers he knows. Some don't use phones or computers or any sort of technology. If you want to contact them, you send a ghost.

"Yes. I seldom venture from my woods, and then only to procure supplies. This trip to Springside is quite an adventure for me."

He speaks so formally that it's clear he hasn't had an actual conversation in a while. I wonder what it is he does out there, alone in the woods, then decide not to ask. I'm about to suggest the Springside Pancake House—which isn't actually adventurous, but the all-you-can-eat will keep him fed—when the door chime rings out once again. I suppose it's too much to hope for that it's an actual customer.

It is. Springside is being overrun by necromancers. Prescott Jones stands in the doorway, the toes of his wingtips just touching the invisible line of my ward. He's doing that on purpose. The smile on his face tells me so.

"I won't dare cross a ward, not with Reginald Weaver around to bear witness. I value my life more than that."

Nigel snorts, but Reginald's expression is devoid of humor.

"You should never violate a ward. No true necromancer does."

I've heard of necromancer justice—retribution, as Nigel calls it. If Reginald is the one who dishes it out, no wonder most necromancers respect wards.

"Katy." Nigel waves a hand. "This is my friend, Prescott Jones."

"We've met," I say, but Prescott doesn't budge from the entrance, so I add, "Would you like to come in for some coffee?"

Prescott needs no more from me. He's across the room in a moment and has Nigel in a tight embrace.

"Oh, it's good to see you. So good. I thought we'd lost you there for a while."

"I thought I'd lost me," Nigel admits.

Prescott holds Nigel at arm's length. "And I see that love agrees with you. You look like you should."

I pour Prescott a cup and refill Reginald's and Nigel's. I can't help but agree: love has done wonders for Nigel. His hair is still pure white, a legacy of his addiction that will never go away. But he isn't as gaunt as he was last fall, and his eyes never appear glazed over, focused on nothing, like they used to. You can see his beauty now. Both brothers are terribly handsome—all olive skin and lush eyelashes.

The thought draws my gaze to Malcolm. He hasn't joined the group, and when I offer up a cup of coffee, he shakes his head.

Malcolm never turns down my coffee.

A moment later, he nods toward the front door and slips out without the three other men noticing. Something tightens in my chest. I've repaired rifts between these two before. I know they love each other. But this time? I'm not sure I can fix this, not before the wedding on Saturday.

"Orson's not going to like this."

The proclamation—from Prescott—pulls my attention away from Malcolm and the door closing softly behind him.

"Not like what?" I ask.

"So many powerful necromancers in one place," Prescott says. "He'll think you've recruited us for the ghost army you're amassing."

I wrinkle my nose—all the consideration Orson Yates truly deserves. "I'm not amassing an army, and I'm pretty sure you know that and he knows that."

Prescott laughs. "Of course I know that. So does he. But you've already seen how he operates. Orson finds the truth inconsequential."

A thought occurs to me, one that involves Orson Yates, his version of the truth, and Prescott. "You knew my mother, right?" I say to him.

"Yes, both your parents."

"And you knew she was a necromancer?"

"I was ten, but yes, I remember that. It was ... she was ... remarkable."

"Was your mother a necromancer?"

Prescott laughs at this, but it's a soft laugh, filled with the warmth of reminiscence. "My mother was old school. She kept the house, kept all of us from killing each other, and only took a job after we all graduated. There were five of us. She should've received hazard pay."

"You didn't answer my question."

Prescott glances away. "It's ... she never practiced the craft, so no, technically she wasn't. We ... those of us who do—" He waves a hand, indicating the group of us. "You take it for granted." He looks to Nigel now, and Reginald, his gaze searching. "The sensing and the communication, it's like any skill. If you don't use it, it fades."

Nigel nods, but Reginald purses his lips as if he doesn't quite agree.

"Why aren't there female necromancers?" I point to Nigel, who does an excellent job of avoiding eye contact. "Do you have any female necromancer friends? Did you invite them to the wedding? According to Orson Yates, the last woman necromancer in his association was my mother. That had to be—"

"Twenty-five years ago," Reginald says. "And I can't answer your question, Katrina Lindstrom, except to say that life is unfair."

"Is it deliberate?"

"Depends on whom you ask," Prescott says. "In the case of Orson Yates, I'm going with yes."

"What about your grandmother?" Nigel's voice is gentle, as if he knows this is a wound that hasn't healed. "Clearly she knew about necromancy. If she wasn't one in her youth, then she certainly had the skills to be one. Why didn't she ever tell you?"

It's a question that keeps me up at night. Before Malcolm and Nigel came to Springside, I'd never heard of this sort of necromancy, speaking to ghosts, partnering with them for fun and profit, using them to do your bidding. Although I'm capable of talking to ghosts, I seldom do so necromancer style, by inviting them inside my head. I prefer my way, which more often than not resembles a game of charades.

"I don't know," I say. It's this that hurts the most. Why didn't she tell me, if only to warn me?

The men fall silent. I open my mouth in hopes of steering the conversation back to lighter things, but Prescott claps his hands together.

"So, bachelor party. There's going to be one, right?" He nudges Reginald and then Nigel. "I have an excellent bottle of scotch that says there must be a party."

Nigel shakes his head and laughs.

Reginald rubs his eyes. "I'm still recovering from your last excellent bottle of scotch."

"Oh, come on," Prescott says. "Just you, me, Reggie here, and we'll even let Malcolm tag along."

At the sound of Malcolm's name, Nigel scowls. I take that as my cue to pour a fresh cup of coffee and head for the door. Before I can leave, Reginald touches my shoulder.

"You take one brother, and I'll handle the other. I've done this before." He winks. Or at least, I think he does. It's a there-and-gone sort of gesture, one that seems out of character.

Almost.

I step outside. The sun is already heating the sidewalk beneath my feet. Malcolm is sitting on the curb next to his convertible, head in his hands. Maple syrup from the Pancake House is floating on the air. Traffic is light, the only real noise the bell of a bicycle ringing out.

It's not a bad morning to sit curbside. So I do, easing next to Malcolm. He doesn't move.

"Hey." I hold out the cup of coffee.

I get a half-sigh, half-growl in response.

I wave my hand across the top of the coffee cup in an attempt to force the steam in Malcolm's direction. It doesn't really work. I look ridiculous, but that's the point. At last Malcolm glances up and gives me a smile.

I offer him the cup. After a moment of hesitation, he takes it. Something inside me loosens. This feels, if not like a victory, then progress.

"I'm sorry," Malcolm says. The words come out with a rush. "I should've told you what was going on. I started to, a hundred times, then I'd think, well, one more month, and then it won't matter."

"Why didn't you tell me? We're partners. I should know these things."

"I didn't want you to worry. I knew you'd suggest cutting costs or not taking a salary, or something." With this last, his gaze fixes on our storefront. The sun strikes the gold lettering of K&M Ghost Eradication Specialists and the words glow.

"It's quite a bit of overhead," I say. "Isn't it? That's the right word? Overhead?"

"Yes. That's the right word, and yes." He sighs. "It's overhead."

"Then maybe—"

He holds up a hand, stopping my words. "Every time I think we should, I remember how you looked that day when you first saw it."

I remember tracing the letters with a finger, marveling at how amazing they were, and how amazing Malcolm was for making the whole thing a surprise.

"I must have stood outside and stared for half an hour."

"You did, and I stared at you," he says

I turn to him now, my eyes dazzled by the gold lettering and the sun.

"I'd never made someone that happy before," he adds, "and I wanted to keep on doing it. Still do."

"We have that small business loan, don't we?"

His mouth turns grim.

"Oh ... that's what you've been paying with your own money, right?"

"The interest rate isn't terrible, but it adds up. And Malcolm-backed loans are currently at zero percent."

I'm pretty sure that's a joke and that I should laugh, but I'm feeling out of my element. "I wish I were better at this. You do so much for the business, and I don't really contribute—"

"Katy, you're the reason we even have a business. Do you remember what I said that first time you showed me how to release ghosts? I'm all sizzle." He bumps my shoulder with his. "And you're the steak."

I turn toward him. His lips brush my forehead and then come to rest on the tender spot next to my eye. My hand finds his, and I trace his fingers, travel the path of a fading scar left over from our last eradication.

"Still, you shouldn't have to do this all on your own. I could take a business class." My voice is low and a little breathy. It's definitely not a profit-and-loss sort of tone. "But that would probably cost money."

"It probably would."

"Would you show me, then? Walk me through the basics? What would happen if you got sick?" That isn't out of the realm of possibility. A few months back, Malcolm ended up in the hospital with broken ribs and a concussion. "I should know what to do."

"I'd love to, especially if we end each session with an evening kiss."

"Oh, I think we could." I draw out my words as if the idea needs great consideration. It doesn't, of course. "Besides, I didn't get my morning kiss yet today."

"You can blame my brother for that." He sighs again, his breath warm against my cheek. "Damn. My brother."

"It's the wedding," I say. That's true, mostly. "Nigel's nervous, and I don't blame him. There's the age difference that everyone's talking about, and of course, Harold was actually well-respected in town."

Malcolm snorts. "I get it, but I don't. Everything I've heard makes me believe he was nothing but an ass and never deserved Sadie."

Everyone has been talking. Whispers about how it's too soon after Harold's death. Whispers about a younger man and an older woman—I think those might hurt the most. Doubt shadows Sadie's expression when she thinks we're not looking. And while both brothers have been accepted in town—and Malcolm is everyone's favorite—technically, they're still strangers.

"It's almost like Harold is still haunting them," I say.

"You're right. Nigel's lashing out, and I happen to be handy. Under the circumstances, I would too." He nudges my shoulder again. "I think I already have. Last winter, anyone?"

"You're lucky Chief Ramsey didn't make you spend a night in jail."

"At least I got a few good punches in."

I hold back a sigh—and the worry that goes with it. I doubt we've seen the last of Carter Dupree or Orson Yates, but as the weeks have slipped by I've thought of them less and less. It's been wedding talk and sprites and the occasional stubborn ghost. It's the Springside I remember so well from when I was growing up.

Despite everything, I feel warm and content in the morning light. I close my eyes and lean in to Malcolm. We could spend the day right here, on the curb, the sun baking our heads.

A single whoop from a police siren has my eyes shooting open. In the street in front of us, a patrol car is idling. The window rolls down. I squint and can just make out the bulky shape of Police Chief Ramsey.

"Got a call about some inappropriate PDA," he says, his manner gruff, no-nonsense.

"PD—?" I begin.

"Public displays of affection," Malcolm fills in for me.

"We're not even holding hands," I say.

"Not hold them somewhere else."

Chief isn't budging, so Malcolm pushes to his feet and tugs me to mine. I peer into the police car. I can't get a read on Chief or even see his expression. All I have is the stern tone of voice and the posture that tells me this is nonnegotiable.

"You're kidding," I say to him anyway.

"Nope, I'm not. And in my day"—he jabs a finger at Malcolm —"we'd at least take our girl out for breakfast."

With that, the window rolls back up and the cruiser rolls down the street. I stare after it and watch the brake lights flicker before turning to Malcolm.

"He was kidding, right?"

"I think..." He laughs. "I think Chief has an odd sense of humor. Or he's trying to set us up. Or both." He holds out a hand. "But it's not a bad idea. Breakfast?"

"Can we afford breakfast?"

"I can afford the Pancake House. My treat."

The second my fingers touch his, he pulls me close. The sun has warmed his skin and that enticing mix of Ivory soap and nutmeg fills the space between us.

"Morning kiss?" he whispers, mouth inches from mine.

"Isn't that a public display of affection? Chief might come back and arrest us."

"Let him try."

CHAPTER 2

I T'S ONLY AFTER we've devoured platefuls of pancakes and Malcolm has left to pick up his tux and Nigel's that I notice the worry in our waitress's eyes. Annie's topping off my orange juice, and as she does so, she leans over and whispers.

"I'm covering for Belinda."

Belinda is my roommate—well, some of the time. Lately, she's been Gregory's roommate. When she's working the Pancake House, Malcolm and I make it a point to sit in her section. But she isn't here this morning.

"She didn't show up, didn't call in, isn't answering texts." Annie takes her time straightening the napkin holder, the salt and pepper shakers.

"She wasn't—" I begin. "I mean, I think she stayed over at ... a friend's last night."

Annie rolls her eyes. "Right. *Friend.* Thing is, we don't want her to get in trouble, lose her job, that sort of thing."

I don't want that either. Belinda has been ghost- and alcohol-free for months now, coming up on a year. The job here means so much to her. I can't imagine her blowing it off. And things have been so quiet that I can't imagine it's a ghost causing this trouble. Then I think of Carter Dupree and the orange juice Belinda spilled all over him and consider: maybe it could be.

"Could you check on her? I would, but—" Annie shrugs. "I'm working her shift."

"I will."

I check my phone. I have twenty minutes before I need to be at the dressmaker. That should give me enough time to stop at Gregory's apartment. I reach for my bag, but before I can pull out my wallet, Annie holds up a hand.

"He paid. Of course he paid. And the tip was..." She shakes her head as if the tip was so large, words alone can't describe it. "If you don't want him hanging around." She nods at the window, at the K&M Ghost Eradication Specialists storefront across the street. "You let us know. The girls in this town would line up for him."

"I'll keep that in mind."

I leave the Pancake House weighed down by worry and maple syrup.

FROM A BLOCK AWAY, I can see the bright yellow van Gregory drives. Even after all these months, he still hasn't removed the black lettering on the side that reads:

Ghost B Gone
Gregory B. Gone, Proprietor

I'm still not sure how he managed all those ghost "evictions"; he has no sense for anything otherworldly, and I suspect it was the other members of his crew who found the haunted locations—or simply used a bit a stagecraft to manufacture them.

How he feels about substitute teaching at Springside High School? I don't know. But I think he's here, permanently, since I'm pretty certain I know how he feels about Belinda.

I walk the one flight up to his apartment. I rap on the door. I wait. I lean forward, as if that will help me hear the telltale signs that someone's home. I'm debating between knocking again and turning around to leave when the door opens.

What I notice first is the long, flowing silver hair. Next is the robe, only because it doesn't fit the wearer's form at all. She's draped in it, like it's a Halloween costume. If she spread her arms wide, she might be able to fly.

I know this woman standing across from me. The last time I saw her, she kissed my cheek and then—unwittingly, it's true—unleashed an entity on me, Malcolm, and the rest of Springside.

"Terese?" I say.

A frown clouds her brow, but a moment later, a smile blooms across her face. "Katy, right? Gregory's been telling me all about the wedding. You must be so excited. I'll see you there. I'll have to run home, of course, for something to wear, but I'm his plus one."

I stand there, open-mouthed. I'm sure this is why Terese feels obligated to fill the space with so many words. I can't think of anything to say. Well, I can, but remarking that Gregory has an invitation because he was originally Belinda's "plus one" is most likely a conversation killer.

"Gregory," Terese calls over her shoulder. "Come see who's here."

I'm still standing in the doorway, speechless, when Gregory emerges from the hallway. He's wearing a pair of jeans ... and nothing else. In his hands he holds a towel and he's using that to dry his hair.

When his gaze lights on me, he freezes. The towel slips from his grip and lands on the floor. His mouth hangs open. I'm fairly certain that in this moment, our expressions are nearly identical.

"We were just talking about the wedding." Terese turns to me. "Did you need something from Gregory?"

An explanation might be nice, but I doubt it's forthcoming. I mouth a few things that aren't really words, then inspiration strikes.

"Actually, I was going to talk to him about the haunted locker at the high school, but I'm running late. I have to be at the dressmaker. So ... you know ... some other time."

"Oh, too bad. We were about to sit down for some coffee, and you're more than welcome to have a cup." She laughs at that and then shakes her head. "What am I saying? My coffee can't compete."

I have a single thermos left in my messenger bag—Kona blend, made with fresh beans from the Coffee Depot. It takes me all of half a second to reject the idea of offering it up.

"I'm sure your coffee's fine," I say. "But I really need to..." I gesture down the hallway, hoping for a quick way out.

"I understand. I'll see you at the wedding if not before."

Terese gives me a friendly wave. Gregory, who stands a foot taller, mouths what looks like an apology over her head. I'm in no mood to accept it.

Because if Belinda isn't here and if she isn't at work, I have no idea where she might be.

THE WOMAN DOING my final fitting doesn't mind that I have my phone out and I'm texting with the agility of a fourteen-year-old girl. My messages to Belinda go nowhere. I try Malcolm because I need to talk to someone.

Katy: Terese is in town.

I wait and wait. I can tell he's responding, or at least thinking about responding.

"Did you get taller?" the woman says to me around a mouthful of pins.

"I don't think so."

"Lose weight?"

"I just ate a big plate of pancakes at the Pancake House."

"Huh. Something's not right. Turn."

As I do, a message from Malcolm pops onto my screen.

Malcolm: Terese as in Mistress Terese of Ghost B Gone?

Katy: That's the one. She's staying with Gregory. Or at least, she's at his place and wearing his bathrobe.

The woman has me turn again, my dress swirling. It's a color best described as ice pink, and I'm not sure whether it makes me look elegant or like a four-year-old.

"Hold still," the woman says. "I need to take in this seam and I don't want to stab you."

Malcolm: Oh. That's ... bad. Belinda?

Katy: Can't find her, she isn't answering and skipped work.

Malcolm: Want me to look?

Katy: Would you?

Malcolm: Of course. You don't even have to ask.

I remain as still as I possibly can. This is easier now that Malcolm is out searching for Belinda.

"There. Got it. Why don't you head out and show Sadie before you change?"

The skirt of my dress held high in one hand, phone in the other, I tiptoe out of the fitting room and over to the larger one, the one they use for wedding gowns. Sadie is standing on a pedestal, while the owner of So-Sew Springside, Marguerite, inspects the dress's train.

"Katy, dear." Sadie holds out a hand to me.

I tiptoe a few more steps and grasp her fingers.

"Aren't you something?" She beams at me. Her flushed cheeks, the pink highlights in her salt-and-pepper hair, and the blush color of her gown conspire to make her appear a decade younger. "Malcolm won't be able to take his eyes off of you," she says.

"Well, he'd better if he doesn't want to trip while he's walking down the aisle."

Marguerite snorts a laugh. "She's trying to get you up on this pedestal."

Well, yes, she is, and has been playing matchmaker ever since Malcolm came to town.

"I think Nigel's the one who's going to have trouble walking down the aisle," I say. "You look incredible."

Sadie presses a hand against the beadwork of the bodice. "It's not too much?"

I give my head an emphatic shake. "Not at all. He wants this. You know that."

Sadie had the big wedding—with Harold. From what I gather, they did everything his way. This time around? Everything is mutual, from the size of the guest list to the filling between the layers of the cake (raspberry cream—pink, of course), to the location (Springside Community Center, not the country club), to a single attendant for each of them. Malcolm is Nigel's best man, and I'm Sadie's lone bridesmaid and maid of honor.

Assuming, of course, that Nigel starts speaking to Malcolm before Saturday.

"And the boys are ... fighting again?" she asks, although it's not really a question.

I'm not sure how she knows this, but she does.

"I'm setting the table for five tonight, or so Nigel informs me," she adds. "Nigel, his friends Reginald and Prescott, you, and me."

Oh. So that's how she knows. "He's not very subtle, is he?"

"No, he's not. And I wish..." She trails off and shakes her head, curls bouncing.

"I'll talk to him," I say, although I haven't had much luck brokering a peace between them.

They don't have much practice being friends. From what Malcolm has told me, while they were growing up, they were always in competition with each other. Each left home at eighteen, meaning to strike out on his own and earn acclaim as a necromancer. These days, they work together, and while they both work hard, neither has mastered the *together* part. I sometimes think the only reason they try is because of me.

"Or maybe," I add, now that I've given it more thought, "take me off your list. Malcolm and I might have some work to do tonight."

We might, of course. We might get an actual customer with an actual ghost. Or I can start learning about profit-and-loss statements and taxes in between evening kisses. This last sounds like an excellent way to spend several hours.

"Try to make the dinner if you can," Sadie says, "because no matter what Nigel says, I'm setting the table for six."

I nod, tiptoe from the dressing room, and check my phone.

Malcolm: No luck so far.

~

I'M HALFWAY TO K&M Ghost Eradication Specialists when the

obvious hits me. I can't find Belinda because she's in the one place I haven't really checked:

Home.

I swing my truck around, certain this is the answer. She snuck in sometime last night, and now she's upstairs, in her room. Belinda Barnes, former Springside High School homecoming queen, isn't the sort of woman who cries her eyes red over a guy.

She might, however, like something to punch. Or some coffee. I don't know if she wants my company, but at the very least I can brew her a pot of one hundred percent Kona and offer up the couch cushions.

I'm so intent on this plan that I nearly miss seeing the necromancer in front of my house. I stop the truck in the middle of the street, shift into reverse, and back up.

There, on the sidewalk, a smirk on his face, is Carter Dupree. I don't bother parking. I kill the engine and climb from the cab. At the last moment, I grab my messenger bag. True, a metal thermos isn't much of a weapon, but it's better than nothing.

"Looking for someone?" he says.

I'm not about to admit anything to him. "If I were, it wouldn't be you."

He makes a face. I reach for the phone in my back pocket.

"Don't even think about calling your boyfriend," he says. "Unless you want me to kick his ass again."

For the record, it was a draw.

"Maybe I was going to call Chief Ramsey."

"And maybe I'll call my very expensive lawyer."

That's not an idle threat. I wish it were. But the BMW parked a few feet from my truck tells me Carter can afford an expensive lawyer. I know Orson Yates and the Midwest Necromancer Association can. I don't want to get Chief in trouble, so I leave my phone where it is.

For now.

"Do you ever read the ghost forums, Katy?"

I peer at Carter. This change of subject is too innocuous to be anything but double-edged.

I go with, "Sometimes."

Actually, scanning the ghost forums is part of Nigel's job. Combing through the misinformation, gossip, lies, and delusions on the forums could be a full-time job by itself. Add in the rest of the Internet? There's something about the Internet and ghosts that brings out the fraudulent and the frenetic.

"You know," Carter continues, as if he's telling me a slightly interesting story, "there are a lot of people upset that Ghost B Gone stopped webcasting. Apparently it had a lot of fans." He shrugs as if this fact is amusing.

It is, in a way, since Ghost B Gone never truly managed an eviction. The ghosts—mainly sprites—just got bored and left.

"Anyway, there's these rumors going around about Gregory and some blonde piece of fluff. Seems Mistress Terese has a lot of fans as well, and they're kind of outraged by this. I thought she might be interested in those message threads, so I sent her the link. She did the rest."

He raises his hands, palms skyward, as if this is some grand achievement on his part. I suppose it is, if your aim is revenge.

"You must be so miserable," I say.

His smile fades before rebounding. Now it looks a little strained. He points to the BMW. "Right. I'm the miserable one. I'm not the one whose business is failing and who can't afford a decent car"—he looks me up and down—"or wardrobe."

"Only a miserable person could enjoy hurting people the way you do."

This time, the smile doesn't fade; it grows sharp, dangerous-looking. He holds up his hand and makes a fist. It's a deliberate motion, but not aggressive—not yet, anyway. I've seen this move before, although I don't know what comes next. I suspect nothing good.

He lets each finger unfurl and as it does, the air around us starts to shimmer.

Goose bumps prickle my arms. The space around us is thick with the otherworldly. I'm not sure what registers first—the wave of anger rolling off this thing Carter has unleashed, or a single word, a command.

Duck!

I do, hands over my head. Even so, when the blast hits, it topples me to the sidewalk. The force knocks Carter off his feet. He flies through the air and lands in the middle of my front yard.

The ghost he's just released whips about, collecting twigs and pebbles in its wake, ripping tender leaves from the trees. Every time Carter tries to sit up, a gale force shoves him back down.

Grit stings my eyes, coats my lips. The ghost strikes anything it can. It rattles the picket fence, shakes the recycling bins. It crashes into the garbage. One can tips, spilling coffee grounds across the driveway.

Stale, days-old Kona blend fills the air. This fuels the ghost's anger even more. I'm puzzling out why when the obvious hits me.

It wants some coffee.

I tug the thermos from the messenger bag and crouch over the cup, shielding it from the debris in the air. I sniff, test the coffee with a finger. Still hot, strong and stout, without any sugar or half and half. I hope this ghost likes its coffee black.

I stand and hold out the cup. "For you. You can have the whole thermos. I can even make you a full pot, but you have to let me inside and you'll have to let go of Carter."

Not that I'm all that concerned about Carter, but I don't want him permanently pinned to my front lawn.

The whirling subsides. I take a tentative step forward. I feel as if I'm coaxing a wild and wounded animal from a trap. Its distrust thickens the air so much it's hard to breathe, and a lingering sadness fills me. This isn't your ordinary nasty ghost. I've encountered plenty of those. This is something else, something intentional.

"What have you done to this ghost?" I direct these words at Carter.

He props himself up on his elbows, the move slow and cautious. "I don't know what you're talking about."

The ghost surges toward the coffee, then, just as quickly, retreats. I try again, urging it forward with one hand. It skitters backward. After we've done this dance a few times, I set the cup on the sidewalk and take a few steps back.

"There," I say, keeping my voice gentle and encouraging. "It's all yours."

The ghost still hesitates. It doesn't point at Carter, not exactly. While strong ghosts can sometimes manifest humanlike forms, this one is in no state for that. But I feel my gaze tugged in his direction.

"I'll take care of him," I say to the ghost. I march over to where Carter is sitting on my lawn. "I don't know what you did to this ghost, but I want you to leave now."

He peers around me, his brow puzzled. "I don't know what you're talking about. It's just one of our reserve ghosts. We use them for ... whatever."

Whatever? I don't know what that means, and I'm not sure I want to. "I think it backfired this time."

Carter wipes his sleeve across his nose. The linen comes away streaked with bright red. A deep purple bruise is forming beneath one eye.

"Go," I say, "unless you want to stick around and have it kick your ass."

I stand between Carter and the ghost as he stumbles down my lawn to his car. He leaves us in a blast of loud music and a patch of burnt rubber along the asphalt. When at last it's quiet, I turn to find the cup nearly empty and the ghost huddled and scared.

I approach first with slow steps, and when that doesn't seem enough, on hands and knees across the sidewalk. I hope none of my neighbors are at home to witness this. Tiny pebbles prick my palms. I scrub them clean on my jeans before pouring a second cup.

"Here you go," I say. "It's all yours."

I'm out of my element with this terrified and damaged ghost. I sit back on my heels and consider what to do.

It's then my phone buzzes with a text message.

Malcolm: Still nothing. Any ideas?

I shield my eyes with a hand and study my house. The curtains are drawn across the window of Belinda's room. That doesn't really mean anything. We do it to keep out the heat.

Katy: Not sure, except now Carter Dupree is in town.

When the call comes mere seconds later, I'm not sure why it startles me. I'm not sure why I put the phone up to my ear. Malcolm's voice blasts from the speaker, and I wait until he's calm —or reasonably so—before I try again.

"Katy, what on earth? Are you okay? Where are you?"

"I'm fine, really. I'm outside my house, and Carter is gone. He didn't violate my ward, which I guess is to his credit."

I really hate to give Carter Dupree credit for anything, but it's true. Other than being blasted up and over the ward, he played by the rules—or at least the ones for wards.

"I'm coming right over." Malcolm's voice is frantic. "No, wait. I'm stopping at Springside PD and talking to Chief about a restraining order, then I'm coming right over. Or you come here. Or—"

I'm about to say something—with luck, something that will calm him down—when another voice joins the conversation.

"Easy, wild man."

The words are muted, but definitely directed at Malcolm. What sounds like a tussle follows. There's a scrape and a chorus of words I can't make out except for: "Let me talk to her." After a pause, Nigel comes on the line.

"Katy, I'm guessing you're okay," he says.

"I am." I fill in all the blanks for him and before he can even ask, say, "Sadie's still at So-Sew Springside. You don't have to worry."

"Trust me, this time around I'm not the one who's worried." He clears his throat. "It's all we can do to restrain him."

"Well, actually, I am kind of worried, but it's about this ghost."

It's letting me crouch next to it to refill the thermos's cup, but I'm running out of coffee fast.

"What about it?" Nigel sounds unconcerned, as if necromancers routinely unleash ghosts on unsuspecting people. "It sounds like one of Orson's attack ghosts, probably meant for Belinda."

Okay, so they probably do. "It's more than that. It's wild, and angry, and I'm not sure how to describe it, but ... damaged."

"Damaged? How so?"

I search for a way to explain what I feel whenever this ghost draws near enough that I can sense it. "It's the difference between an animal that's fierce and nasty because it's a predator and one that's fierce and nasty because it's been abused."

Silence greets my words.

"Nigel?"

"Yeah. Still here."

"I don't know what to do. I can't capture it and set it free somewhere. I don't think that would solve anything."

"It won't."

"Then—"

"Katy, do you have any idea who Reginald Weaver is?"

I blink, wondering what that has to do with my ghost problem. "Your friend ... mentor ... a necromancer?"

"He's one of the foremost necromancers in the state, probably the nation."

Through the speaker, I hear more of those muffled words.

"Oh, yes, and Prescott too. He's no slouch."

"Can they help me?"

The booming voice of Reginald Weaver fills my ear.

"Katrina Lindstrom, keep the ghost where it is. We will be there soon."

CHAPTER 3

I POUR THE LAST drops of coffee from the thermos and hope it's enough to placate this ghost. It hasn't shown additional signs of aggression, but then I've kept it full of Kona blend. I'm not sure what will happen after it finishes this last cup.

I'm still crouched on the sidewalk next to the ghost when two cars pull up: that flashy yellow one and a far more practical, although equally expensive, Land Rover.

Nigel and Prescott hop out of the yellow car. Nigel surveys the area and then points to Sadie's house.

"I'll be over here if anyone needs tech support."

Prescott squeezes his shoulder. "Good man."

From the corner of my eye, I track Nigel's progress up Sadie's porch steps and inside her house. His spine is straight, shoulders square. If he has any regrets about the life he used to live, they don't show.

This, I think, is a good thing.

Malcolm jumps from the Land Rover and rushes to my side. I hold up a hand, urging him to slow down.

"It's skittish," I say.

And, yes, the ghost wavers but otherwise remains in place.

Malcolm kneels next to me, his hand cupping the back of my neck, his lips next to my ear.

"Are you okay?" His whisper is fierce and frantic. "Be honest. I swear to God, if he hurt you, I'll—"

"I'm fine. Really. You're overreacting."

"I don't think I am."

"Everyone else does."

Or rather, Reginald seems completely uninterested in our ongoing drama. He stands at the edge of the ward around my property and appears to be inspecting it and my house, paying particular attention to the damage caused by the ghost. Prescott catches my eye and there's nothing but amusement in his.

Even the ghost loses some of its fear. I know an otherworldly laugh when I hear one.

"See?" I point toward the ghost. "Even it thinks so."

Malcolm manages a laugh of his own, one filled with self-deprecation. "Okay, you're right. I'm overreacting." He glances around the yard. "And you can clearly take care of yourself."

The last of the coffee is gone. I've served up coffee to everything from sprites to an entity so powerful I'm not sure you could call it a ghost. Most don't suck down an entire thermos's worth of the stuff, not even when it's Kona blend.

But this thing? It wants more, or at least that's my guess when it worms its way into the thermos.

"Do you want that pot of coffee I promised you?" I ask.

The thermos rattles and rolls along the sidewalk and bumps to a halt at my knees.

"I think that's a yes," Malcolm says.

Prescott surveys the street. "We should take this inside, and someone should move Katy's truck."

I hand Malcolm the keys and scoop up the thermos. I'm on the porch steps—alone—when I glance behind me.

Both Prescott and Reginald are standing on the sidewalk. Okay, so Prescott's wingtips are flirting with the edge of the ward. I suspect this is something he's known for. Reginald, however, is a respectful distance back. I suspect that's something he's known for, as well.

"Really?" I ask.

"Really," Prescott confirms.

So, once again, I invite them inside. Malcolm dashes up the stairs behind us. Before we can follow them, he pulls me close. It's an awkward hug—him, me, the screen door, and the ghost in its thermos.

I think he might question me again. Worry is radiating from him. It's there in the way his muscles tense as he holds me. Instead his lips come to rest on top of my head and brush strands of hair. When he does speak, his voice is low and warm.

"You smell like sunshine," is all he says.

WE'RE HALFWAY to the kitchen when a thought strikes me. The jolt of fear has me skittering to a halt. I turn, point, but Malcolm has already read my mind.

"You start the coffee. I'll check to see if she's home." He dashes up the stairs, and his footfalls echo overhead.

If Belinda is home, we'll have to send her next door—at the very least. If this thing in the thermos is some sort of attack ghost meant for her, we'll have to think of something to keep her safe. I peer into the depths of the thermos.

The ghost is cowering inside. I don't talk to ghosts, not the way Malcolm and the other necromancers do, but I don't need to do that to sense their feelings, their overriding desires. And right now, all this ghost wants is safety.

That's not something I've encountered before.

In the kitchen, I hand Reginald the thermos and start the coffee. Malcolm returns as I'm measuring out the grounds. He clears the threshold and then staggers backward as if the aroma from the freshly-ground beans has struck him in the chest.

"One hundred percent Kona?" he asks, eyes full of hope.

"I think we need it."

"When you say 'we', does that include humans as well?"

"Maybe," I say, but the scoop I'm holding should give him the answer—as long as he keeps count. I'm making enough for five humans and one ghost. I'll insist someone run a cup over to Nigel.

"Belinda?" I mouth.

He shakes his head.

I don't know whether to be relieved or worried. "You don't suppose Carter has another attack ghost, do you?"

"Doubtful." Prescott hovers over my shoulder, and if Malcolm isn't counting the scoops, he certainly is. "Good God, that smells like heaven."

The kitchen in my old Victorian is cramped. With three men crowding around, the space feels even smaller. Reginald's so tall he jostles the pots and pans hanging from an improvised rack. Most of the counter space is devoted to brewing coffee and has been for as long as I can remember.

"So, you don't think he has another ghost?" I peer into the percolator, compare the amount of water with the grounds I've measured out. I go with a touch more filtered water.

"It's hard to manage more than one unless you're unusually skilled," Prescott says. "Carter isn't unusually skilled."

"Last time he tried, at least in Springside," Malcolm says, "he ended up unconscious and lost both his ghosts to Katy." He's pulling half and half from the refrigerator, and when he turns and confronts our stares, he nearly drops the container. "What? It's true. You captured Harold—"

"Actually, *you* did."

"*We* captured Harold's ghost, and then you made a pact with Delilah and set her free."

"Oh, Delilah." Prescott folds his arms over his chest and leans back against the counter. He shuts his eyes for a moment, a smile playing on his lips. "She's one hell of a ghost. I was wondering where she went. Anyway, I think it's safe to say that Carter came to town with one ghost. He lacks the skill for anything more."

"But where you find Carter with an attack ghost, you'll also find the man holding his leash." Reginald is still clutching the thermos. He strokes the sides gently, as if he's calming the ghost inside or coaxing it to come out.

"I don't think so, not this time." Prescott shakes his head. "Not with me, and not with you here. Orson's not that foolhardy."

"Are you certain it's foolhardy? Nigel can't fight. Malcolm is a youngster, and Katy untrained. That leaves you and me. In one place. How hard would it be to take one—or both—of us out?"

"Is he going to—?" I begin.

"No, he's not," Reginald says. "At least, I doubt he will. I suspect it's another show of power. However, we shouldn't discount a move on his part, especially when we're distracted by wounded ghosts and upcoming weddings."

Reginald's words reassure me—to a point. I glance at Malcolm. His expression is grim, but when he sees me staring, he offers up a smile.

"Don't worry," he mouths.

But I think maybe I should worry, and a lot. I'm completely out of my depth with all this necromancer talk. I know ghosts, and I know coffee. I decide to concentrate on that, brew this ghost the best cup it has ever had, and maybe send it on its way healed, or mostly so.

The mood in the kitchen shifts as the aromatic steam fills the air. Prescott's shoulders loosen. Malcolm no longer looks so grim. The thermos wobbles in Reginald's grip.

When at last I've poured a cup for everyone, I think that maybe one problem is solved. The ghost emerges from the thermos and slips into the steam rising from its cup. As it does so, some of its fear slips away. It's like an exhale, a sigh of relief.

"This is quite good," Reginald says, the rim of the cup poised at his lips.

Prescott rolls his eyes. "What he means is, it's the best damn cup he's ever had. Katy, this is incredible. Really. You must be channeling all your power as a necromancer into brewing coffee."

"I'm not a necromancer." I swallow my sigh with a sip of coffee.

"You should rethink that," Prescott says, his tone dry.

"Well, this little one would agree." Reginald trades his cup for the one the ghost is basking in, easing it from the table with gentle hands. "It knows Katy's wishes, which is why it would like to speak to Malcolm."

Prescott makes a face. "Malcolm?"

Malcolm shoulders Prescott out of the way—a slight that only paints an amused smile on Prescott's face—and steps forward.

"Ready?" Reginald says.

Malcolm nods and reaches out. His touch is tentative. He shuts his eyes, mouth open ever so slightly.

"Technique, Malcolm. Technique," Prescott chides. "Ghost catching has made you sloppy."

Only the barest tensing of his jaw tells me Malcolm has even heard Prescott's words. A moment later, he steps back, eyes wide open.

"Katy, it's one of our ghosts!"

"Oh, so, you *are* amassing a ghost army." Prescott. Again.

Malcolm throws him a scowl. "I mean, it's a Springside ghost. They captured one from town, on purpose. That was supposed to make it fiercer because it would blame Katy for not protecting it."

"I suspect that backfired," Reginald says.

Malcolm nods. "It attacked Carter purely out of revenge, but it recognized Katy. I don't know which ghost it is. I couldn't get a good enough read on it. It's still pretty damaged." He looks to me. "Are we missing one?"

We have our regulars, it's true, those ghosts who either live such a quiet existence that we seldom eradicate them or those who are town fixtures that no one seems to mind—too much.

"I don't know." I review my last several calls. Naughty sprites at the long-term care facility. A ghost that was hoping to inspire awe at the community theater. I think it was going for *Phantom of the Opera*, but the effect was more irritating than terrifying.

Malcolm takes the cup and holds it in front of me. "You don't have to go all necromancer," he says. "Just do that sensing thing you do."

I reach out a hand. This isn't necromancy. At least, I don't think it is. I've always done this, gauged the feelings of ghosts, their driving desire, their personality. I close my eyes and concentrate on the cold sensation engulfing my fingertips.

I know this ghost. And then I know what it is Orson Yates and Carter Dupree have done.

"This is Chief Ramsey's ghost," I say.

"Chief has a ghost?" Malcolm tilts his head as if he needs a new perspective on the ghost still basking in the steam.

It's a fair question. Chief hasn't exactly embraced the idea of the otherworldly. He is, though, a bit more open these days. But he could barely sense the ghost that's been haunting his gardening shed, so he might not notice if it went missing.

"It haunts the watering can in his gardening shed," I say. "It never did much more than rattle the handle, and you know Chief."

Malcolm gives me a crooked grin. "Yeah. I do."

"May I?" Reginald holds out his hands for the coffee cup.

The ghost has returned to swirling in the steam, although I think a fresh serving might be in order. I pour another cup and the ghost abandons the first for the second. I hand both the cup and the ghost over to Reginald as gently as I can.

"I'm afraid this little one isn't the first to be abused by Orson and his association." He pauses and then nods as if he can hear the ghost without the trick Malcolm does.

He raises his gaze to mine and says, "It thinks the world of you, Katy."

"I don't really do anything," I protest. "I brew coffee and catch them. I've never bothered with this one because it's never caused any trouble."

"Ah, that's just it," Reginald says. "You maintain the order of things between humans and ghosts here in Springside. Things would be far worse if either side got the upper hand."

Malcolm cups my shoulder and gives it a squeeze. "Told you so," he whispers in my ear. "You're the steak."

"You know what a nasty ghost can do," Reginald continues. His gaze lowers to the cup still cradled in his hands. "Now you've seen what it is Orson Yates does."

"What do we do with it now?" I ask. "It doesn't seem ... strong enough to release."

Despite all the coffee it's sucked down—and it has made a full thermos and half a pot evaporate. I can't imagine driving it out to the nature preserve and letting it go, or even taking it back to its watering can.

"It isn't strong enough," Reginald confirms. "With your permission, I'd like to take it back up north when I leave. Prescott, go out to my truck and grab one of the cedar boxes."

Prescott's lips twitch as if he's contemplating a refusal. But he leaves without a word and returns with the box, all without comment or complaint. When he places the box on the kitchen table and opens the lid, the scent of cedar joins that of the coffee.

"Little one," Reginald says, voice low, mouth even with the rim of the coffee cup where the ghost is now floating. "Would you consent to spending some time in this box? You will be safe in there. No other necromancer will be able to breach its seal. I will take you home, and when you're better, if you wish, I'll bring you back to Springside."

The air shimmers as the ghost rises from the coffee's steam and eases into the cedar box. The inside is unvarnished but smooth.

The whole thing feels safe, and I wonder if that's part of the seal Reginald has placed on it. Right before he lowers the lid, I blow the ghost a kiss.

Prescott bursts out laughing. My cheeks flame even as Malcolm's grip tightens on my shoulder. He throws Prescott another scowl.

"I didn't—" I begin, but my throat is tight. When Prescott holds up a hand, I'm glad for the excuse to stop speaking.

"It was just so charming. No wonder Orson can't figure out what it is you do. It's the opposite of everything he is and believes." He points to the percolator. "It would never occur to him to brew a ghost a cup of coffee, never mind send it off with a kiss."

Reginald studies the box. "No, it wouldn't. That, of course, is his great weakness, and why he isn't as powerful as he thinks himself to be." He turns to me. "Katrina Lindstrom, thank you for your hospitality. Your coffee lives up to its reputation. With your permission." He raises the box. "I will take this little one some-where safe."

"Is that what you do?" I ask as I see both Prescott and Reginald to the door.

"It's not all I do, but lately, I seem to be running a rehabilita-tion center for the ghosts Orson or one of his associates have damaged."

"Could I visit your woods sometime? Learn how to do that?" I glance at Malcolm, whose expression has gone startled. Maybe I shouldn't blurt out every last idea that pops into my head, but this seems like a good one. "Maybe we could help some of the meaner ghosts instead of simply driving them out of range."

Reginald chuckles. "And here I thought you weren't a necromancer."

He leaves us with that, and says nothing else on his way out the door and down the porch steps. After a quick kiss on my cheek, Prescott follows. It's only after the exhaust from their cars has settled, and it's quiet again, that I turn to Malcolm.

"Is that necromancy?"

He shrugs. "I honestly don't know. Nigel studied with Reginald, but I never have. My grandfather was my mentor, in the same way you learned catch and release from your grandmother."

"What about your parents?"

I'm so used to being on my own—with or without my grand-mother—that the fact that Malcolm and Nigel's parents aren't here for the wedding hasn't seemed odd, until now.

Malcolm sighs. "Let's see. Our father? Somewhere in South America. Or possibly the Falklands, but really, who knows? It's likely he hasn't heard about the wedding yet." He glances over his shoulder at Sadie's house before turning back to me. "Nigel had me send that particular ghost pretty late. I think it was on purpose."

I nod, although I really don't understand.

"And our mother. In Paris. She sent along a blue silk handker-chief for Sadie's something borrowed and something blue. She does approve of the whole younger man, older woman thing, so there's that."

"Oh." My voice sounds so small. I don't know what to make of this information or even how Malcolm feels about it. I want to say something to ... comfort him, I guess.

That must show on my face, because he laughs and tugs me close. "Don't worry. It's ... the way things are."

I peer up at him. "The Armands as free agents?"

"Something like that. My father never approved of Nigel's choice of mentor, which caused a rift. My mother had an affair, and that caused another, as you can imagine. By the time I needed a mentor, everything had fallen apart, so my grandfather stepped in."

"I'm sorry," I say.

"You know what's crazy? I'm not. Not anymore. I feel like I'm building a new family here in Springside. I mean, there's you, of course."

Here, I think I detect a hint of a blush, and my own cheeks burn again.

"But it's also everyone else, Belinda and Gregory—well, when he's not acting like an ass—Sadie, the residents at the long-term care facility. Even Chief Ramsey is starting to grow on me."

I like the idea of building the family you want rather than the one you ended up with. You can always expand, add new members. They don't, strictly speaking, need to be human.

"I'm wondering if we should go check on some of our family," I say. I think of the ghosts that might be missing, and of course, Belinda. "The human and the otherworldly."

Malcolm's lips find the top of my head again, and it's a shivering thing, this almost kiss of his.

"I think maybe we should."

CHAPTER 4

M Y PHONE RINGS at three in the morning. The sound
jolts me upright in bed, heart pounding. I grope the nightstand, missing the phone on the first three tries. My limbs ache
and my head is fogged with sleep despite the adrenaline racing
through my veins.

When I answer, my mouth is so dry, I can barely say hello.

"Hey, it's me. I'm sorry to call so late."

The voice makes my eyes shoot open. "Belinda! Where ... what?
I mean—"

"Before you can ask, yes, I'm okay."

"I'm assuming you're not here." I strain my ears, but I already
know the answer. If Belinda were here, she'd just knock on my
bedroom door.

"You'd be right."

"Or Gregory's?" I hate to go there, but I want to know where
she is.

She snorts. "No, I'm not there either. I'm at my mom's,
actually."

I don't have a response for that, even if my thoughts are

catching up to the rest of me. Belinda and her mother get along—
up to a point. But there are several reasons she lives with me, and
her mother tops that list. I stretch to turn on the bedside lamp,
then squint in its glare. But the light chases away the dark and
makes the house feel not quite so empty.

"Yeah, I know," she adds when I don't respond. "But I couldn't
exactly bring Carter Dupree back to your place."

"You ... what?" My voice has returned, but I don't have any
words for *that*. Carter and Belinda? "What's going on?" I ask at
last.

"Apparently there are some badass necromancers staying at the
bed and breakfast and he didn't want to sleep there tonight, not
after what happened with that ghost."

"You know about that?"

"Yeah, he came into the Pancake House an hour before close."

"Annie was worried," I say. "She asked me to look for you."

"I know, and thanks. I took her shift to make up for ditching."

I scoot up and plump the pillows behind me. I still ache from
trekking around Springside with Malcolm, and I suspect this will
be a very long conversation. A dozen questions swirl in my head; I
really don't know which one to ask first. Gregory and Terese?
Belinda and Carter?

"Can we start from the beginning?" is the one I choose.

"So, yeah, I guess maybe we should." Her sigh fills my ear. "So,
I get off shift the other night and Gregory's not there to pick me
up. I think, no big deal, I'll walk to his place."

I know what's coming and I cringe. "Ouch?"

"Yeah. That. Terese was there, which was why he didn't pick me
up after work."

"He could've said something, called, sent a text?" I can't help
wondering if Belinda was greeted with the same sight I was: Terese
swimming in Gregory's robe with him half-dressed in the
background.

"It's complicated. I think I told you they were together for a long time. He was totally on the rebound. I knew that going in. If this works for them, who am I to stand in their way?" Her voice has the breezy quality of someone trying to convince themselves of something.

"Malcolm thinks he's an ass."

Belinda laughs. "He's the best. Tell him I said that next time you see him. Unless, of course—" Here, her voice turns sly. "All you need to do is nudge him."

"Don't even start on that. This is about you and Carter Dupree, for some reason."

"I'm going to get him off your back." That breezy quality turns steely.

"Don't be crazy. He came to town to hurt you. He had an attack ghost. He could have another for all we know."

"No, I was just a bonus. There's something else going on, and if I have to cozy up to him to find out what it is, I will."

"He's not going to tell you anything."

"See, I think you're wrong. Something happened today, with that ghost, and it's changed things for him. Do you know he's never been attacked by one?"

"Never been...?" My voice trails off.

I simply can't believe it. I started working with my grand-mother when I was five. By the time I was eight, she was taking me with her on all her calls—even the bad ones. Getting attacked by ghosts is part of the job description.

"How can that be?" I ask.

"The way he was raised, I guess. It's all that necromancer stuff Malcolm and Nigel always talk about. Anyway, I thought he was going to break down at the Pancake House. I kept bringing him plates of pancakes until he looked semi-normal again."

"I don't like this. It could be a trick."

"Let's say it is. I'm a lot stronger than I used to be. A lot of that is thanks to you. I'll be okay. Trust me?"

"I really don't think—"

"You don't have to do it all yourself, you know," she says, that steely quality in full force. "The rest of us can help."

I hear the echo of something in her words, something I told Malcolm, perhaps.

"I'm just worried," I say.

"Don't be. I don't have many talents, but I do know how to get information out of guys, especially guys like Carter Dupree. Let me handle him."

"Do I have a choice?"

"Nope." With that, Belinda hangs up.

I stare at my phone until the screen goes black. I want to call Malcolm, but it's much too early. Even a text message will wake him up, so I refrain.

But I'm wide awake. I throw back the comforter and consider the empty side of my bed. I wonder how long it should stay empty. Both *not long* and *too late* fill my thoughts, competing for my attention. I don't know which one is right. Instead of thinking about either one, I head downstairs and brew the first pot of coffee of the day.

SPRINGSIDE at six a.m. is an incredible thing. I walk downtown because I don't want to disturb the quiet with the barely muffled sound of my truck. I want to take in the air, gauge it, search for what should be there—and what shouldn't.

Last night, Malcolm and I concluded that we might be missing some ghosts. The wild ones that haunt the old barn were absent. But, they're unpredictable, and I don't visit the site often enough to know their habits.

Fortunately, Sadie's sprites are still in residence. These days, they spend most of their time at the long-term care facility. They amuse Mrs. Greeley, and Mr. Carlotta's ghost keeps them in line.

Queenie, as he calls her, was there too, a bit put out about her babysitting duties, but otherwise the same as always.

Of all the ghosts in Springside, that's the one Orson Yates cannot be allowed to capture. We both know the entity's name, although I'm the only one who can speak it and actually invoke the thing. But that one single word, in the hands of an unscrupulous necromancer? Nothing good would come of that. She's a strong ghost, but what would it take for her to give up that knowledge?

I don't know. I don't like the overabundance of necromancers in Springside, even if I do trust Nigel's friends.

I'm a block from the Springside Police Department when Chief Ramsey appears on its steps. He catches sight of me and possibly raises an eyebrow, although he's too far away for me to really tell.

I pull a thermos from my messenger bag and hold it up. It's a peace offering. I've used it before. Somehow, it never loses its effectiveness.

Chief sweeps an arm toward the station's door before heading inside. I jog the rest of the way, thermoses jangling at my side.

Chief is already in his office by the time I enter the station. On the sideboard in the reception area, yesterday's coffee has formed a charred sludge in the bottom of the carafe, burner still on low. For a few moments, I stare at the mess, uncertain whether I should do something about it.

"Ignore it," Chief calls from his office. "That's what I do."

"It's just so wrong."

That earns me an actual laugh. Those from Chief Ramsey are pretty rare.

"I have some Kona blend," I say.

"I might actually break a few laws for Kona blend."

I uncap a thermos and pour the coffee into a cup. It's then that the two sprites that haunt the police station come out of hiding. They swirl in the steam and between my fingers and make such an annoyance of themselves that I pour them a cup of their own.

That, of course, is exactly what they want. In truth, I don't mind. I'm glad these two are still here and still causing all sorts of trouble.

"There's strangers in town," I tell them. "You know what that means."

One lazes back and forth in the steam. The other one dances about. Neither is listening.

"It means you need to be careful."

The cup wobbles.

"Don't spill that," I say, "because you're not getting any more."

The cup rights itself.

What sounds like a cough comes from Chief's office. He may be more open-minded about ghosts these days, but not enough to believe in these two. I top off his coffee, and since it's always best to lead with your strengths, I enter his office coffee cup first.

I hand the cup to him and wonder again about showing Penny how to brew a decent pot. Or Chief. There's no law that says the police chief can't make his own coffee.

The Styrofoam cup looks tiny in his grip. He shuts his eyes and inhales. For a moment, his face loses its careworn expression.

"It always takes me back," he says. "Did you know that your mother would brew pot after pot when we were studying for finals?"

I give my head a slight shake.

"Well, she did. This?" He raises the cup. "Must run in the family. Every year, a bunch of us would end up crowding around your grandmother's dining room table, and we'd spend half the night cramming."

I know so little about my mother, and these tidbits Chief shares always take me by surprise and leave me without words. These are small kindnesses, these glimpses into my mother's life. I wish I had a way to repay him.

"She was the only reason any of us got decent grades." He sighs and takes a sip. "But I'm pretty sure you're not here to talk about my GPA."

"Carter Dupree is back in town."

Yes, I know Belinda can take care of herself. And maybe I should trust her instincts on this. But I've seen how vindictive Carter can be, and I know where there's one necromancer with a nasty ghost, there are probably others.

"Ah, yes, and sporting a black eye. Please tell me that wasn't Malcolm's handiwork."

"It wasn't, actually."

Chief cocks his head. "Yours?"

"Not ... exactly?" I'm not sure how to explain an attack ghost to him. He barely believes as it is. "It did happen on my front lawn."

"Did you strike him in any way? Fist, rake, tree branch?"

I shake my head. "I didn't touch him at all."

"Good. Any witnesses?"

"Sadie wasn't home." Here, I shrug. "I'm not sure about anyone else. Most of them work during the day."

What would that attack ghost look like to someone watching from behind their living room curtains? A mini-tornado in my front yard? How would someone rationalize Carter flying through the air? Really, I hope there weren't any witnesses. It would just make everything that much more difficult to explain.

"Actually, I'm more worried about Belinda."

Chief's mouth forms a hard line. His brow darkens. So he must know as well. Springside is a small town, after all. By now, even the ghosts must be gossiping about Gregory, Terese, and Belinda.

"She's not drinking, is she?" he asks.

"I don't know. She's staying at her mom's."

"You two aren't fighting, are you?"

I shake my head. "She's trying to help me with ... something, but I'm not sure she should."

His frown deepens. He was close to her father, and I know he promised to look after Belinda when her father died. She hasn't made that easy.

"I'm not here on any sort of official business," I say. "I'm asking as a ... friend. You know, if we're both looking out for her? Maybe everything will be okay."

"I'll take you up on that." He stares at me, a patented Chief Ramsey stare, the sort that makes you think you've broken some obscure law. Then the look softens into an almost-smile. "Friend."

As I'm on my way out the door, he calls after me.

"Katy, you be careful too."

I halt, hand on the doorframe. "I will. I always am."

"I don't like that Carter Dupree is back in town."

If Chief only knew. "I don't like it either."

That earns me a laugh, but it's short-lived. "I want you to report anything out of the ordinary, no matter how small."

"Of course."

"I'm serious."

I'm about to turn around, to look at him again, but his tone shifts, and something about it keeps me frozen in place.

"I'd like to think your mom wouldn't mind if I looked out for you too."

His voice is rough, and I'm gripping the doorframe so tightly, my fingers ache. I don't dare turn around now, so I squeeze my eyes shut and give my head a vigorous nod. I hope that's enough.

I leave before discovering whether or not it is.

It's Friday, and the moment Malcolm walks through the door of K&M Ghost Eradication Specialists he pulls me into a hug and whirls me around the space. My boots thump against the reception desk and my skirt flares outward.

I'm not dressed for work, but that doesn't really matter. We made it through the week without another ghost incident. We made it through the week without Nigel and Malcolm having another fight. I made it through the week without a glimpse of Carter Dupree.

Even better, in a little more than twenty-four hours Sadie will walk down the aisle and marry Nigel. Nothing else matters.

"What's the occasion?" Malcolm asks.

"Occasion?"

"You're wearing my favorite outfit."

"This is your favorite?" True, I don't have a wide range of outfits, but if I had to guess, I'd say Malcolm's favorite involved the skater skirt.

"Well, you know how I feel about the skirt."

Yes. Yes, I do.

"And the boots are totally kickass, but it's those socks that get me every time."

I own exactly one skirt but many, many over-the-knee stockings. It's a cost-effective way to create a new look—or so I tell myself.

"Well, I have to wear the bridesmaid dress tomorrow." I roll my eyes. I'd really rather not wear the bridesmaid dress at all. "So, I figured I'd go with this today."

Malcolm blinks. "Wait. Assuming you weren't Sadie's maid of honor, would you wear your skater skirt to the wedding?"

"Why not? It's really all I own." I extend a leg and touch the stocking's pattern of smiling daisies. "I'd go with something else, though, something fancier, maybe with sparkles."

His lips twitch. He has an extensive—and expensive—wardrobe of his own. He's never uttered a word about mine. Until maybe now. I brace myself, but for what, I'm not certain.

Instead, he cups my face and gives me one of those sweet dark-roast smiles of his. "Just one of the many reasons why I love you."

All of a sudden, I can't breathe. I can't move. I don't know how to respond. No, that's not true. I do know. I know exactly what to do. My problem is, I'm frozen in place. I can't get my arms to throw themselves around his neck. I can't get my lips to kiss his.

I can't get the words I need to say to leave my mouth.

His thumb travels down my cheekbone. His expression is

nothing but tender. I shake my head, but I'm not telling him no; rather, I hope he'll understand I've lost the ability to speak.

"Shh. You don't have to say it back. You don't have to say anything. Okay?"

"But what if I want to say something?"

"Oh, well, that's fine, too."

He pulls me close, and I bury my face against his neck. It's warm here, and that mix of nutmeg and Ivory Soap is both exotic and so familiar.

"I love you, too," I say against the sensitive skin of his neck. "I have for a long time."

"That's why you didn't need to say it. It's obvious."

"It is?"

"Seriously, Katy. People don't go around sacrificing themselves for others, or putting the other person's happiness first if they don't love them. You were going to step aside and let me partner with Selena again, if I wanted to. Am I right?"

I nod, and it's a miserable sort of thing. In that moment, I feel pathetic. I'm not so noble that I don't mind the mention of Selena. Malcolm notices. Of course he does.

"Hey, I know, I know." His lips brush my forehead. "I've had my moments with Carter."

True, but Carter was never a part of my life the way Selena was with Malcolm.

"Chief warned me that if it happened again," he adds, "he'd toss me in jail for the night."

"He didn't!"

"He did. I think it was supposed to motivate me."

"To do what?"

"Not sure, really. But right now, the only thing I want to do is this."

He kisses me then, and it's a dark and dizzying thing, much more an evening kiss than the normal morning one. In this moment, I'm thankful for so many things—that Nigel is off work, that I picked today of all days to pull on the skater skirt, that my heart is so full and that I could be so happy.

"I wish I didn't have to go to the bachelor party," he says several minutes later.

We've settled on the reception desk. The couch is more comfortable, but from our perch on the desk, we can see the storefront window and the gold lettering of K&M Eradication Specialists. My head rests on his shoulder, and we take turns tracing the scars on the backs of each other's hands.

"What do necromancers do at bachelor parties?"

"Show off, mostly, and drink, and then show off some more."

"The one with the most ghosts wins?"

"Something like that. I guess tonight we'll just drink Prescott's scotch and listen to him brag."

"It could be worse?" I say it like a question, too, because maybe it couldn't.

Malcolm laughs. "Yes, it could, but around them, I will always be Nigel's 'baby' brother. There's no escaping that."

I lace my fingers with his. "If it gets too bad, we could always text."

"There's an idea." His lips brush strands of my hair and his breath is warm against my scalp. "Better make sure your battery is charged."

CHAPTER 5

T HE TEXT COMES at midnight. I'm not surprised, really. I guessed Malcolm might have a better time than he thought he would. When I read the message, I know that's true.

Malcolm: We're having a ghost issue. We're all drunk. None of us can catch it.

Katy: Nigel? Is he okay?

Malcolm: Fine. But it would be better if we got it out of here. Would you mind?

Katy: It will take me a few minutes to brew some coffee, but I'll be over as soon as I can.

Malcolm: You're the best.

It's only as I ready the percolator that I wonder which of Springside's ghosts is causing the trouble. A naughty sprite? That seems likely. Still, if it's something more robust, it could be harder to catch, especially if I'm working solo. I pull out the Kona blend, start up the coffee, and then text Malcolm again.

Katy: Is it a sprite? Something more? One of our usual suspects?

My message sits there. No response. No notice that it has even been delivered. There could be a dozen reasons for that, starting with our spotty cell phone service in Springside.

The steam from the Kona blend is enough to clear my head, although I pour myself a to-go cup anyway. I pull the field kit together, adding in a container of sugar and a thermos of half and half just in case.

I'm halfway through my to-go cup and wide awake by the time I reach Malcolm's apartment building. Low lighting illuminates the stairs, but otherwise all the windows are dark—except one.

I stand on the sidewalk out front and stare up at the window of Malcolm's apartment and wonder if anyone is sober enough to buzz me in. The night air is cool, and I raise my chin in an attempt to get a taste of it. I don't sense anything otherworldly, but there's enough distance between the ground and Malcolm's apartment that I might not. It might only be a sprite, and their presence is so slight as to not be there at all sometimes.

When I turn to head inside, a figure blocks the path. I let out a yelp and leap backward. My heart races. The thermoses jangle in the field kit. I'm reaching for one when the figure across from me grasps my wrist.

Instinctively, I jerk back, but his grip is firm.

"Easy, there. The hangover's going to hurt bad enough." The voice is low, amused. "I don't need you adding to it."

My eyes adjust. I match a face to the voice, although in the dark, it's hard to pick out his features.

"Prescott? What are you—?"

"Malcolm sent me down to let you in."

"Is he ... is everyone okay?" I glance around, uncertain.

"Fine, fine, but we could really use the services of K&M Ghost Eradication Specialists."

Malcolm would come down himself to let me in. That's the way he is. I doubt a couple of glasses of scotch would change that. He *might* send Nigel, if only to get him away from the ghost.

Prescott? No. Prescott isn't the sort of person who allows himself be sent on errands, especially by a baby necromancer or whatever he thinks Malcolm is.

For a moment, we remain like statues. In the slight breeze, I catch a hint of Kona blend, although that's only because the steam has scented my hair. What I notice most is the thing I don't smell.

Scotch. I've never been much of a drinker. Alcohol and ghosts don't mix. But I know the odor. I've caught the hint of it on Belinda far too many times not to.

Prescott is still holding my wrist. His grip is strong enough that I know, if I try to jerk away, he'll tighten it. But my left hand is free. I can use that to grab the canvas field kit, swing it around, and use the element of surprise to break free.

As soon as I think that, I wonder: when did things change? When did Prescott become someone I need to get away from? My arms and legs break out in goose bumps. I pulled on the skater skirt, thinking Malcolm would like that. Now I wish I'd chosen a pair of jeans, something more practical.

I think of Chief Ramsey and wonder if I should have alerted him. But a ghost crashing a bachelor party isn't out of the ordinary.

Except I don't think there's any ghost to catch.

With as much stealth as possible, I weave the fingers of my left hand around the strap of my bag. It's awkward, but it's the only shot I have.

I swing the bag, hoping the trajectory will connect with Prescott's head or neck—anything that will throw him off balance.

"Oh, no, you don't." Prescott ducks, and the jumble of thermoses glances off his head. He swears.

For one blissful moment, my wrist is free from his grip. I take a step, prepare to run, and crash into two people behind me.

"Grab her," he calls out.

Each seizes an arm. I open my mouth to scream only to find it stuffed with a handkerchief.

"None of that." Prescott rubs his head, fingers investigating the bump my collection of thermoses gave him. "Really, Katy, all you need to do is cooperate and everything will be fine. I give you my word as a necromancer."

It's not like I can agree—or disagree; not with my mouth full of high-end linen. My eyes water, and I can feel my pulse throbbing in my neck and in my temples. I want to gasp for air, but that only triggers my gag reflex. A muffled whimper finds its way around the handkerchief.

"Here." Prescott steps close. "If I remove this, do you promise not to scream?"

I remain absolutely still.

"The deal is this. You're coming with us—one way or another. You can ride in the backseat or the trunk. If you scream, you end up in the trunk. Understand?"

I nod.

"Are you going to scream?"

I weigh the options. I'm better off in the backseat, although, in truth, I'm better off not going at all. My gaze is drawn to Malcolm's window and the light illuminating the drawn shades.

Prescott follows my gaze. "Out cold, I'm afraid. Scotch will do that to Reginald. And Malcolm's in no condition to ride to your rescue, although I know he'd love to. You've put a spell on that boy." He turns to me. "So, what will it be?"

I glare at him. Really, how does he expect me to say anything with his handkerchief in my mouth?

"Yes, of course, forgive me. Let's try this again. Will you remain quiet?"

I inhale as deep a breath as I can manage and hold it for a moment. If I must go with them, then the backseat is better than the trunk.

I nod.

Prescott removes the handkerchief. I sputter and cough. I suck in a deep lungful of air but don't break my promise.

"Let's go," he says to the men at my side.

They haul me toward a car, not Prescott's flashy two-seater but a black sedan with dark windows. One man opens the door while the other grips me tighter. He places a hand on the back of my skull so I won't bump my head. The slight pressure tells me I'm supposed to duck.

Instead, I let my knees buckle. I'm in full-on damsel-in-distress mode. I don't cry out, but I give a little yelp. Despite the man holding me, I collapse to the ground under the strength of my own weight.

For one precious moment, my hands are free. I snake one into the messenger bag and tug out a thermos. I push it beneath the car where a tire won't hit it when we leave, but where no one will notice it either.

It's not much of a clue, but Malcolm will recognize the thermos, and anyone who opens the cap will recognize the Kona blend. I'm hoping that someone will be Chief Ramsey. I'm hoping he'll know what to do.

"Careful, gentlemen," Prescott says. "We don't want to break her, not yet, anyway."

I don't know what that means, only that it sounds ominous.

I'm yanked clear off my feet and half-shoved, half-helped into the car. The two men sandwich me into the middle seat while Prescott sits in the front next to a third man, the driver.

I glance behind me and wonder if the trunk might have been the better option.

We're on the outskirts of Springside when the man to my right pulls out a blindfold.

"That won't be necessary," Prescott says.

"Orders."

Prescott surveys the man before turning his gaze toward me. "I apologize, Katy." He nods at the man. "Go ahead."

With my sight cut off, I hear everything—the slight jangle of thermoses near my feet, the whir of tires against asphalt. I catch the overly spiced scent of someone's cologne. After a few turns and a few miles, I lose all sense of direction.

After a few more turns and a few more miles, I feel truly lost.

I AM LOST. With the blindfold, I can't tell how long we've been driving, but my legs ache. I'm folded in on myself in the middle seat. Every time I accidently brush against the man on either side of me, I curl my arms in closer to my body. I clutch my hands together to keep them from trembling.

I squeeze my eyes shut to keep from crying.

The ride is silent. No chatter. No radio. Perhaps it's the quiet that makes the otherworldly buzzing against my ear more pronounced. The presence has been along for the ride this entire time, but I've only just now felt it. Perhaps because it wants me to.

Perhaps because it's Prescott's naughty sprite Frederick.

It caresses one cheek and then the other, a ghostly version of a kiss. Each time it lands, it sucks up a tear. It feels like an apology.

"Frederick," Prescott snaps.

Frederick whizzes around my head before shooting off. I'm left with a single word echoing in my mind.

Sorry.

The car swerves into a turn and then rocks up and over what feels like a very large speed bump. From there, the ride turns rough. I'm thrown against each man in the back seat more often than I'd like.

Then everything stops.

The lack of motion leaves me feeling off-balance. I miss the hum of the tires. I miss the stasis the ride offered, the place between before and after. The car doors open and spring air rushes in, the cool morning bathing my raw cheeks. Through the blindfold, I detect the hint of a sunrise.

One man grabs my arm and yanks me from the car, the force of it resonating in my shoulder. I stumble forward and reach for the blindfold only to have someone slap my hand away.

"You're kidding me," Prescott says. "It's hardly necessary at this point. Hold still, Katy."

Fingers tangle with the blindfold's knot and strands of my hair. The material slides from my eyes and I squint into the morning light. Prescott balls up the blindfold and tosses it on the ground.

"Your part in this is done," one man says to Prescott.

"Oh, yes. Of course it is." The corner of his mouth turns up, but it isn't the sort of smile you should trust. "Thank you for reminding me."

A bemused expression passes over the man's face before he grabs my arm again. "Let's get her inside."

"You first, gentlemen." Prescott sweeps an arm toward the door of a building.

No. A warehouse. I lurch forward under the insistence of my escorts. My feet trip each other up as I stare at the structure. I've seen this place before. It's the warehouse Selena showed me, as dingy and gray as her memory of it. The man yanks me forward, and I have just enough time to glance behind me at Prescott.

He winks.

That doesn't make me feel any better. He isn't along to save me. This isn't some sort of ruse. He is a world-class necromancer with an agenda.

The men lead me to the center of a large open area inside the warehouse and secure me to a support pole near its center, wrists bound behind me. I suspect I'm some sort of sacrificial lamb for whatever Prescott's agenda may be.

When Orson Yates emerges from a hallway directly across from me, I'm absolutely certain.

~

AS HE WALKS TOWARD ME, Orson's dress shoes tap against the concrete floor. The sound echoes against the walls and the ceiling far above our heads. Around the perimeter of the room, men are stationed a few feet apart. I've lost sight of Prescott. And although I'm not alone with Orson Yates, it very much feels that way.

He halts a few paces from me. Out of spitting range, I note. Not that I'm that petty.

Actually, I am.

"I'm so sorry that it's come to this," he says.

He doesn't sound the least bit sorry.

"You could've cooperated. You could've been a part of this, like your mother was."

Yes, my mother, who died under mysterious circumstances. I strain against the zip tie that binds my wrists. My shoulders ache and the plastic is so tight, my fingers feel numb. The pole is cold and rough against my spine. I don't know if the metal edge is jagged enough to cut through the tie, but I ease my wrists back and forth in the hope that it can.

"I will ask you this once," Orson says, his words measured. "Invoke the entity. Do it now."

He doesn't say *or else*. It's there in his tone. I suppose he could hurt me, starve me, but he can't do too much of either—I'm the only one here who knows the entity's name. I'm the only one who can invoke it. Maybe that has put me in danger.

But it's also the only thing keeping me safe.

I remain silent.

"Invoke the entity, Katy."

"And here I thought you were only going to ask her once." Prescott's voice slices through the quiet, that amused tone present as always. "You have to understand what motivates an individual. Clearly, you have no clue about Katy."

Prescott walks closer as he speaks, and Orson turns from me, enough that I can see the tic in his left eye spasm.

"If she wasn't impressed by your show of force, why on earth would she respond now as the victim of that force?" Prescott stops a few feet away from Orson and shakes his head in mock dismay. "You've bungled this from the start."

"I don't recall asking for your opinion."

"But I recall being asked for my help." Prescott strokes his chin. "You want to know how I would've handled it? I would've approached Malcolm. As a necromancer, he's far more susceptible to this sort of thing. Convince him that he'd not only win untold riches, but also the affections of a certain ghost catcher?" Prescott raises his hands, palms skyward. "Really, it's no more difficult than that."

At the mention of Malcolm, my stomach seizes. I want to glance around. I want to make certain he isn't here, but I don't dare.

"You must be confused," Orson says. "Only Katy knows the entity's name."

I try to make myself as small and inconsequential as possible. It hasn't occurred to either of them to ask me *how* I know the entity's name. Do they think it's something my grandmother told me? Did my mother somehow know its name—and died because of it?

My insides turn to ice. My legs tremble. I'm a terrible liar. If they think to ask me, I'm not sure I can concoct a convincing story. So I pray they won't think to ask.

"Courting Malcolm would've been a waste of time," Orson continues. "He's not ... clever enough to woo the name from her."

Prescott closes his eyes and rubs his temples. "Because courting

Katy has obviously been a good use of time. Rudimentary psychology, Orson. That's all this is."

"You want to see psychology in action?" Orson snaps his fingers. "Bring him out."

A door creaks open. Two of Orson's flunkies emerge dragging a third man between them. His head droops and his feet scrape along the floor. I can't see his face, but his hair is that deep ebony I know so well. This time when my stomach seizes, I think I may lose all the coffee I drank earlier.

I bite my lip to keep from crying out. When the men are halfway across the floor, Orson holds up a hand. They halt.

"Right there is fine, gentlemen."

They release Malcolm and he crumples to the floor, his head making a sickening thud when it strikes the concrete. It's then that I can't help it. It's then that I can't hold anything back. I forget my vow to be small and inconsequential. I scream.

"Malcolm!"

He pushes to his elbows before collapsing. His face is turned toward me now. The moment he registers my presence, his expression shifts from mere pain to something more, something darker. The defeat in his eyes is like nothing I've ever seen.

A line of bruises mars his cheekbones, and one eye is already swollen shut. His nose appears broken, and his bottom lip is split open and oozing blood. His right leg is twisted at an unnatural angle. I yank against the zip tie, but only succeed in making the plastic tighten around my wrists.

"There you go," Orson says. "Psychology 101."

"Orson—" Prescott begins.

"You doubt my methods? Let's see how well they work." Orson walks toward Malcolm. "It's too bad, really, that Nigel interfered all those years ago. Malcolm's not terribly clever, true." He kicks Malcolm in the stomach, and I flinch as if I've been struck. "But he would've made a good soldier."

"Leave the boy alone." Prescott's voice sounds steady, but it's very much a lone voice in this warehouse.

"Oh, I'm going to. There's someone else here who's eager to do the honors." Orson pulls a switchblade from his coat pocket and hands it to one of the men who dragged Malcolm into the room.

It's then that I take notice of this particular man. I was so focused on Malcolm that I missed the gleaming blond hair, the fading bruise beneath one eye. Carter Dupree accepts the switchblade and raises his gaze to stare straight at me.

He mouths something. My vision is so blurred by my tears that I don't know what he's said. A curse? A taunt?

"Slowly at first," Orson says. "We don't need to rush through this. It may take her a while to have a change of heart." He turns and addresses the men assembled around the room's perimeter. "Tell me, does anyone here know how long it takes to bleed out from a single slashed wrist?" Orson glances about, a schoolmaster expecting an answer. "No one? All right. Let's experiment." He turns his attention back to Malcolm. "Carter?"

For a moment, I swear Carter hesitates. For a moment, I think his lips move—in a whisper, in a prayer, in something nasty directed at Malcolm? Again, I can't tell. Salt from tears stings my cheeks. I throw myself against the pole, but it's a useless gesture.

When the tip of the knife touches Malcolm's wrist, I cry out.

"Stop! I'll invoke the entity. Just stop. Don't ... do this to him."

"Katy, no!" Malcolm's voice is ragged. He coughs, and his entire body shakes with the effort. "Once they have the entity, they'll only kill you ... and me. It will look like ... murder-suicide."

I jerk my head around, searching for Prescott. A glimpse of his expression should tell me whether or not this is true. But he's vanished, faded into the dark recesses of the warehouse, or perhaps he's left altogether.

"Carter..." Orson prompts.

Am I the only one who senses Carter's reluctance? The knife

tip again grazes Malcolm's wrist. He recoils. Orson steps forward and crushes Malcolm's fingers beneath the sole of his shoe.

"There you go, my boy," he says to Carter. "Have at it."

I won't let there be a third time.

"Stop! I agree. I'll invoke the entity."

Orson eases his foot from Malcolm's hand. "Ah, now, see? I knew you could be reasonable."

"Katy, it's not worth it." Malcolm pushes against the floor again, but he's too injured to even crawl.

I wait until he looks straight at me. "You're worth it," I say. "It'll be okay."

I don't know that, of course. In fact, I doubt very much that things will be okay. But once I've invoked the entity, we'll all have bigger problems to deal with. It won't be pleased; this I sense without even speaking its name. And by invoking it now, I may be killing us all.

But if, in the chaos, Malcolm might escape? Well, that would be worth the price.

"We're waiting," Orson says.

I jut my chin toward him. "Are you sure?"

"Am I *what?*" He laughs and then turns and encourages everyone present to do the same.

Everyone does, lockstep, the laughter rising to the pipes and vents over our heads. Everyone laughs—except Carter.

"Yes, my dear." Orson is still chuckling, his words thick with condescension. "I'm quite sure."

"It's not going to be like you think."

"I doubt you know what I think."

That, at least, is true. I won't even pretend to understand Orson Yates or what he wants.

"And I'm still waiting," he adds.

I take a deep breath. It doesn't do much to clear my head. My hands throb. I tug against the zip tie again, but there's no escaping it. I do my best to calm my heartbeat, to focus on that one word Mr. Carlotta's ghost shared with me so many months ago.

My mouth is dry, and I lick my lips. Then, I say the entity's name. "Momalcurkan."

I speak as softly as I can. No one needs to remember it, assuming any of us live to do so.

An unearthly stillness descends on the warehouse. At first, I think I've misspoken. I expected fire and brimstone, for the roof to be torn clear off. But something about this quiet feels more ominous than that.

"This isn't the time for pranks," Orson says. The sole of his shiny loafer inches toward Malcolm's hand. "Speak the name."

"She did."

The words are no more than a whisper, but they penetrate everything. I feel them vibrate beneath my feet, along the pole I'm tethered to, in the air around us.

"Then show yourself!" Orson demands.

I can't help it. I cringe against the pole. I know this entity, and it doesn't like to be bossed around.

Laughter ripples through the air, the sound of it menacing and cold. "You're right, my dear. I don't."

Like always, it can read my thoughts.

"I also dislike being invoked when I have no wish to be."

A spot on the cement floor liquefies. Dirt and concrete swirl to create what looks like a whirlpool. Its span grows, inch by inch. At first, I suspect I'm the only one who notices, but I can't stop staring to check. The rotation is hypnotic, and it reminds me of the mark this entity once made on my cheek. Although the blue cast of that has faded, I now feel it pulse beneath my skin.

Someone shouts. Orson spins around. I can't see his face, but I suspect he's gaping. He stumbles backward, away from the pool. Switchblade in hand, Carter darts off. The whirlpool expands until it touches the soles of Malcolm's feet.

I cry out, not that I can stop this thing. But perhaps I do, because the whirlpool's diameter remains static. Instead, a behemoth emerges from its center. The thing's surface is craggy and dark, like it has been formed from something elemental, from pieces of the Earth's mantle, or something much older than the Earth.

It turns its eyes toward me. They glow like lava, and its gaze burns. "I know you prefer a different incarnation, my dear," it says, "but I have work to do."

"Now!" Orson shouts.

From the perimeter, one of the men comes running. He must be one of Orson's necromancers. From his gait and the way he spreads his arms and opens his mouth, I know this:

He must be trying to capture the entity.

As soon as I think it, another thought strikes me:

He must be the most foolish person on earth.

But his aim is perfect. The craggy mass vanishes the moment the two collide. A grin spreads across the man's face, a look of undeniable pride at what he's accomplished.

"Well done!" Orson calls out. "Stand by, everyone. Stand by. We may need to do a handoff in short order."

The man takes one step and then another before he starts to stagger. What happens next is difficult to track. His hair fades from brunette to gray to pure white. He ages a good sixty years in a matter of seconds, taut jawline sagging into jowls, folds of skin obscuring his eyes.

He reels, his gaze accusing Orson before it lands on me.

I mouth, "I'm sorry."

He nods once before a bright flame consumes him. The entity peels away from the man a moment before his form disintegrates into a pile of gray ash.

"How many more children do you plan to throw at me, Orson?" The entity oozes forward. "You have very few whose desire is pure enough to hold me for more than a few moments. Indeed, there are very few in this room who could hold me at all."

Orson casts about. It's a jittery motion, and his gaze is just as frantic. From where I'm tethered, it's hard to see the perimeter, but I get the sense of people slipping away, the soft echo of footfalls down some distant corridor.

Certainly Orson is one of those whose desire is pure enough. But he simply stands there, mouth open, hand extended toward the entity as if he could hold it in place while he conjures up Plan B.

"Is my desire pure enough?" a voice asks.

The entity swings its head toward the far corner of the room. From the shadows, Prescott emerges. He strides forward, looking as pulled together and confident as he did on my sidewalk six days ago.

"Ah, Prescott Jones." The entity draws out the s, like the hiss of a snake, and I think yes, that more than fits Prescott at the moment. "You are opportunistic and conniving—admirable traits for a necromancer."

"But is my desire pure enough?"

"I think you know it is." The entity glides forward.

The contrast between its movements and its form is disconcerting. I blink, trying to fight my sudden dizzy spell, but I slump against the pole instead.

"But here's my conundrum," the entity continues. "There are others in this room whose desire is just as pure, perhaps even more so. Why should I limit myself to you?"

"Because you know it's going to be good." Prescott hasn't lost his poise, and the grin he gives this thing is downright seductive.

"Yes, it would be. I'll grant you that."

I'm so caught up in this exchange that the sensation of fingertips moving along my arms takes me by surprise. I yelp and jerk against the pole. I don't know who's behind me, but I want nothing to do with them.

"Shh, Katy. It's me." The words are low and tense, but spoken with a slight southern drawl that I recognize.

Carter Dupree?

"I thought—" I begin, not certain exactly what I thought, only that I'd never see Carter again.

"That I ran off like a coward?"

Well, yes, and that.

"Next on the agenda," he says. "First, I'm going to cut the tie. Hold still. It's so tight I'm afraid I'll end up cutting your skin."

I glance about, nervous someone will notice us, and that someone will alert Orson. But everyone is focused on the entity and Prescott and their little passion play. Orson stands like a man transfixed, one hand still extended, the other in his suit coat pocket. I can't see his face, so I don't know if he's concocting another plan or simply mourning his lost chance at the entity.

"Why are you doing this?" I whisper.

Carter doesn't respond. All I hear is the scrape of blade against plastic.

"You're on the list, aren't you?" I say. "How many people does the entity have to burn through to get to you?"

"Not enough. But, yeah, I'm on the list. But that's not why I'm doing this."

"Then—?"

"I don't want to go through life as a pathetic little shit."

In that confession, I hear the echo of Belinda. It's exactly the sort of thing she'd say, and Carter is exactly the sort of person she'd say it to.

Prescott has taken a step closer to the entity. His arms are hanging loose at his sides, but the tips of his fingers are twitching. He looks like an athlete about to perform a major stunt.

The knife slips through the zip tie and the blade skitters down the pole. A clang echoes. I hold my breath and Carter ducks, but no one glances our way.

"Don't move." He grabs my wrists so I can't pull my hands to me. "You still need to look tied up."

I know he's right, but rush of blood into my fingers is excruciating, like tiny needles of fire. Carter rubs my hands between his, his touch oddly tender.

"There," he says. "Better? Can you move your fingers?"

I try, bending the fingers and frowning with the effort.

"You should be okay in a couple of minutes," he says, "and then you can do what you need to do."

"What I need to do?" I repeat the words, but I don't know what they mean.

Before us, in the center of the warehouse, the entity and Prescott appear locked in negotiation. Their words are too quiet for the rest of us to hear. Orson has crept even closer, although his gaze darts around the perimeter now and then. I suspect he's looking for someone in particular, someone who's standing right behind me.

"You need to capture that thing," Carter says.

"I ... what?"

"Think of the power it has. Think of the kind of power Orson wants to wield. He wants it all: money, political sway. The world's bad enough—we don't need him adding to its problems."

"Prescott—?"

"Do *you* trust him?"

I barely know him, and since he's the reason I'm here, I can't say my trust extends all that far.

"I don't know what he'd do with that sort of power," I admit. But, judging by the way Prescott's grinning, I can't suppose it's anything good.

"Me neither," Carter says. "That's a problem. Then there's you. I don't know what you would do, but I know what you wouldn't. That's enough."

"But I can't—"

"There's no one else, Katy. No one but you."

He's right, of course. Malcolm's too injured. Besides, he was once this thing's willing sacrifice. I'm not sure he's capable of capturing it.

"Assuming I can capture it and it doesn't burn through me, then what?"

"Get it away from Orson."

"I don't know how," I say. "I'm not a necromancer. I don't know how to capture it."

"Just focus on what you want most. Don't second-guess. Go with that one thought—that's the pure desire—and then do what Perry did."

"Was that—?" I nod toward the pile of ash.

"Yeah."

"Were you friends?"

"Kind of." He rubs my hands one last time and then gives my fingers a squeeze. "Good luck."

He's gone before I can crane my neck to watch him leave.

Both Orson and Prescott are focused on the entity. I glance around, but no one is guarding the perimeter of the warehouse anymore. Slowly, I ease my hands in front of me and then, at last, rub my wrists and fingers myself. The skin is raw and swollen. I flinch at my own touch. My fingers still feel thick and numb.

Orson has eased even closer. He's given up looking for Carter, and his full attention is on the entity. Prescott's gaze has never strayed. They've both forgotten about me, but there's one person here who hasn't.

Malcolm.

My eyes meet his. He tries to push to his elbows again, but his arms tremble and he collapses. It takes all my willpower not to rush to him, gather him close, and find a way to get us out of here. For a moment, I contemplate doing just that. The two of us walking out the door and not looking back. We would leave this mess behind us.

The thought of it brings a spate of tears to my eyes.

With gritty palms I push away the tears and take a step forward, not toward Malcolm but the entity.

He shuts his eyes and shakes his head. "Katy, don't."

I don't know if he says these words or if I merely hear them in my head.

"I have to."

"Please." He tries to push up again, but he's far too injured.

I know that if he could, he'd follow me. This might be the only time when I'm glad he can't. Someone will find him and take him to a hospital. He'll be safe.

"Goodbye," I whisper. "I love you."

Then I turn toward the entity and break into a run.

CHAPTER 6

I'M A FEW SECONDS into my sprint when I know it's no good. My thoughts splinter into half a dozen, and then a dozen. And then I lose count of all the things I want. Because I want it all: I want Malcolm healed; I want Springside safe; I want all my ghosts back. I want Nigel and Sadie happily married.

My hiking boots clomp against the cement floor. This is hardly a stealth attack. First Orson and then Prescott turn at my approach. Orson looks livid. Despite the dim light of the warehouse, his face appears bright red. He must know it was Carter who betrayed him, cut me free. Prescott holds up a hand as if he means to stop my advance.

"Katy, no! You don't know what you're doing." Prescott takes a step, a move meant to block my access to the entity.

In that moment, Orson barrels into him, slamming Prescott to the ground and clearing my path to the entity. Like that, I'm there. I rise up on the tips of my boots, spread my arms wide, open my mouth, and dive forward.

My world shifts as if I've plunged into deep water. I panic, claw at the air. The warehouse around me is bright, as if someone has switched on all the lights or opened the roof to let the sunshine stream in. I see minute cracks in the cement and imperfections in the ceiling's paint job.

I whirl and stumble. I want to cry out, but can't find my voice.

Shh. Relax, my dear.

The voice echoes around me, through me. I spin, inspecting the far corners of the warehouse that I know, logically, I shouldn't be able to see, but I can't find the source of the words that echo in my head.

"I don't know what to do." I half-cry, half-speak these words. No one's listening. Orson and Prescott are circling each other. Orson has what looks like a walkie-talkie in one hand and what is definitely a pistol in the other.

Right now, you need to run.

"But—"

You're in no shape to take on Orson's reinforcements, my dear, or his bullets. So run, and believe you can run faster than you ever have before.

The panic subsides just enough that I can see at least a dozen men file into the warehouse. Orson shouts and gestures with the pistol. My gaze zooms in on Malcolm, still on the floor.

"Malcolm—" I begin.

I guarantee his safety, but I can only do so if you run.

I have no choice. I do what the voice inside my head commands.

I run.

I FEEL the sun on my face, my hair streaming behind me. Grass and trees and fences blur. Tears flow from my eyes, carve tracks to my ears.

I don't think it's possible to run this fast. Somehow, I am.

I run until the warehouse is no longer even a dot on the horizon behind me. I run cross-country where no car can follow. I find myself in a wooded area, pine needles raking my cheeks and bare arms, soft earth cushioning my footsteps.

Slow down ... it's time to slow down.

I can't. All I can think of is the mess I've left behind, the fact that I left Malcolm, and yet I can't get my legs to stop moving.

My power might be supernatural, but you are very human, my dear. You will hurt yourself if you keep up this pace.

I stumble, my arms flailing, and the jerky movements slow my momentum. The words echoing in my head slow me down even further until, at last, I clutch a slender birch tree for support.

I cling to it, the papery bark rustling beneath my grip. I take heaving breaths, and I feel the miles I've run in the ache of my legs, the blisters on my feet.

I wait.

My heartbeat slows. The sweat that pours off my skin cools me until I shiver. It's good to stand still, to clutch this slender birch. It's almost peaceful. But the anticipation of what comes next haunts me. Will it hurt? I think of Perry and how his eyes accused us.

Oh, yes. It will hurt.

My dear, what are you doing?

"Waiting."

Whatever for?

"For you to burn through me."

Laughter reverberates in my mind. It's one thing to have someone laugh *at* you. But inside you? I shake my head as if that would dislodge this thing.

Let's review this morning's events, shall we?

"I don't think I have a choice."

Oh, my dear, I knew you'd be a delight. Now, tell me. Why do you think I'd burn through you?

"My desire wasn't pure enough."

Orson's certainly wasn't. He wants too many things—and he knows it.

Why do you think he lined up so many children in an attempt to hold me? There's no way he can. He wants that which he can never have.

"Immortality?"

That would be in the realm of possibility. No, he wants youth, specifically his own youth. That's something I'm unable to give.

"Then how...?" I'm not sure what I'm asking. How was Orson going to use the entity if he couldn't control it himself?

He thinks he can leverage me the way he would an ordinary ghost. Up to a point, he may have been correct. But not just any necromancer can hold me.

"Is that where Prescott comes in?"

Ah, Prescott Jones. Now there's a necromancer with an unwavering desire.

Something clicks. I see what it was that Orson wanted all along. To use me, both to call the entity and have it reside within me—to do his bidding, whatever that would've entailed.

"So when I wouldn't cooperate and join his club, he looked for another way?"

Precisely.

"And Prescott convinced him he was that way?"

Opportunistic and conniving. Admirable traits for a necromancer.

I don't even need to ask. Of course Prescott never had any intention of honoring the deal he made. Orson was simply a means to an end.

And so was I.

I'm not sure where this leaves me, other than stranded in some unfamiliar woods, waiting for a powerful entity to burn through me. I wonder if anyone will be able to find my pile of ash.

So, tell me, my dear, what was it that you wanted?

"I wanted everyone to be safe, Malcolm, Springside, the ghosts. I want Nigel and Sadie married." I glance around, gauge the slant of the sun through the trees. It's only hours until the ceremony, assuming there will still be one. "I kept thinking what might happen to the world if Orson or Prescott captured you and ... see? Too many things."

That laugh reverberates in my head again. *My dear, that's all part of the same desire. Of those assembled in that rather nasty warehouse, yours was the purest desire of all.*

I'm not sure I believe that. In fact, I'm expecting a trick.

Ever the skeptic.

I sigh. It's bad enough that this thing could always guess what I was thinking—now it has a front row seat.

It's part of the pact.

"I'm not a necromancer."

In this particular case, you are, and we have a pact. I admit, it's a unique experience. Everything inside here is so ... benign.

"That sounds insulting."

Not necessarily. Besides, benign isn't banal. If I've been used for evil in the past, it's because I've been captured by evil men—and women. Women can be powerful necromancers, present company included. But they don't do a great deal of capturing. I've always wondered why that is.

"They're too busy doing other things?" I suggest.

The entity laughs again. I press a hand against my head to stop the throbbing.

"Not so loud."

Forgive me, my dear.

"And why so polite?"

In part because we've made a pact. I ... adjust my persona depending upon the necromancer.

"Do I want to know what your Prescott persona would be?"

In a word? No.

This time, I laugh. And I can't believe I'm laughing, that this thing has made me laugh, that it's made me curious. I can't say I like it. It once took Malcolm. It nearly killed Nigel. And just this morning, I watched it destroy someone.

But I'm intrigued.

And scared.

But not fearful. I know, in this moment at least, that it won't hurt me—or anyone I love. That's something.

"Now what?"

I believe you're due at a wedding.

"And Malcolm?"

We can return to the warehouse. Anyone with bullets or an agenda is now gone.

I turn to face the way I came, a hand still gripping the birch as if it's the only thing holding me up.

"I don't know where to go."

Oh, but I do.

"Do I need to run again?"

That would be fastest.

I retie my hiking boots, adjust my socks, and then pull in a deep breath.

"All right," I say. "I'm ready."

You've been ready for a while, my dear. It's about time you accepted your ability as a necromancer.

I run so fast that the air buzzes in my ears. I run so fast I can pretend I haven't heard the entity's words.

THE WAREHOUSE HAS the feel of a building long abandoned. I walk through the area where I was held, but the space is empty. There's the cut plastic tie and strip of duct tape hanging loosely from the support pole, as if someone has torn something away. On the floor a few feet away there's blood.

"Malcolm?"

My voice bounces back at me, too loud, too desperate.

"Is he here?"

I direct this question at the entity, but the presence inside my head is oddly silent. No, it's more than that. The entity is no longer there. I don't know when, exactly, it peeled away from me, but I can tell now that it has.

I turn in a slow circle, as if I could somehow spot it in the warehouse.

It's gone, but instead of relief, nothing but dread fills me.

My footfalls follow me as I walk the perimeter of the space. Every few steps I spin around, certain someone is following me.

No one is there.

The wail doesn't register at first, although I'm not sure why. There's nothing else to hear but my own breathing and the sound of my hiking boots striking the concrete. The cry is quiet and plaintive, but also familiar. I halt in my trek, tilt my head, and listen.

The sound grows louder, as if a chorus of voices has joined it. I know this cry. I've heard this cry all my life.

Ghosts.

They're here—I look around—somewhere. I jog toward the door Orson's men dragged Malcolm through. I push and it opens slowly, hinges creaking. I grope the wall for a light switch. The overhead lamp flickers on and its hiss and crackle fill the air in between the cries of the ghosts.

The corridor is lined with doors, each shut. I try the first, and while the handle turns, I can't open the door. That's when I'm struck with a double sensation—a ward, warning me to back off, and the shimmery outline of a containment field.

I ignore the first and concentrate on the second. Within moments, its hold wavers and then shatters. The door flies open. An otherworldly blast knocks me against the opposite wall as a group of ghosts streams out.

Several ghosts head straight for the open air at the end of the hallway. A few swirl around me, peppering me with icy kisses. I reach out a hand as if I could pet them. These are Springside ghosts, every last one. I jump to my feet and start in on the other doors.

I've just removed the containment field from the last door when the ghost inside comes barreling out. This one is so strong that we tumble across the floor. Even with the noise of my boots thumping, I hear familiar ghostly laughter.

"Delilah?"

She surrounds me so completely I'm encased in mist.

I know I won't understand her answer, but I ask anyway. "How did they catch you again?"

Her form vibrates, and it's dark and angry. But then she swoops around me, plants a kiss on my cheek, and shoves me—hard.

"What the—"

She keeps shoving, and this is no sprite I'm dealing with. The only option I have is to trip over my hiking boots and try to figure out where she wants me to go. She encourages me down a second hallway, more dank and dark than the first. I slap the wall for the light and it barely illuminates a path in front of me.

The doors here are open, all but one. Something about that feels wrong. I stop and peer inside a room. It's several degrees colder than the air in the hallway, and there's what I can only describe as psychic residue within its space.

I think of Chief Ramsey's ghost, how scared and scarred it was, and wonder if it spent time in one of these rooms.

Delilah won't let me contemplate that for long. She shoves again, and again, I trip down the hallway.

The door at the very end is locked, not with a containment field, but truly locked. I rattle the handle to no avail. I don't have anything with me to open it with, but Delilah continues to push me against the door.

"Okay, okay. I get it," I say to her. "Just let me..."

What? I test the door again. It swings inward, or would if it were unlocked. The wood sounds hollow when I knock on it. The handle is flimsy and the lock jangles. I consider my boots, the door, and how much space there is for a running start. Enough, I decide. I back up, push off the opposite wall, and aim my heel at a spot below the lock.

The thud echoes, but nothing budges. The jolt makes my leg

ache from heel to knee and all the way to my hip. Delilah swirls around me. I hold up a hand before she can crash into me again.

"A moment." I suck in a breath. "I'll try again in a moment."

I back up for another run. I wince as my boot connects with the door, but this time something gives. The wood splinters. I kneel at the door and rattle the handle again.

Something clicks. I'm so relieved I won't need to take another run at the door that I let my forehead rest against the wood. The door creaks open and I fall forward with it.

There, on the floor in front of me, is Malcolm.

I crawl to him. My fingers find a pulse at his throat, and his soft exhale warms my cheek. I roll him gently onto his back and check his injuries.

At first, I can't see any. I squint, then stagger to my feet and switch on the overhead bulb. It doesn't add much to the light already streaming in from the hall, but there's enough that I can check for all the wounds I saw earlier.

They don't exist.

Well, not entirely. Beneath where his lip was split open, there's the tiniest of scars. The bruises along his cheekbones have faded to a dull yellow, and I can only see them because I know to look for them. A tiny bump mars his near-perfect nose. His leg, so mangled earlier, appears straight, resting as it should on the ground.

His dress shirt is tattered and torn and covered with rust-colored stains. I peel it back carefully to reveal his ribs.

Here, too, are only the remnants of wounds.

I sit back on my heels, a hand still anchored to Malcolm's chest. Instead of relief, terror zips through me. I can't account for this, and I search for the source of this magic, for the trick, the trap.

There's nothing but Delilah's soft swishing about.

"Thank you," I say to her.

Healed or not, I can't imagine what would've happened to Malcolm if I'd left him behind. I brush strands of hair from his forehead and then stand.

I have someone else to thank.

I step into the hallway. Except for Delilah and a few other ghosts milling about, I'm alone. I know that. I say the words out loud anyway.

"Thank you." I direct the words toward the sky, although why the entity should be up—and not down—I don't know. "I wanted Malcolm healed, and you did so." I squeeze my eyes shut to stop the tears flirting at their corners. I don't know why it means so much that he's whole and well and will be able to stand up for Nigel today, but it does.

"Thank you," I say one last time before ducking back into the room.

I FIND A KITCHEN AREA, some bottled water, and grab a fistful of paper towels. I sit at Malcolm's side and bathe his face and hands in the cool water until his eyelids start to flutter. All at once, his eyes fly open and he shields his face with a hand to block the glare.

"I'm sorry," I say. "I had to turn on the light to make sure you were okay."

"Katy?" His voice is rough and full of disbelief.

"It's me. I'm here."

"Katy?" He pushes up slowly, first to his elbows, and then to sitting.

"Yes, it's me. I'm here." I sound like an idiot, repeating myself. But giddiness bubbles up inside me because Malcolm is awake and whole.

He touches his temple and winces as though he expects it to hurt. He probes his cheekbones, his nose, and runs his hands along his ribcage. Gingerly, he bends his knee and inspects his shin.

"I ... remember being a whole lot more injured than this."

I nod. "You were."

"And I remember thinking"—he squeezes his eyes shut—"that I'd never see you again."

"Do you still hurt?"

I'm contemplating a dash for the kitchen area to search for some ice. In fact, I'm crouching to do just that when Malcolm's fingers wrap around my wrist, anchoring me in place. His skin feels right against mine, not cold and clammy, not heated with fever.

"If I think about it," he says, "I can remember it, remember them beating me, but it feels more like it happened in a dream than real life. I didn't know who they were or why they were doing it until they dragged me into that room and I heard you."

He cringes again, and I think I must as well. That's not something I care to remember. But his pained expression fades and he brushes a strand of hair from my cheek. His touch is so gentle it's like he's afraid I might shatter.

"Did they hurt you?" he asks, and something about his voice tells me he's bracing for the worst possible answer.

I hold out my wrists. "Only where they…"

I turn my hands first one way and then the other. I feel the ache from the zip tie, but the burns are gone. Malcolm holds my wrist close and runs a finger along the line where the plastic bit into my skin.

"Right here," he says. "This is from where they tied you up. You can barely see it."

His finger traces a path that sends a shiver through me. He tugs me close so I'm in his lap, his arms around mine. It's safe here in this pocket of warmth he's created, even in this dank room, even if the aroma of stale sweat and scotch reminds me of how we both got here.

"What happened today?" he asks. "What happened after they forced you to invoke the entity?"

I exhale and sag against his chest. "I'm still not sure. It's almost like I need a scorecard to keep track. First, Prescott betrayed Orson, then Orson had a gun—"

"Are you serious?" A gun? He was going to shoot Prescott?"

"I think so, at some point. But Prescott and the entity seemed to be negotiating, and Orson just stood there. It was weird."

"Oh," Malcolm says. "Of course."

"Of course what?"

"A ghost or entity is most vulnerable right after making a pact with a necromancer. The deal must be set. If something happens to the necromancer before that, things ... get out of balance. It's possible Orson could've contained it without too much effort. He was waiting for Prescott to make a move."

"And the entity was waiting for me."

His arms tighten around mine. "What happened, exactly?"

The story comes out much like that of a dream, nonsensical except to the dreamer. As I speak, I feel Malcolm react as if what I'm saying makes sense. He nods, murmurs something to himself. When I've finished, he shifts and takes my face in his hands.

"Where's the entity now?" he asks.

"I don't know. I got back here and—" I wave a hand toward the door and start to turn that way, but Malcolm tugs me back.

"Look at me, Katy. Look at me right in the eyes."

I relent and allow myself to simply stare into those dark eyes of his. In the dim light they appear nearly black. I want to erase the worry I see there, but for the moment hold still.

He searches my face, runs his finger along my left cheek. From the way he traces the mark so perfectly, I know the faded blue reminder of that encounter remains.

"Do you sense it?" he asks.

"No. I got back here and it was like it had vanished. Delilah helped me find you—"

"Damn, they caught her again?"

"They did." I search the air around us for something other-worldly, but don't detect anything strong enough to be Delilah.

"She might be gone by now, and even though it had vanished, I thanked the entity for healing you—"

"Wait." Malcolm scoots back as if he needs to survey my whole being. "You *thanked* the entity?"

"It healed you. Malcolm, you were—"

"Close to dead. I know." His lips compress into a hard line, but almost immediately soften. "Maybe that's it," he says. "By thanking the entity, you honored the pact. It needed to get away from Orson just as much as you did. It healed me, and you." He brushes the tender underside of my wrist with his lips. "You thanked it and set it free."

"Do you think that's it?"

"Maybe? I don't know. Reginald might, and so might Nigel."

"Who's getting married in ... how many hours?"

Malcolm scoots me back and pushes to stand. When he offers a hand and I take it, he pulls me into a hug.

"Cell phone?" he asks.

"Nope."

"Same here."

"There's a kitchen area. There might be a landline."

Without another word, we leave the room. On our way out, I shut off the light and close the door. It seems like such a silly thing to do, and the hinges screech as if in agreement. But it feels good to shut all that behind us.

In the kitchen, Malcolm picks up the receiver of the phone that's hanging on the wall. The whole thing sheds a layer of dust. He blows on the keypad and creates another cloud.

But then he turns to me, one of his sweet, dark-roast grins on his face.

"Dial tone," is all he says.

CHAPTER 7

"R EALLY?" MALCOLM GLANCES at me and raises an eyebrow. "Do we warrant a police escort?"

I don't know if we warrant it, but one is winding its way up the long road to the warehouse. The lights of the patrol car are flashing. It's leading the convoy, followed by Reginald's Land Rover. Dust billows behind them, painting the clear air a dull brown.

We've only just stepped into the sunlight after spending the last hour huddled over the phone in the kitchen area. We took turns relating the tale, from Malcolm's kidnapping—in the guise of a faked pizza delivery—to mine, to the entity's appearance and then everyone's disappearance.

Nigel's and Belinda's still-panicked voices filled the line, punctuated by Reginald's more measured tone. We learned how Nigel had found my thermos and called Chief Ramsey when he couldn't find Malcolm, how Belinda had called Nigel when she discovered the guest room Carter was staying in was vacant and I wasn't at home. How Reginald had sent ghosts to track down Prescott, Malcolm, and me—without any luck.

During all of that, Malcolm held me close, his cheek next to mine, his lips brushing the sensitive skin at the corner of my mouth. His sigh was half worry and half relief, but toward the end of the call, held nothing but elation.

Now, as we stand here in the sun, I feel it too, even if a patrol car is making its way toward me.

Both vehicles pull to a stop in front of us. Nigel and Belinda spill out of the Land Rover. Nigel staggers a little before lurching toward Malcolm and gripping him in a strong hug.

Belinda captures me in a hug of her own before pulling out her cell phone and aiming it first at the two of us and then at Malcolm and Nigel.

"See?" she says into the camera. "They're both safe."

A strangled cry, a flash of pink, and I know that it's Sadie on the other end.

"I don't know what you said to Carter, but if it wasn't for you," I say to Belinda, "I'm not sure what would've happened."

"Right. *Please.*" Belinda rolls her eyes. "I'm not the one facing down power-obsessed necromancers and scary lava entities."

I open my mouth to protest—because really, without her help, without Carter's change of heart, we wouldn't all be standing here —but she shushes me with a single glance, her *don't cross the home-coming queen* look.

So I don't.

Nigel is holding Malcolm at arm's length now, surveying him for any telltale injuries. "I don't care if you pay me in cups of Katy's coffee from now on. Just don't ... don't go getting yourself killed."

Their second hug is less frantic, but more healing. Malcolm is murmuring something that sounds like "I'm sorry."

I feel the urge to apologize too, although I don't know to whom or why. Then Chief Ramsey steps into view and I know the answer.

He doesn't speak, simply walks toward me and extends my thermos in one hand.

"Yours, I believe," he says.

I nod and take it from him.

"I think I remember saying to call if something out of the ordinary happened?" His tone isn't so much accusatory as it is disappointed and sad.

"I know," I say, and my words are miserable. "It was a trick. I thought it was Malcolm who was texting me."

I don't elaborate. Chief wouldn't believe most of the story anyway.

He pulls something from his pocket and hands it to me. My cell phone. My mouth drops open and I stare up at him in question.

"You need to change your code," he says. "*Coffee* is too obvious."

I turn the phone over in my hands. The last time I held it, I tucked it into the field kit, which ended up on the floor of a dark sedan. "But how...?"

"Someone turned it in," Chief says as if reading my thoughts.

"Someone?"

He shrugs. "Placed it on Penny's desk when she wasn't looking."

"You don't have any surveillance footage of that?"

"Maybe I do, maybe I don't, and maybe, at this point, it doesn't matter."

And maybe he's right.

"Unless we're going to talk about pressing charges."

"Charges?"

"Kidnapping, for one."

I shake my head, not in denial, but because I'm at a loss. "I wouldn't know where to start. I don't think anyone involved will be easy to find."

"That's not your job." He jabs a finger at me. "You got that? Not. Your. Job."

"Can it wait until after the wedding?"

My words find their mark. A rare and genuine smile brightens

Chief's face. "It can," he says. "Besides, I need to walk the bride down the aisle."

Nigel's at my side then, and his expression steals all my thoughts. I forget to thank Chief. I can't do anything but deal with the man in front of me, the man I very much want Sadie to marry this afternoon.

"Katy ... I'm so sorry. I know how Prescott is, but I never imagined he had any sort of agenda, otherwise, I would've never—"

"It's not your fault."

"If you don't, I mean, if you'd rather not—"

"Not what? Not be part of the wedding?" Once again, my mouth hangs open. I glance about, hoping for some help.

Malcolm's eyes are uncertain, and his skin holds a pallor. Belinda frowns. Reginald steps forward, abandoning his spot in the shade of the Land Rover. He places a hand on Nigel's shoulder, securing him in place.

"My friend, you're handling this badly." Reginald turns to me. "What Nigel means is, he'd understand if all you want to do is return home and not attend the wedding tonight."

"But your wedding saved me." I point at Malcolm. "It saved us. It's all I could think about. Carter said I had to hold one thought in my head to catch the entity, but I couldn't. It was Malcolm and you and Sadie, and everyone. My last thought was about the wedding. But it worked, and now that's all I want to do."

Reginald places a gentle hand on my shoulder. "In other words, she is very much looking forward to the wedding."

I can't help but crack a smile, and Nigel gives me one in return.

"Will you?" Nigel says to Reginald.

"Of course, with her permission." He turns to me. "Katrina Lindstrom, I ask your permission to search for the entity. Do you grant it?"

I nod. "Yes, please. I think it's gone, but I don't know for certain."

"See? She's willing," he says to Nigel. "A good sign."

Reginald positions himself across from me. His form blocks the sun. He's as big as Chief Ramsey, and I sense Chief himself stir, move forward, as if he doesn't quite trust Reginald.

As Malcolm did, he takes my face in his hands and stares into my eyes. His scrutiny unnerves me. I want to pull away but, at the same time, resist that urge. This is important. And if the entity isn't truly gone, I want to know.

"Malcolm did this," I say. "He checked."

"I have more years of practice than your young beau."

A blush erupts in my cheeks, one I'm certain Reginald can feel beneath his fingers. At last his gaze shifts from my eyes and centers on my left cheek. He turns my face toward the sun and draws a thumb along the perimeter of the faded blue spot.

At last he steps back. "I detect nothing."

Nigel exhales. Malcolm's eyes brighten, his natural color returning.

"That's no guarantee," Reginald adds. "This is an entity, and an ancient one at that, not a ghost. The rules differ."

"You only deal with ghosts?" I ask.

"I try to. They can be capricious, but their wants are few and often predictable." He nods to the thermos I'm still clutching. "As you already know. Dealing with an entity like this is more like dealing with a very powerful, very exacting human being. You mentioned that you thanked it?"

"I did."

"Perhaps that was all it needed."

"Then we're good to go?" Belinda strides forward. She surveys each of us, hands on hips. "Because there's a wedding in a few hours and a maid of honor in desperate need of a makeover."

Nigel laughs and pulls both Malcolm and me into a hug. Reginald looks serene, if somber, and even Chief manages a smile.

Before we leave, I uncap the thermos. Steam rises into the air and against my face. The Kona blend is perfect drinking temperature. The thermos itself is one of a set of precision-made German ones designed to do just this—keep the coffee hot for as long as possible.

When no one is looking, I set the thermos on the ground, cap at its side. I'll buy a new set, I decide, to replace the one I've lost. And I will leave this one behind because I don't need a reminder of this place.

As we drive off in Reginald's Land Rover, I turn to peer out the back. A glimmer streams from the dark recesses of the warehouse. And around the thermos, I swear I see at least one ghost dance.

CHAPTER 8

THE BRIDAL CHORUS might be the most wonderful thing I've heard all day. I've just reached the makeshift altar when the first strains fill the Springside Community Center ballroom.

Nigel is a statue as he waits for Sadie to walk down the aisle. Only the slight tapping of fingertips against his thigh betrays his true state. His pure white hair matches his tuxedo shirt, and the tux itself looks tailor-made for him.

And then there's his brother. I sneak a glance at Malcolm and feel my cheeks burn brighter than my dress. He's always pulled together, but this takes it up a level. His hair gleams like ebony, and between the jacket, shirt, and bowtie, he looks as if he's stepped out of a fashion magazine. I predict there will be a long line of women at the reception wanting to dance with him.

He catches my gaze and gives me a wink. Then he tilts his head as if he's considering me, the ice-pink bridesmaid dress, and the single pink rose I'm carrying. He raises an eyebrow, nods, and mouths the word, "Nice."

And I'm blushing all over again.

I know when Sadie begins to walk down the aisle on the arm of

Chief Ramsey, because a gasp goes up behind me. I'm not supposed to turn to look, so I don't. Nigel appears petrified in place.

And then she's there, the blush-colored wedding gown like pink foam, the two dozen pink roses in her bouquet, and the pink highlights in her salt-and-pepper hair bathing her in their glow. When Nigel turns and sees her, his entire demeanor changes. The smile vanquishes the worry from his face, and the love in his eyes is so intense, I feel it like a stab in my stomach.

This. They almost lost this. *We* almost lost this. This moment. I suck in a breath and I swear I don't release it until after Sadie and Nigel have recited their vows, after the judge has pronounced them husband and wife, after Nigel has kissed Sadie and they're heading back down the aisle in a shower of rose petals.

I nearly sag against Malcolm when he takes my arm and we follow them.

"You okay?" he whispers.

I manage a nod.

"Fair warning," he continues. "I have it on good authority that the bridal bouquet will be headed your way like a heat-seeking missile."

That makes me laugh.

"You're beautiful," he says.

"So are you."

"But you know what?" He leans down, his lips next to my ear in an almost-kiss. "My favorite is still the skater skirt with the hiking boots."

SADIE'S SPRITES have behaved themselves for the entire ceremony and reception—until now. I allowed them to attend as long as they didn't cause trouble. But they have all the willpower and attention span of a pair of toddlers. I track them overhead as they flit among the ballroom's light fixtures. When they land on the floor they are the "breeze" that kicks up the rose petals. When a centerpiece on one of the tables starts to wobble, I know I will need to act soon.

I scan the dance floor. Sadie is dancing with Nigel, her head on his shoulder, his lips in her hair. Belinda is swaying in the arms of Jack Carlotta, who drove down from Minneapolis for the ceremony. Her eyes are closed, her expression content, even if her smile is wistful.

Maybe because at a table not too far away, Gregory and Terese are sitting side by side, fingers laced. Her gaze tracks the sprites as they careen around the room, and her face is lit with amusement. Gregory? He's oblivious, as usual.

I'm not sure I like these new-old arrangements, but I'm not sure I dislike them either.

Malcolm is executing a stately foxtrot with one of the women from the long-term care facility. There really is a line, and where he's finding the energy—after everything—to dance with each of them amazes me.

But it means I can sneak into the kitchen area and dig out the carafe of Kona blend that I promised Sadie's two sprites.

The kitchen is still in chaos, with dishes everywhere, slices of cake wrapped up for later, empty bottles of champagne and sparkling grape juice. Splotches of gravy speckle the countertops. Somewhere in this mess is a bowl of sugar, and in the fridge a container of half and half. Sadie's sprites like their coffee sweet and light—to match their personalities—and will refuse anything else. If I'm not precise, I'll end up with a coffee-colored bridesmaid dress.

I line up sugar, spoons, two cups, and the carafe itself. I'm turning for the refrigerator when an otherworldly blast propels me against it. My body thumps against the side, hip striking the door handle. I'm pinned in place, cheek against the cool surface, my hands immobile.

I can't move, can't speak. I take tiny breaths since at the moment, I can barely breathe. Icy fingers clutch my throat and tighten their hold inch by inch. It's a slow thing, this choking off of my air—and deliberate. I know this thing that has me in its grip, and it wants that acknowledgement.

It's the ghost of Harold Lancaster.

I open my mouth to scream, to call for help, to alert Malcolm, but nothing emerges. With eyes closed, I work to contain my panic and conserve what little air I have. It's not letting me speak, so I can't negotiate. Even if I could, Harold is one of the rare ghosts that hate coffee. After a moment, his hold wavers—slightly. He can't hold me off the floor and choke me all at once. When his grip lessens, I work my hands beneath me, hoping to push from the refrigerator and break the ghost's grasp. I freeze when footfalls sound behind me.

"It seems someone was left off the guest list."

The voice is smooth and controlled and belongs to Orson Yates. I'm not sure whether to be shocked or impressed that he has the gall to show up here. Chief Ramsey is in the next room, and while he might be in his dress uniform, he's certainly capable of slapping on a pair of handcuffs.

"You may have noticed that he's quite upset about that—and with you." Orson tsks, and the sound plays counterpoint to his shoes striking the linoleum floor. "I can't believe you, of all people, left a poor, defenseless ghost out in the middle of nowhere, in all that cold and snow. And you accuse me of cruelty."

He's at my side now, his face even with mine. "I only give them what they want, after all. That's more than you ever do."

With Orson's proximity, the hold on my throat grows ever tighter. My vision tunnels, and I know I'm not getting enough air to either fight or think. Waves of hatred wash over me, but at the moment, I know this: if Harold's ghost is here with me, he can't ruin Sadie's wedding.

"We'll deal with the rest of the wedding party later," Orson says, as if he's reading my thoughts. No doubt that small relief played across my face. "It'd be a terrible thing for Nigel to relapse before the honeymoon even started, but I think I can arrange that. As for your blonde friend, the one who got under Carter's skin? Oh, I have a particular ghost in mind for her."

I manage a muffled cry but nothing else.

"And, of course, Malcolm. This time around, he won't make such a miraculous recovery. But first you will die knowing you caused all that."

I try to shove against the refrigerator door. I try to draw a breath. My throat is closed. My lungs burn for air. Tears sting my cheeks, the skin raw.

"Let her go."

The words are inexplicably calm and soothing. While I recognize the voice, my panicked, oxygen-deprived mind can't put a name to it. Who is here in this room with us? Is he here to help?

"Think about it, my friend," the voice continues. "You are not truly angry with her, are you? She is not the one who engineered your pain, is she?"

The grip on my throat eases slightly. I gulp in a breath, and it rasps against my windpipe. My fingertips claw against the refrigerator's smooth surface. I can't find purchase, but that doesn't stop me from trying.

Something glimmering and cool touches my cheeks. Sprites—two of them—swoop around my face, dry my tears. Their presence registers and so does this new voice. I know who's responsible for my rescue. Sadie's sprites must have alerted Reginald, who now speaks to Harold's ghost in low, even tones.

"You're too late," Orson says.

"And you're not welcome here," Reginald counters. "As you already know."

"What? Did you place a ward around a *community* center?"

"I don't need to. You have no true power. Not over this ghost, not over anyone here."

Then, as if Reginald has commanded it, Harold's ghost releases its grip completely. I sink to the floor as it ricochets off the refrigerator and arrows straight into Orson.

He stumbles backward, and there's a crashing that I hear more than see. A dish shatters and pots clatter, but I don't check the damage. I'm concentrating on the floor, on pushing myself to my feet. The sprites swirl about me. In my current state, I can hear them clearly. Their chatter fills my ears, full of concern—and suggestions on how to fix my dress once I do stand.

Harold's ghost has gone beyond murderous. The gale it creates around Orson tears tiny pieces of his suit from his body, yanks strands of hair from his head.

Reginald claps twice, and the otherworldly cyclone stops all at once. The ghost retreats, returning to him, much like a dog might return to its owner.

"It's over now," Reginald says to the glimmer caught between his outstretched hands. "You can come with me and find the will to heal."

From the other side of the room, laughter rings out. "Is that what you do with your time? What *is* it you do, exactly, Reginald? Run a ghost rehab center?"

"What I spend most of my time on is fixing your mistakes and repairing the damage you do. You waste your talent."

"Odd. I was thinking the same about you."

"You have a single chance to leave," Reginald says. "Not only does this ghost want to destroy you, but the police might wish to arrest you."

"Whatever for?"

"Kidnapping, I believe. Assault, perhaps. I'm not sure of all the charges, but I'm certain they're serious."

"Yes, and when the story comes out about ghosts and entities and the like, I'm sure it will hold up in the courts. That's why we get to do what we do. The world is filled with nonbelievers." Orson adjusts his suit coat jacket and tugs at his cuffs so they shoot past the sleeves. "Trust me, I am not a man you want to fight in a court of law."

I listen with dismay. I know Orson is right. Chief has a hard enough time grappling with evidence of the supernatural, even with the two sprites that haunt the police station. Then there's everyone else in the system. I wouldn't ask him to put his reputation on the line, not for this, not when we can deal with Orson ourselves.

At least, I think we can.

I cast a quick look at Reginald. He's still holding the ghost between the palms of his hands. Malcolm and I once went up against someone who claimed to be a ghost whisperer. She was a fraud, of course. But Reginald? That's exactly what he does. Emotion drains from Harold's ghost. It quivers, and it's not anger that I feel roll off of it, but a deep exhaustion.

"Leave," Reginald says. "This fight is over, and if you persist, I promise you, the retribution will be swift."

"Really? You think you can gather enough necromancers to counter me?"

"I know I can."

"Perhaps you can, but I doubt they can counter this." Orson shuts his eyes. A second later, a word emerges from his mouth, a word only I should know.

"Momalcurkan."

"No." I whisper the word and look in panic to Reginald again.

His face appears waxy. I don't need to explain what that means. He recognizes the name for what it is, for what it can do.

But how? Orson was standing too far away to hear me speak the entity's name. I said it softly on purpose, to keep something like this from happening. An image of myself tethered to the pole fills my mind, and then, the zip tie curled at the bottom and a strip of duct tape flapping by a spot above my head.

"He recorded me," I say quietly.

Orson laughs. "Indeed I did, and thanks to you, I will forever have this entity at my disposal."

"It's not going to be happy," I mutter.

Orson scoffs. "Its happiness is not my concern."

Already, a spot on the floor is swirling as if it's made of liquid. Sadie's sprites zip past my face, each planting a quick kiss on my cheek, and zoom from the kitchen. I don't blame them. If I could zoom out of here like a sprite, I would.

The form that emerges from the spot is not the craggy, lava-eyed beast of the warehouse, but something more human, its shape bathed in a cloud of inky smoke. The smoke solidifies until at last what could be a handsome man in a well-tailored suit is standing in the center of the kitchen.

"You'll pardon my tardiness," the entity says. "I had to dress for the occasion." It turns to me. "And, my dear, I am always positively giddy to see you, although you do have more sense than to invoke me twice in one day, unlike some people."

Orson launches himself across the room. I scramble, but I'm too weak from my encounter with Harold's ghost, my ballet flats too slick against the linoleum, my dress too cumbersome. He reaches the entity first, spreads his arms and opens his mouth wide.

Reginald moves to my side as if together we might be able to fight Orson once he's united with the entity.

But instead of capturing it, instead of the entity vanishing before us, Orson simply passes through. His momentum carries him forward and he smacks the kitchen floor with his hands and knees.

The entity's form solidifies further, or at least the foot he aims at Orson does. The toe of the entity's shoe connects with Orson's backside. The force propels him against a row of cabinets. Dishes and pans rattle inside.

We're making so much noise, I'm certain someone else must be able to hear. I glance over my shoulder at the swinging doors, peer through the small window. The wedding reception beyond is going on as if the four of us are trapped in an invisible, soundproof room.

"That was part of your desire, was it not, my dear?" the entity says. "A perfect wedding for your friend?"

"We still have a pact?" I ask, and I see the same question reflected in Orson's eyes, an incredulous expression clawing its way through the pain.

But I don't truly need to ask. My connection to this thing runs through me. I feel it now. I touch the faded blue spot on my cheek and wonder why I couldn't feel it before.

Reginald hangs his head. In shame? In despair? I can't tell, but this certainly isn't his fault. An entity this strong could hide itself from all of us. Reginald said so himself.

Across the room, Orson swears. When it gets personal, the entity flicks a hand in his direction and sends Orson slamming against the cabinets once again.

"Cease. You will not speak of my necromancer like that."

Orson staggers to his feet. "But the pact ... after—"

"After we escaped your murderous children? You expected Katy to sever the pact. Did you not orchestrate the entire encounter, even to the point of letting Prescott Jones believe he could double-cross you? It would be far easier to secure me from her than it would be from him."

Orson blinks and sways. He reaches for the counter, and when his palm makes contact, sags into the support.

"But you had to make certain, didn't you?" the entity continues. "No sense invoking me if I'm still claimed. That gets ... messy." It raises its hands, indicating the kitchen around us. "But you hoped Katy would be happy to be rid of me, isn't that right?"

"Actually, I was." I see no point in lying. This thing has always read my thoughts.

The entity laughs, and it's a strange, hollow sound. "That's why I left you alone. I'm an acquired taste, even for the most experienced necromancer."

"The pact was severed," Orson says. "It must be. The exchange was made; each side benefited. You should be mine."

"And yet, I'm not."

The entity walks about the kitchen. Anyone peeking through the window would think the four of us are simply standing in here, chatting about the wedding or refilling our champagne glasses. They would think the entity was an exceedingly handsome man, although they wouldn't be able to recall his features once they glanced away.

When it stares at me straight on, all I can see is a swirling black void. I want to blink or glance away myself, but I can't. It holds me in its non-gaze for a moment and then stalks toward Orson.

"I'll grant you that humans have only graced this planet for a short duration. Still, in all that time, not a single necromancer has bothered to display any gratitude. Until now. The pact remains. No, the pact is strengthened." The entity raises a finger. "Take note for next time."

"So, if I have a pact with you," I say, choosing my words carefully, "then no one else can. Is that right?"

"That's correct." It's Reginald who says this. He turns toward the entity. "Don't put this burden on her. Let her go. You can retreat to another plane and end your interaction with humans."

"Why would I do that? I haven't had this much enjoyment in eons. Besides"—he sweeps a hand in my direction—"it's entirely up to Katy."

I can't sever the pact, not with Orson standing there, not with Orson anywhere. I can't risk it; I can't risk someone finding the recording of the entity's name. I'm stuck with this thing, possibly forever.

"Oh, really, my dear. Stuck? I'm crushed."

I glower at it, and the thing has the audacity to laugh.

"Katrina Lindstrom, this is far more serious than you realize," Reginald says.

I shake my head. "No, I realize."

"It will want things from you."

I imagine it will.

"Your life won't be your own."

That, too.

I turn to Reginald then. "Do you know of some other way? If I sever the pact, then Orson will invoke the entity and use it to do who knows what."

"Or your friend here might be tempted to do the same," the entity says. "Oh, Reginald, think of the *good* you could do with me at your disposal."

Reginald goes waxy again and refuses to meet my eyes. Orson snorts. I see the temptation, feel the tug of it myself. Even now, the urge to flick my wrist in Orson's direction and have the entity dispatch him is nearly overwhelming. It would be so easy, so simple.

So wrong. The world doesn't work that way, and what you get you must pay for eventually.

I won't pay like that.

"Oh, this is going to be interesting," the entity says.

Before I can contradict it, Malcolm bursts through the kitchen doors. His eyes are wide with panic, and when he spots Orson, his expression turns downright lethal. He launches himself across the room.

Malcolm might be younger and stronger, but the last time I saw Orson, he had a gun.

"No!"

My voice rings out, and the world stops. Or, at least, part of the world does. Malcolm is frozen in midair. Orson has one hand in his suit coat pocket. He's always so calm and smooth that, at first, I don't realize he's frozen as well.

That's when I notice the bulge in his pocket.

The entity glides across the floor. Its hand appears to dissolve as it infiltrates the fabric of Orson's suit coat. A moment later, it pulls out a pistol.

"We can't leave this here, can we?" the entity says. "A round in the chamber is far too dangerous, what with children and sprites about."

The entity holds the pistol in its outstretched palm. A thousand tiny cracks form on the surface, then those splinter into a thousand more. The pistol shatters into nothing but a handful of dark grains.

The entity brushes the last bits of black sand from its hands and then inclines its head toward me.

"You see, my dear? A pact isn't such a terrible thing."

My heart races. I feel gutted, and I really don't know what's worse—that I've nearly lost Malcolm twice in one day or that I'm forever beholden to this entity for saving him.

The entity stalks toward me. It knows me, must feel my ambivalence toward it. Of course, it doesn't have an expression; there's nothing but that swirling black void where a face should be. So what it thinks, what it feels, will remain a mystery.

"It has been a rough day, has it not?" it says.

I give a single, numb nod.

"And you haven't danced once with your young man." It casts a glance toward Malcolm, still suspended, still trying to come to my rescue. "He is awfully pretty. I can see why you're so taken with him." It gives me a once-over. "But not like this."

Then, like a fairy godmother, it waves one of its hands. The wrinkles vanish from my dress. A tear along the hem repairs itself. I feel the sticky residue of salt leave my face, lips smoothed with a fresh coat of gloss, hair contained in a chignon.

"There we are. You're a picture, my dear." The entity touches my cheek, the left one, and I feel nothing but the void. "As for the rest, I believe the three of you can handle things."

In a puff of black, inky smoke, the entity vanishes.

Orson lets out a long gasp and clutches at his empty pocket. Malcolm's feet hit the floor with a thud. I rush for him, wrapping my arms around his before he can launch himself at Orson again.

Then the four of us—Malcolm, Reginald, Orson, and me—stare at each other. At last, Reginald clears his throat.

"You had the chance to leave, Orson Yates. Now you have another. This time, I suggest you take it."

Orson pats his suit coat, his trousers.

Reginald shakes his head. "It's gone. You'll have to buy yourself a new one if you wish to shoot someone."

Orson flicks a murderous glance in my direction.

"And don't blame her. She didn't invoke the entity." Reginald regards me for a moment, then turns back to Orson. "Think of where your greed has led you. Perhaps it's not where you wish to be."

I'm still clutching Malcolm tight, but now he turns in my arms and scrutinizes my face. "The entity?"

"He knows its name," I say. "Others do too." I nod toward Reginald. "Orson recorded me, so really, anyone could know."

Malcolm's gaze flickers about the kitchen as if he's aware of missing something crucial. "Then it isn't gone."

I shake my head. I want to cry, but can't find the tears.

Malcolm breaks from my grasp and strides across the room. He collars Orson, twisting the fabric of his suit coat in a tight grip.

"This is where I make a joke about taking out the trash," he says. "But I'm not really in the mood for jokes." He yanks on the coat and drags Orson from the kitchen.

In the quiet that follows, Reginald speaks. "This isn't over for you," he says.

"I know."

"The entity finds you intriguing."

"That isn't good, is it?"

"I'm afraid not." He releases a long breath. "You must tell Malcolm what happened."

"I will."

I peer through the window into the ballroom, where the reception is still in full swing. Nearly everyone is dancing. Nigel twirls

Sadie, and I feel the bass thumping beneath the soles of my ballet flats.

I will tell Malcolm. We'll figure out what to do, together. But now? I want him to come back so we can rejoin the party. I want to dance at Sadie and Nigel's wedding. I want to drink champagne that matches the rose petals. I want everything in the room beyond, and certainly the entity knew that from the start.

Malcolm returns to the kitchen, winded, his gaze anxious until it lands on me.

"Katy?"

I hold out my hand. "Let's go dance."

"But—"

"Nothing's really changed, and Orson's gone, right?"

"Oh, yeah. He's gone."

Malcolm's expression is more than a little self-satisfied. I decide not to ask about the circumstances of Orson's exit. Instead, I nod toward the reception. "Then I want to be out there."

Before we can leave the kitchen, Reginald touches my arm.

"You must tell him," he says, his voice so low it only reaches my ears.

"I will."

But not tonight.

CHAPTER 9

THE SONGS HAVE SLOWED, and the crowd on the dance floor has thinned. An hour ago, Sadie tossed her bouquet at me. It went off course, and Chief Ramsey was nearly the lucky recipient until Sadie's two sprites intervened.

At the last second, and in a spray of petals, it split in two. I caught one half, Belinda the other. It makes me wonder what the sprites know that we don't.

Malcolm has shed his tuxedo jacket. I've left my ballet flats beneath a chair. He's held me close for the last five songs, and no one has tried to interrupt us. My head is resting against his chest and I've been playing a game where I tug at the end of his bowtie to loosen it.

"You've got to stop that," he says, repressed laughter rumbling beneath my cheek.

"Why?" I go for wide-eyed innocence. I'm not certain it works.

"Because I actually don't want you to stop."

Oh? *Oh.* I smile to myself before peering up at him. "What if I don't want to stop either?"

He slows our steps. "Katy, after everything that's happened today, I don't think—"

"Well, I do think, *especially* after everything that's happened today." I wrap my arms tighter around his neck. "I don't want to let you go, not after everything that's happened. So, will you stay with me? Stay the night? In the morning, I'll brew you some Kona blend."

He laughs and pulls me closer. I don't push the idea. I think, maybe, he needs to live with the notion for a few minutes. As a precaution, I cast my thoughts upward. Something about the entity has been bothering me. I suspect our connection goes back much further, before the warehouse, before it marked my cheek, before its appearance at the mausoleum.

Ah, very astute, my dear.

I can't imagine what the connection is, or how far back it goes. I won't ask. I doubt it would tell me, anyway.

You're correct. I won't.

But I want it to tell me one thing.

Do I have tonight? I send the thought skyward, through the pink balloons that are bobbing along the ballroom's ceiling, and into the warm spring night.

The echo of that metallic laugh fills the room. To everyone else, it must sound like the community center's ventilation system groaning to life.

Yes. You have tonight.

Relief washes through me. I clutch Malcolm ever closer.

Enjoy.

I sigh. I could really do without the commentary.

"Katy?"

Malcolm murmurs my name against my hair. His voice is tender and warm. The fragrance of rose petals mixes with his nutmeg and Ivory Soap scent, and the combination is a heady thing that makes me sway.

"Are you sure?" he asks, the question tentative.

"I've never been more sure."

I can't imagine pushing him away, even if—in the long run—that might hurt him less. At the thought, my heart feels sore, like it's bruised itself against my ribcage. But I want Malcolm to know how much he means to me.

No matter what, we'll always have this. Tonight is ours. That's more than enough.

And it will be worth everything that comes after.

SNEAK PEEK: GHOSTS AND CONSEQUENCES

COFFEE AND GHOSTS, SEASON THREE, EPISODE 1

My business partner is kissing the back of my neck. Since we spent the night together, this isn't much of a surprise. I'm curled next to Malcolm, his arm draped over my waist, his rich, nutmeg scent warming the air. I want to laugh at the audacity and joy of it all, but don't dare make a sound, don't dare move. His kiss is a soft, shivery thing. I don't want him to stop. So I remain absolutely still as morning light filters through the drapes and bounces off dust motes in the air.

I'd be lying if I said I didn't love this.

I'd be lying if I said I wasn't worried.

But I am. This is new. Our business is still new, not quite a year old. Beneath the joy is a thin wire of dread that insists this happiness can't last. We've made a huge mistake mixing business with pleasure, and once I confess what happened at Nigel and Sadie's wedding reception last night, it will change everything; it will change *us*.

I will confess. I know I must. But not before coffee. No one should talk about business or pacts with (possibly) demonic entities before coffee.

Malcolm's lips continue to explore the nape of my neck. I'm pretty sure he's awake. True, he's an expert kisser. Even so, no one has so much skill that they can execute what he's currently doing while asleep.

I've vowed not to move, but my toes begin flirting with his. They find the sensitive arch of his foot, and I'm rewarded with his exhale against my neck.

"You awake?" he says, voice low and still warm with sleep.

"I'm guessing you are," I say.

"How are you?"

The simple question betrays so much with its tone: *Are you okay? Was last night okay? Did we make a mistake?*

I'm sure there must be other doubts I'm missing, other things he's feeling. I go with a single word reply.

"Good."

"Hm. You were that last night, too, if I recall."

Now I turn to face him. I'm rewarded with that sweet, dark-roast smile, his eyes, shining at the sight of me. I can't help wondering: how did I get so lucky?

"I think I promised you some Kona blend," I say.

"You did, and I plan to collect. But first, I think I need my morning kiss."

Morning kiss. Evening kiss. It's how we juggled being business partners and a couple, although that was before we moved the arrangement into my bedroom.

"Well, we turned the lights off after midnight." I peer up at him, trying to school my face into absolute seriousness. "Technically, that's morning, so we've already had our morning kiss."

"Doesn't count unless the sun's up." Malcolm tugs me closer, folds me into his arms.

It is, by far, the longest morning kiss on record.

I'm not sure how many pots of coffee I've brewed. Thousands, certainly. On most days, I do it without thinking. Unless we're up against a truly powerful ghost, I don't need to pay attention to the particular blend (although Kona works best to eradicate ghosts) or how precisely I measure the water.

This morning? My hands tremble—just a bit. I'm in Malcolm's tuxedo shirt. The tails skim my knees. Even with the cuffs rolled, the sleeves knock against things with a sweep of my arms. When I sprinkle coffee grounds all over the counter, I set down the scoop, close my eyes, and try not to cry.

"Hey." Malcolm's voice is gentle in my ear. He moves behind me, wraps his arms around mine, and then cradles me against his chest. "Don't worry. I think it's impossible for you to make a bad cup of coffee."

"I could if I tried," I insist.

"That's just it. You gotta *try*. Just toss in some Kona blend. You could make brewed mud this morning. Trust me. I wouldn't notice."

"You sound like you're in a good mood, Mr. Armand."

"I'm in a very good mood." He turns me in his arms and places a kiss on my nose. "I've never been in a better mood."

Something inside me loosens. Tension drains from my shoulders. I eye the coffee scoop and vow to make Malcolm the best damned cup of coffee he's ever had.

Only now I realize that it's okay if it isn't.

By the time the scent of Kona blend fills the kitchen, and Malcolm has two cups and the half and half ready to go, I feel like myself again. We'll drink our coffee, clear our heads, and then we can tackle the big problems left over from last night. We can do this, I'm certain.

Just as I think this, footfalls sound above our heads. Malcolm and I glance upward and then, at the same moment, our eyes meet.

"Belinda?" he says.

I give my head a little shake. "I didn't hear her come in last night. Did you?"

He opens his mouth as if to answer, then shuts it tight. I take that as a no. Because treading above our heads is more than one pair of feet. We could make a dash for the stairs, but we'd only meet whoever is on their way down. We could hide in the living room, but that seems cowardly.

Malcolm studies me, then he glances down at the T-shirt and boxer shorts he's wearing. His lips twitch. Before I can say anything—or toss him one of my grandmother's old aprons—Belinda charges into the kitchen.

"Okay, okay." Her words come out rushed, like she's trying to convince me of something she knows is wrong. "Before you say anything, I just want to say that I'm not..."

She stutters to a halt. Her gaze flits to Malcolm and back to me. For a brief moment, her mouth hangs open. But this is Belinda Barnes, so the shock is quickly replaced by an impish grin.

"Well, it's about time. High five?" She holds up a hand. "I think this deserves a high five."

Malcolm snorts. I scowl.

"There will be no high fives," I say, willing my cheeks not to flame. They do, of course. My entire face is on fire. Even my knees feel hot.

This only makes Belinda laugh. "Fist bump?"

I tilt my head and glare. It's then I noticed her attire, remarkably similar to my own. The man's dress shirt is a pale blue, and since she's six feet tall, hits her mid-thigh.

Then the shirt's owner clears the kitchen doorway, and the whole situation goes from slightly awkward to fairly mortifying.

Jack Carlotta stumbles over the threshold, not that there's anything on the floor to trip him up. To his credit, he swallows his shock almost immediately. Maybe that's a lawyer thing. Before he does, I see a flash of ... something in his eyes. I can't tell if it's regret or guilt or simply shame.

Once upon a time, Jack, Belinda, and I attended high school together, and once upon a time, Jack and Belinda were *the* couple. You know the kind—star athlete and homecoming queen. That was also before the ghosts started tormenting Belinda, before the drinking, before Jack left for college.

And before he started asking me out on a regular basis. By text message. I still have one on my phone from only a few weeks ago. I've never said yes. He's never stopped asking.

After last night? I'm guessing that might change.

Along with the warm scent of coffee, the air is thick with embarrassment. It's my kitchen, which I suppose makes me the one responsible for starting a conversation, offering my guests breakfast. I glance at Malcolm, but his brow is clouded with a low-grade glare aimed in Jack's direction.

They've never really liked each other.

"I have Kona blend!"

I blurt the words, and they ricochet in the tiny space. Then Belinda tips her head back and laughs. The sound of it slices through the embarrassment to the point where even Malcolm cracks a smile.

"Pour us some coffee," Belinda says, pulling on one of my grandmother's aprons. She winks at me. "And then get out of here. Jack and I will make brunch."

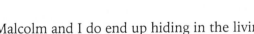

Malcolm and I do end up hiding in the living room. A racket comes from the kitchen—the clatter of pots and pans, the sizzle of veggie bacon, and the aroma of biscuits baking. I cradle a cup of coffee, and if the steam doesn't do much to cool my cheeks, at least it clears my head.

Malcolm paces. He's set his cup on the mantelpiece and pauses after each lap around the living room for a sip.

"You know," he says, after he's logged at least a quarter mile.

"This isn't the way I pictured the next morning. I was hoping to cook you breakfast in bed."

"I still had to get up to make the coffee," I point out.

He makes terrible coffee. For the life of me, I can't figure out why since he's so good at everything else.

"I make okay coffee," he says.

"No, you don't."

"I do. Ask Nigel."

"But—"

"I've been faking."

"Why would you...?" I trail off, my mind whirling at this new bit of information. "But we've spent hours in the kitchen."

A sheepish expression lights his eyes while that dark-roast grin spreads across his face. "Yeah, that was kind of the point. At first, you know, before ... everything." He waves a hand toward the ceiling and the general direction of my bedroom. "I just wanted an excuse to spend time with you."

I tilt my head and go for stern. "And then it got too complicated to explain."

He raises his hands in surrender. "I know, I know. Bad habit."

I grumble a sigh, and he laughs.

"Forgive me?"

"I'll think about it."

I'm expecting him to log another quarter mile around the living room while I do. Instead, he shakes his head as if he's shaking away a thought—and the laughter that goes with it.

"What?" I ask, bracing for another confession.

"I was just thinking that we should text Gregory and Terese and invite them over for the most awkward morning-after brunch ever."

Now, I do laugh and pat the spot on the sofa next to me. "Sit?"

He does, and not too much later, I'm snuggled in his lap. His chin rests on my head, and I'm flush against his chest. His heartbeat is a strong, steady thing against my back.

"Am I forgiven?" he whispers.

"Still thinking about it."

His laughter rumbles beneath me. I'm a terrible liar, and he knows it.

I contemplate the front lawn, the spring morning. I let my gaze drift. At first, the shadow doesn't register. At first, that's all I see, a shadow stretching across my lawn. It takes a few moments before it attaches itself to the man who is so clearly casting it.

He stands on the sidewalk midpoint between my house and Sadie's. In the past months, I've seen so many necromancers stand in that very spot that I'm pretty sure he's one as well.

True, he isn't pulled together as most others I've met. His canvas trousers are the color of damp sand, worn and patched. His hair is shaggy, dipping beneath his collar, and far more gray than black. He carries a backpack slung over his shoulders. But there's something in the way he tilts his chin, tucks his hands so casually in his trouser pockets that pings sudden recognition.

I don't know him. Certainly I've never seen him before, but he's familiar in a way I can't pinpoint.

"Malcolm?"

"Hm?" It's barely an answer. His lips are too busy brushing against strands of my hair, and his fingers are intent on caressing my arms through the long sleeves of his shirt.

"I think there's a necromancer on my sidewalk."

The caressing comes to an abrupt halt. His fingers curl around my arms, and he holds me steady.

"Where?"

I part the shutters to give him a full view of my front lawn, the sidewalk, and the necromancer whose gaze is doing a slow and steady survey of my house.

Malcolm doesn't speak. He doesn't move. He is so still that dread curls in my stomach. Up until now, a necromancer on the front walk has been a harbinger of bad things. Still, this particular necromancer doesn't look all that dangerous.

"Am I right?" I prompt.

"Yeah." He exhales. "You're right. That's a necromancer." With his grip still on my arms, he eases me from his lap. "That also happens to be my father."

WHAT THE HECK IS COFFEE & GHOSTS?

Coffee & Ghosts is a cozy paranormal mystery/romance that is told over a series of episodes and in seasons, much like a television series. Think *Doctor Who* or *Sherlock*.

Ghost in the Coffee Machine, which I think of as the pilot episode, began life as a short story that first appeared in *Coffee: 14 Caffeinated Tales of the Fantastic.*

Once, a very long time ago, I wrote a murder mystery that involved a ghost. During the research phase, I came across a tidbit about catching ghosts using coffee and glass jars. The novel never went anywhere, but years later, when I saw the call for submissions for Coffee, something clicked. Katy, her grandmother, and their business of catching ghosts with coffee and Tupperware (a far more practical and, frankly, safer option) were born.

Not too long later I realized that I wasn't done with coffee and ghosts—or rather, they weren't done with me. They demanded their own type of storytelling as well.

Serial fiction is exciting and fun to write. It's different from a novel in that each episode has its own story arc but also supports a larger one for the season.

I've recently consolidated the episodes into three season bundles. This makes both finding the episodes and binge-reading them much easier.

I can't tell you how much fun it was to write COFFEE & GHOSTS, and I want to thank you for reading and coming along on this journey with me.

ABOUT THE AUTHOR

CHARITY TAHMASEB has slung corn on the cob for Green Giant and jumped out of airplanes (but not at the same time). She spent twelve years as a Girl Scout and six in the Army; that she wore a green uniform for both may not be a coincidence. These days, she writes fiction (long and short) and works as a technical writer for a software company in St. Paul.

Her short speculative fiction has appeared in *Flash Fiction Online, Deep Magic,* and *Cicada.*

ALSO BY CHARITY TAHMASEB

Made in United States
Orlando, FL
10 February 2022